THE
LIVING
GOD

To Gerri,
Nothing is Impossible.
Kaytalin Platt

KAYTALIN PLATT

Published by Inkshares, Inc., Oakland, California
www.inkshares.com

Edited by WriterTherapy
Cover design by Tim Barber of Dissect Designs
Interior design by Kevin G. Summers

ISBN: 9781947848931
e-ISBN: 9781947848429
LCCN: 2018937930

Second edition

Printed in the United States of America

For my father. Thank you for teaching me that girls are every bit a strong and capable as boys and never wavering in your faith that I'd achieve my dreams. I miss you.

And for Kathy, my friend and soul sister. You helped make this book possible. Thank you for being my friend, writing confidant, partner, and ally for over a decade.

ONE

EARTH DOES NOT understand the curse of time. It knows not the ravages of age, as it simply alters its form to endure. Rocks weather to dust, and that dust layers to weave stories of the past. Earth cradles the remnants of millennia. The living walk upon it and the dead are buried within it. The world belongs to the earth, and it returns to it, sheltered in sediments that defy time.

All things are bound by time, but not earth. Not usually.

Today the earth bent to time's will as limber as a young sapling. The soil, muddied with blood, dried. Red stains swept back to the dead, their wounds closed, and their bodies rose from the sand.

The frozen scene worked backward. Every hack, slice, and arrow drew away. Soldiers sheathed swords and mounted horses. Fires snuffed out, and thatched roofs regrew thin spindles of straw. The frightened faces slacked and reformed smiles, while the soldiers rode backward out of the city and up the hill to the trees.

Each one passed a lone figure standing on the drying earth beneath the arched stone gate. Her eyes glowed white hot, and light wrapped in tendrils about her hands. She turned her head to the blue sky, to the birds flying in reverse and the dark receding clouds. The Time Mage convulsed with a wet, drowning gasp, and blood dripped from her nose to curl over her lips. She fell, digging her fingers into the soil, and vomited. The white light was snuffed from her eyes, and the world restarted anew.

The quiet of lapsed time broke with laughter that silenced in confusion. The dead felt at their wounds in panic and, finding none, looked to the red-haired woman sick upon the earth. Behind her, past the tall wall and up the hill, soldiers mounted on horses burst from the forest.

"Run," she said to them, lifting her head. Green eyes burned through her disheveled, curly hair. "Run!"

Screams tore through the crowd, and the villagers scattered. They scooped up children, grabbed their wives and their valuables, and fled. The stronger and braver of them snatched what insufficient weapons they had and greeted the army as it rode into the city with brandished swords and Adridian flags boasting the angry face of a gray dragon stitched to black cotton.

Instead of fighting, they warded off the threatened villagers and circled around the kneeling woman. The horsemen, all adorned in armor, cloaks, and helmets, numbered in the hundreds. So many were there that not all of them could fit within the village, so they spilled outward and lined the brick wall.

"Saran!" called a soldier upon a black horse. "You're a fool." He slid from the saddle and landed with a thud next to her, where he knelt and dragged her into his arms. He wore leather armor, unlike the bulky metal of most soldiers, and a fierce steel helmet in the visage of a dragon. She rested against the soft leather breastplate, letting her tense muscles relax in his arms, and smeared the blood from beneath her nose with a quivering hand.

"Let go of that traitor, Ahriman," said another. The man the voice belonged to lifted the helmet from his head, revealing a narrow, scathing face, and threw it hard to the earth. "The king will be notified of this. He will deal with your treason."

Saran turned her heavy eyes up to the angry soldier and then she shut them with an exasperated sigh, burrowing against the man who held her. She wished the world away with all her might, but upon opening her eyes again, everything remained the same. It always remained the same. "How fortunate that I am of a position that is protected." The arms around her tightened, and her gaze lifted to the red eyes peering through the helmet's narrow slit.

"Idiot," her savior whispered, and only she could see the edge of a smile pulling his cheeks high.

The angry soldier continued, "We had the upper hand. We had the element of surprise. Now, because of you, the scum have run off!" The soldier's arm slung out toward the hills. Behind him, villagers scattered for shelter in the forest.

"Yes, the campaign is a complete failure, Lord Marki. I suspect we should just head home." Saran pushed away from Ahriman and used his shoulder to steady herself as she stood.

Lord Odan Marki slipped from his horse, rage turning his face a terrible shade of red. Marki's bony fist, wrapped in a glove tipped with pointed metal barbs, swung for her skull. His fist rattled through the air only to be snatched up by another soldier next to him.

This one wore no helmet and the same less-restrictive leather armor as Ahriman. He stood tall among the other soldiers, with a broad build and long coal-black hair pulled taut behind his head. His blue eyes settled with warning on Lord Marki.

"Mind yourself, Odan. That's a princess you're about to scar, and I doubt the king would take kindly to it, no matter what foolishness she's done," said the man with a deep rumbling voice. When Odan calmed, the soldier released him.

"If you think your title protects you from retribution, you are gravely mistaken," Odan growled, knuckles cracking as his fists tightened at his sides.

"It seems my title doesn't afford me much more than protection," replied the princess, casting them all a dark glare. "What other royal do you know who is addressed so informally and threatened with physical harm? Hmm?"

The wide arc of soldiers shifted with a rumbling clank of metal as they gave a halfhearted salute, bashing their gloved hands against their metal or leathered chests. She appraised them all, watching as they sat like stiff iron statues upon well-bred warhorses. She blamed her father for their forgetfulness. He insisted they know her as their own on the battlefield. He wanted her to earn their respect as a warrior before earning it as their future queen, just as he had earned it long before snatching the throne from the previous king. However, there were certain drawbacks to her whimsical status. Odan Marki's lack of respect, for one.

"My apologies for the improper address a moment ago," came the courtly voice of Keleir Ahriman as he rose to stand next to her. "I was concerned, and it wasn't intentional."

"You are forgiven, Lord Ahriman," Saran said, nodding to him. "And so are you, Lord Marki. I understand how important this battle was for you. Its success would have marked your rise among the ranks and been quite the notch for you. However, our informants were wrong. There were no rebels here."

Odan's face darkened to crimson, his eyes bulged, flashing bright cyan with power, and his hands shook. Frost licked across the earth from where Odan's feet touched it toward Saran, turning the dirt snowy white. She stepped away just as it reached her.

"Back to camp. We'll return to the capital, and then you can complain to the king of my slight against you, Lord Marki," she told the Ice Mage. She turned her back to them and let the exhaustion wash across her face. She wrapped an arm around her queasy stomach and walked back toward the village wall. The world rippled before her eyes, like something seen through the bottom of a whiskey glass.

"You shouldn't be walking. Where's your horse?" Ahriman asked, reaching for her arm. She evaded his touch with narrowed eyes. He drew back his hand and clanked his fist against the hard metal sword hilt at his hip. "Princess! You should not be walking."

Saran stopped short, letting out a heavy sigh. She turned back to scold him for his concern, but her legs quivered, and she keeled sideways. Ahriman dove and slipped an arm around her waist before she hit the earth. She met his eyes again as he lowered his head to her ear.

"Ride," he said, voice firm and quiet. "Please." He did not look down at her, nor did he offer to carry her. He helped her stand and guided her to his horse, where she drew herself into the saddle. Lord Ahriman climbed into the saddle behind her. "I'm porting Her Highness back to camp. She spent too much of her Life and needs rest to recover what's been lost."

Heatless, bright orange flames sprouted from the earth and tangled like vines over them, and the fire of Keleir Ahriman's Gate stole them away. A mile or so away, under the shade of clustered trees near the entrance to a large camp, the earth caught fire. A horse with two riders emerged, struggling to gallop out of a hole made of embers and molten rock. Once on even ground, the fire around them snuffed out, leaving the patch of dirt, leaves, and grass void of any signs of it having been there at all.

The mostly empty camp had a few servants going about their duties. The servants did not look up or notice Saran and Keleir appearing just at the outskirts of the farthest row of tents. The two Mages waited just to be sure they had not been seen before the Fire Mage guided his horse behind a cluster of brush near a rippling creek. Shadows hung heavy beneath the thick, leafy canopy, allowing them to hide easily in their dark clothes. On a branch hanging low over the trickling water, a hawk watched them approach.

Saran slid from the horse, and her escort dropped heavily next to her. He placed his hands on her shoulders, turning her to him so abruptly that her head spun. Pain splintered through her skull, and she closed her eyes tight with a groan.

"If you didn't smell like vomit, I'd kiss you," Keleir said, one hand curling behind her neck and the other brushing through her unkempt hair. The pressure of his hand against her aching skull felt surprisingly refreshing. "That was foolish."

"Innocent people were dying." She flashed her eyes open, taking in the fearsome dragon helmet and the red eyes peering through it. A wiry smile sprouted on her tired face. "And I could wash my mouth out."

He drew from his pocket a tattered red cloth and wiped the drying blood from her upper lip and chin, a gentle touch for someone wearing such a fearsome mask. "How are you feeling?"

She closed her eyes, wavering on her feet, and assessed her body. Saran didn't have to answer him—he already knew how she felt. Just as she could sense everything about him. Still, she knew he liked it when she said it with her own words. "Exhausted. My skull is splitting open from the inside."

Keleir pursed his lips together and curled his hands against her cheeks. "If you ever do something that dangerous again, I'll . . ."

"You'll what, m'lord?"

Keleir shook his helmet loose from his head. It clanked once against the earth and then rolled into the mud at the edge of the creek—he'd spend the afternoon scrubbing it. His stark-white hair brushed against his shoulders and strands of it fell across his face. He was a handsome young man, despite the misleading color of his hair, with a strong jaw and unsettling red eyes. It was a visage that most people on her world feared. It marked him as a man touched by a demon, and while that was frightening on its own, he was also a man who had been gifted by the Core, the life of their world, with the element of fire. He drew her in and rested his chin at the top of her head. "I don't know. But it will be fearsome and vengeful."

"Vengeful?"

He nodded, pressing a firm kiss to her aching temple. His arms squeezed tighter around her, and his voice wavered ever so slightly. "You could have died. Don't ever push that far again. Know your limits, Saran D'mor. You are not immortal."

The princess frowned. He wasn't wrong. She had used her power longer than necessary. But she had wanted to leave the village as they'd found it. They were well into the fall rains, and it would take weeks for them to repair the damage. By contrast, it would only take her a day or two to recover what she'd lost in giving them back their homes.

Saran could hear the sound of hooves in the distance, still too far to feel the thunder of the army galloping toward them. She wanted to stay in his arms longer, to rest there where it was safe. She fed off the strength he radiated and used it to soothe the ache in her head.

Keleir caught her just as she drew away. "Yarin won't look past what you did. Not this time. It was blatant treason, and there is no way to justify it or convince him it was a mistake like all those times before . . ."

"I will deal with those consequences. The most I'll get is a scolding, I'm sure."

The Fire Mage shook his head. "What if it is worse?"

Saran flinched, remembering the harsh crack of a rod against her spine, the hard thud of a boot in her gut. "Then I'll deal with that as well. I could not see those people die, Keleir. I'm tired of pretending I don't care. It was worth the risk."

Keleir frowned at her, and she felt his disappointment ripple through the air like a cool breeze. "But not worth your life."

Saran didn't argue, partly because he was right and partly because her mind could not tolerate another moment of standing. She touched his cheek lightly, just as the army began to emerge through the brush. The princess turned and crossed the smoky camp, picking her way through the cluster of tents and trees, before collapsing through the front flap of her own.

Inside the tent, Saran listened to the sound of the army riding back. She heard them dismount and disperse to their individual areas while she lay against her bedding with her hands pressed to her skull.

Even with the conversation finished, Saran couldn't help the bubble of worry Keleir's warning brought. Most of her life she'd been her father's good and faithful daughter . . . at least as far as he knew. *Sometimes we do what we hate to do what is right,* Madam Ophelia, the castle healer, would tell her. But more and more she grew sick of the act, and the closer they got to their freedom, the less she cared about keeping it up. The careful façade she'd woven around herself had crumbled, and she knew that if she didn't piece it back together soon, the elaborate ruse she'd cultivated most of her life would be undone—and with it, their plan of escape.

TWO

AT NIGHT THE camp quieted, save the sound of crickets and snoring. Saran's tent was modest for a princess and comfortable enough for two slender people. Fur and embroidered pillows draped the floor, the only luxury she allowed herself past the military-issued wool blankets and understuffed pillows. Her traveling clothes sat folded neatly at the entrance, and she lay beneath the furs wearing a thin cotton dressing gown.

The night air had cooled enough to chill, and she burrowed down against the soft fur until it covered her nose. She couldn't sleep for the aching in her head, and nothing could drown out the snarling, growling, horrible snores of the soldier sleeping in the tent next to her.

A shadow moved along the canvas and around the front of her tent. Her heart leapt up until she registered the prickle of power in the air that told her Keleir was close and growing nearer by the second. Then he fumbled in. He pressed a finger to his lips and slid along the fur to lie by her side.

"Are you mad?" she hissed at him, feeling his warm nose brush against her cheek. His arm curled over her waist and drew her tight against him. He felt hot, like fire. Not surprising, given it was his element. The chill that had settled over her dissipated in the presence of his heat.

"It's near morning, and everyone is sleeping. Even the dolt left to keep watch. I couldn't sense you sleeping, so I thought I'd pass the time with you."

Saran sighed, choosing not to waste energy with arguing. "Why aren't you sleeping?"

The Fire Mage pursed his lips together and shrugged. "And you?"

She touched the bridge of her nose. "My head is pounding to the point I wish to bash the rest of my brains to mush and end the pain. Were you having nightmares?"

Keleir curled his hand along her side. "I dreamed."

"Of him?"

He looked away. "Of him."

"What—"

"I'd rather not," Keleir said. "Not tonight."

Saran nodded and shut her eyes as the Fire Mage settled down next to her, tucking his face in the crook of her neck.

"Do you remember when you were a child and you'd first come to the palace? You had such terrible nightmares that your screams kept half the orphanage awake."

"Aren't you a little young to remember this?"

"I can remember it enough. I remember that I'd snuck out one night to visit Leila . . ." Saran paused at the sad memory of her now long-dead friend. "And I went by the boy's dormitory out of curiosity. I heard this great wailing, so I crept inside and found you rolling on a cot in a closet where the older boys had stuffed you to muffle the noise. You looked miserable and frightened. I remembered how Madam Ophelia would hug me after having a nightmare, so I crawled into bed and gave you this great big hug."

"Please don't finish this story." Keleir rolled onto his back, staring up at the canvas ceiling with an immense frown.

"You woke up, wrapped your hands around my throat, and nearly choked me to death," she said, laughing. Keleir let out an exasperated groan.

Saran snickered and rolled over him, lying across his chest. "Now I can do this and live."

"If that is a fond memory of me, I've been doing something very, very wrong." Keleir's jaw tightened. He reached up and brushed his fingers through her tangled ringlets. "I have come a long way since then. I am master of my body now—I have been for some time—and I thank you each day for it."

Saran smiled, snuggling closer to him. Whatever connected them, whatever this feeling was that lit her soul aflame when he was near, it had brought them together. She had saved his soul from the creature inside him, and in that she had given him a new life.

She thought back to their first meeting five years ago—at least her first meeting with *Keleir* and not the creature inside him, the Oruke. It was weeks after the healers had mended her fire-ravaged body. She'd been burned, almost to death, reaching inside him to make his soul whole. At first she'd been utterly terrified of him, convinced he was still the creature that wanted her dead. But he wasn't, and he'd vowed to repay her, vowed to atone. They'd quietly worked side by side against her father ever since.

Saran's gaze drove into the canvas tent. Eyes wide with fear that she squelched before Keleir could sense it. No, it was more complicated than that. What she had done to save him . . . it tied her to him, to his sanity, and to his control over the Oruke. She had to be near him, and because of that she had learned to love him out of necessity. But somewhere along the way, she'd truly fallen for him.

Saran lay for an hour or more listening to the rhythm of his heart. With daylight creeping ever closer, she turned her thoughts to the next day.

"Tomorrow night, while the others sleep, we'll leave to meet Darshan," she said, settling on her side next to him. "I don't know how Father will punish me for what I've done. It may mean I can't meet with Darshan afterwards, so it has to be tomorrow, before we get back to Andrian." Her words were a faint whisper pressed to his ear. The brush of her lips sent a shiver through him. Now planning escapes into the night to plot against the king was the last thing on his mind.

"Aye," he said. He paused before adding, "I won't let Yarin harm you."

"It has been a long time since Father had me beaten. He's gotten more used to psychological torture . . . which is why you have to stay away from me, Keleir. I do not want him knowing that I care for you as strongly as I do. He will use that against me."

The Fire Mage turned his red gaze on her, glancing side-long as he took a deep breath. "He knows we're friends. He will not know we are lovers, but you cannot deny our friendship. We've been friends for five years. Since you gave me back control over this form."

Saran nudged him with her nose. "Go, before someone wakes and finds you leaving . . . and do not port! You'll set my covers afire."

"I don't think that's true." Keleir sighed. "But I'll take the slow way if you insist."

THREE

THE ARMY TRAVELED for the length of a day in a line three men wide and two hundred men long, with servants handling horse-drawn supply wagons trailing behind them. A gloomy gray sky poured rain in a torrent, soaking through wool cloaks and leather armor. Not a single joyous person remained among the lot of wet and travel-weary soldiers. By nightfall they were well and truly miserable.

They came to a large field where the army spread out, and the servants started pitching tents and building fires to warm chilled bones and prepare food.

Saran watched with a somber frown as her servant wrestled with the wet canvas. He grumbled curses under his breath in a language she barely understood, one derived from a homeland somewhere across the First and far from Adrid. She knew that if she wanted to, the Core would grant her the gift of understanding, but it felt like an invasion of his private grumbling. He had brown skin, perhaps Droven in origin. But Droven men were large and built like great stone walls, and her servant had the framing of a malnourished mine worker. He stopped his wrestling and turned his dark eyes on her.

"I don't think the Princess of Adrid should have her tent on the outskirts of camp. That's all I'm saying, Your Highness." He was a thin boy, barely a man. Saran pitied him even as she appreciated his loyalty. She had no choice when it came to servants. She'd rather not have any at all, but he had adamantly volunteered for the position when the roster went up in the great hall. She suspected he thought it better to serve her than the others.

"When I need a washroom, I shall not lift skirts or draw down pants among men. I will have discreet access to a bush, and no one will talk me out of it."

The servant blew air through his nose and, shaking his head, went back to pitching the tent. She had no need to understand his language; the sideways glance he gave her proved a perfect translation for his garbled speech.

The battlefield is no place for the sole heir of a kingdom, least of all a woman.

War. Battle. Her father had granted her the freedom to fight among men without question. The King of Adrid took pride in a powerful heir, one who commanded respect among his military and was feared by his people. He didn't consider the possibility of losing her in battle. His breast was too full of hubris, too high on his own glory to assume that he would ever know failure.

Near her tent, a few soldiers fought with damp wood in the hopes of building something to warm themselves with. They'd managed to start a withering flame and were taking great care in coaxing it to a fuller life. Saran rubbed heat into her arms as she sat around the fire with them, watching as they burned shredded pieces of fabric from their own packs in the hopes of keeping the flame hot.

Keleir's tall form stepped out from the crowd and up to the pit, where he waved his hand over the flame. The fire roared up in a great whoosh, startling the soldiers bent so close to it. Except for a hooded form sitting on a wet log across from him, the gathered men gave a great yelp and abandoned the pit. Saran sat perfectly still, enjoying the rush of heat over her cold cheeks. She chuckled as the startled men found another pit to invade, one with fewer Mages around it.

The princess's gaze fell on the seated man who chose to stay in their company. She saw the edge of a smirk pull at his lips beneath the shadow of his hood. "Rowe," she said, greeting him with a smile. He lowered the cloth now that the mist had stopped and the fire burned warm. He was the same tall, broad man with blue eyes and black hair, who just the day before kept Odan from breaking her nose.

He gave a gentle nod in her direction, folding his arms and bracing them across his drawn knees. "Princess."

Keleir took a seat on the split log between them, a self-satisfied smile plastered on his handsome face. "Pity they didn't stay. The fire's quite nice now."

Saran chuckled and held her hands up to the flames. "Thank you. We are lucky to have a Fire Mage on days like this."

"We made camp early today," Rowe said. "I guarantee the men will be drunk and singing within the hour. Sleeping soon after."

True to form, the men did exactly as Rowe promised. The clouds parted to a bright, moonlit sky full of stars, and they danced beneath it in fits of laughter.

Saran ducked off to change into dry clothes. When she returned, Rowe and Keleir had big, wide grins and pints of ale in their hands. Keleir held two, drinking from one and holding out the other for her.

"Pickings are slim now. All that's left is piss ale," he said, lifting it higher. "Drink up and sit down. Food is almost ready."

Saran arched an eyebrow and turned up her nose at the foul-smelling liquid. "You really know how to sell a drink, Lord Ahriman. Unfortunately I'm not so eager to get drunk."

"Pour it out," Keleir whispered from behind his mug with a mischievous smile. "That's what I'm doing."

Her lips parted, but his narrowed gaze clamped her mouth shut. Rowe gave her a wink from across the fire, drunkenly slinging out his arm and sloshing the ale across the earth.

"I've had three of these! I feel nuttin'."

"Then have three more!" someone shouted from far back in the camp.

Saran laughed, taking up the ale and pretending to sip. She choked on a gag from the smell, and after faking her drink, she gently placed the mug near her boot. They spent the rest of the evening laughing at Rowe, who, while not truly drunk, gave a good show of acting so. He stumbled around from person to person, draping his long arm over their shoulders and leaning all his weight upon them. He would speak for a few minutes and go to another who caught his eye. Eventually he skipped clumsily back to the fire, dropping his empty mug by a log. Then, with a huffing laugh, he stumbled around the fire and held out his hand to Saran.

"Dance with me!"

Saran stretched her legs across the earth, comfortably leaning back. "No." Her green gaze fluttered up from the fire, narrowing on him. "You're drunk."

"Dance with me." He pushed his hand farther toward her, curling his fingers in and out.

Music filtered down from the other end of camp. It had been playing all night without her noticing, but suddenly the sound seemed so much louder. Soldiers stood together in a group playing lively tunes with mismatched instruments.

Rowe stared down with bright eyes and a handsome smile. He nudged her with his hand and then reaffirmed his commitment by motioning to the small area with just enough room to dance. They were near in age, and both only a few years younger than Keleir. Looking at Rowe's dark hair and bright eyes, it was hard to imagine them brothers. Then again, Keleir looked little like any man she'd ever seen. She wondered if the Fire Mage would boast the same black hair and blue eyes had the Oruke not stolen him as a vessel.

Saran huffed. "Fine!" Lumbering to her feet, she kicked over the full mug of ale as she passed.

Rowe curled his arm around her waist, giving a rough tug forward, and grinned devilishly down at her.

Saran's green eyes lingered on him as his hand smoothed down her lower back. "Watch it, my lord. I'll turn that arm to dust."

Rowe's grin broadened, and he carried her off, spinning about the fire with little care for falling in. She laughed as he tugged her along, not sure of her feet in this unrehearsed number. It was the type of dance one did in a bar after too many drinks, and Saran was unaccustomed to such merrymaking. She wasn't too familiar with courtly dances either, as her father did not host the same balls and banquets that other rulers might throw from time to time. Saran was not the type of princess who attended etiquette classes. She ate like a commoner, danced like an invalid, and fought like a man.

Abruptly the musicians transitioned into a less brassy song. Their instruments, poorly tuned and unevenly distributed, left the air filled with a shrill wailing song that wasn't fast enough to waltz to, but too slow and bad to enjoy.

Rowe led her in slower circles near the fire. His hand curled gently around hers while his hips swayed close. His face beheld a dreamy smile and his eyes roamed over her.

"What is this?" She sighed, aware of the intimacy in his movements.

"Keleir told me you were concerned that people might think you lie with him," he whispered into her ear. "So I'm letting them think you lie with me."

She shot a dark glare to Rowe's older brother seated nearby. "This isn't any better."

"It's better than him, isn't it?"

"No." Saran pulled her hand away and stepped back. She stood straight and regal, her head held high as any royal's. Pride was the only thing she shared with nobles. "Thank you for the dance, Lord Ahriman . . ."

"Blackwell," he corrected. Reminding her that while he shared the same blood as Keleir, he did not share the same cursed name. Ahriman, a surname given to all children born with an Oruke inside them, was Mavish for *darkness*.

"Lord Blackwell," she whispered, going back to her damp log.

Keleir eyed her from where he sat and brushed his drying white hair from his face. She knew he'd heard their exchange, but he made no move to justify his brother's willingness to throw himself before a sword. Rowe's nature could be self-sacrificing and noble, just as much as he could be exceedingly selfish.

"Well," Rowe exhaled, stretching. "I've been shunned by a beautiful woman and had more than enough to drink. I'll sleep now."

"Don't feel so bad, lad," said a soldier as he patted Rowe's shoulder. "I know a couple of pretty castle maids who will be happy to comfort you when we're home."

Rowe cupped a hand over his heart. "Thanks for the kindness, but I'm afraid I only have eyes for one."

"Oh, stop the melodramatics," Saran spat. She glared across the fire at him. "You are lucky I danced with you at all. If it weren't out of pity for hurting a drunken man's feelings, I'd have left you be. I'll not pity you again, that's for sure. Now off with you. Sleep the drink off, you louse."

Rowe's blue eyes narrowed, and his lips pressed into a tight line. He gave a gentle nod. "Forgive me." He left through the parting crowd, much like a wolf with his tail between his legs.

Keleir took a real gulp of ale, wincing at the taste. "Well, that was lovely."

Saran angrily tossed a twig into the fire. "I won't have him sacrificing himself to preserve our . . ." She tossed another and another, never bothering to finish her sentence.

Keleir nodded. "I do not want him sacrificing himself either. He gets these ideas in his head . . . I don't know where they come from. I wish he'd consult me f—"

"He gets them from you. If you would not tell him about our conversations, he would not feel it necessary to throw himself upon the sacrificial altar to preserve our . . ."

Keleir let out a heated laugh. "You can't even say it."

"What?"

The Fire Mage leaned toward her with a tight smile. "Our relationship."

"Shh!"

"If you say it, someone might hear. They might drag me off with a bag over my head. You're afraid I'll be assassinated or tortured by your father. After all, it would be one more thing he has to control you with." The fire grew taller and wider. It ate up the wet earth as though it weren't soaked and muddied. "I do not fear him or his Ekaru priests. If I wanted, I could slay him in a breath, and you know it. I could go there tonight and end this war."

Saran bent and searched the Fire Mage's eyes. She found the dreadful black of the Oruke sweeping across the whites. She called to him.

"He's a weak, pathetic, old, and diseased man who hurts you because he believes he has power over you. I will not stand for the fear you have of him. It is misplaced. He is *nothing* to be afraid of!"

"Keleir!"

The Fire Mage stiffened, and the black that had threatened to take him over receded in a flash.

"Calm," she whispered, touching just beneath her eye. A signal to him that he needed better control. She wanted to wrap her arms about him and ease his rage in the way only she could. The anger did not belong to him—not entirely, at least.

The Oruke's malicious presence writhing inside him fueled that rage. That sliver of connection, that blind and consuming rage, was the only thing the creature could slip out anymore since she'd walled it away.

Keleir touched his cheek. He swallowed hard and gave a harsh nod, burrowing down into his cloak and glaring at the weakening fire.

Once Keleir seized control of his anger, Saran turned her attention to the neighboring group gathered around the fire next to them, wondering just how much of the conversation they'd heard. When she met their eyes, they looked away, one by one, until all of them buried their heads in music and ale for the rest of the night. An agonizing silence settled between Keleir and Saran. When the silence grew too uncomfortable, she stood, tugging the cloak tightly about her shoulders, and headed off to the comforting darkness away from the fire.

Night drew on, and the camp went quiet. When only a few remained awake, Saran emerged from her tent and went into the forest where Rowe and Keleir waited, cloaked in wool and shadow, among the trees.

"Wear your hood," the Fire Mage ordered, tugging the dense fabric over her head.

"They already know who I am," she countered, but she let the hood stay as he settled his warm hands on her shoulders.

"Darshan might, but there could be people in that camp that do not understand why you're there. I don't want them thinking they have an opportunity to assassinate the Princess of Adrid. It will end our relationship with the rebels if I find I have to put my sword through another's heart. Do me this favor."

She scowled. "I don't really think anyone knows what the Princess of Adrid looks like."

"They know she has hair of fire. That's enough."

"Lots of people have this color hair."

"Are we going to stand here all night arguing about the covering of one's head, or are we going to go plan a coup?" Rowe asked, crossing his arms. "You can work out what you really want to argue about later."

Saran nodded. Her eyes glowed white hot, and the earth beneath their feet disappeared in a circle of light and mist. It swallowed them and deposited them in an open field hundreds of miles away. They settled near a wide ruin circle, where the grass stood hip high and wafted in a cool breeze. Fireflies floated about the field and in the dark forest around them in yellows, greens, and oranges. It was quiet, as silent as any tomb, and much warmer and drier than their camp.

Rowe swatted at an annoying horsefly as it buzzed too close to his head. "This doesn't look very populated. I think you miscalculated, Saran."

"I did not." She smiled and pointed to the stone arch along the wall, motioning for them to follow.

The ruins were the span of a small village. A wide, short wall built from medium-sized granite rocks, standing three feet high in most places, surrounded remnants of a tower that once stood twenty stories high over the lush countryside of southern Adrid.

"This used to be a great school for Magi before my father had the teachers slaughtered, the children abducted, and the building burned some forty years ago. Now the ruins hide a secret." Saran tried to imagine what the tower looked like long ago. It had been a time when children born gifted by the Core with elemental magic were delivered to be apprentices at the school. The Core chose and gave her gifts indiscriminately. No one really knew why some were born with an element and others weren't. It was long believed that the Core gave gifts as they were needed, though it was anyone's guess as to what they were needed for.

Saran held her hand to the stone arch leading into the circle of ruins, tilting an ear to the opening. "Can you hear it?"

"I hear nothing but crickets and wind," Rowe said, folding his arms with a skeptical arch of his brows before he angrily swatted the fly again. "And this damn creature." His eyes sparked a bright blue, and as he swiped his hand through the air, electricity crackled across his flesh and a tiny bolt of blue light zapped the horsefly midswoop.

"I know! Isn't it beautiful? I've never heard of a masking spell so clever or so large. Come here, and I'll show you," the princess said, motioning for them to follow. She stepped through the opening beneath the stone arch and disappeared.

Rowe, in a panic, dashed after her and blinked out of sight.

Keleir stood quietly, admiring the arch where Saran and Rowe no longer stood. Instead of rushing after them, he looped around the wall and hopped over it. He landed in the empty plot of land visible from the outer rim and waded through the tall grass. The Fire Mage ran his fingers over the blades, pulling at it and twirling the slivers of green between his fingers. After he surveyed the wide circle and hopped back over the wall, he went straight through the arch.

The potent scent of food and campfire greeted him as strongly as if he'd run into a physical wall, a far more appetizing smell than their dinner earlier. Warm light flooded the space where hundreds of small campfires sat between cabins and tents. Torches lined a long, wide walkway leading to the back of the camp where a gigantic canvas tent had been erected. The people were happy here, dancing and talking with smiles upon their faces much the same as the soldiers they'd occupied time with earlier. But this was different. It seemed like genuine happiness, despite their poverty. It baffled the Fire Mage, and being so interested in their merrymaking, he barely noticed the armored guard patting him down or stripping him of the sword at his waist.

Perhaps it was the quickness with which the man went about it or the careful way he did it so as not to bring attention to himself. When Keleir peered down at him, the man's face was white with fear. It was then that Keleir realized the person who should have covered their hair was him.

"Careful where you put your hands," Rowe warned the man inspecting Saran.

The princess frowned at his protectiveness and turned her attention to the guard, who searched her as professionally and unfeelingly as any that had come before. "We will see Darshan. I sent a bird, so he is expecting us."

The guard led them down the long, lit path to the massive tent at the back of the encampment, where he opened the flap and motioned them to enter. Saran passed through the threshold of fabric and into a wide stone room far larger than the expanse of the tent she'd seen outside.

They stood in a circular great hall with a towering vaulted ceiling supported by wide wooden beams. Tall, narrow stained glass windows lined the walls, each one depicting a different Mage with a different element. While it was night outside the tent, daylight filtered through each colored pane until the glass cast glittering jewels across the polished white marble floor. No furniture adorned the room save a wide table with parchment maps strewn across the top and two candelabras stationed at opposite corners. An older man, well past fifty, hunched over the maps, drawing wet lines with his finger that turned to inky black paths.

Saran coughed, easing toward the table and lowering the hood that covered her head. "Ishep Darshan," she said, smiling as he snapped to attention like a ghost had called his name. "I'm sorry, I didn't mean to spook you. You seemed very into your mapmaking."

"Saran D'mor . . ." he whispered, coming round the table, dressed in traveling clothes, a pale shirt, and brown pants. His speckled salt-and-pepper hair faded into a short white beard. "Forgive me, Princess. I was not expecting you until later in the week."

"I sent a message two days ago about my change in itinerary. I guess it didn't reach you."

Darshan frowned. "I received no communication from you. But this is a pleasant surprise. I was just going over the maps for Salara."

Saran followed him back to the table. "Salara is just what I came to speak with you about." Darshan lifted his eyes to the two men with her, letting his gaze settle on Keleir with an uneasy cringe. "Perhaps we can speak in private?"

"Are we going over this again?" Saran muttered.

"It is not that I do not trust him," Darshan said, frowning. "I simply do not trust what is *in* him. He is cursed."

Saran didn't need to look at Keleir to know he tensed at the accusation. Just as she sensed her awake or asleep, she sensed him. Each movement he made, the feeling of him, felt like a ripple in the air between them. She locked her eyes on the rebel leader and did not look away.

"I have secured the Oruke within to a confined place inside him. It has not broken free in five years. It will not. He is in perfect control." And he would stay so, as long as there was magic in the world and as long as she lived.

Darshan pressed his hands together. "I understand that, and it is comforting. However, how do you know?"

"How do I know what?"

"That it is he and not the Oruke?"

The princess stared into his aged, ocean-blue eyes and struggled not to look back at Keleir in question. Her faith would not waver simply because one man didn't believe it possible. She believed. She had to. She was the master of Keleir's salvation, and if she didn't believe, then no one would.

Darshan settled back as if to sit, and a wooden chair appeared from thin air to catch him. "When an Oruke takes a host, an unborn child, it takes a host completely. It is rare, if not impossible, for one to be born with their consciousness still intact. So how do you know, Your Highness, that the man behind you is not the Oruke having played you so very well all these years?"

The princess glided her fingers across the tabletop, letting her gaze follow their path. "Because, Ishep, the Oruke wants me dead." Keleir's presence tingled stronger in the air. "He has a sick fascination with it, actually. He wants my blood pooled on the floor beneath him. Out of all the people in the world, when I am near him, it drives him mad. He makes no sound decisions. He is overcome with bloodlust and rage. He's told me this, while his hands were around my neck, choking the life from me."

Darshan swallowed hard and turned his eyes to Keleir as if he expected some horrible monster to spring out from behind his flesh.

The princess straightened with a smirk. "If it brings you any comfort, Darshan, I can assure you that in the five years since I locked him away, the things that Keleir Ahriman does to me are nothing close to murder. He is in control. The Oruke inside him fights for freedom, but Keleir is in control."

"How long do you think he can maintain that control?"

"Forever," Keleir said, narrowing his eyes on the questioning man. "I can maintain it forever."

"I hope you are right," Darshan replied, and then he turned to the Fire Mage's brother. His face softened fondly. "Rowe, my boy, how are you? Have you heard anything from Her lately?"

Rowe touched his head. "No. She's been quiet. I've not heard anything in several months."

"The Prophetess comes and goes as She pleases, I suppose. She offers help when we need it most. Be thankful to have been chosen to hear Her voice. Now I suppose we should get on to matters. You can't be here all night." The four crowded around the table over the map.

"In four months, my father will move on Salara," Saran said. "At that point, the army will be away from the capital, making it the perfect time for an assault on the city. You will have to transition the militia from Salara to Andrian. When the army arrives in Salara, they will only find villagers there. However, this risks the villagers, since there will be no one to protect them. Without protection, the Salaran's lives will be sacrificed. You have to be willing to risk that for this plan to work, and I'm not. My father is sick; his illness has exacerbated his deranged mind. Madam Ophelia, our head healer, says he has very little time left. We could save more lives if we wait for him to die." Saran's eyes met Darshan's. "If we follow this plan of divide and conquer, even if you take the capital and the throne, you will lose rebels, but you will lose more villagers. Thousands are going to die. If you keep the rebels at Salara, they can defend the walls and defend the people."

Darshan frowned, shaking his head. "He has been sick for many years. He has not died yet. I have waited long enough . . . and you are not married yet. There are whispers that your father intends you to wed the Alar in the south. As border quarrels are often a prelude to invasion, Mavahan has been incredibly aggressive of late. The empire is weak. We do not have time to wait for him to die. We must act now."

Saran's brows knit together. "Father has made no mention of marrying me off to the Alar. I doubt he would want to merge his kingdom with someone he could not control. Not to mention, it would leave no one to govern his throne at his death. The kingdom will be thrown to the proverbial wolves."

"There is another whisper," Darshan said, eyeing Keleir, "that he will marry you to the Alar and adopt a son, a Mage, one powerful and feared, one close to his heart."

The princess laughed. "There are none close to his heart." Even still, her knuckles curled over the table as she stared at the maps. She'd heard none of these whispers, and she lived in the very palace where they were born. Her gaze fell on Rowe, and then Keleir, and both men shook their heads.

"How did you come to hear this?"

"From a chambermaid who often sits at the feet of your father in his study. She goes by Betha. The Mage to take his place, whose real name has been forgotten for another, was brought before him as a child and raised within the palace walls. He who bathed in blood: Lifesbane."

The wood of the table groaned beneath Keleir's grip. "I have not worn that name for many years, Darshan."

Ishep folded his arms across his chest. "Doesn't change the fact that you're a murderer. You might have staved off killing innocent women and children for the last couple years, but the king still admires your brutality. He will adopt you as his son, and you will be king in his stead, and I will not allow that. I will not allow an Oruke control of an army. The devastation would be unimaginable. Therefore, we will attack the palace on the same day that the army goes for Salara. Lives will be lost, but it will be worth it in the end."

"If what you are saying is true, and there is a threat of invasion from Mavahan, then upsetting the ruler of Adrid will open a floodgate of opportunity for the Alar. Perhaps this is not the time to think of destabilizing a kingdom when we could very well be wiped out by another overzealous king?" Keleir hissed. "We have heard nothing of this Alar. This changes a great many things."

"It changes nothing. There will be no destabilization. Saran D'mor will sit upon the throne. She is respected. The people will follow her."

Rowe's lip curled with a sneer. "They will kill her. The people know her as a warrior who fights in her father's army. They do not know that she fights to save their lives in battles, instead of ending them. The legends that follow her name are not ones of glory or honor. The people do not see anything but another brutal savage set to inherit the throne. As soon as Yarin is deposed, they will seek her head too. If not that, then the nobles will move in and place themselves in power. They will want to fashion it so a man takes the throne. Either one of them or a son."

"I have no desire to be queen," Saran said, eyeing Darshan. "You know this. We discussed it. I would step down and pass the power to you. I would get to live my life as I wish it. The people respect you, Ishep. They love you. They will follow you. They will not follow me, nor do I wish them to."

"The threat from Mavahan changes everything," Keleir added. "Their army has grown in the time that we've been at war with our own people. We should not ignore the possibility that deposing Yarin will bring war from the south. Perhaps we should give this more time and more thought?"

"I will not," Darshan said, standing. "That will leave more time for you to be named heir to the throne. You may not be Lifesbane now, but you could very well be again. I do not trust you, Keleir Ahriman. I do not trust the Oruke inside you. The Prophetess doesn't trust you either. She chose your brother to warn us of your coming."

Keleir slammed his hands upon the table, and Darshan jumped back an inch. Black seeped into the corner of Keleir's eyes and then quickly dispersed. "I am not that man anymore! And I am not some monster whispered of in prophecy."

"Are you so sure?" Darshan asked in a quiet whisper, watching as the Fire Mage struggled to reign in his anger.

Keleir stiffened, standing straight, and stared hard at the rebel leader before he dropped his eyes to the maps strewn across the tabletop. "I'll wait outside."

Saran started after him. "Keleir!"

Keleir lifted a hand and waved Saran off, ducking back through the fabric hanging across the door.

"He is a danger," Darshan said. "You know what has been deemed by the Prophetess. No matter your feelings, Saran and Rowe, his destiny is beyond your control. He will bring devastation to this world."

Saran shook her head in fierce denial, staring down at the floor. Blinking the mist from her eyes, she turned a stern gaze on Darshan. "I will ensure he does not."

"You will fail." The old Mage frowned.

A wistful smile tugged the corners of her mouth. "I will die trying, and if such a thing should happen, it will have been better to die having tried than to abandon him and let him fall freely into darkness."

A long silence passed between them, with Rowe biting his tongue and curling his fist to keep from punching the old man across the table. After the air grew too thick with tension, Rowe righted himself and went to his brother. Darshan stared at the doorway as if hopeful that the Lightning Mage would return. When he did not, Darshan bent his head and ran his finger across the map, painting a watery line that eventually turned to black ink.

"I will attack the palace the day the king attacks Salara. We will kill the king and put you on the throne. You have the most command of the army in that area and will be able to quell any upset that might happen once he is dead. After a month, when we get word to the armies stationed in outposts throughout the kingdom that the king has died and you are queen, we will make a transition. Whether by marriage or avocation. Agreed?"

"No marriage, Darshan. I have already chosen the man I'll spend my life with. The more concerning matter is, what if Mavahan invades?"

"Mavahan is a kingdom of men who do not believe in the Core, the Prophetess, or the Magi. They are surrounded by a great desert and live in the Deadlands. They have no magic, and no concept of how it functions. Those who cross our borders and feel the Awakening will have no idea how to hone that ability or use it to their advantage. We will crush them because of their ignorance. I have no doubt about this. Are we in agreement?"

"I believe we are, if you are so unmoving to compromise." Saran straightened and folded her hands together. "There is another problem that we should discuss. I am to be punished, and I do not know how. I will send word once I've received it. It may not change your plans, but I need you to know so you can alter accordingly."

Darshan nodded, and his gaze grew soft. "I hope . . . I hope he does not hurt you."

Saran lifted her knowing gaze to him. "You know how he punishes those he cannot kill."

The older Mage's brows knit, and a dark cloud came over him. "Your mother was very strong, Saran. You are stronger. That is why she sought so hard to save you from him. She knew that you would do what she could not . . . in the end. I know she did."

"Are you saying that to discourage any self-doubt I have?" Saran laughed at his mortified expression. "Do not worry, Ishep. I do not intend to make suicide the escape route from my father."

Darshan choked on the awkwardness of her words. "Good! Well, be off. You have stayed here longer than intended, I assume. Be safe, Saran D'mor. The Three need you."

Saran jolted. It had been ages since someone mentioned the Three out loud. Months since she, Keleir, and Rowe bothered to explore them in the little free time they had. Saran thought about the gleaming metal towers of the Second and how their civilizations faded sparsely into beautiful rolling green hills. The Second was slowly being devoured by its people and their wars. She could do little to help that world.

Then she thought about the Third. She thought about their gleaming glass cities that covered every inch of the world's surface. She thought about the oceans that had turned yellow and acidic and all the life that had once lived in them now washed dead upon the shores. She thought about Roshaud, the president of the Third, a man her father kept in good company, a man that made her stomach twist with disgust. For a second his black shadow loomed tall over her, as it had when she was a child. Then it was gone, and the fear with it. She could do nothing to help that world either.

Darshan believed her to be something she was not. He believed her to be the Equitas, the counter to the Oruke in prophecy. A savior for her world and the ones beyond. But the Three didn't need her as far as she was concerned.

"Just this one, really," Saran said with a smile. "Just this one."

Outside Keleir and Rowe stood close, muttering between themselves. The Fire Mage had kindling in his eyes, and their orange glow was a better sight than the seeping black he displayed in times when the Oruke battled for control. At least this anger was all his own.

"Rowe, go on ahead. We'll follow closely behind. I need to speak to Keleir a moment," she said, once in the quiet field outside the hidden fortress.

Rowe nodded, and a crackling electric-blue portal swallowed him up.

Cool wind tossed Saran's red hair into her face, and she tugged it back behind an ear, lifting her eyes to the smoldering Fire Mage before her.

"He knows not of what he speaks," she said, reaching for his arm.

He drew away, pursing his lips into a tight line, and stepped a half circle around her. "He knows exactly what he's talking about. I'm slipping, Saran." He turned his face to the stars and scratched angrily at the back of his head. "I can feel him clawing, grasping. He gains more ground with each passing year and ever more quickly as of late. I'm angry. I'm angry all the time."

"I'll push him back," Saran said, recovering the ground she lost when he drew away. "I won't let him have you."

"He already has me! I can't escape him because I am him. I am Lifesbane. I am a murderer and a monster. I have killed *so* many people, Saran . . . and eventually I will kill more."

"You are not a murderer! It was not you who killed those people."

"Yes, Saran, it was. It was me." He curled his fingers in her hair and cupped her cheeks. "You love me and you see me as no one else ever will. You know my soul, and that blinds you to what I really am. You cannot see the beast because you only see me. But I am the beast. We are one and the same."

She shook her head, pressing in against him. Her hands lifted to his face and she held him as he held her, looking deep into those swirling pools of red. "You cannot have him," she told the Oruke because she knew it could hear her. "He is mine."

Keleir kissed her, curling his hand at the back of her head and his arm around her waist. He drank her in until he could no longer go without air, and drawing away, he said, "When this is finished . . ."

"We will leave," Saran said. "The three of us. Like we planned. We'll find someplace peaceful, and your anger will be quelled. All this blood and war does you little good."

"We could leave this world altogether . . ." Keleir appraised her. "We could go to the Second or the Third, if we're really desperate."

Saran frowned. Neither of those options suited her, especially not the Third. "Let's not talk about this now."

Keleir's jaw worked, but eventually he nodded and drew her close. "I won't let your father marry you off to the Alar," he whispered, his lips brushing against her jaw.

"We'll be good and gone before he can, far away, over the mountains, on a lake perhaps, with a cute cottage. We'll fish and hunt and read all day. I'm sure you and Rowe can find plenty to entertain yourselves with." She smiled at the wiry grin that broke out across his face. But then he paused, and the grin fell away. He set his eyes on the dark trees around them, staring off into a place that only he could see. It was like he could hear or see someone she could not.

"If—" Keleir clenched his jaw. His eyes flickered around with thought. "If it takes over—Hey, don't shake your head. Listen to me, this is important. If it takes over, run. Don't try to save me. It will be too late. There will be nothing left to save. Run. With Rowe. Go as far away as you can. I don't want you to die by my hands, even if I'm not the one controlling them."

Saran blinked her eyes, turning them to the stars to avoid him seeing her tears. "Run," she said, laughing, watching the world blur. "I'm not good at running."

"I know. I've borne witness to your clumsiness." Keleir smiled for a while longer, watching her as she refused to look at him and show him her tears. "Run, Saran D'mor. Run from me. As far away as you can get. Run from this world so that I may never find you."

Saran's jaw set, and she turned away from him, swaying into the high grass and running her fingers along the sea of feather-soft tips. She turned back to him, tears gone. "You speak as if you've already lost."

His lips twitched, and he pressed them to her cheek in a soft kiss. "I was lost all my life until I found you. As long as I have you, I'll never be lost again. As long as I am who I am and as long as I am with you, I am a found man."

She drew back and curled her fingers in his. "I can feel your presence in the very air around me, and you can feel mine. We are connected. My soul to your soul."

"Do you think I'm your soul mate?" Keleir grinned. "Romantic."

Saran scowled.

Keleir mused, "Maybe I am. Maybe that's the feeling. This electric connectivity when we are near, and maybe that's why he hates you so much. You are the redeemer of my soul, Saran. You balance me."

"You are a clever wordsmith tonight, m'lord."

"Some nights I feel inspired." He clutched her hand tighter.

"We should go. The sun will rise soon."

Keleir shook his head. "Not yet." He curled his fingers around hers. "Can we go somewhere—"

"Keleir . . ."

"A Window is open. Let me take you somewhere. Just for a minute."

Saran knew what he wanted to do. He wanted to leave their world, if only for a moment. He wanted to run from time, to run from the lives they had. Soon, she thought, they would no longer be bound by their oaths to Darshan. They would have the freedom to be whoever they wished and to go wherever they desired. For now, she'd let him pretend that they were free . . . just for a minute.

Windows to the other worlds only opened near sunrise and sunset. If he wanted to show her something on the Second, the morning before she faced her father's wrath was as good a time as any.

"All right," Saran whispered, giving him a gentle nod.

Keleir wrapped his arms tight around her waist, and his eyes glowed with orange embers. Fire crackled up around their ankles. It wrapped around them, heatless and brilliant.

FOUR

THEY REAPPEARED IN dark shadows between two long metal boxes. The earth felt hard as stone beneath their feet and was dyed the color of pitch. Flashes of colorful lights blinked up in the night sky, and the sound of screams and laughter filtered out from the other side of the boxes. The screams and laughter were accompanied by music and the roar of metal against metal. The sun had just begun to set over the horizon and blanket the area in night. The last tendril of sunlight glimmered through the trees opposite of the flashing lights.

The air was warm, like where they'd been on the First moments before, but thick with humidity. It was too hot for the leather armor they wore, but they wouldn't be here long enough to justify shucking it.

Keleir took Saran's sword and sheath and tucked it under one of the metal boxes before following suit with his own. "Let's not get arrested again," he muttered before taking her hand and leading her out from behind the boxes and into the warm lamplight.

Except, they weren't lamps . . . that's not what they called them here. They called them streetlights, and they were electric. Everything here was electric.

Saran's eyes lifted to the sky and the colorful glittering lights of a giant spinning wheel slowly. The wheel had compartments with people waving down from them. Beyond the wheel were tents and caravans. There were other contraptions that went high into the air and spun around, blinking wild colorful lights and music. Each contraption had a group of people in them that were either laughing hysterically or screaming in utter terror. Hundreds of people moved back and forth down wide paths that led through the area, hopping into lines that wove toward the metal contraptions.

As they walked the path, Saran spotted one line going into a tall, thin metal house with a wolf man painted on the front of it. Words were written in bright yellow lettering near his sharp fangs. Inside the dimly lit house, she could just make out people feeling their way through a maze of mirrors and glass into a dark corridor. The ones who survived exited down a metal slide.

Keleir's large, excited smile lifted Saran's apprehension over visiting the Second. It was the happiest she'd seen him in days, and with how much his control over the Oruke had been slipping as of late, she would indulge his need for fun.

He hurriedly led her through the crowd toward one of the contraptions in the shape of a giant spinning top decorated with large, colorful flashing lights. Along the way she caught the name of their location on a banner dangling over the path.

Welcome to the Greater Gulf State Fair.

A fair. Fairs on the Second were far busier than those on the First. But then again, Saran had never really seen a fair in person. She'd read about them, heard stories told by older Adridians. A fair hadn't come to the capital since her father took the throne.

A fair in Adrid would also have never possessed metal machines or lights and music as brilliant or overwhelming.

Keleir rushed them into a long line waiting to enter the giant metal top. She curled her arm in his, drawing closer to him. The people moved around them like a sea of water, pressed in close. Too close. The thickness of the crowd and the wild noise made her uneasy. The world felt too loud to enjoy, but Keleir's calm presence kept her planted firmly in place.

She rested her head to his shoulder, peeking out from behind her curly hair.

When the eyes around them noticed Keleir's peculiar hair and eyes, they simply glanced away as if it were nothing at all. No one looked at him with fear or hatred here. She suspected that's why he liked it so much. Despite their technology, despite the inevitably dying world that he despised, he found peace amongst the nonconformists on the Second.

Keleir taught Saran and Rowe how to visit this world. Visiting the Second used to be a skill and luxury prevalent among Mages of the First, but as the last of the old wise ones died off and Yarin refused to continue the practice of passing knowledge down to the new generation, those with the ability to use Windows to move from one world to another were few and far between. Yarin didn't want to risk the people under his thumb seeing a way to evade him, and Saran couldn't deny that she had thought of escaping to the Second herself many times. Something always held her back.

Keleir knew how to travel between worlds because the Oruke had taught him as a child. He never spoke about the things the Oruke had shown him on those trips to the Second. But when his mind had finally become his own and he had full control over his body, Keleir had taken to journeying to the Second for fun. Then he taught Saran and Rowe the rules of traveling, and the three had, at one time, spent endless nights exploring with gleeful joy.

That was, until Saran noticed that the longer they spent in a place with a failing Core and dying magic, the harder it was for Keleir to maintain control over the Oruke . . . or rather, the harder it was for her to maintain the spell she'd woven around his soul.

"We don't have much time," Saran whispered. "If we miss our Window and don't return, I'll be locked in the dungeons."

"One ride," he replied, smiling at her. "I just want to show you one ride, and then we'll be gone before the Window closes."

Saran turned an uneasy gaze to the spinning metal top.

"Cool costume, dude!" shouted a teen in oversized clothes as he ran up to Keleir with a raised hand. Saran drew her arms away and prepared for the attack, but Keleir simply lifted his arm and smacked his palm flat against the other's hand.

The teen passed them by without so much as a second glance.

But Saran's nerves were lit with tension.

Before they reached the guardian of the spinning top, who seemed to be collecting small pieces of paper from each person who wished to enter, a group of young girls bounded up to them. Saran nearly thrashed them all, but Keleir pulled her arms tight to her sides in a tense hug.

"Can we get a picture with you guys? You look amazing!" shouted one.

"So cool. Who are you supposed to be?" asked the other.

Keleir nodded to them. He spoke to them kindly in their language—English—but never really offered them any answers. The girls gathered in a tight cluster that sent Saran's panic wild. Keleir squeezed her tight, and they all faced a woman Saran assumed to be the mother of the girls. The woman held a thin rectangle up before her face.

"Smile! Karlie, smile!"

A flash of light blinded Saran, and the girls ran off with a giggle, disappearing as fast as they'd arrived.

"Thank you!" the mother called as she hurried after them.

By this time, they were next in line. The ride's guardian flexed his hands for them to come forward, and Saran stepped dizzily along with Keleir, blinking the blinding colors from her eyes. The Fire Mage fished a small gold piece out of the pouch at his waist. "I don't have a ticket," he murmured, "but this is real gold."

"Sure it is," the man muttered.

"It is," Keleir insisted, his native Adridian accent thick in the air. "I promise."

"Need a ticket each," the ticket man replied. "No ticket, no ride."

Saran squeezed Keleir's arm and noted the disappointment in his eyes. Her eyes lit white. The entire fair went silent around them. The brightly lit wheel, with its dangling baubles filled with people, stopped spinning. The metal contraptions that flung and whizzed about froze midswing or flip in the air. The patrons stopped walking midstep, and the ticket man paused as he tried to pass the gold piece back to Keleir.

Saran looked at her lover with blinding white eyes and a clever smile. She reached into the man's pouch and drew two slivers of paper.

The world restarted with a loud roar of music, screams, and laughter. As the man passed the gold piece to Keleir, Saran held out the slivers of paper. "Here. Tickets. He likes to stay in character," she said, the English words falling unpracticed from her tongue.

The Core's gift of magic allowed them many things. One happened to be the ability to pick up on foreign languages quickly—where magic was available. As they were born of the

Core, the life of the planet, and all languages derived from life, the Core allowed them the ability to learn those languages as easily as a sponge absorbing water.

But Saran had never practiced it as much as Keleir. So while she knew the words, Keleir spoke them with far more skill.

"Whatever," the man muttered and took the tickets from her. He motioned for them to enter the ride.

Keleir took her hand and guided her in. It was dark inside, save for a bright purple light in the ceiling that caused all white fabric to glow. Keleir's hair shone like a bright purple beacon that made Saran laugh and reach up to touch it. He laughed too when her teeth glowed purple, and he drew her to a place on the wall where two empty plush mats were available for them to lean against.

"What is this?" she asked him, flattening out against the mat.

"It's what flying feels like," Keleir replied. "What I imagine flying feels like."

He reached out and grasped her fingers, curling his around hers.

The round room filled with people. They all pressed against the mats on the walls, and the door closed. Saran felt nervous being locked in such a dark space with otherworld strangers, but Keleir wasn't afraid.

So she wouldn't be either.

The top began to move, slowly at first and then faster. The faster it moved, the more the air felt like a physical force pressing against her. Saran clutched Keleir's hand tighter. The force pinned them to the walls as the whole contraption changed angles, tilting from one end to the other.

An excited laugh escaped Saran's lips when the wall slid upward and then down. She tried to lift her head off the mat and couldn't. She tried to reach her hand toward the purple light in the ceiling but could barely get her fingers off the mat.

Saran turned her head to Keleir, feeling the force press her cheek into the mat. He was already looking at her, a big, wide grin on his face. His teeth glowed purple.

Saran laughed. She laughed so hard that her eyes watered with tears. Keleir laughed with her, and the two of them, hands clasped, learned what it felt like to fly.

Eventually the spinning slowed, the tilting stopped, and the pressure against them ebbed until they could lift their heads from the mat. Saran's belly felt queasy, and she didn't want to rise off the mat until she knew she wouldn't vomit.

Keleir slid close to her, pressing his lips to her cheek. He pulled her with him from the ride and out into the droves of people exploring the fair.

"That was the first ride I ever went on when I came here the first time. I stumbled upon the fair while blindly porting as far as my eyes could see on one of my first trips to the Second without the Oruke in control. The fair only comes here in the fall, I think. When I came other times, it wasn't here."

Saran wondered why Keleir had never taken them here. Rowe would have loved everything about it, right down to the screaming metal and blaring music. Both of them could handle the busyness of the Second far better than she could.

"We need to go," Keleir said, tugging her back toward the darkness where they arrived.

Saran wanted to go on another ride.

She wanted to know more about the big wheel with the flashing lights. She wanted to know how high she could go in it. Saran wanted to eat the ugly cake coated in sugar she kept seeing people snack on. She didn't want to go back home. She didn't want to be a princess. She didn't want to be punished for saving people who would never see her as anything but an enemy.

But Saran nodded and followed along. They could not stay. Keleir, especially, could not stay. Even if she had the ability to hold back time, she couldn't do it forever. She could move it forward, backward, and freeze it, but only temporarily. There were some things not even she could stop time from eroding, no matter how hard she tried.

FIVE

THE CAPITAL OF Adrid sat atop a massive hill, bordering on the edge of a six-hundred-foot cliff overlooking the Andrian Sea for which the city was named. Like many towns in Adrid, it had once been prosperous, a mecca to those seeking knowledge and wealth. Now, poverty stricken, most of the inhabitants and shop owners fled some years ago for neighboring cities or other countries, hoping to rebuild the wealth lost from taxation and a declining economy. Once filled with happy people, it now stood as nothing more than a glorified military fort.

The castle sat at the back of the city, at the crest of the cliff. Its towers wove up into a gray sky like narrow fingers grasping at the dreary clouds. Most of the castle was in fine shape, save for the older wings. The brickwork on the east end of the castle, the oldest, was crumbled, and some of the towers teetered more in the breeze than others.

The quiet city sat walled away from wide grassy plains, once lush in farmland and vegetables. Small farmhouses dotted the fields, most collapsed upon themselves, while the fields were overrun by waist-high weeds. The road that led into the city stood in such a state of disrepair that massive ruts filled with muddied water replaced the cobblestone paving.

The army passed along the trail toward the city in a slow, somber pace, more like a funeral procession than a formidable force. The wagons and horses limped along the beaten path, avoiding the deeper holes when possible, until they reached the threshold of the city.

Heavy iron gates opened with a low groan while soldiers in the gatehouse struggled with the heavy crank to lift it high enough for the wagons to pass beneath. The harsh weight of invisible chains latched around Saran's arms and legs as the iron clashed to the earth behind her. Her prison door now closed, the cold stone walls squeezed in around her. She took deep breaths to calm her rattled nerves and reminded herself that it was merely temporary. A promise she made every time she returned, which she always did.

"We welcome you back," said a burly soldier from the bastion wall. He clanked his armored hand against the stone before rapping it across his breastplate. "Did you paint the earth red with blood?"

Odan turned on his horse to glare at Saran. His hateful smile transformed into a grin too wide for his narrow face. "We had a problem with one of our Mages. It will be dealt with shortly."

Saran's eyes rolled. Once they were well into the city and at the foot of the castle steps, she passed the reins of her horse to the stableboy. He always waited near a guard who sat at the base of the steps and fed the great fire basins that sat upon short stone pillars at either side of the grand staircase. The guard gave her a curt nod as he splintered wood with a sharp hatchet and tossed it into the fire.

Saran turned to Odan. "I'm not worried."

"You should be," Odan said, working the gloves off his slender hands. "I wonder, has the king ever had you whipped? I'd very much enjoy the sight."

"Scarring a royal heir is not his prerogative, especially one he wishes to barter like chattel for the right marriage proposal. Shall we?" She motioned with a quick wave of her hand for him to ascend the stairs ahead of her.

He blinked and did not move, looking very much like a man who thought to be set on fire any second. Saran sighed. "If I go with you to accept my punishment, rather than have you tattle like a scorned child, it ends all of this quicker. I desire a hot bath and a warm bed, and I can have that as soon as I'm done catering to you." Saran snatched the leather gloves from her hands and motioned again for Odan to walk ahead of her. "It was a long road, and I must atone for what I did to you, correct? What difference does it make if it is now or later?"

Anxiety welled in her, but her face revealed nothing but a confident woman. Saran had practiced hiding her fears and sorrow behind a mask of aggression and bravado, and as always Odan Marki bought it. The Ice Mage snarled, turning with such melodramatic fervor that his long cloak slapped in the light breeze. Saran smiled and sauntered up the steps behind him.

In the grimness of a cold, dark throne room, where the windows hadn't been cleaned in years and cobwebs hung from forgotten chandeliers, Saran lifted a bored gaze from the rough-cut granite floor. Her jade eyes fell on her father as he hobbled back and forth before his throne, his cane clacking hollowly along with him. The throne sat upon a wide, low podium, flanked by huge iron bowls full of burning coal, a decorative touch that matched the staircase entrance to the palace outside. The orange flames flapping in the bowls cast a harsh, hot light across the king's wrinkled, angry face. At either side of him, at the foot of the podium, stood his personal Saharsiad—Mage Hunters—paid to defend him should any of his underlings seek to use magic against him.

For a long time, King Yarin D'mor paced in silence while he listened to Odan's recounting of the village fight. The Ice Mage spoke of how, just as they'd achieved the upper hand, the princess left her horse and reversed their progress with the gift the Core granted her—time. When Odan's story concluded, her father lifted his eyes, his lip twitching with a snarl. The words seemed to fail him until his whole body shook and they rattled out of him in one angry burst. "You conniving, traitorous bitch. Do you know what you've cost us?"

Saran clasped her hands behind her back, observing his anger quietly. Though used to his intimidation, she felt a sense of dread when his half-blind eyes settled on her, knowing part of her would always be the little girl who feared him. "There were no insurgents in that village. We were slaughtering innocent people. Frankly, Father, if I may be perfectly honest with you, you don't deserve any praise from people who are starving."

Yarin glowered at his daughter, nails scratching furiously at his dry flesh. He had aged much from the disease that riddled his body. Once a proud, robust man, he sat withered to a dry husk, with loose skin hanging over rotting bones.

He paused his self-mutilation to lift a finger at her. "If you were any other soldier, I'd have you drawn and quartered for such betrayal. But you are my daughter. You are the heir. I need you."

Saran's gaze settled on him, and her mouth opened before she could reign in her words or her temper. "You only need me as a bargaining chip for the proper marriage proposal. You couldn't care less what happens to me after that. Just as you cared so little for my mother. She was a path to the throne and a belly for your cursed child!" Her eyes burned as she glowered at him. The ache of that truth weighed heavy in her heart. He had always hated her, she thought, because he wanted a son.

"Oh, shut up, Saran. Stop being melodramatic," the old man hissed, scowling as he paced back the opposite direction.

"It's true, isn't it? I bet it sorely disappoints you every day that she bore a girl to your crown. Whenever you look upon your daughter, do you not weep for a son?" Her vision blurred with angry tears, and she quickly blinked them away, focusing on reclaiming the mask she wore so well before him.

"Shut up, Saran!" Yarin reared and slung his cane at her.

The princess's eyes flared with white light, and the cane aged to dust well before striking her.

The room hushed. The advisers to the king slunk back while the Saharsiad stepped forward. Yarin appraised his daughter as a farmer would the prospect of putting down a lame horse. "Saran, you have used your power to thwart me. I allowed you freedom. I allowed you to learn your gifts. I allowed you to work alongside the Magi in the battlefield. You have threatened your own kingdom with this betrayal, and I cannot forgive it. You must be punished. Until such time as I see fit or until you have proven yourself noble to your father once more, I am restricting your powers and confining you to the castle."

Saran's gaze narrowed, and a dark chuckle escaped her. "I won't allow that."

"You have no choice." The king nodded.

A harsh grip took her hands behind her back, and a metal band clamped around her wrist. Her knees buckled at the cold, depleting drain of magic as she was cut off from the Core. Saran twisted and tugged her arm from the soldier, examining the metal manacle around her wrist. It was thin and flat, scribed with runes that blocked her connection to the Core. Nostrils flaring with fury, she tugged on it, bit at it, and screamed when nothing she did could tear it from her.

"Take it off!"

"You are not allowed to the leave the castle. You are, however, allowed to roam it. Do not do something to risk losing that privilege as well. Ponder your mistake and make sure that you understand your place here, Daughter."

Saran stopped short of snatching him up by his robes. She heaved angry breaths, clenching her fists at her sides. "The people you crush under your boot won't take it much longer. You have months at the most. They will raid this castle, and they will string you up on the rafters." She backed away from him. "Perhaps I will have to join you. Should it come to that . . . I will gladly swing alongside you."

Yarin's lips drew back with a sneer. "Guards, drag my daughter back to her room. She isn't to leave or receive a single meal until I decide otherwise."

The guard near her gave an apologetic look as his hands curled around her arms and tugged her from the room. "You sure don't know when to quit," he muttered, releasing her once the door closed.

"It is a personality flaw I'm working through." Saran rubbed her wrist and the annoying metal bracelet. "You don't happen to have a key to this, do you?"

"King Yarin has it, or he has given it to someone to hold on to. I'm afraid you won't be using your element anytime soon, Your Highness."

The guard did as instructed and guided her to the opulent room she occupied on the southwest side of the castle, perched on the cliffs overlooking the sea. The room's rough-cut stone walls were draped in rich tapestries, the floors were polished hardwood, and the space was filled with intricately carved furniture.

Once inside, the guard took hold of the door and drew it closed. He paused a moment, giving her a sorry look before casting his eyes down in shame. "I have to lock you in. I am sorry."

Saran gave him a soft nod. He closed the door, and moments later it locked with a click. Now alone, she set to prying at the metal band around her wrist until it cut into her skin. She tried everything, even pouring oil over her flesh and dragging the manacle over her hand as far is it would go. Nothing worked, no matter what trick she tried or what she pulled against. In the end, she only hurt herself.

Frustration boiled over into rage, and the princess stalked across her dim room to the ornate chair by the empty fireplace, falling into it with a growl. She needed the Bind off. Without her power, everything would slowly unravel. Without it, she wasn't sure how long Keleir would be able to keep the creature inside him locked away. She had to convince her father to end her punishment—and quickly.

Hours passed while Saran fiddled with the band that blocked her magic, until sunset made her room grow dark. True to Yarin's word, no one brought food. The maids who normally visited her in the evening hours to light the candles and run a bath didn't show either. Not that Saran cared much for that, since she hated someone fussing over meaningless tasks for her. Instead she lit her own candles and took a cold sponge bath with a basin of stale water near the bed. She used the small hatchet near the fireplace to split wood into kindling, which she used to build a fire for light and warmth.

Boredom set in not long after that, and she paced her room over, wrapped in a loose, flowing cotton robe. She examined every object in her room as if it were the first time, running her fingers over books and trinkets that littered the cluttered shelves.

She'd collected a trinket from any place she visited on the Three, but more than half of them had come from the Second.

They were little mementoes from the places she'd gone to with Keleir and Rowe when they found time to hide away there. They would go just at sunset, and being unable to return until dawn, would attempt to function the following day with no sleep. The nights they didn't sleep were worth it. They were not beholden to anyone. They did as they pleased.

But they always came back. Rowe sought redemption from his past. Keleir stayed for Saran. Saran stayed because . . .

She lifted one trinket from the shelf, a two-inch-tall green woman with a crown, a book, and an arm outstretched toward the sky. The statue's hand was broken off. Saran couldn't remember what the statue once held, but she did remember that it represented freedom.

The balcony door creaked open, and a rush of cool sea air fluttered into the room.

Keleir closed the glass doors behind him, moving from the shadows into the candlelight. "I didn't know he would banish you to your room without supper like a child."

Saran stared at him in shock, dropping the trinket and curling her fingers over her heart. It cracked against the floor. The air lacked the familiar ripple of power. She should have sensed him the moment he appeared just outside her window. The vacancy nearly tore a cry from her. "Keleir," she breathed, slipping her arms around his waist and burrowing against him.

"Something's wrong . . . You don't feel right. Actually I don't feel you at all . . ." His red eyes narrowed on her, his fingers brushing over her cheek.

She lifted her arm to show him the silver band around her wrist. "It looks like I won't be leaving this place any time soon, unless we do it the hard way." Her eyes, full of concern, looked him over. She touched his face and hair lightly with her fingers, examining him as if she were looking for something broken. "How are you feeling?"

Keleir grabbed her arm as she lowered it, pulling her wrist closer for inspection. The red in his eyes lit like embers in the breeze. Dreadful horror stole his expression. To Bind a Mage was the cruelest of all punishments. "He *Bound* you?" Darkness crept into his voice, dropping it an octave lower than normal human tongue. "I'll rip him apart slowly until he tells me where the key is."

"Keleir," she whispered, grabbing his hand and prying out of his tightening grip. She locked her hand with his, fast and tight, while she brushed fingers through his hair to soothe him. "Breathe. Calm. Please you weren't well yesterday. You were too close to the edge. Don't let it gain any more ground than it already has. Don't give it an opening." *Not now, not when I'm like this.* His red gaze settled slowly, his breathing returning to normal, and he framed her face in his hands. Concern creased his brow.

"It will just take a little longer," Saran whispered, her voice as calm and smooth as placid water. She was used to this rage. Like a lion tamer calming a beast, she used her words and her touch to mellow his storm. She needed him, above all, to be calm. "Rowe will be patient."

"I am not patient."

She arched an elegant eyebrow at him, a smirk tugging at her lips. "Oh, I'm quite aware of that." She wrapped her arms around his neck and tilted her head up to him. Slowly his lips found hers in a wash of heat, while strong arms drew her up against him.

"You need a distraction," she said, pressing her forehead to his. Her hands snaked up his chest and unbuckled the clasps to his leather armor, dropping it at their feet. The metal clasps clanked harsh against the floor. Keleir sighed as her soft hands slipped under his dingy white tunic, lifting it over his head. He sought her wrists, grasping, pinning them behind her back as he drew her in for a kiss.

"I have missed you," he whispered, his forehead pressed to hers. "Being so close on the road and yet unable to truly be with you . . ." He kissed her, hot and long, and drew her ever tighter into him as if he wished to merge her soul with his. A moment later he pulled away and gave a roguish smile. "I'm serious, I will kill Yarin and rid you of that thing. Tonight."

Saran frowned. "Do not be so willing to shed blood—even if he is deserving of it." Knowing that her serious tone drew them increasingly further from the playful mood she attempted to weave, she washed the thoughts from her mind and focused on things that usually quelled the beast in him. "It will be hard to help you undress without hands, m'lord. You're hindering my attempt to distract you from your anger." The princess tugged idly against him.

Keleir snorted. "I could just burn the pants off."

Saran scoffed.

The Fire Mage chuckled, releasing his grip. He lifted his arms slowly out to his sides. He relished the sensual look she gave him while her hands snaked over his belt and drew it away. When he stood bare before her, his hands went to work drawing the cotton robe from her shoulders and gathering her light weight into his arms.

They worshipped each other with hands and mouths until they tangled together among the furs and silks of her bed. The wrestling ended with Saran mounted atop him, riding along a wave of ecstasy, while Keleir withered beneath her. He sought handfuls of flesh, and his mouth traced wet lines across her chest. Then, once they crossed the threshold of heaven, they lay in the quiet dark of her room, the moonglow bathing over them through rippled panes of glass.

Saran nuzzled into the crook of his warm neck. "Do you think he heard?"

"Hmm?"

"The guard outside. Do you think he heard?"

"If he did?" Keleir asked with a laugh. "You're already confined to your room like a child and cut off from the Core—what would it matter if your father found us now?"

"Your head on a spike," Saran replied. "I'm pretty sure that matters to both of us."

"The only reason I don't kill him is because you have restrained me. But if he doesn't release you from that contraption tomorrow evening, I will find my restraint sorely lacking."

"The Saharsiad," Saran reminded him. "They'd kill you or you'd have to run for a very long time."

"We're already going to run, Saran," Keleir said, sitting up over her. "What difference does it make whether he dies tonight or after Salara? People will still hunt us. They will hunt you for your title, and they will hunt me for the Oruke . . ." Keleir's brow furrowed. "But they will not find us. Not if we go someplace no one would ever dream to look."

"Keleir, please . . ."

"We could go to the Third."

Saran pursed her lips together, thankful for the shadows to hide her frustration. He couldn't go to the Third. Her power wouldn't work there, and he'd eventually . . . It wasn't a guarantee, not by any means, but if they were there, the spell she'd woven over him would be gone.

"We can't go to the Third."

Keleir brushed fingers across her cheek. "On the Third, without magic, I wouldn't be like this. I wouldn't have this . . ." He cupped a hand over the gruesome star-shaped scar on his chest and the intricate demon-faced tattoo that decorated it. "I wouldn't have it, and it wouldn't constantly seek to control me. I'd escape the horrible visions of our future, and I'd live in peace with you."

Saran wanted desperately to believe that. "Peace? On the Third? We'd end up slaves to Roshaud or living in the slums."

"So? I know the slums aren't what you're used to, Princess, but I think we could build a nice little home in the underbelly of Roshaud's city. We might even start a kingdom of our own among the poor and disillusioned."

Saran smiled, running fingers up and down his arm, and then across his chest and over the mark of the Oruke. Tears brimmed her eyes.

"What is it?" he asked.

"Nothing." She sighed, pressing kisses to his lips. "It's nothing."

"You don't believe I'd last there, do you? You think the Oruke would be the one in control."

"No. That's not it," she lied. Saran pursed her lips together and drew the man she loved into a warm hug. She whispered to him, "If it comes to that, we can go to the Third. I will live with you in the slums."

"And a fine slum queen you'll make," he replied, pressing a kiss to her temple.

SIX

SARAN SAW NO need to change into proper clothing. Her door was soundly locked, and the guard told her it would remain so until her father decided otherwise. Knowing the old man, he could very well die before giving her freedom.

The time she spent locked away allowed her the benefit of quiet, enough to organize her thoughts and plot a way to get her magic back. She knew if she seemed too desperate for it, her father would only take pleasure in withholding it longer. However, if she wasn't urgent enough, she might not get them back before things began to really unravel.

Saran lounged in her robe near a small fire, reading a book that she'd pored over several times in the past few years. Her gifts were well beyond its advice and the limits that it set, but she read it anyway, as if it would inspire her to other feats not heard of by Mage or mortal. The thick book, with its tattered leather cover stained from the oils of a thousand hands, smelled of old parchment.

She distracted herself with researching elemental enchantments, anything that might help her unlock the Bind herself. She ended up stalled on the page concerning Alikons, elemental creatures formed using human or animal hosts as a starting ingredient. A Mage could reach into the heart of a living creature and force their elemental magic into it, creating a monster that would blindly and willfully follow their commands. Alikons didn't last long, not on record at least. Like the spark of an ember, they burned out quickly. It was also taboo and borderline forbidden to perform, especially on a person, and it came with the adverse effect of the creator being tied to the pain and loss of their creation. Her fingers roamed over the spell, frowning deeply before turning the page. The frown didn't last long.

Out of all the books on the shelves, this was her favorite. It reminded her of when she learned magic alongside Rowe in a small group of young Mages, though she had mostly taught herself. Mages learned by apprenticeships, but she'd converted their common elemental spells for earth, water, fire, and wind for her own use. There were no books on time magic, and there were no tutors to offer her guidance. Her father would have been the only Time Mage to teach her . . . but he never did. It was possible that he couldn't, given his illness. What Saran knew she garnered from reading books and mimicking others.

Saran met Keleir many years before meeting Rowe. The head of the orphanage quarantined him often because of his violent nature. Rowe arrived years later as a teenager, when he Awoke to his gifts. Eventually only Rowe could be near the infamous Ahriman Lifesbane without a terrible catastrophe ensuing. They fought alongside each other and, even as teens, earned a bloody reputation. Rowe never explained if he understood that he'd befriended the Oruke and not Keleir. Rowe didn't say much of anything about that time other than to express a desire for redemption.

Rowe could not bear the weight of bloodshed like the Oruke. He would do the bidding of his king without question, but he mourned each life that left by his hands. When he grew into a young man, the weight of death hung so heavy upon him that he would not eat or drink. He shriveled to a husk, sickly and near death.

Saran had forced water through his parted, dry lips and coaxed soup into his belly. No one could make him eat, not the sternest maid in all of Andrian, except the daughter of his king. There, under candlelight, in the dark and cold military-issued room, she fed him little by little for days until he gathered the strength to sit.

His men thought he'd been cursed, but he told Saran the truth. He'd murdered, and he deserved the slow and agonizing death that starvation would surely bring him. On that day, while she fed the Lightning Mage, they bonded over a unified hatred for the cruelty of her father's regime.

Afterwards, she introduced him to Darshan, who had often snuck into the castle when she was a young girl. Darshan had loved her mother, and Saran suspected that he thought of her as a daughter. She wondered what sort of person she would have become if not for the influences of Ishep Darshan or the resident healer, Madam Ophelia. She might have become her father. Sometimes Saran feared she still would.

The princess jumped as the balcony door blew open in a rush of cold air, far too chilly for the afternoon temperature. Frost licked across the hardwood floor, up the drapes and tapestries on the wall, and snuffed out the fire she read by. Her breath rushed from her lungs in hot fog about her face.

The princess closed the book and placed it on the small table near her chair. She drew the robe tighter against her chest and glared down at the dead fire. "Do you mind?"

Odan Marki bowed deeply between the open doors, a clever smile plastered on his thin face. "Apologies, Your Highness."

She scowled, folding her arms across her chest in an effort not to shiver at his chilly entrance. "I suppose because I'm

Bound you wish to seek retribution for the slight I made against you? You were deserving of it. You know that, don't you? Those were innocent people."

"In the eyes of our princess perhaps, but not the eyes of our king," Odan mused.

She exhaled a tight breath through her nose, turning her attention to the dead fire, where the frost that touched the embers began to melt. If she had her element, the fire would reignite and Odan would be a frozen statue adorning her chamber for as long as stamina sustained her. Though Keleir would argue it a waste of her Life.

Odan closed the doors behind him and went to the fire, where he knelt and pressed kindling between the dimly glowing embers. In a matter of minutes, the smoldering brush lit and fire warmed her bare feet. He sat silently, poking at the fire until it regained its former warmth. Then he stood, sweeping a bony hand over his blond hair. Cyan-colored eyes fixated on her, and a cruel smile hardened the edges of his pinched face.

"You think your status protects you, *Princess*? It doesn't," he said. "I don't fear you."

"You say that while I currently lack the power to send you back to be swaddled by your mother. Oh yes, you can be quite fearsome when you target defenseless people, can't you? Women, children . . . Bound Mages. I could still wipe the floor with you, magic or not. Don't throw your words about, expecting me to cower at your feet. You will be sorely disappointed, Lord Marki."

Odan sneered, fingers flexing at his sides with the urge to smack the smug look from her pretty face. He turned his gaze away to gather what shreds he could of his control and spotted the silver platter and crumbs of food sitting atop an engraved tray. His sneer transformed into a brilliant smile, like a lily opening to the sun. "He visited you, did he? Brought you food?"

The princess stiffened and opened her book. "Maids like me. Unlike certain nobles, I do not drag them kicking and screaming into my room for the night. They often break rules to make me comfortable when my father is being a child."

"A maid didn't bring you that." Odan grinned, stepping around her chair. He shoved the tray and silver plate to the floor with a loud clatter, scooping up the folded parchment hidden beneath.

Saran jumped to her feet and marched to him. He lifted the letter, admiring the paper, and then let his gaze settle on her. "I sometimes enjoy sitting on your balcony at night, you know."

She seethed, reaching for the letter. "I will be sure to make it so no Gates form there after today."

Odan snatched his hand away, taking a step back. "I sit there, wondering what it would look like to kill you. To be named your father's heir. At any rate, I witness many things while perched on the railing. For example, I see Lord Ahriman—"

His head cocked sideways with a loud smack before he could finish, and Saran drew her fist back for another blow.

Her hand broke on impact with an iron-hard shield of ice that formed over his face. She drew it to her chest, choking back a scream. Had it not been for pride, she might have cowered with tears. Instead she glared at him, calculating how easy it would be to throw him from the balcony he trespassed so frequently.

"Give that back," she said, nodding to the letter.

"I'm going to show this to your father immediately and let him know what his daughter does against his wishes and behind his back. We'll see how much he treasures you or Lord Ahriman then."

Odan turned for the door, and Saran lunged at him, wrapping her good arm around his neck and planting her knees in the small of his back. She drew back with all her weight, bracing against him for added leverage. She choked him as hard as she could until he stumbled back and fell on the bed, gagging.

Odan grabbed hold of her broken hand, squeezing tight. At first the princess refused to yield. She gritted her teeth, tightened her grip, and held as fast as she could. But then the shattered fragments of bone cut nerves and she released him with a strangled wail.

The Ice Mage lurched up from the bed, whirling on her, sword in hand. Saran's own lay across the room, leaning against the stone fireplace. Again, had she her element, it would have been within her grasp in seconds.

Odan laughed at her helplessness. "What was it—"

Saran kicked him square in the jewels and, when he doubled over, planted her foot in the center of his face. Odan's nose crunched under the force of her kick, and the Ice Mage fell back against the tapestry-laden wall. His sword clanked to the wooden floor. Saran rolled forward, bending to scoop it up, but ice glued it to the boards. He returned her kick, leaving them both heaving on separate sides of the room, nursing bloody noses.

The Ice Mage used frost to cool the fire that reddened his face and stifled the blood with a cloth from his pocket, while Saran curled the hem of her robe up against her nostrils, glaring across the room at him.

Odan waved a finger at her as he blotted his nose. "You won't tell who hit you."

Saran sneered and immediately regretted it, already feeling the tightness of swelling in her skin. "What makes you think I'd obey you?"

Lord Marki held up the bloodstained parchment in his hand and shook it in the air.

The princess rested against the ornately carved bedpost, feeling the sharp edges dig into her skin. She leaned harder against it, if only to distract herself from the throbbing of her face and broken hand. "What else is it you want? Not tattling about how I soundly kicked your ass can't be your only bargain."

Odan grinned, looking mad with a river of blood staining his upper lip and chin. "Oh, there are a great many things I want from you."

Saran scowled at him. "I'll take that note to my father myself before I indulge whatever depravity you can muster from that twisted brain of yours."

"Truly? Then let us go together." Lord Marki bowed, sweeping a thin arm to the door.

Saran took a step to her wardrobe, seeking to draw on something a little more substantial than the dressing gown.

"Do you think your father will have him beheaded or quartered? After all, your price is severely diminished now. Not many kings make offers for power in exchange for used goods."

She paused, her hand resting on the wool cloak hanging just inside the wardrobe. Saran glared daggers at the wooden door. Her hand fisted the fabric as her eye caught the glint of metal just under the wardrobe roof. Seconds turned into minutes while she toyed with her choices. Freedom for her lover and his brother was mere months away and all lost if Odan called her bluff.

She imagined Keleir Bound and disemboweled for treason. No matter how much Yarin favored the Fire Mage, he would not tolerate this betrayal.

Couldn't she swallow her pride? Was it such a heavy price to pay? And when the blasted Binding left her wrist, she'd make sure that Lord Odan Marki became a pillar of dust at her feet.

Saran drew her hand from the wool coat and ran it across the roof of the wardrobe as she shut the door and turned to Odan, her shoulders slumping in defeat. "If I do this, you will keep our secret?"

He nodded once and tucked the parchment into his waistband. "I'm glad you finally see reason."

The princess said nothing, but she held his gaze long after he wanted to look away. "I guess it heals your pride to have such control over me?" she asked, lifting her broken hand up to her chest. "Does it make you feel better?"

"You are caught in a narrow passage now. If I tell your father, Lord Ahriman will surely be punished. But if you tell Keleir about our arrangement, while he might kill me, I daresay he'll abandon you for giving in to me. He is not a forgiving man, and he won't forgive you, no matter your reasons."

Saran's face became a blank slate even while her insides twisted into knots. "A week," she spat. "You have me for a week and no more. Then it ends, and no one says a word to anyone."

Odan reached out and curled his fingers in her crimson hair. "Agreed."

The princess glowered at him. Then her glower brightened into a smile. Firelight caught the glint of a dagger. She plunged it into his shoulder, at the curve of his neck, before he could even flinch. Odan howled, reaching up to draw the blade free as her good hand snatched the parchment from his waistband. She tossed it into the fire, watching the flames lick up around it.

"You . . ."

"I'd visit a healer quickly if I were you," Saran said, stepping around him and plopping down in her chair. She reached to the table and drew her book into her lap, opening to the marked page. "I think I nicked something vital." She smiled as he stumbled, dripping blood across the floor, onto the balcony, where a wash of icy wind stole him away.

The princess waited a short while before opening the door to her room. It took a bit to pick the lock, especially with one hand, and once the door opened she found the guard sound asleep. That explained why he'd ignored all the commotion. She nudged him awake and sent him after a healer and an enchanter to make sure that Lord Marki never graced her bedroom balcony again. Unfortunately that also meant that Keleir would not be able to either.

The bracelet around her wrist kept the healer from using magic to mend the bones of her hand. Instead Madam Ophelia wrapped it in bandages and gave Saran a bag spelled by an Ice Mage to press over the aching bone.

"This elixir isn't so much magic as it is herbal. It will help ease the pain and the swelling, Your Highness," she said, handing her a cup of hot tea. "Your nose isn't broken. There will be light bruising and a little swelling. The bleeding has stopped."

"Thank you," Saran said, curling her fingers around the warm ceramic cup and lifting it to her lips.

Madam Ophelia gathered her tools into a leather sack and stood straight. She was a prim woman, with gray hair slicked back into an overly tight bun that pulled the lines of her aged face smooth. "Are you ready to tell the guards who attacked you so that they may meet justice?"

Saran sipped the tea. "I have dealt justice to him . . . a measure of it. I want him cowering in some corner, glancing over his shoulder, wondering when and if there will be more. No, I am not ready to divulge his name. But when I am, palace guards will be of little use to me."

The healer grinned, a dark and happy smile that sent a little shiver down Saran's spine. "Men," Madam Ophelia said, bending closer. "It is a great pleasure to see a woman make them quiver. I long for you to take the throne, Your Highness. For then they will know the true power of the Grand Feminine, the power of woman, the power of a queen. Please call me if you require any further assistance."

"Thank you," Saran murmured, watching the woman exit as another servant entered. This one did not move with the careful, poised grace that Madam Ophelia carried so naturally. He poured sweat, heaving great puffs of air into his lungs as he slid and almost fell to a stop at her feet. He collected himself, standing straight and tall with his chest puffed out.

"Princess," he gasped, clapping his heels together and bowing deeply. "The king requests your presence in the throne room. The Alar has sent representatives to court."

SEVEN

KELEIR DRUMMED HIS fingers against the wooden table, staring off at the wall as his brother scarfed down his breakfast. The full dining hall had long tables with men and women seated at them, eating the morning meal. Everyone had a plate of food except for the Fire Mage, who had chosen to give his to Saran that morning.

The grand hall stood fifty feet wide and one hundred feet long, with towering ceilings and tall, wide windows lining one side, allowing bright morning light to drift warmly into the room. The thunder of voices reverberated off the ceiling, concealing all individual conversation in a haze of white noise. It made Keleir comfortable enough to speak of secretive matters without worry of being overheard.

"She didn't get dinner?" Rowe asked, taking a breathless gulp of juice.

"I retrieved something from the kitchen last night and brought her my breakfast this morning. I'm not going to let her starve because her father's a bastard. We should just kill him and blame it on his disease."

Rowe nodded while trying not to laugh at his brother's candid and remorseless suggestion. "Wonderful idea. Then you can spend the next hundred years hunting for the key he hid in Prophetess-knows-where."

"I doubt he even has the key."

"Exactly."

Keleir stole a piece of bacon from Rowe's plate. "We should torture it out of him."

"Yes, torture is often misconstrued for natural death in the end."

The Fire Mage scowled and reached across the table for another piece of bacon. "You are really killing my glory today, Brother. Can't you agree with anything I say?"

"Someone has to be your conscience when Saran isn't around. It might as well be me." Rowe smacked Keleir's hand away. "Get your own!"

"I had my own. I did a charitable thing and donated it. One more piece."

Rowe dragged his plate closer to his chest with a feral growl, his lip curling up like a dog's. Bright blue eyes bored into his brother. "No."

The Fire Mage drew his hand back and observed the possessiveness with a coy smile. "You need a woman. It's weird to protect food like your one and only love."

"It is my one and only, at the moment. I am deeply invested in this. Why don't you invest in some of your own, aye?" Rowe took a big smiling bite. "Or go find your woman."

Keleir grinned, settling back in his chair. A faint rosy glow spread across his cheeks as he looked away. "She *is* confined to her room all day."

Rowe bit his bacon and made a suggestive glance to the servant heading their way. Keleir righted himself on the bench and wiped the pleasant look from his face. The servant walked to the end of their table and gave a deep respectful bow. "Lord

Ahriman, Lord Blackwell, I've been asked to summon you to court. The king requests the honor of your presence."

The Fire Mage's red gaze flicked to the servant. "Oh, it is we who are honored. Tell the king we will be there shortly."

Rowe finished his breakfast, and the two men headed for the throne room, though neither of them rushed the journey. Court could be painfully dull, and the two, while favored among the top of Yarin's Mages, were rarely needed. Court happened on rare and special occasions, as most of the nobles had given their land rights away or lost them in Yarin's drive to consolidate power. As such, the event often felt somber and unproductive. While it seemed odd for them to be asked to join, neither questioned the summoning of a mad man. Nothing the king did as of late made any real sense at all.

The various methods from the Third that King Yarin used to prolong his life gave him an adverse reaction to sunlight. Because of this, he kept the throne room dark with thick, heavy curtains drawn over the windows to blot out the light. Even without the curtains, light would have found it hard to penetrate the layers of dirt caked upon the panes so thickly that they appeared frosted. It was a large room lit by torches and candles, with wide, round pillars and narrow skeletal arches peaked to vaults holding up the lengthy ceiling. Today a red carpet lined the center of the room from the heavy wooden doors to the steps leading up to the old king.

Court did not have many participants, and usually only a handful of nobles clustered about the king. That morning soldiers, servants, and nobles lined the tattered red carpet, chattering among themselves and filling the normally vacant room with enough noise that it echoed off the arched ceiling and reverberated from the walls out into the hall.

"What's all this?" Rowe muttered to his brother as they paused at the open door.

Keleir shook his head, scanning the faces within view until his sight traveled down the length of the aisle to the king. Three tall men stood near him, all adorned in gold and white robes. They were tan of skin, black-haired, and they wore the traditional headdresses of the Mavahan people.

Saran spotted Keleir and Rowe at the threshold of the roaring throne room. She stopped next to them, peering bewildered inside. Having never seen such an enormous crowed gathered, Saran couldn't possibly imagine why they would all be there . . . until she spotted the Mavish men. Her heart dropped to her boots. "Well, a lot of people have come to see me off. That's nice, I suppose." Nervous jitters traveled through her legs, and she thanked herself for dressing in skirts, as that would hide their tremble. Anxiety wrapping around her heart competed with the pain of a broken hand and the ache of a damaged nose.

"You aren't going anywhere," Keleir muttered, turning his gaze on her. His eyes darkened at the flush around her cheeks and nose. "What happened?"

Saran touched her face with the tips of her fingers and then reached down to the sleeve of her dress and drew it over her bandaged hand. "It's a rather long story, one better discussed later when there aren't eyes watching."

Keleir shook his head, reached for her arm, and drew back the belled fabric hiding her bandaged hand. Embers lit in his eyes, and his jaw set tight. "Tell me now."

Rowe coughed and nodded down the lengthy aisle to the king sitting impatiently upon his throne. Rowe wobbled in a nervous fashion, heel to toe, before stepping off. "Come, Yarin is glaring at us."

Saran nodded and stepped after Rowe. Keleir gaped at her and followed quickly in her wake. "Saran . . ."

The princess ignored him and smiled at the rows of people greeting her. She bowed her head to those who offered her that courtesy and tapped her breast with her fist to any soldier that saluted.

Keleir caught her by the elbow near the end of the aisle.

Saran froze, her gaze darting out to the hundreds of eyes on them. She could feel her father glowering at her from his throne. She met the Fire Mage's angry gaze, allowing the hardness in her eyes to speak for her. The Fire Mage paused, glancing to his fingers wrapped too tightly around her arm, and then to the soldiers and nobles with their curious gazes and craning necks. "Forgive me, Your Highness," he whispered, bowing deeply before going to his brother's side.

"Daughter," Yarin croaked as he motioned for her to take her place at his right.

Saran ascended to stand next to him as one might approach their own execution. She held a regal form but took no pleasure in the act. When she reached her appointed place, she turned to face the crowd that had gathered. Not until that moment, while overlooking them, did she find it within herself to truly be afraid.

Soldiers lined the red-carpeted aisle at the back of the room, while the nobles stood in rows toward the front. Representatives of the Mavahan Empire, adorned in their silks and jewels, lined the right front of the podium, while Keleir and Rowe stood to the left.

"Father," Saran whispered, bending low to his ear. "What is this? What are you doing?" Again she felt a tremble in her legs, so she locked her knees, refusing to show any sign of fear or weakness before the people ogling her. She narrowed her eyes on the Mavahans. She imagined herself stuffed unwillingly into an ornately carved wagon, whisked across the dry, sandy dunes of their country, and gifted with a smile to the Alar, their king. The prospect of an unwanted marriage was the least horrifying thing about being sold away. What frightened her more than these men, more than the idea of living in the Deadlands, forever cut off from the Core, was the fact that she had all the power in the world to stop it—if only her father had not Bound her.

"I am securing the future of our kingdom, Saran," he said, a sick smile pulling on his baggy face. "We both know I'll soon be dead. I won't leave it to be stripped of everything I worked so hard for."

Panic raced through her. She clenched her fists tight at her sides and watched her father as he slid forward and struggled to stand. The cane in his hand wobbled as he thrust his disease-riddled body up out of his throne. He took one step forward and lifted his hand to silence the room. His subjects quieted. The silence became a physical weight wrapped around her neck. A thousand protests bubbled inside of her, threatening to burst out of her mouth and further dissolve the little autonomy she had left.

What could she do? What could she say? She was a woman. A daughter. A bargaining chip. She could easily be described as the most powerful Mage in her father's possession, and yet he used her as nothing more than a dowry for peace. No matter how much she argued or screamed, it would not change the fate he had planned for her, whatever it might be. In order to be truly free, one of them, she or her father, would have to die.

It wouldn't be hard to kill him. If his people knew the truth, if they knew just how fragile and powerless he really was, they'd rush the throne and rip him to pieces, if only for a chance to sit one second on his throne. The princess eyed her father, the words balled like a hard knot in the back of her throat. If she spoke them . . . Her gaze flittered to Keleir and Rowe. If she spoke them, what would she lose?

"It is no secret that your great king will soon return to the Core. Had I not been the great Mage that I am, nay, the stubborn soldier, I'd have gone a long time ago," King Yarin began. "The time has come for me to lay the foundations of your future in stone so that you can take comfort. Many years have passed since Saran came of age, and my advisers have pleaded with me to ensure my lineage and marry her to a worthy successor so that the next King of Adrid would be accepted by the Core. It is time that such succession was established and such union announced. Hear me, people of Adrid, and know my word as law. Any man or woman who questions this decree, or who makes any attempt to sabotage what I have ordered, shall be executed as a traitor. Listen well and know that my daughter, Princess Saran D'mor of Adrid, will wed the feared warrior Lifesbane, and he will be your king."

Saran heard the words. They fell from his lips to a muted crowd. Even as her mind registered them for what they were, she could not believe that he'd said them. She blinked and stumbled a step forward. Her hands shook with rage that splintered through her heart only to be doused with realization. Not the Alar. Not Mavahan. But Keleir. Adrid.

The throne room erupted in a flurry of voices. Some soldiers cheered in the distance where the shadows of the dark room obscured them. All became white noise to Saran as her green eyes settled on Keleir in shock.

A Mavahan representative bowed deeply and took a respectful step forward. He did not lift his head but opened his hands in a great parting of peace and with a forced smile spoke to the king. "That isn't what we discussed, King Yarin, for the better part of six months. We would not have agreed to travel for a month only to see you promise the hand of your daughter to a common lord within your court, one not even of noble birth. The princess is to wed Alar Dago, as we agreed that she would."

Yarin's cheek twitched, and he hobbled close to the edge of the podium, bending to look at the representative with his half-blind eyes. "We agreed? I don't remember. I have this poor diseased brain, you see. Did we already sign a marriage contract?"

"We were to sign it upon our arrival. Princess Saran will leave with us this evening, as agreed."

"No contract? What madman thinks to come collect a bride that has not been signed for? Has your Alar sent me payment for her hand?"

"The payment, King Yarin, is in the form of peace. I assure you, that is the most luxurious and expensive gift our Alar could ever bestow you," he hissed.

Yarin straightened, his face creasing with anger. "I need no such gift! I have all that I need here."

The representative bowed deeper, as if he meant to touch the floor with his forehead. "The Alar will not take this well. You promised a queen. In exchange for your daughter, he would open trade and relieve the strangling grip on your kingdom. You would no longer fear invasion."

"There is no need for the Alar to relieve a strangled grip," Yarin said. "Lifesbane will. Go back to your Alar. Tell him the name Ahriman Lifesbane and watch as he quivers at the sound of it."

The Mavahan man grew darker with rage. "Why waste our time by calling us here? What purpose does your announcement serve, if not to plant seeds of war?"

"I wanted you to see him for yourself," Yarin said and motioned to the white-haired, red-eyed man. "Ahriman Lifesbane, future King of Adrid."

Saran took a cautious step forward, resting her hand on her father's hunched shoulder. "You're marrying me off to Keleir?"

Yarin grinned. "If anyone can rein in your willfulness, it is he."

Saran tried not to laugh. If her heart weren't hammering, if she didn't fully believe it a dream, she might have. However, when she looked out at Keleir to share her happiness, there was something terribly wrong. She could see it in his eyes, in the way he clutched his chest as if his heart were threatening to bound out from behind his ribs. The Oruke was speaking to him.

"Your Majesty, might I suggest that the princess be married to my brother, Rowe?" Keleir's voice rang over the murmur of the crowd. His winced and forced his quivering hands at his sides. His voice rose above the loud room. "While he does not possess my deadly reputation, he is less likely to be controlled by an Oruke and more trusted by your people."

"What?" said Saran, Yarin, and Rowe as one.

The king shook his head at the Fire Mage. "I'm giving you a kingdom, Lifesbane, and I'm giving you my daughter . . ."

Keleir turned a disdainful glare on Saran that made her stomach twist into knots. "I'll gladly take your kingdom. I don't want your daughter."

Rowe choked.

Yarin laughed.

Keleir continued, "She's willful, spoiled, and uncontrollable. I need someone that will bend to my whim, someone who will listen to me. A wife should be submissive to her husband. Saran is anything but."

"You will marry her," the king said, falling into his throne. "It is decided. It is law. You will control her—I have no doubt about that, Lord Ahriman. She will break under you."

Keleir snarled, curling his fists at his sides. "If it is my king's wish."

Saran's brow furrowed. Her heart pounded, and she felt at the Bind around her wrist. She needed it off. Off. Off. Off!

Yarin nodded. "It is your king's command." He turned his gaze to Saran and waved her off before addressing the crowded room. "That is all. Go."

Saran brushed past Keleir and Rowe on her way to the door but didn't bother to spare either a glance. When she'd abandoned the room, the nobles and soldiers began to file out behind her. The Mavahan representatives turned to the king without a word. They bowed low to him, in more respect than he deserved, and backed out of the room.

Rowe stalked after Keleir as he faded to the back of the crowd and into a dark corner of the throne room. The Fire Mage bent near the wall, clutching his chest, and heaved great gulps of air into his lungs.

Rowe placed his hand on Keleir's shoulder and gave it a harsh squeeze. "What the hell was that about? The king just gave you permission to be with her. He gave her to you, and you tried to pawn her off on me? In front of her? I don't want to be king any more than you do, but did you stop and think what that said to the woman you love?"

Keleir fell against the wall, craning his head back. His brow glistened with sweat, and his hand clutched at his aching chest, nails trying to claw out the thing inside him. "It is happy,

Rowe. The moment the king named me his successor and gave me Saran as a wife, the Oruke was happy. I have never known happiness from it. It hates her . . . and it is happy."

EIGHT

THE PRINCESS POURED herself a generous glass of Levlin whiskey, hoping that enough of it would drown the throbbing ache in her hand. By the second glass her chest felt warm, but her hand still screamed. The healer's tonic had worn off hours before, and she'd sent her guard for more. He'd yet to return, though he'd been gone long enough to go and come thrice.

The door to her room opened in a sweeping groan.

"Prophetess, yes!"

Keleir closed it quietly behind him, lifting his gaze to her disappointed face. It still felt unsettling to view him there before her and not feel him in the room. Had she been without the Binding, she would have known immediately that it wasn't the guard returning with her aid.

Often an overconfident man, the Fire Mage entered the room one quiet step at a time, as one might approach an unfamiliar canine. "I didn't think he'd keep you locked in after giving you away. I'll talk to him about it."

Saran fell into her chair, holding a cold glass to her bandaged hand. "Do that, will you? Why don't you speak to him more about how I should marry your brother while you are at it, hmm?"

He frowned and, shaking his head, draped an arm across the mantel. "It's not . . . It is complicated."

She smiled. "Complicated? We've been hiding ourselves away for years. Today my father announces to the whole kingdom that I am to be yours, and you call me a spoiled, willful brat whom you want nothing to do with. Then, as if that didn't cut deep enough, you try to pawn me off on Rowe. It was so very uncomplicated, Keleir!" She jumped from her chair and went for the balcony, letting the rush of cold sea air calm her racing heart.

He followed and braced against the railing with his forearms, casting his gaze to the sea and the setting sun. The last threads of daylight lit her hair afire, and the wind tossed it like angry flames about her head. He enjoyed the sight and found peace watching her fight to contain it behind her ears.

"Something happened when your father made that announcement. The Oruke felt joy. I was afraid, Saran. I've never felt it that happy, especially where it concerns you."

The princess turned her eyes upon him, strands of red brushing across her face. "And is it still so full of joy?"

"It is silent," he said, rubbing his chest. "For the most part."

"That beast craves power, and to be king is power, Keleir. It was more than likely happy about that than happy about having a wife, especially me."

"I know—I mean, I understand that now. At that moment, I was shocked. I didn't know what to think or what I was feeling. I only wanted to protect you from him."

Keleir grasped her bandaged hand hidden beneath the sleeve of her robe. Saran yelped and drew it trembling to her chest. For the longest time, the two lovers stared at each other, each trying desperately to read the other. Without their connection, they had to rely on more human means of deciphering the other's thoughts. Keleir reached for her good hand, taking it lightly in his fingers, and guided her back to her chair out of the wind.

"Let me see," he said, his voice warm and gentle.

Saran nodded, taking the edge of her sleeve and drawing it up to her elbow. He peeked around the loose bandaging, cringing at the smell of strong healing herbs. Her hand quivered in his light grasp, aching at such a gentle touch. She desperately longed for the numbing herbs that Madam Ophelia provided.

"Are you ready to tell me?" Keleir asked, his voice too calm.

"Odan's been watching us, Keleir. I'm not sure for how long. He found the note you left me this morning and he meant to take it to Father. We fought, and it ended with a knife lodged in his shoulder. It seems that there was no need to worry about it after all. The letter, I mean . . . given how things turned out."

"I'll have Yarin remove the Bind so a healer can treat you." He released her hand, his fingers brushing along her jaw. His eyes darkened, the ruby red deepening as he stood. "And I'll go speak with Odan."

Saran rushed to her feet. "Don't kill him."

Keleir's unreadable face transformed with a wicked grin. "I have a reputation to maintain, my love." He swept his arm around and bowed deeply before turning for the door.

Her heart lurched up into her throat, and she nearly choked on her words. "Don't!"

The Fire Mage stopped at the door, his fingertips grazing over the cool metal handle. He froze, and she raged, needing to know what he thought, what he felt. Slowly he turned back to her, questioning eyes appraising her.

"Don't kill him."

"Saran, he attacked you. He hit you. He broke your hand. I'm going to kill him before he does worse when my back is turned next."

"I know. I understand. But don't do it. He isn't . . . You've gone a long time without killing, despite what you say. He isn't worth it." She went to him, taking his hand and pulling him away from the door. "Stay with me instead."

He frowned. "You don't want me to kill Odan for the same reason you don't wish me to kill Yarin. You don't want it to tarnish whatever polish you forged on me when sealing away the Oruke. Do you think if I kill him I'll lose what is left of my soul?"

"Keleir, you are not a murderer. "

He leaned forward, his face pressing close to hers. He smirked at the startled look she gave him. Even after all these years, when he got angry, it proved hard to tell the difference between the Oruke and Keleir. "I am a murderer," he whispered. "Please stop pretending I'm not."

"You are *not* a murderer *anymore*," she corrected. Saran straightened her spine and hardened her face. She believed with all her heart that the Keleir she'd brought back from the darkness was not a killer, and so far, after five years, he'd done nothing but prove her right. Still, a dark cloud of guilt followed him for the actions not done by his hand. No matter what she told him, he would forever take ownership for the murders committed by the Oruke.

Keleir shook his head and moved past her to the chair she'd occupied. He fell into it as if the heavy weight of that guilt were two hands shoving hard against his shoulders. "Having not killed in five years does not absolve me of the sins that came before. It doesn't remove the blood from my hands. People know me as Lifesbane. They fear me. My village feared me long before I garnered that reputation."

Saran frowned, remembering the long, painful tale of his childhood. His village had been superstitious and cruel. Every child born with an Oruke was marked by white hair and red eyes, but Keleir had also been born with a birthmark on his chest, right over his heart. It looked more like thousands of carefully woven knots in the form of a rabid, monstrous face. The village elders had ordered his mother and father to remove the mark. They believed it would sever the Oruke's hold over their son. His father held him down, and they cut the mark from his chest, skinning the flesh away. It only came back darker, and each time it returned they held him down again and removed it. Now the mark remained, as black as any tattoo, but behind it was a gnarled and messy scar, like the shape of a layered eight-pointed star.

The last time the village cut it from him was the night Keleir Awoke to the gifts the Core had blessed him with. In anguish and consumed with newfound and unlearned power, he'd killed his father with magic. To kill with magic was considered a terrible crime by the Core, and one with a single price: a life for a life.

The Core claimed Her price, and while it should have killed Keleir, it did not. But it did give the Oruke total control over Keleir's body for thirteen years, up until the point Saran brought Keleir back from the darkness.

She knew his story as well as any folktale. He'd told it to her on numerous occasions when his battle with the Oruke became particularly trying. Her heart ached for him, knowing no way to help him without her magic.

"You can clean me up, wash me off, keep me dry for five years, but it doesn't change what I am or what I did," Keleir whispered.

"You should see your face," she said as she brushed her fingers against his cheek before squeezing his hand. "Someone with eyes so sad cannot be a monster. You feel remorse, Keleir. You hate what was done by your hands, but it was not you. It was *him*. It was the Oruke. You died, and for thirteen years the

Oruke had control of your body. I turned back time enough to rebuild the wall between your soul and his. Technically I resurrected you. But I can't do that again. What I did should have been impossible to begin with. If . . ."

"It nearly killed you," he whispered, brushing his hand over her hair. "You saved me, risked so much for me, after all that I'd done to hurt you."

"*It wasn't you.* I saw you, buried in him . . . screaming. I can't do it again. Which is why you must listen to me and ignore the urge. If you kill again with magic—"

"There are many ways to kill other than magic. What I did to my father was an accident, no matter how much he deserved it. I'm not saying I plan to kill again, I'm just saying . . ."

Saran's face grew stern. "Kill only to protect yourself. Not for vengeance or pleasure. Kill for survival. Use your reputation, if you must, but do not become it. That is all that I ask."

Keleir leaned forward and pressed a kiss to the top of her head. "That is a simple thing to give someone who has done so much."

Saran stared at the fire while he drew her in tight against his chest. She listened to the rhythm of his heart, knowing that the Oruke lay just beneath the surface, knowing that with each passing day the Bind wrapped around her wrist, the Oruke grew stronger. Keleir didn't seek out Odan. Instead they spent the evening together. Making love had always been the most effective means for quieting the darkness in his mind; however, it seemed to do little good that night. Eventually, and more reluctantly for Keleir, they slept.

NINE

"IT IS DYING. Look at how cold it grows. Look what they've done. They take everything given to them and they destroy it. It is not fair that they live, that they feel, and in return they do their world such an injustice. They'll destroy it until there is nothing left. Like the Third—" Before Keleir's eyes, a world of metal appeared. There wasn't a spot of green as far as he could see. Huge turbines worked to purify the air to make the planet habitable. "And like the Second soon will be." The view of the Third shifted into that of the Second, a world of a technology that slowly encroached on the Life of its Core. It was filled with a people constantly struggling to balance their need for consumption with their desire to protect their world from destruction . . . and they were losing.

It all faded, and they stood once more over a dying Core.

"The First is next, you know. You feel it. War is coming, and greed. Parasites. Cancers. They are the bane of life, not you," the Oruke said to the Fire Mage as they stood side by side atop the molten soul of the planet, now frozen in a solid mass of black rock. The crevices still glowed hot with life, but how long before those cracks went dark too?

Keleir lifted his eyes to the man next to him, to the Oruke, but the face he saw was his own.

The Fire Mage's eyes snapped open, and he ran a trembling hand across his damp face, staring up at a dark ceiling. The dying embers of the fire added little light to the black room, but he could see the detail in the fabric draped above the bed enough to remember where he was. He felt Saran's heat next to him, curled on her side near the edge of the bed.

The Oruke moved inside, feeling much like a worm wiggling in his chest. The rhythm in his heart changed with what Madam Ophelia liked to call a palpitation, a term she learned while apprenticing in a Second hospital as a young woman. His head ached with the pressure of the monster beating at the thin walls, desperately wanting to get back in and show him more horrors than he cared to know. "Stop," he whispered, fisting his white hair in his hands. "Please stop."

TEN

SARAN GLOWERED AT the tapestry-laden wall, jaw set tight enough to hurt, while Madam Ophelia rubbed more herbs over her broken hand and rewrapped it with cloth. The healer had a gentle touch when she chose to. She could also be very impatient and harsh, but luckily for Saran, that morning Madam Ophelia had chosen the former method for treating her patient. Even still, it hurt.

The healer lifted her gray eyes to the princess, the corners of her lips tugging upward but never truly forming a smile. "I can't imagine how you feel being unable to heal yourself or having a healer mend you."

Saran admired the healer's handiwork as the woman poured them both a small cup of tea, adding a vial of medicine to Saran's. "It is indescribable."

Madam Ophelia nodded and passed Saran her cup of medicated tea. "I hope you don't mind, I thought I'd join you for breakfast." She motioned for the servant near the door to bring forward a tray of pastries from the kitchen. "I had the cook work up something special for us."

Saran gaped at the tray. "I haven't had scones since I was a teen." Back when they used to have variety in their meals.

Madam Ophelia gave a dry chuckle. "I'm sure you could ask for anything and get it. The servants here are very loyal to you."

Saran sipped at the hot tea, enjoying the warmth of it on her cheeks. "I don't like making special requests of people. I don't like having servants. If I had my way, I'd live in a quiet cottage by a lake."

"But that isn't the hand that fate dealt, unfortunately."

Saran pursed her lips together, exhaling slowly through her nose. "No, I suppose it isn't."

"Your nose is very bruised today. I've brought a paste to cover the coloring. I know you aren't fond of paint, but I think it would do some good to hide the abuse you received from Odan Marki. It is best if the people of this castle see you as untouchable." Madam Ophelia snapped her fingers, and another servant stepped forward, placing a small glass jar filled with tan paint, the color of Saran's skin, on the table between her chair and Madam Ophelia's.

"I didn't tell you who attacked me," Saran mused.

"I guessed."

"And how is Odan?"

"Resting. He won't be troubling you anymore. His recent encounter was enlightening for him."

"Near-death experiences are often so."

Madam Ophelia smiled over her cup of tea. "Aren't they?" She drank and set the empty cup off to the side before folding her hands in her lap. "Still, wear the paint to cover the bruising and long sleeves to cover your hand. The more people think you're invulnerable, the better. The practice has suited your father all these years. Men quiver at his name. If only they knew that with a harsh breeze, they could see him fall."

Saran paused midsip, taking the moment to rethink Madam Ophelia's words before swallowing her tea. "I know your servants are loyal, but even that was bold of you. Not many people survive speaking ill of the king as you just did."

"I'm the king's healer. He's dying. He has a month at the most. Soon you will be queen and you must begin to carry yourself as such. You cannot run from this, Your Highness. It is time to stop living a double life and own up to that responsibility."

Saran set her half-empty cup of tea down and met Madam Ophelia's eyes. "I don't know what you mean by that. I have one life, and that is to be the Princess of Adrid. I have sacrificed a great many things to carry this mantle. Please do not suggest that I live a double life aloud ever again, for both our sakes."

"Of course, forgive me." Madam Ophelia held Saran's gaze, her face a clean, emotionless slate. Her dull eyes bored into the princess's. The healer had the look of a woman who could see you for everything you were and everything you weren't. She rested her hand on Saran's shoulder. "You are without your magic, but you are not broken. Perhaps this is a test of your strength. I find that we are all made better through struggle and that, in the end, we all come out stronger for it. You have great power, Saran, beyond the one the Core blessed you with, if only you had the courage to look past the veil of uncertainty."

Madam Ophelia had been the one to deliver her when her mother gave birth. When her mother died several months after, Madam Ophelia swaddled her, found a wet nurse to feed her, taught her to walk and talk. She mended Saran's bumps and bruises from her father's abuse and her training as a soldier. She taught Saran what to do when she transitioned from a child into a woman the night her moon cycle came. Madam Ophelia, in more ways than Saran could count, had been the only mother Saran had ever known. Saran's first words had been to call Madam Ophelia *Ma. Madam* was too complicated.

Despite these kindly, motherly traits, Madam Ophelia had always ensured a safe emotional distance.

Saran took up the half-empty cup of tea and sipped at it, pondering the healer's words as she gathered her things into a leather satchel. Madam Ophelia bowed deeply to Saran.

I find that we are all made better through struggle . . .

The words sank in the pit of Saran's stomach. How much better could any of them afford to get?

ELEVEN

THE ADRID COUNCIL chambers were lively the day after the king's announcement. The narrow table lined with chairs took the full length of the room. Advisers occupied the well-worn seats that typically sat empty. The king lounged against the far wall, away from the windows and the light. He munched on birdseeds and spit the shells into a clay cup at the corner foot of the table, much to the disgust of the noble seated next to him. He missed often.

The early morning sun tried desperately to come through the dingy, dirty windows. It cast dim colors on the floor from the tinted glass at the top of the arches. Even that bit of light felt like too much. The dull glare tugged at Keleir's nerves, and he sought to avoid it by hiding behind the shadow of a burly noble hovering over the table. Dark circles hung under his red eyes as he glowered at the creature of a man speaking to him.

"Wake up, Lifesbane," said the duke, chuckling and slapping his shoulder. "Did the realization you couldn't run a kingdom keep you up late?"

"Or your inability to wrangle a woman?" said another.

Keleir pressed fingers to his temple as he glared across the table at the laughing man. A dark smile tugged at his lips, and they parted to speak when a loud, resounding crack echoed off the low ceiling. The king lifted his cane and rapped it against the floor a second time, silencing the room.

"Let's see," he said, his voice as rough as the worn brick wall behind him. "Is everyone . . . Where is Saran?"

"You confined her to her room, my king," Keleir droned, settling back in his chair. "She will not be attending the meeting unless you remove the guard outside her door."

The king's leathery face withered with a frown. He cracked his cane against the floor. "Someone fetch that damn daughter of mine before the Seconds get here."

A servant ducked out of the room, and each of the nobles grew silent and stared blankly at the sick man. Keleir slid forward, leaning to the center of the table to peer down the length. "Seconds, my king? Are you saying Second Dwellers are coming here?"

Yarin nodded, wiggling into his chair. "Yes, didn't I mention they were coming?"

Keleir shook his head, glancing to the other members of the council sitting at the table. Those nobles that regularly attended meetings shook their heads at him. The men seated at the table exchanged grave looks between themselves, the sort that only insane men could earn. "Are you absolutely certain Seconds are coming today, my king? Perhaps you are—"

"You are not king yet, Lifesbane," Yarin warned, spittle landing on his chin. "I know what I'm talking about. I do not forget things. I might be old and diseased, but I'm not senile."

"Of course." The Fire Mage nodded and settled back in his chair, curling his hands over the arms.

It would be easy to convince everyone he's senile and kill him. You could marry Saran and take the throne immediately.

"It would be easy," Keleir agreed, glancing up. His insides twisted at the face staring across the table at him. The white-haired mirror of himself smiled a devilish grin, his eyes an inky black. He pressed a finger to his lips to hush the startled Fire Mage.

Shh, said the Oruke. *No one can hear or see me. They'll just think you're talking to yourself. You don't want to seem as crazy as the old man, do you?*

Keleir stiffened.

You don't look well, my friend, he said. *Not sleeping? Bad dreams? They wouldn't be so awful if you'd listen.*

Keleir pressed his fingers to his temples hard enough to dent the flesh. He shut his eyes tight, concentrating on the sound of Yarin's cane scraping impatiently against the stone while he droned on.

You can't ignore me forever. I am part of you. I am you . . . The voice grew distant, fainter, and when he opened his eyes, the same ugly noble from moments before was looking across the table at him. The door to the council chamber rattled open, and Saran wandered in, dressed in a deep burgundy tunic and black pants, with her curly hair piled in a careless mess atop her head. Long strands dangled around her neck and ears. With no room for her at the table, she leaned against the wall between two great windows and cast a dark gaze to her father. "Aye, I'm here. What is it?"

"Perfect," Yarin muttered, wiggling his flat rear in his narrow chair. "Before the Seconds arrive, I'd like to discuss what I announced yesterday. By now, even if you weren't there, I'm sure you are aware that I betrothed my daughter, Saran, to Ahriman. Tomorrow, to make things official, there will be a betrothal ceremony, where Saran and Keleir will be bound to one another. We all know I'm one leg from falling over Death's cliff, so let's not pretend that I have plenty of time to get my affairs in order."

The members of the council nodded. Keleir looked up from the table to Saran, who met his gaze with just the hint of a smile. Her face, less swollen than the night before, appeared to have been smoothed over with paint typically worn by wealthy noble women. "From here out, Keleir and Saran are one. When the Seconds arrive, Lifesbane will be introduced as my Name Heir to be wed to my Blood Heir."

The room nodded slowly. No one whispered how unsure they were about the king's decision, not when Lifesbane had a reputation for keen hearing and a quick temper.

A heavy knock sounded at the door, and a servant hurried to open it. He bowed profusely to the three men waiting on the other side. Two of them were dressed in deep blue trousers and nicely trimmed jackets adorned with medals across the left breast, a uniform commonly worn by Second soldiers. The other wore a sharp gray outfit: pants, a jacket, and a narrow blue strip of fabric dangling from his pristine white collar. Each man had a short hairstyle unpopular among Adridian men, cropped close to their heads, less than half an inch, and slicked down.

"Welcome, gentleman," Yarin greeted them in English. He rose from his chair, arms quivering over his cane.

The three entered the council chamber and gave a swift bow of respect to the king before they fanned out. Three of the nobles at the table relinquished their seats and moved to stand against the far wall with Saran.

"King Yarin," said the Second with the most medals across his chest. An older man with graying hair and a square face. While his lips smiled, his eyes did not. "After our meeting two months ago, I didn't hear from you. I figured you had turned down our offer."

"Never. I simply had to think it over."

"With the Mavahan Alar breathing down your neck and the civil war, it must be hard to think straight. At any rate, we're fully prepared to invest in Adrid's defenses, provided that our compensation is still as we discussed."

"Lords," King Yarin said, waving at the three men. "This is General Pulaski, Sergeant McDonald, and . . . I'm sorry, I don't know you, sir."

"This is our lawyer, Mr. Oswald," the general said, smiling. "You don't have lawyers on the First, so you might not know what they do. Lawyers help us facilitate our business transactions, tie up loose ends, and make sure our contracts are perfect and legally worded. He is simply here to make sure this goes smoothly and that everyone gets what they want."

"And what is it that we want?" Keleir asked, red eyes gleaming. "What is this, Your Majesty?"

"Forgive the outspoken boy. This is Ahriman. Most know him as Lifesbane. He is the future King of Adrid. Power, it seems, has already gone to his head."

Keleir glowered and said in Adridian, "It is not power that causes me to question the appearance of Second soldiers in our world and at our council table. It is a valid question, my king, and one I'm sure all others present would very much like to hear answered—for those who can understand their tongue."

The king squirmed in his seat, huffed, and tossed a dismissive gaze to the Fire Mage.

Pulaski chuckled, clasping his hands together over the table and turning his body to Keleir. "You're hemorrhaging resources, rebels are overpowering your armies, and you've got a foreigner breathing down your neck and threatening to conquer your kingdom. King Yarin approached my government a few months ago with some legitimate concerns. We offered to help. In exchange for weapons, the United States government gets access to a resource-rich landscape. Resources, I might add, that you have no desire to utilize for yourself." Pulaski's faux smile transformed into a condescending grin. "We'll give you boom-boom sticks, and you'll give us your useless oil."

Saran shifted off the wall and around the table. "That is horribly offensive," she said in English, tapping the shoulder of one noble and motioning for him to move. She sat next to Keleir and across from the Seconds, draping her arms over the table. "Referring to your guns as boom-boom sticks like we're illiterate tribesmen."

"Daughter . . ."

"Your weapons do not belong in our world, just as our resources do not belong in yours," she continued, casting her father a dark glare. "It is taboo to bring such items here. We do not need them."

"I think you do," Mr. Oswald said. "Princess Saran, forgive Pulaski. He's terrible with people. How he reached the rank of general with his countenance, I don't know."

Saran cast a glare to Pulaski before nodding in agreement with Oswald. "This world is damaged enough. We do not need your demonic machinery introduced here. What you will give us is the very reason your world is dying. We do not need that influence on the First."

"She's right," Keleir said. "The First has remained secure because we have not embraced the same ideals as those who have destroyed their worlds. Our Core is strong because we have left it intact. I would rather lose the entire kingdom than have this world mined to death like the Third, and like the Second will be shortly."

Pulaski glowered at the Fire Mage. "Lucky for me, boy, you aren't king yet. And as for embracing the same ideas, sure you have. You just don't have the right equipment—yet."

Keleir smirked. "You play the villain quite well, Pulaski. I hope you didn't plan to make a deal today. Even if the king agrees to this damned scheme, as soon as I'm on the throne I will send your weapons back to you, ammunition first if I must."

Mr. Oswald coughed, setting a leather case on the table. "The Treaty of Adrid was signed some two hundred and fifty years ago between your government and the governments of the Second. It states that we will not interfere in your world if you do not interfere in ours, unless explicitly asked, of course. King Yarin asked, and we are offering our interference because of it. The treaty binds each one of us from invading the other. If our government chose to, we could wipe Adrid from the map in a night, and all without the use of magic. Your Magi could do very little to save you."

"I wouldn't be so sure of that." Saran glowered. "Are you threatening us, lawyer?"

"No, Your Highness. I am simply stating the agreement in the treaty so you know what it protects and allows. If Adrid were to break any portion of that treaty, the United States would not be in the wrong for retaliating. If we retaliated, we would turn your world to dust."

Saran turned her attention to her ailing father as he watched quietly, munching birdseeds. "So what will it be, Father? Shall we take our chances against the rebels and Mavahan or the Seconds?"

Yarin mulled over her words. "We're losing the war. If we lose Salara . . ."

"You won't," Keleir said. "I won't allow it."

"Can you promise victory, Lifesbane, after the last unsuccessful missions?"

"Yes," he replied. "I promise you victory—I guarantee it. You will win Salara. The earth will be bathed in so much blood that the rebels will have no resolve left to continue. Of this, I have no doubt."

"And what of your problems with Mavahan?" Mr. Oswald asked.

"I will handle that as well," Keleir said. "I will go to Mavahan and speak to the Alar. I will handle him."

Oswald laughed, along with the other two Seconds. "One man?"

Keleir leaned closer. "Take a good look at me. Do I look like just any man to you?"

Oswald narrowed his eyes at Keleir, appraising the young lord. "Admittedly your hair and eyes are unsettling. On the Second, however, a clever makeup artist can produce the same effect."

"There isn't much magic left on your world, so what I am is a rarity, I'm sure. Therefore, I'll forgive your ignorance. I am what simpleminded men call a *demon*. I was born with the mark of the Oruke. Do you know what an Oruke is, Mr. Oswald?"

The lawyer shook his head.

"An Oruke is a creature created from the forgotten matter between worlds. He is made up of all the leftover energy from the birth of a universe. He is a bodiless being that can only survive in our world by bonding with a newly conceived child. The Oruke accidently, or purposefully, comes to our world by hitching a ride through a Mage's Gate. It enters the womb and melds with the infant. It takes the full gestational period for the Oruke to worm its way in every fiber of the child, eventually destroying its human consciousness and replacing it. What is born is no longer what would have been. The entire child's consciousness is solely the Oruke. They are bloodthirsty, powerful, dangerous, and impulsive. They are not mentally equipped to deal with the array of human emotions, so they feel things ten times stronger. For example, mild anger for you is colossal rage for them. Simple appreciation for a woman can be uncontrollable lust, and, well, there aren't too many stories of sad Orukes. They are incapable of understanding empathy."

Oswald swallowed. "So you are this Oruke?"

Keleir laughed. "Oh, no, I am something much worse. I am a man with an Oruke inside him, with full control of his body, and unlike most Orukes, the Core blessed me with Fire. I have devastated entire villages and armies alone. Should you say my name outside these walls, men will cower and hide with fear. A reputation can be a powerful weapon when utilized properly. So yes, Mr. Oswald, I will handle the troubling affairs of Adrid—without weapons from the Second. If I am not being overly confident, I would suspect that is why our king chose me to wed his daughter and inherit his throne."

Yarin smiled large and proud, leaning back heavily in his chair. "My son," he said, rapping his cane against the table. "It is settled then. While I wanted your weapons, General, it seems my people think otherwise. A smart king heeds the words of his advisers. I'm sorry you came here for nothing."

Saran nearly choked at her father's admission, unable to recall a single time in her life that he'd ever heeded the words of his advisers.

"If I didn't know any better, King Yarin, I would suspect that we came here so you could show off your new heir." General Pulaski narrowed his eyes at Yarin before turning a sneer on Keleir.

Yarin smirked. "It had the advantage of working out that way, but no, I was genuinely interested in your offer, General. But I have more faith in a demon than I do in man."

Keleir smirked but did not meet the king's amused gaze. "Well, if that is all of our business for now, perhaps we should adjourn. We've wasted enough of their time."

"Yes, you have," the quiet Sergeant McDonald replied as he stood up from his chair, holding out his hand. "Though negotiations didn't go well, it was a pleasure to meet the future king."

Keleir eyed the hand in front of him before standing and grabbing the sergeant by the forearm for a good shake. "Perhaps our future negotiations will be more in your favor, Sergeant."

"If we are lucky," he replied.

When the Seconds left, the nobles filed out, leaving the table empty save Saran, Keleir, and the king. The silence grew thick between them while they waited for everyone to clear earshot of the door. Keleir went to the end of the table and sat down to the right of the king with his arms draped across the tabletop, fingers clasped together. "We need to talk," he said, red eyes fixing hard and fast on the old man. "It concerns your daughter."

"You will marry her."

"Oh, I'll gladly marry her. But there is something you should handle first." Keleir glanced away. "Saran, wipe the paste from your face."

"Paste?" Saran chuckled as she took a cloth and gently wiped the flesh-tinted paint from her nose, revealing a tinge of purple and swollen flesh.

"Show him your hand," Keleir continued.

Saran lifted her hand from the long sleeves of her tunic and showed him the bandaged, broken mess. For a fraction of a second, she thought she saw concern flash in the king's eyes. It disappeared, like every other emotion the old man possessed. "What's this?" Yarin asked, sneering. "Did you hurt her?"

"No," Keleir growled. "And lucky for the man who did, Saran has asked me to have mercy. You will remove the Binding so that she may heal. It will remain off once a healer has completed her duties. Understood?"

"Are you giving me orders, Ahriman?" Yarin turned his aged eyes on the Fire Mage. "The Binding will stay on. Saran is not to be trusted."

"You will remove her Binding. I will handle her unruliness. She is to my liking and she will keep to my will."

Saran bristled at his words. Being of willful independence, she couldn't help but feel annoyed, even though they were meant to placate her father.

Yarin smirked. "You admit it then?"

Keleir cast Saran a puzzled look. "Admit what?"

Yarin leaned toward Keleir, turning his face into the younger man's ear. "You love her," the old man rasped. The king sat back, turning a smug smile on his daughter. "Her Binding is as much to keep you in line as it is to keep her. I do not know to what extent she's twisted your brain, but when a man as formidable as you goes from slaughtering whole villages to killing no one, not a single person, in five years, well . . . there are some questions."

"Why make me your heir if you don't think I'm up to your ruthlessness?"

"Because you will be." Yarin smiled. "It is your destiny. If I must leave anything behind in legacy, let it be that I handed the man who would unite and destroy worlds the keys to a vast empire."

Saran and Keleir exchanged bewildered looks before the princess eased forward. "Father, he is not the one the Ekaru priests told you of. Even if he were, I would not allow it. I cannot allow it."

Keleir looked down at his hands and gave a heavy sigh. "King Yarin, you will remove the Bind on Saran." His voice turned frighteningly calm, far too patient for the Fire Mage's personality.

"It will not be removed. She'll die with it on before I allow that. You don't see it yet, but I do. I'm old. I'm crippled. I'm dying. But I have yet to be completely blinded or deafened. I have studied the madness that took my wife enough to know that Saran is a direct threat to your power, and while I cannot keep you from loving her or from wanting her, I can keep her from interfering in your destiny with magic. You are long awaited by your people, Lifesbane."

The Fire Mage seized the king by the neck. "I will not play games with you. Be cryptic again, please. I've wanted nothing more than to slaughter you for the last five years. Please give me a reason." The Fire Mage's eyes kindled blazing orange, and the king's neck sizzled.

Saran lurched up, knocking her chair over, and wrapped her hands around her neck. "K-Kel!"

He released the king and went to her, drawing her hands gently from her throat to find red rings of scalded flesh in the same pattern as the ones he'd left on Yarin's wrinkled skin.

Yarin winced, feigning to touch his blistered skin. "A precaution attached to the Binding. The spell blocks the effect of magic, unless magic affects me. Any harm, magic or not, delivered by another's hand upon me will also be inflicted upon her. Saran is my insurance. She will keep me safe from you until you have accepted your truth."

Keleir couldn't tear his gaze from her scorched skin. "I'm sorry," he whispered and pressed a quivering kiss to her forehead. He fought wave after wave of rage that grew stronger in him with every second he stared at the damage caused by his hand. His veins burned like molten lava, scorching hot and begging for release. He turned to the king, fire crackling in his eyes and a growl on his lips. "What if you die from natural causes?"

"Then she is safe but still Bound. You don't understand how much of a threat she is. Not yet. You will, though, when He wakes."

"Who?"

"The Oruke."

Keleir's fire snuffed out, and his eyes cooled to a deep ruby red. "Tell me."

"When the Three are devoured by their darkness, He will see to the fall of the Corrupt and the rise of the Oru—"

"I know the prophecy, Yarin! Do you not think it was recited to me over and over while the people of my village cut the mark from my chest? I know that prophecy so well I recite it in my sleep. Saran is not a part of it."

"She is," the king said. His old gaze fell mournfully to her. "How unfortunate for my blood to birth the Equitas. I have known for a long time what she is. Her mother knew too."

Keleir stiffened, and Saran stepped up next to him. He glanced to her, but her gaze remained locked on the old king in his well-worn chair.

"Speak no more of the woman you drove to suicide," she spat. "Speak no more of this prophecy or Orukes or Equitases. We define our own destiny, Father. Not you, not demons, and not the dreams of man. There is no such thing as the Living God."

"I killed her," Yarin said. His lips twitched and wobbled back and forth between a cruel smile and a deep frown. It seemed the crazed old king could not decide between being happy or upset at the revelation. "I caught her trying to sneak you away with that damn traitorous Water Mage, Ishep Darshan. She meant to hide you in the Second, and I caught her. She knew what you were. She told me, after persuasion. She had visions the moment you were conceived, and the Prophetess told her that the Oruke would seek to kill you in the hopes of solidifying his future. Don't you see what I am willing to do to make sure He exists? I'm willing to give up everything, even my wife. Even my daughter. The Vel d'Ekaru will rise."

Saran's hand clapped against the king's leathery face hard enough to cock his head sideways and, thanks to her Bind's enchantment, send herself spiraling into the table. Keleir looped an arm around her waist and steadied her against him. She clutched her reddening cheek and hissed at the old man.

"Let's go," Keleir muttered, drawing her away.

"No! I'm going to beat him senseless!" Tears stung her eyes as she glowered at the man she'd been raised to call Father. The man whose blood ran through her veins. A man that had killed her mother and passed the death off as if she'd done it to herself out of desperation and insanity.

"And beat yourself in turn? No. Can't you see what he's trying to do?" Keleir pressed his face into her curly hair and held her tighter. "Do not let him win. Let him die a lonely, old bastard."

Saran shook with rage, glaring at her sickly father, who looked neither pleased nor displeased with the revelation. She found nothing but well-practiced hollowness in his eyes, a detachment that he'd adopted with her the moment he viewed her a threat to all his carefully laid plans, and desperately still, she sought some amount of humanity and affection in that bleak gaze. "Why do you want the world to end so badly? Why do you allow this torment?"

The king tilted his head. Confusion glittered in his eyes. "Perfection is born from torment, Saran. Torment weeds out weakness and strengthens you. Isn't that what you've always wanted, Keleir? A perfect world?"

The Fire Mage's arms tightened around the princess, and he drew her back to the door. Keleir's touch quivered, a shake of fear or dread. "Perfection is unattainable, Yarin."

Yarin's body shook with a great laugh. "And still the Vel d'Ekaru pursues it for the sake of us all."

Saran jerked forward. Keleir lifted her up by the waist and out the door, slamming it behind them.

"Let me kill him!" she seethed, twisting against his strong grip.

"And kill yourself? You are more important to me than vengeance. He's old, Saran. Old and senile and wrong. He'll die soon enough. We will find a way to remove the Binding ourselves, or we will use that old contraption in the dungeon to go to the Third." He took her face in his hands. "Trust me. He's wrong. I am not what he thinks I am, and you are not the Equitas. We are Keleir Ahriman and Saran D'mor, haunted, but nothing more. Do you believe me?"

Saran nodded, but he saw the questioning look in her eyes, he read the words she wouldn't voice, and the Oruke inside him laughed.

TWELVE

"THIS WILL EASE the pain and get you through the ceremony," Madam Ophelia said as she passed a cup of hot medicated tea into Saran's good hand.

"Thank you. Could you bring me more once the ceremony is over? I may have need of it depending on whether I make it out of the room without punching someone." She took a deep swig of the near-scalding liquid. Her hand hurt too much to pay mind to the temperature, and she had little patience to wait for it to cool.

"Certainly," said Madam Ophelia with a pleasant smile. "You look beautiful, I might add."

Saran glanced to the mirror as her handmaiden, Ora, finished the last buttons and ties on the heavily embroidered burgundy dress. The very old and very traditional gown, belonging to one of her great-grandmothers, had all the trappings of a corset and layered skirts, proving to be one of the most uncomfortable things she'd ever worn. "I hate it," she admitted with a sour frown.

"It is a little much, isn't it?" Madam Ophelia agreed, smoothing her hands over the plain dress she wore. Healers liked plain cotton clothes of simple design. They were practical clothes, without the finery of corsets or embroidery or layers of unnecessary dressing.

"I'd rather be in riding clothes—at least they're comfortable." Saran took another sip of medicine. "It's not to say it isn't a pretty dress. It is a lovely dress. I meant no offense. It just isn't . . . me."

"Your hair looks lovely, at least," Madam Ophelia offered with a smile.

"It is lovely . . . Ora does beautiful work. I wouldn't know what to do with it, as you can tell from my usual unkemptness. I am the single worst princess ever produced for this kingdom."

Madam Ophelia smiled, coming to stand just behind Saran. She met the princess's eyes in the mirror. "You were raised by wolves, child. Had your mother survived, she would have taught you the ways of a woman, but instead you were taught the ways of a brute. I mean no insult . . ."

Saran laughed. "You speak truth. I learned to stab a man in the kidney before I learned to put on a dress."

Ora gave a bashful smile as she pinned a gold peacock into Saran's curly hair. "I think you're ready, Your Highness."

The princess downed the rest of her tonic and handed the empty cup to the healer. "Yes, it seems I am. I can't delay any longer, can I?"

"Are you not excited to be engaged to Lord Ahriman?" Madam Ophelia asked.

Saran's lips parted, but the answer never left her. Instead she pursed them together and shrugged her shoulders. "Someone will be king. He is a far better choice than others." She could have told the truth. She could admit that she wanted to marry him. Though she'd never thought of marrying him in the fashion her father intended. Saran loved Keleir, but binding herself to him the Mage's way meant also binding herself to the Oruke, and the Oruke to Adrid. "You could be queen without a king," Madam Ophelia replied. "It isn't necessary to have a man to rule."

Saran smiled. "You are right. I have no need for a king. But I will have need of heirs and, well, Lord Ahriman is attractive and intelligent."

The healer grinned. "'Tis true, Your Highness. Many admire him, though most are too fearful of him to make advances. The ones brave enough to approach are swiftly rejected."

"His brother, however," Ora said with a chuckle, "he's very popular. The servant girls love him, and if the rumors are true, he loves them right back."

Saran's eyebrow arched. "Really now?"

"Oh, yes, m'lady."

The princess smiled. "What a scoundrel."

"If you ask me, a man who thrusts himself this way and that is either senseless or in pain."

Saran froze, turning a careful eye on the servant. "Pain?"

"Yes, Your Highness. If it's not too crude to repeat, they say his body's willing but his thoughts lie elsewhere. Some say a woman he loved spurned him. A rumor, though."

"Rumors always have some basis of truth, no matter how far removed," Saran replied, eyeing herself, a stranger, in the mirror. She couldn't imagine Rowe to be the type of man to take on multiple lovers or even lie with a woman for only a night. If the rumors were true, then she didn't know him as well as she thought . . . or perhaps he'd changed. Her curiosity turned to the hypothetical woman who had stolen his heart and did not return his feelings.

Years ago, Saran had loved him. Part of her still did. But she'd been torn between that love and the developing feelings for Keleir. Saran had never meant to fall for Keleir. Her interactions with him began innocently at first, a means to an end to keep the Oruke inside him at bay.

For a short while, the three had been able to maintain some sort of strange shared love. Then Rowe pulled away. He told her that he loved another. She hadn't pressed him further, partly because it hurt and partly because he insisted she devote herself to his brother. She tried to imagine what sort of woman had stolen his heart and why she didn't love him in turn.

Before she could delve any deeper, the door opened, and an Ekaru priest gave her a careful nod.

There weren't a lot of witnesses waiting in the throne room. Saran felt silly for being adorned in such heavily embroidered fabric for a handful of people. For the amount of time and care the servants put in, she might as well have been married that day. She hated the thought of her wedding if they put such fuss over attire for a simple betrothal ceremony.

Keleir waited at the foot of the king's throne. A man who normally sniffed at the idea of fanciful clothing, he wore a regal tunic and a crimson cloak that draped over one shoulder. His brother stood close at his side, dressed as smartly as the soon-to-be king. The two were engaged in deep, whispering conversation until Rowe spotted Saran and lost the words in the back of his throat. He nudged his brother with a hard elbow and nodded toward her. Keleir's gaze lifted, his head turned, and he met her with tired eyes.

She could not read the emotion on his face. She knew he hadn't slept again, and not simply because he looked exhausted. He'd spent the night tossing, turning, screaming. Whatever that creature said to him tore him apart from the inside out at night, and she could do little to help him with the Bind. She could only obey her father's wishes and hope that he favored her with release. Though that did seem unlikely now, given his superstitions. She needed to prove herself no harm to the Oruke's plans and that she could even support them.

Saran turned her eyes on her father. He'd always been easy to fool. She couldn't remember when she began her act or when she started working against him in secret. Perhaps at eleven, when she was ignored by him and allowed to sit in on his lengthy meetings. At some point, she found a way to make herself useful, to make him proud. She took interest in the military, and he gave her a position in his army. She won battles for him, and he praised her for it. Who would ever suspect that the daughter of the king whispered his secrets to his greatest enemy?

She'd been good at deceiving him, until she'd finally grown tired of the lie. Until it got harder to fix the damage once the armies left the burning cities. But she'd taken the mask off too soon, and she needed to put it back on now. If she didn't, the world would get infinitely harder to fix.

The priest led her to them with his head to the stars, having such a pompous air about him that she thought he might float away. He took great pride in delivering her to the king, and once he reached the foot of the throne, he swooped into a deep bow. "Your Majesty," he said, "I present the Princess of Adrid for her Claiming."

"Yes, yes, get on with it." Yarin sighed, falling back into his throne. He waved the priest off.

The priest stood between Saran and Keleir, taking Saran by the arm. She almost drew away from him but instead clenched her teeth and focused on being the perfect daughter. "Places, please. Left hands together!"

Saran placed her left hand in Keleir's hot palm. The Fire Mage was pale and held deep circles under his eyes, but he smiled for her. His grip tightened protectively around her hand, and he bent toward her ear. "You are lovely."

She pressed her bandaged hand against the tight corset. "I can barely breathe. I hate this dress."

He offered a sympathetic frown, resisting the urge to brush his hand over her cheek. "It will be over soon. Painless, and then you can be rid of it and into something more comfortable."

The priest began his incantation with a cough to clear his throat. He twined gold rope about their arms and wrists, and ended it with a knot over their hands. "You are Bound by Law and by Magic, never to be parted. You swear an oath this day to wed the other. To be faithful. To never waver or turn from one to another. To . . ."

Saran listened to his words, and even with the Bind, she felt the heat of the priest's magic tickle the air. Her heart raced up into her throat, and she stepped toward the priest. "Those are wedding vows. This is a betrothal ceremony."

The Fire Mage cocked his head to Yarin. "Explain."

The king, slouched upon his throne, gave a dismissive wave of his hand. "I have no reason to explain. What you seek is only obtainable through her."

Keleir met Saran's wild eyes, filled with fear and uncertainty. He couldn't deny that he, too, felt afraid for what the king wanted. "What I seek?" he asked, shaking his head. His attention turned to Yarin, his face growing red with rage. He tugged against the rope that bound his hand to his lover. "No more riddles, you decrepit sack of horseshit!"

The Ekaru priest, along with the very few witnesses in the room, gave a horrified gasp.

"Say a word," growled the Fire Mage to the Priest. "One word and I'll burn you alive." He tugged his hand from Saran, but the ropes held them tight together.

"Keleir!" she called, jerking forward against the rope as the Fire Mage stepped toward the King. "Wedding now or later, what does it matter?"

"It matters! I will not give this thing inside me what it wants, what your father wants!" He pulled at the rope that bound them together, shaking with rage. Like a rabid dog tugging against his owner's leash, he thrashed his hand to free himself from her. "My entire life I've followed the path this thing set me on. No more."

Behind them, the priest scolded, "You are not finished with the spell, Lifesbane! Do not remove the Binding."

The torches and candles lining the walls of the throne room roared fierce and hot. "THAT IS NOT MY NAME!" Embers crackled in Keleir's eyes, and he set the cord about his hand aflame, snuffing it out before it touched Saran's flesh. Once free, he stomped up the stairs and snatched the king by his robes, drawing him out of the throne as easily as a man could lift a child.

"Careful," Yarin warned. "Saran bruises easily."

The Fire Mage shook, rage coursing through him hotter than molten lava. It took all of himself not to throw the old man into the wall. If not for the threat to Saran, he would have. Black seeped into the corner of his eyes, and he sneered. "Talk."

"Keleir!" Rowe bounded up the podium and grabbed hold of his brother's shoulder. "Keleir, stop it!"

"I will not," the Fire Mage seethed.

"Stop," Rowe whispered. "Marry her. You've wanted this, haven't you?" His electric gaze fell on the princess, where she stood hopeful and afraid, her hands clasped pleadingly together. He offered his brother a rueful smile. "You love her. Marry her. Marry her, or I will."

The Fire Mage stiffened, glowering at his brother. Of course he'd try to trick him in such a way, always playing the scoundrel willing to whisk her away when it suited him. Keleir shook his head, growling out a sound more demon than man. "I can't . . . If I do this, if it takes me over, she will not have the chance to be with another. It will Bind her to me, but worse, it will Bind her to the Oruke."

Saran edged closer to the foot of the king's podium. She eyed her father and then Keleir. "I know what this means. Shouldn't it be my choice, if the cost is so great? I choose you." She swallowed. "And I choose the Oruke."

"Lovely." Yarin sighed.

The princess glared at the king. "I am not doing this to please you." She immediately regretted her words. Of course she needed to do this to please him.

"Why are you doing it?" Keleir asked, dropping Yarin back into his throne. He shook his brother's hand from his shoulder and turned to her. "Haven't we been happy with what we have? We don't need this, to be Bound in this law. I'd happily marry you, Saran, but not the way of Mages. We don't need that chain, especially with the risk of losing my battle. You will never be able to love another, be with another, as long as this form lives."

"I am Bound to you, regardless of law. Without this Bind," she said, glancing to the manacle around her wrist, "I feel you in the very air around me, Keleir." Her eyes watered. How she missed that feeling. How she missed the kinetic energy of his power in the same room as her, as comforting as a warm blanket on a cold night. "But you're right. If you don't want this, then I will not agree to it."

Yarin tsked them with a wave of his finger. A slow, cruel smile curled the corners of his mouth. "This isn't a negotiation. Finish the ritual. Finish it or face the consequences."

Keleir gave a devilish smirk. "And what are those consequences, my king?"

Yarin stretched his old legs out and reached into his robes. He pulled a dagger from the folds and plunged it into his leg. His face stiffened with pain, but the old man never uttered a sound of distress. He was, after all, used to misery.

Saran buckled with a cry, falling into a pool of burgundy skirts. Rowe rushed from the podium and fell to the floor near her, hurriedly pushing folds of fabric and underskirt away to wrap his hands tight around her bleeding thigh.

The Fire Mage snatched Yarin up. The king chuckled through clenched teeth, and he twisted the dagger in his leg. Saran screamed, writhing beneath the hard press of Rowe's hands. She grasped to pull the offending weapon free but only caught air.

Keleir ripped the dagger from Yarin's wound, messy and quick, and threw it across the great hall where the king could not reach it. Saran withered on the floor, heaving as pain splintered through her.

Rowe cradled her and pressed his wide hand against the hole to try to stop the bleeding. It poured over his fingers and dripped to the stone under them. "It's all right," the Lightning Mage soothed, staring down into Saran's alarmed eyes.

Sweat beaded on the king's forehead. "Finish the ceremony."

Keleir loomed angrily over the crazed old man. "Why is this so important to you?"

"When the Three are devoured by their darkness . . ." the king began before Keleir's hands wrapped around his throat, silencing him. Behind the Fire Mage, the princess choked.

"Keleir!" Rowe roared. "She can't breathe. Stop it!"

Keleir's eyes grew black as pitch. "What does it matter to you if I am king? Why is this so important to you? Answer the question, and I'll release you."

Rowe watched with horror as color left Saran's face and her eyes pleaded with him for air, as if he were the one choking her. Her hands wrapped around her throat and clawed at an invisible grasp she could not reach. Rowe roared. "You're killing her!"

Yarin grinned. He struggled to lift his chin, and with a single breath he hissed, "You are long awaited, Vel d'Ekaru."

Keleir released his grip on the king and let the old man fall back, coughing, into his throne. He backed down the steps and across the floor until he stood near Saran and Rowe, letting his gaze slip to the woman he loved, gasping on the floor in his brother's arms. The Lightning Mage's face turned a ghostly sheet of white, and the black in Keleir's eyes seeped away like a passing storm.

"Finish it," Yarin said. "And no harm will come to her or your brother."

"She needs a healer," Rowe whispered, brushing the curls from her face. Saran pressed her cheek into his chest and closed her eyes wearily. The Lightning Mage turned his angry gaze to his brother. "I told you to stop."

Keleir nodded. "I'm sorry . . . I . . ."

The king straightened in his chair. Blood stained his robes and dripped down his leg to pool beneath his boot. He required a healer as badly as his daughter, and Keleir wondered if the man would sooner sit there and bleed to death than relinquish control of the moment.

"Finish," said the king with the sort of finality that proved the Fire Mage's thoughts correct. He would not escape this without someone he loved being hurt or worse.

Keleir nodded and knelt next to Saran. "Quickly," he said to the priest as he took the princess's left hand in his. The priest pulled from his pocket a second gold rope and tied it around their hands. The Fire Mage tried to ignore the weary look on Saran's face or how the color of her lips slowly returned to their normal shade of rose.

"You swear an oath this day to wed the other. To be faithful. To never waver or turn from one another. To be tied as one for the rest of your living days, and endure pain if you ever knowingly break the oath that Binds you." The Priest turned four shades of green as his eyes fell on the blood collecting around Saran's legs. "As a priest of the Vel d'Ekaru, by my authority as a representative of His will, I wed you. Man to woman. Mage to Mage. Eternal and everlasting." The priest took a small knife from his belt and turned Keleir's hand over, cutting across the palm. He then pressed the hand to Saran's already bleeding leg. "Blood to blood."

After a minute the priest released his grip on the Fire Mage with a disappointed frown. "Usually there is more fanfare, but the Bind is probably keeping the spell from completing. It will need to be removed in order to finish. You will also have to consummate."

"The Bind will remain," Yarin snapped. "The spell will complete when it is removed, and it will only be removed when I die naturally or when I have decided to remove it. Either way, at that moment, it will be time for you to be king and inherit all that is required to ascend to your proper place."

Keleir nodded, as passive as a beaten dog, and did not lift his gaze to the old man. "Let us go, then, if all that is required of us is finished. Your daughter needs stitching."

Yarin threw his hand toward the door. "Go then."

Keleir moved to gather Saran in his arms, but Rowe took her swiftly and stood. "I'll carry her. I think you've done enough for now."

They took Saran to the medical ward on the south side of the palace and let the healers tend to the wound, stitching and bandaging it. They tucked her safely into the medical cot, drugged with herbs and tea, and then Rowe motioned for Keleir to follow him out to the hall. Once the door closed, the Lightning Mage struck his brother soundly across the jaw.

Keleir skidded sideways into the wall, and his head cracked against the stone. He cupped his jaw with one hand and wiped blood from his lip with the other. He did not feel anger at his brother for the hit. In fact, he wanted it to hurt more. He *needed* it to hurt more. "You told me to hit you if you ever willingly hurt her," Rowe seethed. "I kept my promise."

The Fire Mage leaned into the wall, wanting more than ever to be sucked into it. He stared across at his jealous and angry brother. "Are you sure you aren't hitting me for other reasons?"

"Those reasons don't matter. She couldn't breathe, and you *ignored* me. Vengeance meant more to you than her. You're slipping. Anger is getting the better of you."

Keleir cast his eyes to the floor. "I know."

"What do you plan to do about it?"

"I don't know, Rowe."

"You look awful."

The Fire Mage curled his fingers in his white hair and closed his eyes. "The inside of my mind is like a shattered wall, crumbling ever so slightly with each pull and tug the Oruke makes. I can feel the pieces falling right now. It's a constant scratching pain. A . . . headache that isn't quite there. I don't only see him in my dreams, but now sometimes while I'm awake. It's as if the moment Saran was Bound, the wall she built to protect me formed a huge crack, and it's been growing ever since."

"If she were free, do you think it would save you?"

"I don't know. I could be too far gone. She said she couldn't do it again, and I believe her. It nearly killed her once. She might die the next time she tries." Keleir sunk to the floor, stretching his long legs out before him. "I don't want to tell her. Gods, I shouldn't have done this! She's trapped to me."

"And you to her," Rowe reminded. "Though, not yet. You've got to finish the ritual. Remove the Bind and consummate the marriage."

Keleir gave a low, dark chuckle. "I'm pretty sure we've consummated."

"Does that even count?"

Keleir shook his head, tears in his eyes. "No idea."

"Saran has had the shit kicked out of her the last few days. She's not fit to fight if Darshan leads his assault on the capital, and we don't know how long it will be before she is. There's also the risk she'll die if one of his bloodthirsty men puts a sword through Yarin. One of us needs to go to him and let him know what's happened."

Keleir lifted his red gaze to his brother. "What if we leave them to bloody each other and we use the Gate Maker in the cellar to go somewhere else?"

"What do you mean?"

"Saran and I discussed it, though we agreed to wait until after Salara. We want to go to the Third. There isn't any magic there. It may stop the progression of the Oruke. What if we don't wait until after Salara? We could go tonight. Let those that revel in war fight their battles. I'm tired. I'm *so* tired, Rowe. I want peace, both of mind and body. I *need* sanctuary."

Rowe hesitated. "I'll speak to Darshan. You stay with Saran. When I get back, we can talk more about going to the Third. But I'm in agreement for waiting until after Salara."

Keleir's lips parted, but he clamped his mouth shut and stood. "The two of you are very loyal to a man who would happily have me beheaded."

"We are loyal to freedom for thousands of people, Keleir, not to Darshan. You are my brother, and if going to the Third saves you, then I will go. But I need to finish what I started with Saran. Please respect that."

Keleir frowned. Even though he felt part of their little group, he had never truly been part of their alliance with Darshan. It had begun before his merger with them as a man, not as the Oruke. Rowe had always possessed a blind devotion, a desperate need for atonement that led him to do irresponsible and selfish things.

The Fire Mage shook his head and went to the door to Saran's room. "I'm turning into a monster who may very well slaughter all of you for the sheer joy of it. Perhaps you should respect that more."

THIRTEEN

SARAN EYED HER new husband as he sat on the edge of her bed, staring at his shoes. The small, narrow room had a single straw cot, a small table with a candle, and a cabinet of medical supplies tucked into the corner. The tiny light from the withering flame next to her reflected the terrible mood rippling off the Fire Mage. Even without their connection, she could feel it in the air. A black cloud hung around him, and a heavy weight had settled on his shoulders.

"I've not been this unlucky since we were stuck in the Ebon caves fighting off cavern dwellers." She sighed, tilting her head back into the pillow.

Saran could count on one hand the number of times she'd been this damaged and unable to quickly resolve it with magic. One of those included the night she faced off against the Oruke to bring Keleir back from the darkness. It had taken seven healers two weeks to mend her body. By all accounts, she should have died.

The Ebon caves came in a close second as far as damage, and though it had been filled with pain, it was a happy memory for her. It was on that trip that she realized she had fallen for the Fire Mage. He'd protected her, helped her walk, nursed her sickness from the infection. They'd been trapped for days, lost in the caves and fighting off locals who didn't appreciate trespassers, until they wormed their way out of a hole in the caverns and landed on Adrid soil. When their powers returned, Saran mended herself. Keleir, thankfully, had endured the experience without losing himself to the Oruke. In fact, he had said he didn't hear the creature at all.

He referred to that story as proof that going to the Third or running away to Mavahan would save him from the Oruke. Of course she knew the truth. He wouldn't last much longer than they had in the caves.

Her limbs were fuzzy-numb from the herbal tea, and her eyes heavy with sleep. For the moment, her father's damage caused only a slight ache. "At least then I only had a few cracked ribs, a broken leg, and a really infected bite, and that all cleared up right after we got out of Mavahan and I could use my element again."

Keleir's hand tightened into a fist. "In the course of three days you have had your hand broken, your face pummeled, your neck burned, your leg stabbed, and I nearly choked the life out of you. This is more than a little unlucky, Saran." He rubbed his temple, stiffening as her left hand brushed along his back. She curled on her side and dragged her short nails over him soothingly. "I am sorry I was too angry to hear Rowe. I wish I could go back. I wish I could manipulate time as you do and fix all the wrongs I've done."

Saran swallowed the knot in her throat. She needed her power. She missed having the ability to make everything better, to control fate, and to rewrite the history around her. She used it as a shield from all the wrongs in the world, and that shield had been stripped from her. She'd never had a life without magic, and now she had nothing. Not even the strength of her own body. She'd never been this frail, this vulnerable, and she couldn't afford to be any of these things, not with Keleir in such a bad state. Not when she knew him to be so vulnerable himself.

If her powers weren't returned to her soon . . .

"It's fine. Listen, the only reason all of this seems so bad is because I usually heal very quickly. What is the beauty of manipulating time if you can't reverse the damage or speed up the recovery? When I get hurt, I get right back up as if nothing happened. You're not used to seeing me like this, that's all. Honestly I'm not used to being like this. You know how much I hate being the damsel."

"You are hardly a damsel . . ."

Saran smiled, curling her fingers in his tunic. "Look here."

He hesitated but finally turned to look at her. Even in shadows and looking as if he'd not slept in days, he was the most handsome man she'd ever seen. Most would find his appearance unsettling, and yet she'd grown to love it.

"Husband." The word felt odd as it rolled out of her mouth and into the air, where it hung heavy around them. She laughed. "I thought it would sound more natural."

"It is new," he admitted. "It may sound more natural over time."

"I'm sure. Do you want to say it?"

"Husband?"

She laughed again. "No."

Keleir swallowed, reaching out for her good hand. He curled his fingers around it tightly, as if he needed to draw strength in order to speak. "Wife."

The word quivered on his tongue, half-restrained as it forced its way from his throat. His eyes watered as he looked down at her fingers curled around his hand. He blinked and wiped his hands across his cheek to banish the sign of emotion. "I told Rowe that I would sit with you and keep you company, but I have something I need to know. I have to leave you for a little while. I'll be back as soon as I can."

Saran tightened her hold on him. "Where are you going?"

The Fire Mage gave a weak smile. He bent and kissed her lips. "To church."

FOURTEEN

ROWE WAITED PATIENTLY for Darshan in the circular tower-tent. Warm sunlight filtered in through the tall stained glass windows, painting colors across the floor. The colors moved, shifted, twinkled with each slight rustle of the illusionary trees outside. He stared at the floor with a painfully tight grasp on the arms of his chair, watching the colors as they moved.

"Lord Blackwell," Darshan greeted with a smile, falling weary into a chair that materialized behind him.

Rowe jerked from his thoughts, blue eyes flashing up from the floor to meet the rebel leader's curious gaze.

"What brings you here?" the Water Mage continued.

"I've come on behalf of Saran."

"Ah, yes. She did say she would send word on her punishment . . ." Darshan slid to the edge of his chair, resting his arms across his knees. "And?"

"It's complicated. We may not be able to win this war without . . ." Rowe swallowed. "The king has placed a Bind on her. She cannot use her power. The Bind is also connected to his life. If he is hurt, she is hurt. If he is killed, she is killed. The only means of avoiding hurting her is if he dies naturally. We haven't located a key to free her. That is my next goal once I'm through here."

Darshan frowned, settling back in the old wooden chair. "I see . . ."

"If you raid the castle and kill the king, Saran will die with him. Neither I nor Keleir will allow you to kill him if it means losing her. You understand this, don't you?"

"I understand."

Rowe tilted his head. "And your thoughts?"

Darshan pursed his lips together and stared at the floor. Then he pressed his fingers to the bridge of his nose and clenched his eyes. "I loved her mother. Her mother loved me. We couldn't be together because of her forced marriage to Yarin and the rules that come with those rituals. But we loved each other . . . It would sadden my heart greatly to lose Saran, but war often involves collateral damage." His eyes flashed to Rowe's and held them. "We must strike and rid ourselves of Yarin, no matter the cost."

"Then imprison him," Rowe said quietly. "Until he dies of old age or diseases or until we rid her of the Bind. You cannot afford to lose Saran. She is not a casualty of war. Not when there is so much at stake."

"Are you saying this because you love her?"

"No," Rowe groaned. "I'm saying it because I love my brother and he loves her. I'm saying it because my brother is losing the war with the Oruke and he needs Saran to keep him stable. If you take Saran away, the Oruke will consume him, and there will be no one to keep the creature in check. She is his Equitas. I know this to be true. You stand to lose quite a bit if you take her out of the game."

"Game?"

"You know what I mean, Darshan."

Darshan's gaze turned piercing, and his face pinched with a frown.

"Have you had any visions?"

"No. The Prophetess has been quiet. No dreams either."

The Water Mage tapped his fingers against the chair thoughtfully. Rowe fixated on the sound, as if he could decipher what the old man thought based on the rhythm he set. "Your brother is slipping. What is your opinion on the matter?"

"You know what my view of the matter is. I care a great deal for him. I will do anything to keep him. That includes going someplace I do not want to go. He speaks of travel to the Third as a means of hindering the Oruke. He thinks that a world without magic will stop the Oruke's advances and save his sanity. He wants to go immediately, but I want to hold off until after Salara."

Darshan nodded. "How do you know the Oruke hasn't taken control of your brother already? You said he is slipping? What if he already slipped and the glimpses you are seeing now are merely the Oruke slipping up in his act? Of course he doesn't want you to help with Salara. Ridding the king of the throne and his access to it would hinder his plans. He wants the rebellion to fail. It will ensure his succession."

"It has already been ensured. Saran and Keleir were married today. He will be king once Yarin is gone."

Darshan's lips curled with a cruel smile. "How convenient."

"Keleir doesn't want to be king. He didn't want to marry Saran. He only married her because Yarin tortured her. It was mercy."

"The Oruke is good at acting human, isn't he? He knows you and he knows Saran. He knows what you think and how you feel. He is playing you. Of course he wants to take you both to the Third immediately. He will strand you there, without magic to get you home, nor the means of technology to create a Gate. He will leave the two people most likely to stop him in a Deadworld and go about his plans without your threat. He is playing you, Rowe. He has been playing you all along. He fakes this slipping so it increases your desire to save him. But he will betray you."

"He is not playing me," Rowe growled.

"And you know this for sure?"

The Lightning Mage glared at Darshan and hesitated. "No."

"If he is to prove himself to you and to me, he must go through with our plans. He must depose Yarin and relinquish control of Adrid to someone more trustworthy than a monster." Ishep gave a sympathetic sigh. "I understand it is hard to believe. You love your brother very strongly. It blinds. In the end, all the things that Keleir claimed to not want, he did anyway, did he not? He married Saran. He accepted the title of Name Heir. He says one thing and does another. Are those the actions of your brother? Is that the standard you hold him to?"

Rowe's lips pursed. He stared toward Darshan, long, hard, but not entirely at him. He looked past the old Water Mage into his own thoughts. Keleir had been acting unlike himself, and he'd attributed it to the ground the Oruke claimed on his mind. Was there truth in Darshan's words?

"I will speak to my brother about Salara. I will push for him to help fulfill our promise. If he disagrees, then Saran and I will finish this on our own. We will not go to the Third until you sit on the throne."

Darshan smiled softly. "I have every confidence in you, but what will you do if the Oruke doesn't agree with your terms?"

Rowe stood up, smoothing his hands over his tunic. "Then I will kill him. If what you are saying is true, my brother died long ago."

"Your brother died the moment the Oruke entered the womb. He never had a chance to exist. This is the way of Orukes. It is unheard of—impossible—for it to be any other way. If by some miracle the Oruke bonding couldn't be completed or he managed to compartmentalize the creature inside him, it will not change the ending of his story. He is the Oruke."

FIFTEEN

DARK SHADOWS HUNG in the corners of the chapel. The light of a hundred candles littered across the altar did little to combat the impenetrable darkness. Chandeliers hung low and dim, and heavy curtains were drawn over the windows. A priest knelt at the front, before the altar, with his hands clasped and resting across the top. He wore dark robes and a hood drawn tightly over his head. Around his waist dangled several gold trinkets from a rough brown rope.

"Is there a funeral?" Keleir asked, sitting on the front pew with a heavy sigh. He drew his cloak around him like a blanket, admiring the bleak architecture. Keleir didn't think anything could be as bleak as Yarin's throne room, but then again, he had not been to the Church of the Vel d'Ekaru in many years.

"I like the dark," the priest said. He rose. The coal-gray robes washed around his ankles. "At least when I pray. It helps me focus."

"I never understood the point of praying to the Living God," the Fire Mage said. "If He is living flesh, how does He hear your prayers?"

The priest smiled and sat next to the future king. "Ekaru priests do not pray in hopes that the Living God will hear them.

We pray because it keeps us faithful. It keeps us connected to what has yet to be delivered but has long been promised."

Keleir turned his eyes up to the marking of a monstrous face formed from a thousand rope knots painted on a red banner that hung from a golden pole. The flag spilled behind the candlelit altar like a bloody waterfall. He knew the mark well, as he'd been born with it on his chest.

The Fire Mage wondered quietly for a long time why he sat in the pew next to the priest. He'd come here seeking answers about a creature he'd lived with his entire life yet knew nothing about. He'd come for answers to Yarin's riddles, but looking at the man in his gray robes, who side-eyed him in such an eerily reverent way, he doubted he'd get anything other than more riddles.

"You await the Vel d'Ekaru, the Living God."

"We await the redemption of our universe, and the universes beyond ours." The priest smiled and followed Keleir's gaze to the painted banner. "When did you last attend service, Lord Ahriman?"

"I attended as a young boy and as a teen, but Yarin's religion was not mine, and not my people's. I remember some of your beliefs, however."

"Do you know the origins of the First, the Second, and the Third?"

"I know legends."

The priest smiled. "I'm Brother Povish, by the way. We didn't get to be introduced earlier during the ceremony."

Keleir froze, turning a surprised look on the priest. "I didn't even realize that was you. I was . . . distracted."

"It is not your fault, Lord Ahriman. A lot was going on. A lot of blood. It is easy to be distracted by decay. Not to rush you off, my lord—it just seems that you are lost. How may I help you?"

Keleir glanced to the priest and then back to the banner hanging behind the altar. "I need to understand the Vel d'Ekaru. I have come to learn, Brother Povish, about your mighty god."

"To understand Him, we'd have to start at the beginning, and it is a long story . . ."

"I have time." No, Keleir thought, he had very little of that. But if time paid for answers, time he would give. "Start at the beginning."

The priest clasped his hands in his lap and turned his eyes to the altar to begin his tale. "Each land, each people, has their own legends about how the universe formed. Some are based on science, some on myth, and some on faith. But all legends, no matter what view, begin with one initial spark. One loud bang, if you will. We know that there are universes right next to ours, alternate realities where we exist or don't exist. We know of three of these realities, for sure. The First, a lush world full of magic, where the life of the planet is thriving and only just beginning to hear the call of destruction. The Second, new to greed and already seeing the toll it takes on a dying world. Then the Third, well-acquainted with greed. They killed their planet. They mined it dry.

"The Three are without name, as no one lived at their birth to name them. They were born of power and light, and the Origin God gave each a soul, locked with a Key. The First Key is the Body of Life, the power to create or destroy. The Second Key is the Hand of Strength, with the power to control the Body. The Third is the Carrier of Power, which cradles them both. When combined, the Keys have the ability to tear apart universes or create them.

"The Origin God created the first universe, though I don't necessarily mean ours, and from that sprouted others. We could be the hundredth, or the thousandth. As we haven't found the right combination for unlocking others, we have only the Three. Each universe had its own life. Each a copy of the next, with infinite possibilities."

Keleir sighed, trying not to seem bored by the origin of the universe. These were not the answers he wanted, and if this marked the beginning of the priest's tale, he felt that he'd be hours before getting any of the information he'd sat down for. "And what about the Orukes, the spirits between worlds?"

"Imagine bubbles floating in water. Imagine each bubble is a separate universe, a separate world, and the water is the matter that floats between those worlds. It binds them together. The Orukes are the spent remnants of energy that float in that matter. They are fragments of time and space that were lost or ejected at the formation of a universe. They are trapped, tortured creatures without real form. Every now and then, one finds its way into our world, but without any physical form of its own, it is merely a ghost and does not survive long. That is why they merge with a child carried in its mother's womb."

The Fire Mage glowered at the floor. "The consciousness isn't developed yet, so it is easier to take over the form."

Brother Povish smiled. "Not so easy, it seems. You shouldn't hate the thing inside you, Lord Ahriman. It is a gift."

"This is not a gift," Keleir hissed, touching his chest. "This has brought me nothing but misery."

"You fight it. Pain always accompanies futility."

"And I should just embrace it and let it take me over?"

"It wouldn't hurt anymore, would it?"

Keleir scoffed. He turned his attention away from the man to the heavy curtains blocking out the setting sun. The creature had run him for nearly thirteen years, and for what? He'd murdered. Slaughtered. Killed. He'd brought destruction and war. He'd been exalted and worshipped for it, and Keleir hated it. His only redemption came in the form of a woman who'd braved fire and agony to reach inside and make his soul whole again. He would never be that creature again willingly.

"You were never meant to exist in the first place, Lord Ahriman. You are a vessel for something that has been desired for a very long time. You are a vessel for our redeemer and the savior of our universe, the liberator of the Oruke. It hurts, because you are not meant to be alive."

The Fire Mage froze, turning his gaze slowly to Brother Povish. "All this thing wants is death and destruction. How is that your redeemer? It would sooner see you flayed."

"Not I." The priest smiled. "Others perhaps, like your wife."

Keleir growled. "And how is that a good thing? How should I accept that and let it win, if it means to murder someone I love?"

"Because it is for the best. You can't see it. I understand that. My words will do little to shape your view of the matter. Your human emotions cloud you."

"My human emotions are far more reliable than the instability of a creature not equipped to handle them!"

"What I mean," Brother Povish began patiently, "is that your sentimentality toward your own life, to the life of the people around you, and to the world itself clouds you from seeing the truth."

"Then explain to me the truth, Brother Povish. Help me see it."

"You know the truth. He has told you, hasn't he? Shown you?"

Keleir gave a tight smile. "I'd like to hear it from something other than the voice inside my head."

Brother Povish took a deep breath, ending it in a pleasant sigh. He shifted in his seat, as a child would right before receiving a present. The joyful look on his face turned Keleir's stomach. He felt ill and angry. Part of him wanted to kill the priests for relishing in such a thing, and the wiser part of him knew that road led exactly where the priest wanted him to go. "The Origin God created the universe and its planets, and thus sprouted life. From that life grew plants and animals, creatures that existed in an ever-revolving cycle. It was perfect and beautiful, but then it evolved. From the ooze grew a parasite. It started small and innocent enough, as they always do, until it grew intelligent and strong.

"Humanity, Lord Ahriman, is the parasite of the world. It is a virus that rots what it touches. The world revolves in a cycle, and humans spit in the face of it. They underappreciate and overconsume. Just like the damaging cells of a disease in your body, it seeks out the healthy cells and destroys them. Humans devour everything, Lord Ahriman, until there is nothing left. They are selfish, greedy creatures. Even the best of them."

"You speak of yourself. You are human."

"Yes and no. I'm a second-generation Oruke. My father was an Oruke. You are an Oruke, but you refuse to let your human nature be consumed by the righteousness of your redeemer. You think the Oruke is evil, and you hate it because it made you murder, because it craves blood. But you do not realize that what the Oruke does isn't evil at all. It is a culling. It is the same thing as squishing the beetle that threatens to ruin the crop. Humanity is the beetle—the Oruke is just the gardener trying to keep the crops alive."

"If your father was an Oruke, why didn't you worship him as the Vel d'Ekaru?"

"There are many Orukes in the world, but only one of them has lived many times over. The Oruke inside you has seen the end of the Three repeated and has attempted to save it every time. You are the prophesied one. You are the vessel, the body of the Living God."

"But how do you *know*?"

Brother Povish grinned. "Why, because you told us so, Lord Ahriman. A long time ago. When you were boy. You bear his mark."

SIXTEEN

SARAN STARED AT the flickering candle next to her bed. Despite her drowsiness, she lay awake in the medical ward on the small, uncomfortable cot filled with straw and barely big enough for one person. To protect against the draft filtering in from the cracked window above her head, her legs were draped in a blanket little more than gossamer cloth.

She waited for Keleir to return. She let her fingers play with the Bind around her wrist, hating it. Aside from missing the sensation of the Fire Mage roaming near and the light flicker of magical current wafting through the air, each day that she was blocked from her magic meant Keleir would slip further into darkness. The worst part was that she couldn't explain to him why. She couldn't even tell Rowe. If either of them knew what she'd done to banish the Oruke . . .

Saran swallowed hard. Keleir would hate her. He wouldn't understand.

Panic bubbled up in her chest. The urge to run to her father and beg him for freedom consumed her, and yet she could not run. She could barely stand, and Yarin did not take well to signs of weakness. She also had never begged for anything in her life, and she was certain he wouldn't indulge her pleas. He never had before. Her thoughts raced, and the world felt like a giant spinning top that moved too fast for her to control, and . . . she'd always had control.

The door cracked open, and she sat up in bed too quickly. Her head rushed, and she fell back against the pillows with a dizzy whimper. Rowe brushed inside, closing the heavy door behind him. He took a look around the room, sneering. Anger flared in his blue eyes.

"Where is Keleir?" he asked.

"There was something he needed to do. He seemed upset." She shifted, pushing her arms against the mattress to sit up, this time more slowly. "I'm worried about him."

Rowe nodded, taking a seat at the edge of her bed. "I just got back from speaking with Darshan. I explained our situation concerning your Bind." Rowe rested his hands on his knees and stared at the floor. "I also told him about Keleir's plan to go to the Third."

Saran saw the disappointed look rising in his eyes. The past few days were a blur for her, but even so she felt guilty for not telling him. They never made important plans for the future without Rowe along to help. "There wasn't any time to discuss it with you. We weren't trying to keep it secret, but with everything that happened . . ."

Rowe's hands tightened. "He wants to go immediately and not stay to finish what we started."

Saran sighed, tilting her head back. Her gaze turned to the flickering candle, watching the little flame dance in the air. "He's not feeling well. He's scared, I think. Truthfully I'm scared too. But we can't just up and go to the Third. I don't know what will happen if we journey there."

Rowe nodded. "I am worried about more than that."

"Tell me."

"Darshan said some things that . . . has altered my perception of the situation. I don't know what to think anymore. I've never had reason to question my brother's loyalty until today, when you nearly died because of his rage."

"It's not *his* rage, you know that."

"I do, and that is why I'm concerned. Saran, the Keleir I know would never hurt you. He would drop everything to stop from hurting you. He didn't today . . ."

Saran's gaze narrowed on the black-haired man. "I'm not following you."

"What if it isn't Keleir? What if it is the Oruke pretending to be Keleir?"

She scoffed, waving her hand dismissively in the air, even while a bud of terror blossomed in her chest. She squashed it quickly. "The Oruke wants to kill me, Rowe. If Keleir were the Oruke, he wouldn't have shed tears as I lay in this bed. He wouldn't want so desperately to be saved."

Rowe paused at her words. Would the Oruke be so clever? "Keleir cried?"

The princess nodded. "Well, he started to, but you know him."

"We're losing him, Saran. What if we can't finish this in time? Darshan will not trust Keleir unless he helps with Salara. He will view any other action as the Oruke's defiance. He doesn't believe that Keleir has any control." Rowe shook his head. "I warned Darshan about the Bind's connection to Yarin, but I doubt his people will heed that warning. We can't take Keleir somewhere safe from the Oruke. He won't leave you. Not only that, Yarin has some weird fixation with Keleir. If he disappears, he's liable to imprison and torture us both to figure out his whereabouts."

Saran sighed heavily, sinking into the stiff pillow with all her weight. "Fuck, why does this have to be so complicated?

Okay, we'll finish this. We made a vow. When it is over, we will leave it all behind. Until then, we need to find a way to keep Keleir in control. I need this thing off of me." Saran lifted her arm, waving the Bind weakly in the air. "Keleir will be fine. I will fix this. I just need to be free of this thing.

The Lightning Mage nodded, his gaze hard as he stared at the floor.

"Trust your brother, Rowe. Trust me."

Rowe stared at the floor, fisting his hands over his knees. "I . . ."

Saran gave his shoulder a firm squeeze.

Rowe sighed, turning to her and pressing his lips into her hair. "Sleep. You need your strength."

Her hand tightened on him, but he drew away from her grasp. She caught him by the wrist. "You trust him, don't you?"

The young Mage shut his eyes. "My gut is twisting, and all I can believe is that something awful is going to happen. I love my brother, Saran. Even when he was consumed by darkness, I loved him and looked up to him. But I do not trust him. Deep down, I don't think I ever have."

The wooden door behind them creaked, standing three inches open when Rowe knew it had been shut before. In the loudness of his thoughts, he hadn't heard anyone enter.

"Was it Keleir?" Rowe asked, throat closing.

"I don't know . . . I can't feel him. Rowe, if he heard you say that—"

"I'll find him."

SEVENTEEN

KELEIR STARED ACROSS the bay at the glint of the setting sun. The wind blew harshly across the balcony, tossing his white hair about his head to the point that it stung his cheeks and blinded him. When he leaned against the railing, the roar of the wind filled his ears loud enough to war with the voice inside his head.

The powerful Fire Mage slumped forward against the stone, lowering his head and clenching his eyes tight. He buckled to his knees, a broken man, while the priest's words played like a never-ending song, a constant reminder of his doom.

He was the bringer of destruction, the monster that children feared, doomed to hurt the ones he loved, and nothing could stop him. Time would be his undoing, and the one person who could control time no longer had the power. If she could not stop him, then . . .

With longing eyes, he took in the waves crashing against the rocks.

Death is not an escape, the Oruke whispered. *I am here, no matter if your soul leaves this body. It will not die.*

"Can you use a body that does not function?"

Bodies heal.

Keleir glared at the waves. "Why?"

Quiet. Seconds ticked away, and he felt the aching scratch of the Oruke thinking. *This doesn't have to be horrible or painful. Listen to me, Keleir, my brother in body . . .*

Keleir laughed. "We are not brothers."

Let me show you why this has to be.

"You've shown me lots of things, Oruke."

But you won't listen. You won't trust in what I show you.

Keleir lifted his gaze to the ocean beyond the cove. "Death. That is all you show me."

You will see soon enough that the people you love—these humans you want to protect—are as twisted and dark as the rest of them. It was true what the priest said. This world will meet the same fate as the Third. But we can stop them. We can save what there is left to save.

"By killing?"

By redeeming. Some will die, this is true. But what I intend for the world is something much better. Humans are imperfect, selfish creatures . . . but they can be made better. From the ashes of what we must do, they will rise anew. They will rise cleansed and stronger. They will be perfect.

Keleir shook his head. "Perfection is impossible."

Nothing is impossible.

The Fire Mage roared, "I don't want any part of this! I just want to be with Saran and Rowe, somewhere quiet. If the world burns around us, so be it. As long as I have them . . ."

You are part of it, Keleir. There is no escape from this.

Keleir glared at the horizon, his eyes burning. The world before him disappeared into a watery blur. He gripped the banister beneath his hands until his knuckles whitened. "Save me," he whispered to the wind, to the gods, to anyone with the power to stop him. "Save me!"

"You are saved," came a voice behind him. With tears brimming his eyes, Keleir glanced over his shoulder at the man in the doorway. The Oruke stared at him, holding out a hand, sorrow in his eyes. "Trust me. I have never lied to you. I will never lie to you."

Keleir looked away to the cresting waves below. The rocks, jagged and menacing, reached up to him, calling like a siren, waiting with open arms to greet him at the bottom.

Better to be dead, he thought, than hurt the people he loved. Better to be dead than fail to protect them. Keleir turned to the Oruke and sat on the railing, giving a solemn smile. "You want to cleanse mankind? Do it alone," he said to the creature, and he let himself fall back.

The wind roared up around him, deafening in his ears. He was not afraid. Instead a feeling, placid and soothing, coursed through his veins, easing the tension and releasing him from the horrible prison he'd walled himself in. Freedom and peace wrapped about him, welcoming him to his oblivion.

Electric-blue light crackled in the air, and a harsh grip clutched his waist. He fell into warmth and reappeared kneeling on the balcony floor with Rowe hovering over him, shaking him furiously.

"Keleir! Didn't you hear me? Why would you . . ."

Keleir looked at his brother's pale face and then flopped back to lie across the floor, staring up at the darkening sky. Confusion filled him. It replaced itself with realization, knowing that the man in the doorway speaking to him had been Rowe all along. Profound hollowness replaced the peaceful serenity that he'd momentarily found in his ending. This soon faded to resentment. "I heard you . . ."

"Why?"

The Fire Mage didn't answer. His brother didn't trust him. How much would that trust worsen if Rowe knew that he now saw visions of the Oruke in his waking life?

"The brother I know would *never* give up. He would never do something so cowardly as to take his own life. He would never abandon Saran or me!"

Keleir laughed. It rumbled up from his chest like a growl. He stood, dusting his pants. "The Keleir you know is dead . . . dying, at any rate." He turned his dull eyes on his brother. The look sent the Lightning Mage back a step.

Rowe frowned. "Perhaps . . ."

"Trust." Keleir waved a finger at Rowe, an acidic smirk twisting his handsome face. "That's what we lack, right? Fine. I'll prove my loyalty to you, Rowe. When I have, I will do what I wish with what remains of my life, and you may do what you wish with yours. You no longer have to be my shield or my watcher. I was wrong to depend on you so. I see now that it has been too hard on you."

"That isn't . . ." Rowe frowned.

"Go away," Keleir muttered, leaning back against the railing.

Rowe's expression hardened. "Will you throw yourself off the balcony when I leave?"

Keleir looked down at the crashing, frothy waves. "Not today."

The Fire Mage listened to the echo of his brother's boots across the stone floor until he could no longer hear them compete with the sea. He sat with his back to the railing, his legs stretched out before him, until night fell and the world encased him in darkness.

The moon offered little light to see by, so it surprised him when Saran emerged from the darkness of his room, wrapped in a white sheet. She limped, favoring the leg her father injured. Her hair, once done up nicely, now hung half-pinned from all her wallowing. Loose strands of curls tangled in the wind while pain pulled her normally happy face tight and worry creased her brow. Keleir could barely see in the night, but her pain glowed angrily at him. Guilt wrapped like a vise around his heart, and he hung his head so not to see her.

"You should be resting," he whispered, staring at his hands. She stepped between his legs until her feet crowded his vision. She had petite feet, small and narrow, with long toes. Monkey feet, she called them.

"I couldn't rest. No matter how hard I tried. I worried for you," she replied and tugged the blanket tight around her shoulders. "Rowe told me what happened, but he wouldn't let me see you. I had to wait until he fell asleep."

She slipped down to her knees, clenching her teeth against a cry of pain. He turned his face away from the awful expression she made as she knelt between his legs.

"Is it true?"

Keleir nodded without meeting eyes.

"Why?" Her voice crackled unsteadily from her lips. He heard the pain, and it tore his eyes from the floor. A tear rolled down her cheek. She reached up and wiped it, turning her face from the wind so that it tossed her hair up like a shield. "Why would you do that?"

He swallowed the hard lump growing in his throat. "No reason will ever be good enough for you."

She took his face in her hands. "You're right. It won't be. I can't understand your pain, so I can't understand why you would want to leave. But while I can't understand the pain, I can respect it. I can recognize that it is there. I cannot save you from it, but I can help you through it . . . somehow. I can listen. I'm good at listening."

Keleir nodded. His eyes burned. "You are."

"I want to hit you," she said, managing to look at him again. "But I won't."

"You can hit me," he whispered eagerly, wrapping his hands around hers. "Please do."

She shook her head. "No."

Saran leaned forward, making an awful sound as she did. Her forehead pressed against his, and she draped her arms over his shoulders. "Don't leave me. I know that's selfish to ask, and I don't care if it is a lie, but promise me you won't go."

Keleir swallowed and nodded, rubbing his nose against hers. "I won't leave you, I promise."

He reached forward and placed his hands on her hips. He lifted and turned her so that she sat sideways against him, alleviating the pressure on her wound. She let out a tight scream as she moved, biting into the fabric at his shoulder. He whispered, "Sorry," until the tension in her subsided and she breathed with less agony.

When the pain passed, she smirked. "If only I had your tolerance."

"I'm glad you don't. My tolerance comes from several years of practice."

"By practice, you mean torture?"

"Yes." He sighed. "I mean torture. I want you to always be safe."

They sat together for several minutes, listening to the wind howl around them. Keleir's fingers locked around Saran's hand as she snuggled closer to him because his element always provided heat. A human fireplace, is what she called him. "Are you warm?"

"Mm-hmm," she murmured, nuzzling her nose against his neck. "You're very warm."

The Fire Mage gave a self-satisfied smile.

"Keleir . . ." Her voice faded as she admired his face in what little light the stars offered. "I trust you."

His stomach rolled over. He wanted to see her face better, to look into those trusting eyes. He wanted to hear the words over and over, repeated until they blotted out the blackness in his mind.

"I believe in you," she continued.

"Saran . . ." His throat closed. He could barely breathe, half expecting this to fall away into another trick or nightmare, so he held her tighter just in case she slipped away.

"So listen to me, Oruke . . ." She bent her face close to his heart. It raced inside his chest, hammering in his ears. "One day, I will save him from you. I will erase you—this is my vow."

The Fire Mage's jaw set tight, and he looked up to the stars. All day he'd fought these emotions, fought to bury them, to be stronger than he was. Her words broke him as easily as thrown glass. He gasped, hoping a deep breath and swallow would remove the hard brick in his throat. Instead he cried. Keleir wrapped his arms around her and buried his face against her hair, and she cried with him.

"I love you," he choked. "Gods, I love you. I'm sorry. I'm so sorry. I'll be better. I swear it. I'll fight harder. I won't give up. I promise you."

After they calmed and lay against each other for close to an hour, he gathered her in his arms, careful of her leg. "Let's get you into bed." As gentle as he tried to be, her occasional huff of pain stabbed at his heart.

Instead of delivering her back into Rowe's protection in the medical ward, he carried her to his bed. He cared very little for his brother's concern, and Rowe was smart enough to assume where she'd gone when he woke. Keleir let himself be selfish with her. He held her and gave into exhaustion, and for the first time in many days he did not fear sleep.

He would be stronger.

This is my vow.

EIGHTEEN

SARAN LIMPED ALONG as fast as her wounded leg would carry her. The skirts she wore tangled around her legs, and she fought with the fabric to keep from tripping. When she reached the council chamber, she burst into the room to find that the meeting had ended, and the only two people left were Keleir and a servant cleaning up her father's birdseeds strewn across the floor.

"You can't go to Mavahan," she exhaled, wincing as she came to rest against the table.

The servant looked up from his sweeping and, seeing the furrowed, sweating brow of the princess in the presence of her husband, gathered his dustpan and fled the room.

Keleir turned his gaze from the map of Mavahan to his wife. "I have to go."

"No, you don't."

"Saran, if I don't go to fix this, we may gain the kingdom only to lose it to Mavahan. They will not tolerate your father's games, and they will not forget the slight of being denied a queen. When we destabilize Adrid, they will attack us. I have to go. I promised I would make this right."

Keleir pulled out a chair and urged her to sit.

She glared at him. "You're too close to the edge to go to Mavahan. Keleir, you don't know what the Deadlands would do to you right now." Keleir pressed his hands to her shoulders and attempted to guide her down into the chair, but she shook off his hand. "Stop trying to make me sit. I'm standing if we are going to have this argument. You are *not* going to Mavahan."

"I am."

"No, you are not. You could cross the border and be completely lost to us! I can't bring you back again, Keleir. I don't know if it works twice."

"You don't know what you did, remember?"

"Exactly!"

Keleir frowned. She knew that look. His red eyes peered through her, thinking and plotting his next move. Sometimes arguments with him were detailed chess matches, and she didn't have the physical or mental stamina to play right now.

"I don't care what happens to this kingdom," she admitted. "Do you understand me?"

"Rowe cares, and you're lying."

"I won't lose you," she told him. "Don't go."

"I made a promise, Saran," Keleir whispered. "I promised Rowe I would finish this. It's the only way I can prove to him that he can trust me."

Saran knew he understood why she was asking this of him. She also knew that he wanted to go to Mavahan because it *was* a Deadland, and he thought he might find peace from the Oruke there. Saran shook her head, tears in her eyes. "There are other ways."

"Not for Rowe," Keleir murmured. "If I lose the battle with the Oruke . . . I want to have lost it with his trust and with his love. He's my brother, Saran."

"And I'm your wife." Panic filled her eyes. He'd never denied her anything she asked for. He couldn't . . . "Don't go."

Keleir appraised her, his lips working on a retort. Her heart lifted when she realized he would stay, but then he brushed past her and gathered the maps on the table. "I have to do this. It will earn Yarin's favor and perhaps, when I return, I can convince him to give me the key to your Bind."

Tears brimmed Saran's eyes. Would he hate her if she locked him away? How could she possibly hope to stop him from leaving in her current state? She hated feeling so helpless.

"If you return, you might not be yourself. Do you understand that?"

Keleir nodded, not meeting her eyes. "If I stay, I may not be myself."

"I can fix you. I just need to get this Bind off. I need the key."

Keleir clenched his eyes and gathered the maps under his arm. "We both know Yarin isn't going to give that key to you. He may give it to me, though, if I have the right ammunition. If I can lay an entire kingdom at his feet, maybe that will be enough payment for your freedom."

"Keleir, please . . ." She had no idea what he meant by his words, what he meant about bringing an entire kingdom to her father's feet, but she knew that there was little chance that the Keleir she knew would come back to her once that mission was over. If by some chance he did, he would not last long.

"I leave in the morning," Keleir murmured. "I'll be gone three or four weeks."

Pain splintered in her chest, and she clenched her eyes to block him out. Shaking her head, she left him with his maps in the council chamber. Saran nearly made it back to her room before a wave of anxiety struck her. It almost brought her to her knees, but instead she pressed her forehead into the rough stone of the corridor wall.

She heaved deep breaths, unable to wrangle her fear and anger. Her thoughts raced wildly for a solution, but Keleir was right. Her father wasn't going to give her the key, and nothing she'd read about had led to a way of removing the Bind without one. The only way to get it off was to somehow find the key or . . .

Saran lifted her hand, admiring the Bind. She sprang off the wall and hobbled quickly to her room, where she slammed the door behind her. Saran went to the fireplace, to the hatchet tucked against the side of the stone hearth and knelt there with a cry of pain.

Saran reached out with her bandaged, throbbing hand and grasped the hatchet handle. She winced as she forced her fingers to curl around the wood and lift the heavy weight. The princess pressed her opposite hand against the hearth and flattened out her arm against the warm stone.

Sweat beaded on Saran's forehead as she pressed the sharp edge of the hatchet to her wrist, just before the Bind.

"Okay," Saran said. "You can do this." She lifted the hatchet. Her hand barely had the strength to hold the thing. She would need more strength than that to break the bone and sever her hand.

"Okay, okay, okay . . ." Saran pressed the blade to her wrist again, carefully measuring. "Come on, Saran, you've been burned to a crisp by an Oruke possessed Fire Mage. Nothing hurts like that. This isn't going to be so bad. You can do this."

Saran lifted the hatchet high into the air. Her hand trembled violently, and her fingers ached at the grip around the handle. Seconds away from bringing the hatchet down on her wrist, she screamed her rage and tossed it away. The princess cradled her aching broken fist, angry at its weakness and angry at herself for lacking the conviction to follow through. How many hits would it have taken with such a weak strike? Two?

Three? Couldn't she endure that? What if she bled out before she'd even finished hacking her hand off?

Was her only option really to wait until Keleir returned? To hope that her father would gift them the key? She doubted any of that would come in time, and even if it did . . . Keleir would finally know the truth of what she'd done to save him.

NINETEEN

"SARAN, IF YOU don't sit down, I'm going to strap you to this chair," Rowe muttered, looking up from his book. He sat in the overstuffed chair by a dead fireplace, reading with the help of a tall candle on the tiny table next to him.

Saran kept pacing. "I'm exercising the muscles. I'm tired of being stiff."

"You should rest."

"I don't want to rest!"

Rowe clamped his mouth shut, turning a page. Several long minutes passed, with the silence of Saran's room accented by irritated huffs as she strained to exercise her healing leg.

"He's coming back," Rowe muttered.

The princess scowled at him. "What if it works? What if he can stay there and be free of the Oruke?"

Rowe pursed his lips together and glared at the book. "Then I assume you will abandon this place and go to him. That is what you do when you love someone, right? He's been gone two weeks, not a lifetime."

"Mavahan is a Deadland. What I did to save him shouldn't hold there. If by some miracle it does, why would he return?"

"Well, it is easier to follow him to Mavahan than the Third, isn't it?"

"I should have gone with him or in his stead. I'm the princess."

"You couldn't travel in the state you were in. Infection still affects you, just like all the other mortals in the world. Mavahan is desolate, hot, and horrible. Sure, getting to the outskirts is easy, but you can't Port across the desert. You'd have to ride in the hot sun and frigid nights for three days, and that's if you don't get caught up in a storm. Sand in that wound wouldn't be pleasant, I imagine."

"You should have gone to Mavahan with him."

"Keleir asked me to stay behind and keep an eye on you. Odan's out of the medical ward, finally recovered from his blood loss, and you were in no shape to deal with him should he be foolish enough to seek retribution a second time."

"Is it wrong of me to wish he were dead?"

Rowe glanced up from his book. "Odan clearly deserved whatever he got, but I don't think a good person wishes death or pain on anyone. It seems Keleir is rubbing off on you."

"And you are innocent?"

"I am reformed."

Saran scoffed.

Rowe chuckled, but he did not turn his attention away from the book.

The princess fell into the chair across from him and began to drum her fingertips over the wooden arm, watching the Lightning Mage stare at his book. "You aren't reading, are you?"

"I'm trying," he said, turning the page.

"Is everything all right? You've been irritable for days."

The lord looked up from his book, closed it slowly, and rested his hands across the top. "A lot has happened in the last few weeks. A lot of things I need to digest. My brother got married, and he's losing his mind. He attempted suicide. My best friend, who is married to my brother, has been battered and is being held captive in her own home. Meanwhile, I have a rebellion to finish, and the two people I need help from the most are incapable of delivering. When the rebels come to kill the king, they will also kill my friend. My brother will lose his soul to the Oruke, and I will have to kill him. The two people I love most in this world are slipping through my fingers, and I'm unable to do anything about it. I'm torn between saving them and saving my own soul."

Saran blinked at him, swallowing his words as quickly as he let them loose. "Saving your soul?"

Rowe's jaw tightened. "Nothing. Go back to your pacing."

She didn't. Instead she sat quietly and watched as he opened the book and began to read again. His eyes scanned the page quickly, flipping pages far faster than someone indulging in reading for pleasure.

"Reformed," she whispered after several seconds of observation. "That's why you're angry . . . You're upset that the plan isn't coming together, that we might not be able to fully pull off this upheaval? You are still convinced that the only way to redeem yourself from the things you did is to liberate the people you tormented? If you don't, will you consider every act since you *reformed* a failure?"

The Lightning Mage had spent the last seven years, since she nursed him back from the brink of starvation, attempting to do everything in his power to atone for what he'd done by Yarin's command. No amount of sacrifice seemed to ease his guilt, and he had always been willing to sacrifice anything, even the safety of those he loved, if it meant salvation for his soul. Rowe could be incredibly selfless, but in this one instance, in this one desire, he would burn the world and everyone in it to fix what he had done in his other life. Rowe's brow twitched.

His cheeks flushed with either embarrassment or anger; it was hard to tell with him. "That isn't what I meant."

"What is more important? Redeeming your soul or your brother's? You had control over your actions. Keleir had no control over what the Oruke did with his hands."

Rowe slammed the book shut with a loud thump. "Which is exactly why my sins are greater! I had control! I had free will! I used it to torture and kill." Rowe's eyes sparked with electric current as he glared across the room at her. "I know very well I'm more of a monster than my brother ever will be. He has no control over what is inside him, but I created my own demon. I must atone for it. Setting this world right is the only way I know how."

"At what expense?"

Rowe looked away.

"The Prophetess speaks to you. Isn't that enough redemption? She chose you to carry her words across time, Rowe. She chose to speak to you alone. Doesn't that mean you've been forgiven?"

"She hasn't spoken to me in months, Saran. No dreams, no visions, no voices. Nothing. I'm forgotten. The most crucial part of our plan is about to unfold and not a single whisper from the woman who set me on this path." Rowe tossed the book across the room. It slapped against the stone wall, shaking Saran in her seat. "I feel like all of this is unraveling and I'm trying desperately to hold the threads together."

The princess stood up and went to him, placing a hand at the top of his head. "We will figure this out. We have months before you travel to Salara. I'll handle this side of our plan. When this is all over, you will find your redemption, and I will save Keleir's soul."

Rowe looked up to Saran and nodded slowly. She pulled him in, hugging his head to her belly before she bent and placed a kiss to the top of his head. "It will be fine," she assured, though the tone of her voice said otherwise.

Rowe shook his head and set his jaw tight.

"The rebels will kill Yarin. They will show him no mercy, and because of that damned Bind they will kill you too. I cannot . . . that is not negotiable for me."

"Have a little faith in me, Rowe Blackwell. I may not have magic, and I may be tied to a bag of bones, but I'm not helpless. I'll handle my part. You handle yours." Rowe's disapproving sigh bristled her nerves. She folded her arms, careful of her healing hand. "So if you don't trust Keleir and you don't trust me, who do you trust, Rowe?"

Rowe stole another book off her shelf. "I trust you," he said. "I do not trust those around you, and yes, that includes my own brother."

"Keleir would never hurt me."

Rowe turned and placed the book back on the shelf. "I think I've read everything in here. I'm going to the library."

"Just like Keleir, running away when the conversation gets difficult. You two really are brothers."

Rowe turned to her from the door. "Do you enjoy prodding me? Are you so bored with your confinement that you are taking pleasure in tormenting a friend?"

"I didn—"

"You didn't mean to. You might hate being a princess, but you sure do have the same high and mighty attitude that all royals carry. You have no claim over me, Saran. I do not have to bend to answer your questions like a servant."

Saran blinked at him, an ache splintering through her heart. "I've *never* ordered you to do anything. Never." She took a step forward. "First you try to throw your life away by pretending to love me, and then—"

Rowe laughed, low and deep and with so much malice that her insides squirmed. "I'm going to the library," he said as he threw open the door.

Saran nodded faintly, sinking down into the chair he'd occupied earlier.

TWENTY

SHADOWS HUNG LIKE tapestries in the lower levels of the palace, far into the depths of the cliff, where the caverns that sailors used as a shipyard met the bay. Water dripped from stone walls, and moss grew thick and heavy in the cracks. Torches lined the left side of their path, a wide hall leading to an old wooden door at the end. At either side of the door stood an armor-clad soldier, his helmet drawn down over his face.

"Why the guards, Father? Are you worried your old friend may murder you?" Saran asked, her green eyes flickering to the back of the old man's head as he hobbled before her.

"Nonsense," he said.

Saran paused, her lips tugging with a smirk. "Ah, you're being the showman again. What is it we are bragging about today?"

Her father didn't reply. Instead he gave a harsh crack of his cane against the wall, and the guards opened the door for him.

The dark room had long stalactites hanging from the ceiling, dripping calcium upon the dank floor. At the back of the room, upon a metal podium with rusted grated stairs, sat a large metal ring, eight feet in diameter. Affixed to the old, worn ring was a metal box with corroded knobs and rusted red dials.

The contraption did not belong to the First, a fact made more prominent by the red wires stretching from the metal box to the base of the ring. Long ago, the president of the Third had gifted the technology to his friend, the newly crowned King of Adrid, so that they could visit and easily trade goods.

When Saran was little, Yarin often made several trips throughout the year, sometimes staying several days. At first they went for casual visits, but then they returned for healing. Yarin used their science to prolong his life until it became clear that no amount of science or magic would save him from the inevitable.

Time magic was one of the most powerful elements known to man. It was also the most volatile and taxing on the body. Magic came with a cost even with the most basic of elements. All Mages needed a short recovery period to renew the lifeforce spent using their power. The more power used, the longer it took to renew.

The power to control time was rare and not written about or studied. No one knew what it did to a Time Mage over the course of their usually short lives. Saran knew because of her father, his illness, and the fact that he had dragged her along to the Third for every treatment. When a Time Mage used their power, they recovered their stamina, but the hidden toll never repaired. Tumors had grown thick in her father's brain, and even when he had them removed they inevitably returned with each use of his element. He'd finally stopped using his power altogether, or perhaps he had lost it in his treatments.

Saran tried not to think about the ache in her skull whenever she pushed herself too far. She tried not to imagine that she, too, had those things growing in her head, threatening to drive her as mad as her father.

"Lord Brenden," Saran greeted as her father took his place at the foot of the podium steps. Lord Brenden, an old Lightning

Mage, had a thick gray beard and long, thinning hair. His blue eyes crackled with the same electric intensity that Rowe's possessed as they looked the princess over.

"Lord Brenden is here to open the Gate, as Lord Blackwell seems to have disappeared for the past two days," Yarin muttered, waving a careless hand over to the Lightning Mage standing near the metal ring.

Saran forced a smile. "Thank you, Lord Brenden. Your services are appreciated. My father has a hard time expressing his gratitude."

Lord Brenden's lips drew up into a smirk, revealing a row of rotted teeth. For a lord, he had little personal hygiene. His robes were tattered, for he had no wife to mend them, and his nails were overgrown and cracked, with dirt caked beneath them. Once, he'd been a great noble in her father's court, but when Blackwell came along to replace his Lightning Mage skills as a better user of the element, he became irrelevant to the king.

Yarin stood, all his weight heavy upon his wooden cane. He glowered at the empty wall beyond the metal ring for several minutes and then tilted his head ever so slowly to the old Mage near the console box. "Yes, my daughter is beautiful. Yes, she addressed you. Now that the shock has worn off, could you be good and do your job, Mevog?"

Mevog Brenden's smirk twisted into a snarl. His eyes glowed bright blue, and his fingers crackled. He directed them over the metal box and touched the surface with his nails. Electricity crackled down through the red wires. Cold blue lights flickered to life at the bottom of the ring, igniting one by one on either side, from bottom to top. Mevog twisted a dial, keeping his electric hand upon the console. A soft whir rippled through the room, and electric waves flicked along the interior of the ring with an ever-increasing pace until they collided, tangled, and weaved into a tight white netting.

The edge of a wide, low metal contraption emerged from the feathering light, and Saran stepped to the side as a morbidly obese man upon a floating chair squeezed through the ring and into their world. Yarin took a hobbling step to the left as the hovering chair breezed down the steps to the stone floor, followed by three wide men in plastic suits and two very thin men in chains.

"Can't go a minute without slaves, Roshaud?" Saran asked with a sneer, letting her gaze flick pointedly to the starving men with their necks and hands bound in manacles.

"Princess," the large man replied. "Lovely as ever."

Saran straightened and gave a sweeping curtsy to the president of the Third. Never had she met a more disgusting human being in her entire young life, even counting her father. Roshaud held a gift for cruelty that Yarin could never live up to. The president of the Third took delight in kidnapping men and women from other worlds to use as slaves on his own, to perform tasks that his people had become too apathetic to maintain or, at the very base of all slavery, for sexual subjugation. They were disposable, and when they grew too sick from the food the people of the Third consumed with years of built-up immunity, they were slaughtered and quickly replaced by another round of kidnappings.

But why kidnap, when you could make pacts with other world leaders, like Yarin, to reap and claim the unwanted? For years now her father had been feeding Roshaud the rebel outlaws that filled his prisons or allowing Roshaud's men to roll into a village and claim the leftovers after a crushing confrontation.

Along with being a wretched human being, Roshaud was the poster child for his diseased world, a man too sick to walk upon his own legs. It was a curse derived from his appetite for cloned food on a planet that no longer had any source of nourishment from an original species of animal or plant. He and his people had killed their world, and now they survived on artificial sustenance, recreations of creatures that had long since gone extinct, and as a result, as a side effect of their science, it turned their bodies into blubbering, useless piles of tissue. It slowed their metabolisms, increased their hormone levels, and reduced their bone strength and muscle tissue.

The men who followed him, other than his slaves, were only slightly smaller. They waddled on their own legs with the help of metal braces powered by packs strapped to their backs.

"Curious," Saran said as she rose from her curtsy. "Will you be able to fit through the door on that?"

"I was hoping for a faster means of travel now that I'm here, my lovely," Roshaud said with a smile, running his hand over his bare, round belly. He sat, dressed in comfortable plush pants, bare feet and chest, with a faux fur orange vest. Hair matted his chest in thick waves and traveled beneath the vest to his back. He had numerous chins spilling beneath his face, and thick sideburns curling to cut a sharp line where a man's jaw might have been. The top of his head was clean-shaven, and from his ears down he wore a long mane, braided and curled over his shoulder.

His entourage wore plastic seafoam green suits marred by black symbols of their rank across their arms and shoulders, and each had their rank tattooed in black across the top of their shaved heads. The slaves were shaved as well and wore their rank as burns on their right cheeks. Their clothes were dingy gray jumpsuits, and each had a number painted on their left breast.

"I would offer you a Gate to make your travel easier," Saran said with forced courtesy, each word strained and overtly patient, "but unfortunately I'm not able to."

Roshaud's beady black eyes leered at her, and he grinned. "Someone trapped you?" His eyes flicked to the Bind at her wrist. He knew exactly what it was; she could see that in his eyes. Saran wondered how many Bound Mages had been sent to him by her father.

"Come, sit on my lap and tell me all about it, just like you did as a girl," Roshaud said.

Yarin laughed and smacked his cane against the president's chair. "Don't flirt, Roshaud. That is a married woman you speak to."

"Oh?" Roshaud gasped and turned his attention to the king. "You didn't invite me! I am appalled at you, Yarin D'mor! We have been friends too long for you to forget me. Who did you give her to, without my consent? Saran has been dear to me since she was small enough to bounce upon my knee."

Saran's jaw tightened, and she glowered down at the president. Even after all those years, she remembered the horrible moments she'd spent in his company as a child, no matter the hours it had taken to wish such memories away. Though disgust twisted her stomach, she smiled at the revolting man and proudly proclaimed the name he'd most hate to hear: "Keleir Ahriman Lifesbane."

Roshaud's gaze darkened on the king, and he turned his chair slowly back to Saran. Bristling anger rolled off the jealous president, who might have hoped at some point to convince her father to give her to him as a means of keeping their wretched treaty going for years to come.

She straightened and smoothed her hands over her stomach, as triumphant as the last standing warrior upon a battlefield marred with blood, a warrior who knew just how to cut her enemy deeper. "He's a good husband. Strong. Fit. He'll make a fine king and a fine father."

The president nodded, letting the anger rest in his eyes. "Good," he said. "Well, shall we? I haven't visited in a while, and it seems there is much to catch up on. Where is the future king, anyway?" The president glanced around, searching for Ahriman. Saran suspected that if he had the means, he'd drive any manner of object through the Mage's heart for taking what he thought belonged to him.

"He is on a diplomatic mission to Mavahan," Yarin said, guiding Roshaud into Mevog's glittering electric portal, just off to the side from the Gate Maker they'd arrived through.

"Do come, Saran," Roshaud called when she did not move to follow.

The princess shook her silver Bind in the air. "It doesn't work with magic," she told the president. "But fret not, *old friend*, I'll meet you there shortly."

"What's with this Binding?" she heard the man ask her father as they disappeared through Mevog's Gate.

Saran set out on the long walk to the council chamber where they would receive Roshaud as their honored guest and treat him to freshly cooked steak, potatoes, and wine. She nearly vomited in her mouth at the image of him gnawing on the meat, the juice spilling across his chin to pool on his hairy chest. So engrossed in her dark thoughts, she paid little attention to her path. The castle corridors were burned into her mind, a mental map trekked so often that she never really thought of where she was going, only where she needed to be.

She struck an immovable force, smashing her nose up against hard muscle and leather armor. Saran grabbed at her face with a whimper and turned a watery gaze on the black-haired tower in the middle of the hall. Rowe shook his head, clutching a stack of books in his arms. The library door swung closed next to him.

"Have you truly been in there for two days?" Saran asked, pressing fingers lightly over her sore flesh.

"No," the lord said, curling the books under his arm and resting against the stone wall next to him. "Maybe half of the two days."

Saran stepped around him. "Must have been very interesting reading."

"Where are you off to?"

"I'm off to be the good daughter and entertain our guest, the president of the Third. Hopefully, if I'm well behaved, I get to have my Bind taken off."

"Roshaud is here?" the Lightning Mage asked, his boots clacking against the floor as he raced to catch her.

"Father invited him for dinner, I suppose to show off his brilliant decision-making skills, as he has been doing as of late. Keleir isn't here for him to brag on, so I must bear the brunt of his boasting. At least I get to see the hate in Roshaud's eyes every time Father mentions Keleir's name and *husband* in the same sentence." Saran turned her smile on Rowe. "You should have seen it! Had he been a Fire Mage, he would have burst into angry flames."

"I'll accompany you. It has been a while since I've seen the president."

Saran shrugged. "Mevog is attending to your Gate duties."

Rowe frowned. "I don't like that you have to be put in the same room with Roshaud."

"He's a disgusting human being, but as he cannot lift himself from his own chair, I doubt I really have anything to worry about. I'm not a child anymore. The most he can do is leer at me across the room."

Rowe scowled at her. "Nor do I want him leering at you either. Let me help deflect some of his attentions?"

Saran hated being fussed over, and while Keleir partially understood, Rowe had always possessed an inability to grasp her loathing of it. The insistence that she needed a protector bristled her nerves. "Why fear that a man without the ability to walk would hurt me? I've gotten along just fine without a bodyguard. Please enjoy your reading."

"Saran . . . stop."

The princess slowed her pace and turned to her friend. She appraised the concern in his eyes and felt ashamed of her words. He knew the darkness in her thoughts, the memories she'd overcome, the hatred she had for the president of the Third. He didn't want to protect her from Roshaud . . . he wanted to be the distraction from the specter of her past. A distraction from someone who had hurt her deeply, who had been allowed to hurt her by the one person who should have protected her most—her father. "Sometimes we have to do things we hate. We all have our monsters, Rowe, and only we can tame them. You can't do that for everyone you love. Accept it and focus your energy on your own. I'll be fine."

TWENTY-ONE

WAVES OF SANDY dunes spread out for miles before hardening to a dry, cracked earth around a sandstone city. The tall walls were topped with elaborate mosaic tiles and narrow alcoves. To the east of its walls, the city bordered a wide, slow river that wove from the tall glacier mountains of northern Tomorro all the way to the dry seabeds of south Droves, the kingdom that shared Mavahan's southeastern border. Four tall, spindly towers lifted to a cloudless blue sky, each tower topped with a gold dome that glinted blinding bright beneath a high-noon sun. The towering structures surrounded the palace, a massive sandstone ziggurat erected at the center of the city.

Keleir surveyed the desert from the top of his chestnut-colored horse. The heat bore down on them as heavy as the weight of a mountain. Sweat soaked his clothes and glistened along his skin. He wiped it from his brow and smeared it on the tan pants he wore. "Fucking desert," he grunted, tugging the hood over his head to shield his skin and eyes from the harsh glare.

Despite the heat and its sweltering uncomfortable nature, Keleir felt more peace in the desolate sands than he had in months beneath the cool, tall redwoods and oaks in Adrid. Here, the only noise in his head was his own thoughts. The Deadlands muted the Oruke. Just as Keleir suspected. Here, he was free.

"Your Highness," a soldier called behind him.

Keleir continued on with little recognition for the voice.

"My prince!" the soldier called louder, and again Keleir ignored him.

The young knight rode up from the ranks trailing behind him and slid to a stop in the sand next to Keleir. "My lord," he said, peering through a swath of fabric wrapped protectively around his pale face.

The Fire Mage blinked at the young man and then looked back to the straggling army. "What did you call me?"

"My lord," the man said, bowing his head low.

"Before that," Keleir asked, biting his tongue to keep the edge of frustration from his voice.

"I called you *prince*. Noble law dictates that once a man has married a woman of higher nobility, he is to take the male equivalent title of her rank in succession to the throne. By law you are Prince of Adrid, and we must address you as such. That is also how we will introduce you to the Alar once we arrive," the young man rambled, quick and nervous, nodding toward the glinting palace in the distance. He kept rambling, as if Keleir were not already aware of all the protocols he spoke of. Perhaps it was the young man's only means of communication, this wild incessant chatter. The Fire Mage deeply hoped not. "You've not spoken much since we set out from Adrid, my prince. My name is Sir Luke Canin, your translator and adviser to the traditions of the Mavahan people. I meant to introduce myself earlier, but forgive me, Your Highness—I find you incredibly intimidating."

He almost laughed at the boy. "Call me something other than *prince*," Keleir muttered. "I don't care what."

"I-I'm n-not sure I understand," the young man replied.

The Fire Mage sighed and turned a gleaming red glare upon the shaking boy. "If you cannot, by law, call me anything other than *prince*, call me Ahriman."

"A-Ahriman," Sir Canin repeated, nodding so fast that Keleir thought his head might pop off his shoulders. Canin's eyes glittered with a smile. He straightened in his seat and pointed to the city. "Mavahan representatives will meet us at the gate and escort us to the palace. They view a noble—specifically prince, princess, king, or queen—as close to godliness as they will ever come. Therefore, the men in our troop will stop riding and walk alongside you. Your head, upon riding into the city, must always be higher than ours. To ignore this would be admitting to the Mavahan people that we view our rulers as equals."

"Got it," Keleir said, nodding. "And if we walk?"

"A ruler must always walk three steps before his servants; however in public spaces the ruler is to be flanked with at least one row of guards to each side. When we are greeted by the Alar, you must bow your head but never bow your shoulders, as it is a sign that you are lesser than him."

Keleir smiled. "And what if I do not bow at all?"

"He will take it as an offence and probably have you killed. We are about to enter a city ruled by a king who seeks to invade our country. This is a diplomatic mission, is it not? We should attempt to follow their rules."

Keleir shrugged. "If King Yarin wanted diplomacy, he would have married Saran to the Alar at the Alar's request. We dishonored and embarrassed Alar Dago. He prepared for a queen, and we did not deliver. I doubt he intends any one of us to make it out of that city alive."

Luke Canin swallowed. "But . . ."

"You're walking into a trap, Sir Canin. I'm sure you didn't expect that when you volunteered to follow the future King of Adrid to Mavahan. Don't look so frightened. I have no intention of letting the Alar succeed. Magic or not, I'm very hard to kill."

"While I admit that I have every faith in you. I do not have as much faith in myself. I'm not a fighter, my prince."

"Ahriman," Keleir corrected.

"I'm a simple linguist, a scholar. I'm not very good with swords, and I'm definitely not any good with magic. My sister had the gifts of a healer, but other than that, magic has no home in my family. If I were to come up against Mavahan's famed warriors, I fear I'd be the first to fall."

"And knowing this information, the wisest thing to do would be to turn back, correct?"

"Yes, I suppose it would be."

"And you won't?"

Luke smiled. "I imagine running would bring a lot of shame to my family."

"You're a very noble man," Keleir whispered, staring at the city of their doom. "I find nobility to be rare among Adridian soldiers."

"I believe there are more noble men than you think, my prince." Sir Canin looked back at the soldiers trailing behind. "Adridian soldiers get a reputation for being evil, slaughtering, raping, pillaging thugs. However, consider that soldiers are bred and raised to follow orders. They are taught that the law of their king is the only rule book they should follow. What the king says, goes. If the king says to murder, a soldier murders, because he was fashioned to always obey."

Keleir cocked his head curiously. "What about the human conscience?"

"Consciences can be bred out of men, can they not? Rigorous training and indoctrination can turn the noblest man into a monster. If you are fed a constant diet of hate, the most likely outcome would be for you to eventually embody that. You are, in essence, what you devour, after all.

"Look to the men back there, my prince. Each one had, and still has, the potential for goodness or to at least be better than they are. All they need is someone to show them the right way. They have had a king who glorifies destruction, persecution, and violence against their fellow countrymen. Most of the soldiers in the Adridian army are orphans raised as warriors. They never had the chance to learn love or respect for their fellows. They know only honor and duty to the man who fed them, clothed them, and bathed them in war. They hear only the voice of King Yarin, who feeds them their diet of hate. The king, my prince, is their conscience. What they need is a new one."

Keleir smiled at Luke and tugged the tan hood farther over his head to shield his eyes from the sun. "You speak openly against your king, a bravery I admire. You risk much by not showering that old bag of bones with the praise he doesn't deserve. But I counter your theory, Luke. All men are born with a moral compass of some sort. What say you of those soldiers who follow the orders blindly, who relish in the death and horror and do not feel guilt at the bodies that fall by their hand?"

Luke thought for a second. "I think you are right. Most have a moral compass of some sort, but what if you were never taught right from wrong? Wouldn't your moral compass be skewed, my prince?"

"Call me Ahriman, and I'm not going to correct you again, understood? Next time I'll strike you, and for every time you utter a title other than my name, I will strike you again. Clear?"

"Yes . . . Ahriman."

"Now, before they catch us, answer me a second question, Sir Canin. Why does your moral compass swing a different way?"

"I was raised in a noble house by a loving family. A hard father, but a loving one. My mother can be thanked for my morality. I see the world as it is, not as the king wishes me to see it."

"And you still serve him?"

"I think a lot of people still serve him, agreeing or not. Each has their reasons, but mine is very simple. I serve him in the hopes of outliving the horror. I dream of a better king that will surely take his place. There was a time when I thought I might not see it, and maybe I still won't. I don't know whether you will be a good king, I can only hope that you might."

"That's a fool's hope, Sir Canin. All men of power are corrupt. You will never have a good king, and you will not find it in me. Do you not fear the Oruke that I harbor will set loose a wave of destruction far more devastating than anything Yarin could muster?"

The young knight went silent, his brown eyes appraising Keleir. "My sister says I have a sickness," he began, turning his gaze back to the sandstone city. "Too much faith or not enough sense. She could never decide on which. I'm a dreamer, my pri—"

Keleir's hand collided with the back of Luke's head, knocking him forward in his saddle. The offending hand returned to its rest upon the saddle horn, and the Fire Mage never gave him a second glance.

Luke rubbed the back of his head.

Keleir smirked. "Saran spoke to you."

Luke hesitated. "Her Highness approached me, yes."

The Fire Mage's smirk broadened into a grin. "Lovely woman, my wife . . ." Even if he'd repeated the word *wife* a thousand times in his head, saying it aloud still felt strange. He stole a glance over his shoulder at his men and then looked at Luke in a new light. "I suppose she spoke highly of me?"

"She did. She asked me to look after you, or at least to make sure you didn't, and I quote, 'do something rash that gets himself killed.' I trust whom the princess trusts. She has never led me astray on that."

"Where has she led you?"

"To the same path that you walk, that is all," Sir Canin replied, his voice a careful breath as if he feared some lurking creature might overhear them.

"Ahh," the Fire Mage mused. "So you are a traitor then? Like my wife?"

Luke's eyes lit, and he sat straighter in his saddle. "N-No."

Keleir laughed. "Do not fear, Sir Canin." He turned his ruby gaze to the cowering man and, with a mischievous grin, whispered, "I'm a traitor too."

Luke blinked at the Fire Mage, giving a vacant nod to show the prince that he understood what that meant. He turned his head back to the city.

"You will have your wish," Keleir told the young knight. "You will see a good king one day, but it will not be me. I only hope that whoever it is will remain a good king for a long time. I have not the energy, nor the patience, for two coups."

Keleir drew his horse to a slower pace and allowed his men to collect behind him. Luke gave them the same speech about Mavahan etiquette and instructed them in the way they were to conduct themselves once they crossed the threshold into the city. He did not elaborate on the details of their visit or on how their prince viewed their mission as nothing short of suicide.

Once they reached the heavy metal gates to the city, the soldiers accompanying Keleir went to their feet while he sat stiffly in the saddle. He appraised the tall walls and the iron doors, taking in every detail he could, from the cracks in the stone to the rust on the metal chains lifting the gate from the dry, sandy earth.

The rusted gate, a sheet of heavy metal with rounded bolts, had latches for huge hooks and thick chains to grapple the edges and hoist it above their heads. It moved with slow trepidation, revealing the inside of the city inch by uncertain inch. Half expecting a wall of men with bows and poison-tipped arrows to greet him, it surprised Keleir to find a mirror of his own situation once the door lifted enough to see.

Soldiers lined behind a man of average height. He stood, dressed in gold silks and ruby satin shoes, with his head wrapped in a heavily embroidered cloth. A man of middle age, he had dark, tanned skin and a thick black beard sprinkled with silver.

Keleir slipped from his horse, and a soldier took the reins and guided the creature to the back of the entourage. The Prince of Adrid smoothed his sweating hands against the insides of his thin tan coat and lifted them to draw back the protective hood, revealing a wash of stark white hair.

A deft silence stole the voice of the murmuring crowd behind the Alar and his soldiers. Peasants hung out of their glassless windows to see the foreign royal. At the site of his inhuman features, they shrunk back into their homes and drew their shutters closed.

The Alar smiled, revealing a row of too-white teeth, achieved only by chewing upon the acidic root of the Bagwa tree for hours. "*Ve drago ta vel Jino Adrid. Abla greto sha toma, dres Ipaba, burso dur Ahriman, pres dre cro tugatta.*"

Sir Canin coughed and stepped close to Keleir's side, but not a degree before him. He leaned in and translated quietly to him. "He says, 'I'd heard that the Prince of Adrid, a man who stole my bride, was an Ipaba, marked with the surname Ahriman, but I did not believe it until now.' Ipaba means *Soulless One* in Mavish."

"*Das ze drogo Ahriman cres ba Mavahan?*" the Alar asked.

"Do you know that the name Ahriman originates from Mavahan?"

Keleir smiled. "Great, this is going well already." He took a step forward and bowed his head, keeping in mind not to bow his shoulders to the Alar. "It is interesting that your culture coined the name given to me at birth. Thank you for sharing this knowledge, and it raises my curiosity of why a culture so removed from the power of the Core would be the first to name a creature born from it. Perhaps my coming here will be one filled with knowledge, not just diplomacy. Should we move our conversation to the sanctuary of your palace walls and away from your frightened people?"

Luke translated quickly, his tongue well-trained to the dialect of the Alar, and the king's eyes lit with interest in the young knight. He replied to Luke, who had yet to remove his own hood and cloth from around his face. When the last cluster of indiscernible words left the Alar's lips, Luke drew his hood off to reveal sandy blond hair and pale skin. His brown eyes turned to Keleir, and he smiled. "The Alar wishes us to follow him to a place more comfortable to our pale skin."

Keleir and his men followed the Alar, flanked by two rows of soldiers, to the base of a large staircase leading up to the middle floors of the ziggurat at the center of the city. By the time they reached the top, the Fire Mage counted over two hundred steps, and his men, already exhausted from traveling in the heat, were winded.

Bronze doors opened to a dark corridor, and cool air wafted from inside the ziggurat. The size and massive stone walls kept the interior insulated from the penetrating and merciless heat. As the shadow of the interior stole them inside, cool, stale air greeted their burning skin.

"The Alar says that since we have traveled far and for many days, perhaps we would like to indulge in baths and a rest before meeting formally on his personal veranda this evening," Luke said to Keleir as the Alar snapped his fingers and a procession of female slaves emerged from a narrow hall.

Each servant wore a rust-red dress parted on each side to reveal a narrow sliver of smooth, tan flesh. Bronze clasps held the dresses over their shoulders, and they were drawn tight about their waists by three narrow leather bands. Each woman had smooth black or brown hair pulled up and piled in braids at the top of her head. They wore no jewelry, save a bronze collar about their necks and a thin gold chain around their left ankles.

"The Alar has given his finest slaves for your indulgence, my prince," Luke whispered. "It would be rude to refuse them. It is customary for you, having not brought female servants of your own, to choose two to help you with your various needs while you stay in his house. You do not have to utilize them, just . . . make the best to keep up appearances that you are."

"Choose for me," Keleir said, his gaze glancing indifferently over the women and then settling on the young knight.

"Ehh . . ." Luke's cheeks colored deep rose. He looked the women over and called to the Alar. Two women, one from the middle and one from the very end, stepped out from the line and took deep sweeping bows that brought the top of their braids brushing along the stone floor.

"The remainder of the slaves will be divvied up between your men, who may take one per two of them. A single slave is offered to the person of your choosing who you feel should be honored."

Keleir smiled. "Choose one for yourself."

Sir Canin coughed. "Your Highness . . ."

"You," Keleir said to a woman nearest the Alar, dressed in rust red, but far more conservatively than the rest. He motioned for her to move forward and then swept his hand toward Luke. "Him. My honored. Without him, I am deaf."

The woman glanced to the Alar, and he gave a swift nod. She stood before Luke and gave him a great sweeping bow as the others did. Keleir realized the woman wore no collar and had no chain about her ankle. She smiled at Luke and took his hand tenderly. She spoke to the young knight in words that Keleir did not understand, and then the knight looked to his prince and smiled. Luke's cheeks were a darker rose than before, and he set his teeth in such a way that Keleir could not understand if he felt flustered or angry.

"Her Royal Highness, Princess Velora, sister of the Alar and the Keeper of His House, has accepted your request. She says that she will make your honored welcome."

Keleir swallowed. "Can you ask her forgiveness and explain that I didn't know of her stature in this house?"

"I will not," Luke said, while smiling. "I mean, no, my prince. It would be disrespectful to turn her away now that she has bowed and agreed to your request."

"Great, so I look like an asshole no matter what I do," the Fire Mage murmured.

"No, you look like a prince," Luke replied.

The Fire Mage clamped his mouth shut and followed his two escorts down a wide hall opposite the one the slave girls had entered through. The path of corridors they took were winding back and forth like a maze. He went up steps and then down steps, left and then right, until he swore he'd gone in circles before the two women led him to a thick wooden door at the end of a narrow hall.

The dark room beyond smelled of spices that were unfamiliar to Keleir. The wide chamber had a tall peaked ceiling that mimicked the shape of the ziggurat. From the center fell a beam of golden sunlight on a square ten-by-ten pool of steaming hot water sunken into the floor. Fur rugs littered the floor, and bottles of oil and soap sat clustered on a clean gold tray placed near the pool's edge. At the back of the room, in the shadows, lay a bed of silks and furs upon a wide podium. Sheer crimson fabric hung from a thick bronze ring attached to a metal plate in the ceiling. The fabric gathered in rippling pools about the bed.

His escorts fanned into the room, one going to the tables near the bed and lighting the array of candles littering the surfaces. The other went to the small trays covered in candles around the bath. When finished, the two stood side by side before the bath, hands clasped in front of them. They looked at him as one might a ghost. He realized, as they appraised his strange features, that they had not really looked at him until that moment.

"Thank you," Keleir said, knowing they would not understand him. "You can go. I'm fine. I can bathe."

The chamber door opened behind him, and a tall, broad man carried in the leather satchel that had been attached to the back of his horse. The man dropped the heavy bag in the corner of the room, near a wooden wardrobe tucked against the wall with an ornamental palm. The gruff, dark-skinned man, Droven in origins, bore a bronze collar around his neck. He gave the Fire Mage a fleeting glance before leaving the room and shutting the door behind him.

"As I said," Keleir continued, "I'm fine."

The women nodded but circled around him and began to tug at the fabric he wore. They were experts in removing articles of clothing. By the time the Fire Mage could dance away from them, they had stolen his cloak and belt.

"This is going to get awkward very fast," he said to them, holding up his hands innocently. "I'm good at bathing myself. I know that might not be the custom in Mavahan. I also understand that you have no idea what I'm sayi—hey!" He took a quick step back as the servant girl reached for the edge of his tunic. It took all his willpower not to slap her hand away.

She was a slave, doing as told. How could he punish her for misunderstanding? Especially when her life itself was punishment in its own way.

The two women no longer held apprehensive faces or fear in their eyes. Instead they appeared curious as they approached him. He held up his hands, keeping both at bay.

"No," he said firmly, stopping their advance. He motioned to the door. "Go."

"*Beva ugrad, cre hokator,*" one of the young women said to him, an edge of annoyance tainting her flowering speech. She pointed to him and then to the water. "*Cre hokator.*"

Keleir shook his head. "I have no idea what that means."

The women advanced on him, and he took a step back, nearly falling into the deep bath. "All right! Fine. I've got it."

He grabbed the hem of his tunic and drew it over his head before kicking his shoes off, dropping his pants, and stepping down into the water as quickly as he could. The center of the pool, at its deepest, was at least five feet. The water swelled around his chest. He'd been in the hot sun all day, but there was something soothing about the scalding temperature of the water. He dunked his head and ran his fingers across his scalp to clean the sand from his hair. He stood straight, washing his white hair back with one hand and dragging the other over his eyes.

When he glanced back to the servants, they were down to nothing but the bronze collars around their necks and gold chains about their ankles. Each one held a rag in one hand and a bottle of oil in the other and were stepping down into the pool to join him.

He wasn't a blind man, and he could appreciate beauty when he saw it, but they might as well have poured ice into his bath. He held up his hands and backed away from them, up and out of the stone tub at its second entrance just behind him. He stood, dripping wet at the edge, with hands in the air as they entered the deepest part of the bath and tilted their heads curiously at him.

"I'm clean. Very clean. Sooo clean. See?"

The women looked to the each other and drew the cloths in their hands up to their noses. The edge of a smile pulled their cheeks up as they turned their attention back to him. He found their bashfulness amusing, and the tension in his body subsided enough that he let out a long sigh. "Good, you understand me."

Both of them nodded, holding their long, slender arms out and pouring the bottle of oil into the water. The water frothed around them, and the steam grew thicker in the air. It wafted up in thick pink plumes, filling the air around the Fire Mage's feet and floating up about his waist.

"What . . ." he muttered, inhaling a deep breath of sweet rose. His vision blurred, his legs buckled.

Keleir stumbled, naked and wet, toward the safety of a dark corner, far away from the flowering pink smoke. He focused on Porting away, focused on falling back into his Gate, but instead he collapsed against the hard stone floor.

The beautiful women in the tub ascended the stairs toward him as the pink smoke flooded the floor of the room and rose higher to the ceiling. "*Dako*," said one of the women, smiling behind her red cloth. "*Dako de Ipaba.*"

Keleir fought the heavy weight of his eyes dragging closed. He struggled to stand, only to scrape his skin along the harsh stone with the effort. Darkness crept in, and sleep sucked him under.

TWENTY-TWO

ROSHAUD MUSHED MEAT between his dull teeth in ravenous, open-mouthed gnawing that sent juice and pink blood washing over his lips and down his chin. He hummed a happy tune, as one might on a warm, pleasant spring day while walking in a meadow of flowers.

He wrapped a meaty hand around the pewter goblet, drawing the wine to his lips and gulping in heavy, wet, gasping pulls. His black eyes peered over the glinting chalice and across from him, where Saran sat leaning against the table with her chin propped on her hand.

"Not eating?" he asked, setting the goblet down near his plate and appraising the bored princess with a disappointed frown.

"Forgive me, I'm not feeling hungry," she replied, a pleasant smile concealing the disgust churning her stomach. It was easy to pretend to be pleasant—she'd had years of practice where her father was concerned. It wasn't until recently that her well-practiced facade had finally worn down to reveal a seemingly uncharacteristic conniving nature. At least from her father's point of view.

Yarin sat at the end of the table with Roshaud in the honored space to his right. The king mulled over his food with less relish than the president, watching his daughter with the same appraising stare.

"Eat," Yarin ordered, nodding to the servant behind her. He scurried from the room to the kitchen and returned with a tray of grilled steak, potatoes, sliced bread, and a goblet of wine. He set the plate before her with silver utensils and a sea-blue rag, before placing the goblet down. Once finished, he backed away to his designated corner.

Saran scowled at the meal, listening to the loud grinding of teeth against tendon coming from across the table. Normally not one to be bothered by the sound of chewing, Saran found it nearly unbearable in present company. She stabbed a potato and brought it to her lips, taking a small bite. She smiled and set her fork back down, hiding her quivering hand beneath the table. Saran wrapped her fingers around her knee and squeezed tight, attempting to keep the tension from her face as she let lose what little anger she could without being caught. When she'd gained some measure of control over herself, she let out a deep sigh. "Delicious."

"Very," murmured the robust president. His beady eyes twinkled with a twisted leer. Only he could find eating arousing.

"It is unfortunate that Keleir had to go away to Mavahan," the princess said, taking another bite. She was quite aware of how the sight of eating affected Roshaud, but she could hardly stop if she were to play nice for her father. If she wanted to get the Bind off, she had to make the old man happy. If eating in front of his vulture of a friend would please him . . . well, she'd suffer the leering eyes of a predator for freedom. It didn't mean that she couldn't offer Roshaud his own form of misery in return. "But as he will be king, there will be many other opportunities for you to see him."

Roshaud frowned and swallowed. "That is true."

Saran took another bite before idly moving the food about with her fork. "Although our relationship with the Third may be very different when I am queen and he is king."

"How so?" Roshaud asked.

Saran smiled. "Let's not talk about business at dinner."

"You brought it up, my love," Roshaud replied, painting his face with a smile.

"I did, forgive me. We can talk later." Saran placed the knife and fork at either side of her plate. "Perhaps after dinner we could visit privately?"

Roshaud's face lit up, and he turned his eager eyes on the king at the head of the table.

"Of course," Yarin said. His gaze flashed to Saran with an approving light.

By the time dinner ended, Saran had eaten very little on her plate, but Roshaud had secured two helpings of everything and more than enough wine. The servant cleared the table and refilled each glass. King Yarin stayed only a few minutes longer to speak with his old friend before the inevitable call of wine-induced sleep lured him up from the table and off to his chambers.

"Have no fear, Father," Saran called to the drunken king. "I will see to it that Roshaud makes it safely home."

Yarin waved his hand but paid no mind to her as he closed the heavy wooden door behind him. The whirring of Roshaud's chair interrupted the deep, thick silence that encased the room when the king left.

Roshaud pulled his contraption next to Saran's chair. He lifted a pudgy hand to her arm and trailed the back of his thick fingers over her skin. The princess stiffened, tilting her head and casting her eyes down to his touch.

"What is it you wanted to discuss, my love?" he asked, struggling to move closer to her.

Saran smiled, taking his hand and pushing it away from her arm. "The future."

Roshaud withdrew his hand with a twitch of his fingers and gave her a cruel smile. "It is such a shame you married. I suppose it would be an even greater shame if something widowed you."

"You cannot kill him. No one you control would ever accomplish it, so do not waste your time, Roshaud. I do not belong in your world, just as you do not belong in mine."

The president of the Third ground his teeth together.

"For that matter, nothing of the First belongs in the Third. When my father is gone and another sits on the throne, you will be forbidden from mining the First for slaves. If your people come here to take ours, they will only find their own death."

Roshaud glowered at her. "Such threats? To me?"

Saran let out a patient, heavy sigh. "Why do men assume I make idle threats? Is it because I'm a woman? Not threatening in my disposition? What more can I do to make you heed my words?"

The president of the Third reddened in the face. "I could conquer your puny world and enslave all of your people if I choose. I will make you mine, as you have always been mine."

Saran scoffed. "Truly the delusions of a man who does not understand the world he is in. You cannot get your forces here. Your Gates are too small. Magic would burn your ships. I would rust them to dust and turn your men into infants. If you wish to threaten me, Roshaud, work harder. I do not fear you." The princess let her steely gaze settle on his beady black eyes. She did not flinch.

Roshaud pursed his lips into a tight line and his black eyes looked her over. He grinned. "I do have such fond memories of you as a child, when you were less vocal and my legs still worked." His hand smoothed along the top of her thigh.

Saran stiffened, and for an instant the rigid facade shattered. She looked down at Roshaud's hand, her fingers flexing over the fork sitting next to her plate. She collected the tiny pieces of her mask and put them back together, using rage as mortar. "I am not a child any longer," she reminded him, all too calmly, before plunging the fork into his hand. Roshaud howled, and she twisted the silver for good measure, relishing in the pain that washed over his face. The princess stood, drawing the fork away and placing it neatly back on the table.

Off in the corner, the servant who attended to her retreated farther into the shadows, willing himself to be invisible.

Saran towered over Roshaud while he clutched his wounded hand to his chest. She absorbed the damage she'd done to both the man and their political future. "Perhaps now you will remember."

Saran stepped outside to where Lord Brenden awaited his orders. "See to it that the president of the Third has a safe journey home. There was an accident involving a fork, and he was injured. I believe he'll wish to seek medical attention on the Third." The Mage nodded with a toothless smile.

TWENTY-THREE

KELEIR EMERGED FROM heavy sleep with a ragged, wet gasp. He shot straight up from the floor, brushing his hands across his form as if expecting pieces to be missing. Ipabas were feared among most of the Mavahan people, but also worshipped and revered by others. There were rumors, where Adrid met Mavahan's border, that some would steal pieces of those cursed with Orukes to be used in the only magic available in Mavahan: Dregs.

Dreg magic could be performed by those not blessed by the Core. Because Mavahan was cut off from the life and fertility of the planet, it did not allow for natural elemental magic. The magic available could be harsh and cruel, created from tangible means like plants, waste, blood, and bone. To those Dregs sorcerers, Ipabas were as divine an ingredient as anything in the world, and extremely rare. Those who practiced Dregs believed that parts of Ipabas made their magic work.

Keleir's hands skittered over smooth naked flesh, with only a sparse remnant of cloth draped across his lap. He found all his limbs attached and, for the most part, unharmed. A hand curled at the top of his skull and drew the damp sack from his face, snatching with it a few strands of white hair. Blinding sunlight stole his vision, and he lifted his hands to shield his eyes. In the blur of the light and the effects of whatever those women had drugged him with, he could just make out the Alar sitting upon a stone chair at the edge of a balcony. Next to him stood his sister, Velora, the Keeper of His House. To her right were the women who'd accosted him.

"*Ipaba dre dicaro Vel d'Ekaru*," the Alar said. He stared down his nose at where Keleir sat immodestly on the stone. "*Detoro tag Deka z'Alaru.*"

The balcony was shaded by a heavy red canopy, but it did little to keep out the heat. The stone scalded his skin, even sheltered from the sun.

"He says," Luke's voice piped up. He sat clothed and shackled just behind Keleir. "When this Oruke becomes the Living God, he will seek the Book of Kings. He asks if that is what you've come for."

Keleir rested his forehead against his knee and wiped the sweat from his brow. "No. Tell him I am not the Vel d'Ekaru. Tell him I don't know what book he speaks of, that I don't seek it. Ask him to release you and the others. He may keep me, but no one else should be punished for my sins."

Luke hastily translated Keleir's words, but the dark expression on the Alar's face did not lighten. He frowned and glared down at them. The Alar said another long line of words, so jumbled and fast that Keleir, who had picked up only a few Mavish words thus far, could not even find it remotely familiar.

There was hesitation in Luke's voice. The young soldier shifted uncomfortably against the stone floor. "H-He, eh . . . the fact you do not seek the book does not disprove you are the Vel d'Ekaru, merely that you have not completely turned."

The Alar went on, a clever smile creeping up his face. It was well-known that Mavahan were large followers of the Vel d'Ekaru religion. It was, after all, their language. Vel d'Ekaru, the Living God. It was Mavahan who brought the religion to Adrid, and Yarin who cultivated it. Once, the Alar made frequent pilgrimages to Adrid to commune with the Ekaru priests who waited in the land of magic for the Vel d'Ekaru to be born. Somewhere along the way, the Alar stopped believing. He stopped his pilgrimages, and the relationship with Adrid crumbled.

"The Living God will seek the Book of Kings ravenously," Luke translated.

"You were expecting the Oruke?" Keleir muttered, looking down at the chains he wore. "Would you have bound him?"

"No," the Alar replied in basic tongue. "I would not have lived long enough to do it."

Keleir shook his head, his hands curling into fists. "Then unchain me if you know I mean you no harm! I am not the Vel d'Ekaru. I will never be him. I do not *choose* to be him!"

"It is not within your power to choose or not choose. It is an inevitability," the Alar muttered. "I shared the same god as Yarin for many years until the Prophetess spoke to me as clearly as I speak to you. We are pawns, all of us, in a never-ending war between two creatures of time: the Prophetess with her champion, the Equitas, and the Oruke with his vessel, the Vel d'Ekaru. I will not let the Living God rise."

Keleir relaxed on the floor. "So you plan to kill me?"

The Alar's face twitched. He settled into his seat as if a heavy weight had fallen on him and crushed his limbs to the stone. "Unfortunately I cannot. I wish it were as simple as destroying the vessel, but the Oruke will live on. He is not fully bound to flesh and thus cannot be killed. He needs physical form, through and through, and even then I suspect he can live on. The safest thing to do is to keep you, as you are, in chains and imprisoned, until we find a way to purge the Oruke and destroy it forever."

"Are you sure you're not sore I stole your bride?" Keleir muttered with the hint of a smirk. "Seems like the easiest way to get rid of an Oruke is to kill him. What do you care if he comes back? By the time his next vessel is old enough to cause you any trouble, you'll be long dead." Keleir leaned forward. "Kill me."

The Alar glared down at Keleir and leaned forward in his stone chair. "I would have brought Saran D'mor into my home. She is the Equitas and your destroyer. I would have protected her from you until she was strong enough to face you."

Keleir groaned and stood in all his nakedness, casting his eyes about the room before settling a hard gaze on the Mavahan king. "She is strong enough."

Luke coughed. The sound stole Keleir's attention from the Alar. The young man avoided Keleir's gaze for the obvious reason, his nakedness. The prince, who wasn't the least bit ashamed, wrapped the cloth that had fallen away around himself.

"The Book of Kings," Luke began, swallowing dryly. "It can only be opened by a king. It is a charter, a chronicle of recordings made by the rulers of the First. It exists outside of treaties and war. It never resides in one king's hands for too long, as it contains the secrets of existence. A king, no matter how cruel, has never disobeyed that covenant."

"Until it came to me a year ago from Droves," the Alar muttered. "I will not see it go on to Adrid, not as long as I may live and breathe. Neither Yarin nor his replacement will hold that much power, even for a second." The Alar turned to his sister, the Keeper of His House. "Velora, find the prince something comfortable to wear. He will be wearing it for a very long time."

Keleir took a step toward the Alar, but the guards grabbed hold of him. "You cannot keep me here!"

"I can," the king replied unsympathetically.

"My brother and my wife will not leave me here to rot!" Keleir warned.

"They will," Velora said, her voice soft and musical. "If they think you're content to stay here, which I'm sure was a concern of theirs given your predicament. Don't worry, Prince Keleir, we will send your happy words and encouragement for a better future home to them."

Keleir glowered at her before his expression softened to a wicked smile. "You will find I'm not easily contained, Keeper of His House."

TWENTY-FOUR

WHEN ROWE WOKE, there was a fire crackling warmly in the bedroom hearth. Strange, as he'd managed to fall asleep as the last embers settled into ash. The roaring logs illuminated his quarters well enough to see the glittering gold titles on a stack of books he'd collected atop his desk. It also lit it enough for him to see the young, lithe, bald woman standing at the foot of his bed, her silhouette dark but familiar to him.

Her eyes opened, blinding white that spread until he could no longer see her. The power glowed from beneath her skin, and her clothes melted away until there was nothing left of her but a body of pure, endless light.

"Prophetess," he cried, sitting straight in bed.

"Rowe," the Prophetess greeted, her voice a flurry of low and high chimes all ringing together, like several versions of her speaking at once.

"It has been so long . . ."

Her chin lowered. If it weren't for the light, he wondered if he would have found shame in her eyes. "I couldn't—" The slump of her elegant, glittering form suggested great sadness in place of shame. She held that form for a moment longer before lifting her head and straightening her back, like a woman resigning herself to her duty. She lifted a hand and pointed a sharp, glowing finger at him. "Remember my words, Rowe Blackwell, and know that you will be betrayed. The Equitas cannot exist without the Living God. For the Equitas to live, so must the Living God rise."

Rowe jerked as something hot or sharp scraped his chest. The room went dark, the fire in the hearth now as dead as when he'd first slept. There was no glowing woman at the foot of his bed, no sign that she'd ever been there at all. The only remnant that proved any of it had been real was the thin trickle of blood from the small scrape of a nail. It wasn't an unfamiliar marking, she often left them so he would know the difference between imagination and divine appearance.

He threw the covers from his lap and wrapped his robe about his shoulders before going to his desk and drawing out a leather-bound journal from a squeaking drawer. He opened it, flipping through tattered parchment papers until he found the page he'd written the prophecy on some ten years ago.

The Three will be devoured by darkness, their cities will crumble, and their kingdoms will fall. The rulers of their nations will bring darkness to their lands. When the Vel d'Ekaru rises, the Equitas will come to balance time. They will be forged in pain and born from sleep. They will consume and become the Body of Life, and before them will fall the Hand of Strength and the Carrier of Power. The Soldier from the Eastern Mountains will fight with them, and the Prophetess will be their guide.

It was scribbled in faded ink but legible enough for him to read. He read it over and over before letting his eyes drift slowly to the counter prophecy, the prayer of the Ekaru priests.

When the Three are devoured by their darkness, He will see to the rise of the Oruke. Before the Vel d'Ekaru will fall the Body of Life, the Hand of Strength, and the Carrier of Power. The ashes of the Three will become One, and the Oruke will arrive in droves to purge the sickness from its soil.

Rowe frowned at the passages. They both spoke of the same three artifacts: the Body of Life, the Hand of Strength, and the Carrier of Power. Three legendary keys to the Three known worlds, and all hidden with no record of where to find them, at least none that he knew of. Each prophecy spoke of the hero or the villain gaining control of the artifacts.

The prophecies did little to concern him—he'd read them enough to become indifferent to them. He wasn't sure why she desperately wanted him to recall them. Nothing had changed. His brother had grown darker and had fallen deeper into the Oruke's clutches and closer to becoming the Living God.

What had changed?

Know that you will be betrayed . . .

Who would betray him?

He mulled over the two prophecies, both written from different ideological views. One spoke of a hero, and one spoke of the destroyer painted as a hero. *For the Equitas to exist, so must the Living God rise.* For the Equitas to live, the other had to . . .

He closed the leather journal with a hard thump and tossed it back into the drawer. Rowe and many others had always believed Saran to be the Equitas, the counter to the Living God. If this were true, Keleir would have to succumb to the Oruke or Saran would die.

TWENTY-FIVE

THREE MORE WEEKS came and went as swift as the passing of a storm, leaving just as much damage in its wake. Saran spent long hours on her balcony staring off at the sea, and Rowe took up his training duties in the barracks for the new recruits. They attempted, as best they could, to act as if nothing happened. But both of them, deep down, knew that something was terribly wrong.

When Keleir didn't arrive home as expected, it caused little concern in the castle. Sometimes sandstorms swept across the desert and kept traveling to a minimum for days. When the second week passed from his scheduled return, even Yarin's toes began to tap harshly and impatiently against the floor. By the third week a quiet resolve settled over Saran and Rowe like a pan-warmed blanket.

"We will do what we must," she'd whispered, twisting the Bind about her wrist. "Then we will go find him."

Saran was standing on her balcony, watching the sea, when she spotted the messenger pigeon arrive. She bounded up the well-worn west tower steps, clutching the cotton skirts of her day dress. Behind her, Rowe's boots echoed as he gained ground, taking the twisting narrow stars two at a time, until he caught up to her. "It came from the south," she said, her voice a breathless whisper.

"I know, but do not get your hopes up."

"It is too late for that."

The messenger, covered in feathers and bird dung, sat clutching a fluttering pigeon when they barged through his door. He'd barely begun to unroll the small note from its thin legs when they took it for themselves.

"That's none of your—" The dark look that crossed Saran's face, accompanied by the crackle of lightning in Rowe's eyes, silenced the messenger. "Apologies, Your Highness."

Saran hastily read the letter, two short lines written in careful script.

"I can't return. Let me rest. I never wanted to be king. I'm sorry." Her hands and voice trembled as she read the words aloud to Rowe. She passed the note to him, her eyes awash with tears.

Rowe read the letter for himself. He read it as many times as he could in the span of a minute while Saran collapsed into a dirty chair next to him. "At least we know for sure now," he said.

"Yes," she replied, careful to keep her face away from him. "Now we know."

"It doesn't look like his handwriting," Rowe muttered.

"Would he dictate it?"

"Keleir doesn't dictate anything." Rowe read the words again. "He doesn't mention anything about us."

"Why would he?" Saran asked, lifting her eyes. "He expected the note to go directly to the king. He wouldn't want Yarin to know that we might join him later or that we're so heavily involved with the rebellion. You think I'm a prisoner now? We'd both be Bound or murdered if he knew."

Saran remembered the messenger in the room. Her gaze locked on him, frowning. The messenger, old and thin with wild white hair, backed slowly away. "I won't tell nothin', Princess, I promise. Nothin'."

Rowe's form tensed, and he turned to Saran. "Deliver the message to your father."

"Are you insane? Do you know what will happen if he thinks his prized Vel d'Ekaru won't come back?"

Rowe pressed the note into her hand.

"It is either you tell him Keleir has abandoned you, or you risk him sending the army into Mavahan to retrieve him, which he may do anyway."

Saran glowered at Rowe. "He won't accept this."

"And he won't allow the silence that we've endured for weeks to go on any longer," the Lightning Mage argued. "Go."

Saran growled, shaking her head as her hand curled around the slender note. She said nothing more to the Lightning Mage, leaving him alone with the messenger.

When Rowe could no longer hear the gentle clack of her shoes down the stone steps, he turned to the old, white-haired messenger, electric blue crackling in his eyes.

"I promise," the old man said. "I won't tell anyone."

Rowe stepped toward him, his frown deepening with remorse. "I know."

TWENTY-SIX

YARIN GLOWERED AT the tiny, crumpled piece of parchment lying on his desk. His old brow wrinkled while his cane tapped irritably against the floor. "Run away?" he asked, glancing up at Saran. She stood across from him, her hands clasped in front of her, her sadness concealed by a mask of indifference.

"You have yourself to blame," she whispered. "Insisting he is something he's not. A king maybe, but the Vel d'Ekaru . . ."

Yarin shoved the note away and settled back in his chair with an angry frown. "Tyrinis Dago will not let him stay. Despite our recent disagreement, the Alar will honor the Ekaru."

Saran took the chair across from him. "Why would the Alar honor the Ekaru?"

"We have our differences, the Alar and I, but there is one thing we share: the same god. He may have lost faith, but when he realizes who Keleir is, that faith will be reborn in him." Yarin smiled at his daughter. "Keleir can't escape his future."

The princess hid the uneasiness from her posture, staring bored across the desk at him. "Father." She sighed, resting her hands in her lap. "Can we discuss removing this Bind now? I've learned my lesson. At least I understand my place and why I'm useful to you. You've made Keleir king. I am happy with that decision, and the rebel in my heart has been tempered by the blessing of a strong husband—one that I love. Let me go into Mavahan and bring him home. He will listen to me."

Yarin chuckled. "You can go to Mavahan if you wish, my beautiful daughter, but you will never approach Ahriman again without that Bind."

"What's so threatening about my element?"

"Everything," Yarin replied, leaning his elbows against the desk. "I understand I'm old, and you think I'm insane, but I'm clever enough to know what you did to him. Though it took time to figure it out."

Saran stiffened, an uneasiness rolling through her. She kept the tremble of fear out of her features so that they remained as placid and dark as a stagnant barrel of water. "I did nothing to him."

Yarin waved a finger at her, a crooked smile on his face. "While the Origin God cursed me with the Equitas for a daughter, it has come with the added benefit of you being a terrible liar."

Her green eyes fixated on the old king. "Superstitions will get you nowhere, Father. How sad will you be when you realize all your silly dreaming was nothing but a terrible nursery rhyme, whispered by a diseased mind. I'm not the Equitas. I'm just a woman, a normal—albeit gifted with magic—woman." She appraised him and his fixed face, like someone had taken his aged wrinkled skin and smashed it into an eerie smile and spackled it with varnish. The implication in his eyes was enough. He did not stop smiling, because he had accepted what she refused: that it was all true and there was no escaping it.

Yarin shifted out of his statuesque smile. "Alikons usually don't last very long, at least not five years' worth."

Saran scoffed. "Keleir isn't an Alikon. We've both seen elemental Alikons before, Father, and he isn't misshapen or monstrous. He's human, much to your dismay. The only thing I did was build a wall around the Oruke and his consciousness. I gave Keleir back his body, that is all."

"When do you recharge the link to your Alikon?" her father went on. "While he sleeps? When you make love?"

Saran jolted at his words. Heat burned her cheeks, and she growled, bolting out of her chair. "I should have known not to expect serious conversation from you."

"What you did to him is undone by your lack of connection to him. It matters little what terminology you want to use, lovely child. The Bind will remain until he transitions back into his true self." Yarin fixed his cold and unfeeling gaze, a look far removed from that of a loving father. She was, as she'd always been, a means to an end, just as her mother had been before her.

Saran had wanted a loving father. As a child she'd clung desperately to the hope that he would give her love to fill the absence of a lost mother. He had, in his own demented way, loved her. She suspected that it was the sort of love one bestowed upon their favorite plow, an instrument of fortune and future, but nothing that deserved true fondness.

"Why not kill me?" she asked him, hating the crack her voice made as she acknowledged his indifference to her life.

"Keleir must be king, and in order for him to do so, he must be tied to the land by your union. It is the only way the Core will accept him as a legitimate king. While you are married, the bond between you as husband and wife has not been fulfilled because of the Bind. But I cannot remove the Bind until the Keleir you know has gone away—"

"Why does he need to be king?"

Yarin settled back in his chair, the wood groaning as it accepted his full weight. "Do you think I did what I did to be king for my own selfish reasons?"

"Yes," Saran snapped.

"I loved your grandfather. King Dante Vanguard was my friend. My mentor. But he did not believe in the voice that I heard. He did not believe the truth. The Vel d'Ekaru came to me, just as the Prophetess comes to her chosen champions, and showed me what I needed to do." A gleam entered Yarin's eye, the sort of light that forms when a father meets his newborn child. "I made myself king. I married Vanguard's daughter so our child would have the blood of the Vanguard lineage, so that they would be a true heir, bound to the land and accepted by the Core. The Book of Kings will only open for a true king."

Saran's head swam with his words. She pressed her fingers to her temples in the hope it would help her focus. "What if you'd had a boy?"

"I wouldn't have."

"How do you know?"

Yarin grinned. "Fate, dear child. Our paths were already forged before we were born. You know as well as anyone how time works. All of this has come to pass before . . . in some shape or form."

Saran's throat went dry. She stared aghast at him until the words crawled up and out of her mouth. "W-Why tell me this?"

The first show of sympathy appeared in Yarin's eyes, the briefest of emotions before something else crushed it. "There is nothing you can do to stop it."

She absorbed his words, let them charge maddening through her mind. The princess stood, straightening her spine. "I do not believe in destiny. We have choices, Father. You chose the path the voice told you to tread, and thus it led you to the desired outcome. A self-fulfilling prophecy, the only ones that truly exist. If you had chosen a different path, it would have led to a different outcome. You might have chosen this one, but it doesn't mean I have to follow."

TWENTY-SEVEN

HER HEART POUNDED angrily in her chest as she left Yarin's chambers. She slammed the heavy wooden door behind her and stomped down the corridor. The fever of rage turned the world into a blur of monochrome and faceless humanoid shapes. The princess wandered aimlessly through the castle with no real purpose or destination while her boiling blood tempered.

It wasn't just her father that had driven her rage, though he held most of the blame. She felt angry at Keleir for sending such an impersonal letter. She knew his reasons, and yet she couldn't help but feel the cold finality of those words.

Let me rest.

Saran stood with her back to the stone, staring at the gritty cobbled floor, too lost in her thoughts to notice the rush of servants flooding the hall toward the edge of the west tower steps. Their horrified gasps tore her from her thoughts.

She pushed through the crowd gathered around two soldiers carrying a body wrapped in dingy canvas. The servants whispered among themselves, and she would have bothered to listen had she not noticed the pigeon feathers stuck to the wrap.

"They say he hanged himself," Odan's familiar voice muttered next to her. She felt the cold of his magic against her arm, and her green eyes lifted to his sunken face.

His cheeks, always sharp and high, now had deep dark shadows under them. His eyes were sunken into his head and black with sleeplessness, but his cyan-blue irises still glittered with frost and ice. While his form was depleted, his magic remained as strong as ever.

"Who?" she asked him, careful with her tone. He stood too peacefully next to her, lacking the usual radiant loathing that prickled off him in her presence. Perhaps he had no energy for it.

"The messenger," he replied, tilting his head down to her. "I suppose it gets lonely waiting in that tower for birds, with birds being your only companion. I don't blame him for leaving his miserable life. I would, too, in his position."

Saran glowered at him, but couldn't form the words for a retort. A sick feeling curled in the pit of her stomach.

"Looking green, Princess," Odan muttered. "I figured you weren't so affected by death with how swiftly you tried to kill me."

"Some are more deserving of death than others," she replied. Saran's green eyes narrowed. She curled her fists at her sides and turned away from him. Odan stepped in her path, sickly and feeble. He felt like a ghost before her, paper-thin and translucent. She ducked around him. "Excuse me."

Again he stepped in her path. "I almost died. In fact, the healers almost let me die once I told them who stabbed me. They are devoted to you, aren't they?"

"They believe in the Grand Feminine, a woman of power and influence. I am their future queen, so of course they are devoted to me. How did you convince them to let you live?"

Odan frowned at the floor before he held out his slender hand. "By making a Life Debt." He turned his palm up to her and rolled back the sleeve of his tunic, revealing a black scar running up his forearm. "Madam Ophelia made me swear a Blood Oath on the Life Debt that I would never bring you harm. The debt expires on her death. Unfortunately it comes with the stipulation that I must physically make a truce with you or I'll just keep degenerating."

Saran appraised him. "You look like shit because you've avoided being nice to me?"

"Yes," Odan replied with the slightest hint of amusement. "So shall we shake as quickly as possible?"

"You must really want to live." She held out her hand but did not touch him. "If I don't do this, if I don't agree to the truce, does that mean you die a slow agonizing death?"

"Potentially," he murmured through gritted teeth. "Or maybe it just counts that I try."

Saran slipped her hand into his frigid grip. "You are lucky, Lord Marki, that I am honorable enough to forgive your insanity so that you do not suffer." She shook his hand quickly and drew away. "I accept your truce. Tell Madam Ophelia to find me if she doesn't believe it." She pushed Odan aside gently. "I really need to leave now."

Saran found Rowe in his chambers and at his desk, hovering over one of twenty books scattered across the top. He didn't bother looking up as she closed the door behind her. Only Saran or Keleir would come into his rooms without knocking.

"Did you do it?" she snapped at him, slamming her hands against the desk and bending down to obstruct his field of vision. "Did you?"

Rowe's blue eyes glinted in the dark room, and he settled back in his chair with a heavy sigh. "I made it quick. He didn't feel anything; he only went to sleep."

A sharp resounding crack echoed off the stone walls, and Rowe's head snapped to the left. Her palm burned angrily, as hot as the fire scalding her veins. Her voice quivered with rage. "You're a bastard! You didn't have to kill him."

Rowe righted himself, reaching a hand up to rub the sting from his cheek. "He heard too much, Saran. Keleir would have done the same."

"No, he wouldn't have."

"Yes, he would've, and you know it."

Her chest heaved angry breaths into her lungs and she stepped away from his desk. "He was innocent. Just some old man who had the unfortunate luck of being in the same room as my panicked ramblings. He didn't deserve what you did. He wasn't evil! His only crime was listening to what he couldn't avoid hearing. You could have paid—"

"There is not enough money to keep a man silent in this poor dissolving country. Money doesn't do anyone a bit of good here. You're a princess, but are you wealthy? You wear no jewelry, you have no crown, and your castle is falling down around you. The money that once belonged to your family was lost in war. The only thing that keeps this country afloat is fear and title, and Yarin would have gotten the information from him through fear alone. Whatever threats I could've made would not have kept him silent. I did what was necessary, and I will not apologize for it. You can hate me if you want, but I did it to protect us both."

Saran shook her head, a woeful sadness stealing the light in her eyes. "No," she whispered to him, backing toward the door. "You did it to preserve your soul-saving mission. You did it for yourself."

Rowe frowned. "We're all selfish. Even Keleir. Even you. But I'm not lying, and I took no joy in it." Rowe stood and stepped around his desk. He sat atop it, his shoulders slumping. "She spoke to me, for the first time in so very long. She warned me, Saran. We've been betrayed, whatever that means. In order for the Equitas to exist, the Living God must rise. Keleir cannot return from Mavahan, Saran. If he does, then we've lost him. But if he doesn't, I've lost you."

Saran glowered at him fiercely, jabbing his chest with her finger hard enough to snap the bone. She pointed harshly at him. "Not you too. Not you!"

"Saran . . ."

"No," she spat. "No!" He reached for her and she slapped his hand away. "I am not going to lose him! I'm not going to quit. I'll chop this fucking thing from my wrist before that happens. I do not believe in prophecies. They're riddles. They're lies! There is no such thing as fate or destiny. We choose our paths, Rowe."

"I desperately wish that were true."

"It *is* true."

Rowe folded his arms, dawning a sad, sympathetic stare. She knew by his expression that he chose not to argue with her because he felt it useless. Her stubborn heart would never be swayed, and she would never believe the words of an invisible woman who chose only to speak in one man's dreams.

"Regardless of what we believe, it matters very little now. For whatever reason, Keleir isn't coming back." He waited, letting the finality of that sink in. He read the panic in her eyes, and he imagined the soul behind them bashing against the walls, wanting desperately to shatter free and go where she pleased. "I leave for Salara at the end of the month, and I will attempt to finish our mission alone. I've agreed to supply Darshan with the aid he needs in exchange for his word that Yarin will not be harmed. However, since I trust Darshan's men about as much as Yarin, I want you to try to overpower your father or at least lock him away before someone gets the itch to kill him out of vengeance."

The stiffness in Saran's shoulders melted. The fluttering wildness of her eyes eased into sorrow. "Time has passed quickly."

Rowe nodded. "It has. I was hoping . . . I'd hoped Keleir would come back. If something should go wrong, it would be nice to see him one last time. I want to apologize to him for what happened before he left. It was fear and selfishness talking—I didn't mean any of it." His eyes glossed with tears.

Saran reached out to him, despite her anger, and held him tight. She stared out his window to the balcony, which looked so much like his brother's room. Her thoughts drifted back to the night Keleir flung himself from the railing to escape his monster, to protect them all from it.

She thought about the terrible thing that Rowe had done to keep their secret. She thought about her own deceit and lies. What monsters they had become in the shadows of Yarin D'mor . . . and she feared what they would turn into if they continued to stay.

Her throat grew dry, but she forced the thought aloud anyway. "We should have gone away, like he wanted."

The Lightning Mage nodded, burrowing his face against her warm neck. "I know."

TWENTY-EIGHT

THE BELLY OF the ziggurat prison sat several floors deep beneath the earth, protected from the harsh desert sun. The interior was lit only by torches and a single beam of sunlight filtering down an impossibly long shaft that ran through the center of the structure. It allowed just enough light in to crush the soul of any man thinking it a hint to freedom.

For weeks Keleir watched men attempt to reach the square four-by-four shaft, only to see them end up as broken piles on the sandy prison floor. Those strong enough to reach the shaft were no longer strong enough to press their weight against the sides and shinny up. They always ended up like the rest.

He did not understand Mavish, but he guessed enough from the jesting of those around him that the ones who had been inside the prison the longest found those sad attempts entertaining. They even, by his guess, goaded a few into it just for the primitive entertainment it provided.

The Alar did not offer Keleir the luxury of his own cell, separated from the superstitious Mavahan people. They left him in the common hold, a large cavernous sandy pit at the bottom of the prison. Some—more violent—men sat chained to the walls, but the rest wandered aimlessly with boredom.

Those whose sanity had been driven away spent most of the day staring at the beam of golden sun, muttering to themselves.

When he first arrived, they'd shunned him as an Ipaba, and in all honesty, he couldn't have been happier. He didn't understand their language, and he wanted them to fear him. Fear would keep one of them from starting something Keleir wasn't too sure he could finish. In all his training, he was far better at magic than combat. Most of the men in prison were working slaves, built like giant stone pillars, and dropped in the pit until needed again.

He recognized one of them but made no move to speak to him. He knew the man from the day he arrived, from the room in which they trapped him. He delivered the luggage that Keleir now suspected belonged to some vagabond on the street. Not that it contained anything valuable to him.

The tall slave possessed deep, dark skin the color of rich chocolate, a color in sharp contrast to the bronze collar hanging around his neck and the tan rags around his waist. Despite the rags, his owner kept himself well. He wore a crown of long, tight braids tipped with bronze clasps, the cluster of which were bound together at the back of his head with a leather cord. He held a different rank than the rest, given his clean-shaven appearance—perhaps he was the reason some kept their distance from Keleir.

Those who didn't shy away from the man called him Xalen Okara.

Keleir spent the first week curiously watching the Droven man, for it seemed a much better use of his time than watching men plummet to their death. At first the latter had been interesting enough, but after the sixth one, he grew too disgusted with the lack of intelligence in those that followed.

Xalen paraded around the room with the pride of a king. Perhaps he'd worn the crown of a Droven king but now wore the rags of prisoner. Even if that were not the case, Keleir imagined it so. It made his dull confinement all the more interesting.

His curiosity in the Droven man couldn't save Keleir from his own thoughts, and as a week passed into another, he lost himself in staring at the sunlit shaft with the other prisoners who thought they might escape up it.

The Fire Mage snapped away from his thoughts when the guards brought Luke to speak to him, and it was the first Keleir had heard his own language in weeks.

"They sent a message to Adrid. They forced me to write it—I'm sorry, Ahriman." He bowed to Keleir, but the prince would have none of it. He grabbed the boy's shoulders and held him upright.

"You do what you must to survive. Do not worry. The situation is far from hopeless. I didn't come here expecting a warm welcome. I planned for a lot of scenarios, though not for a massive, impossible cavernous pit to escape from." Keleir's fingers tightened on Luke's shoulders. "Tell me how to get out of here. Tell me whatever deal I must make with them. I will give it."

Sir Canin shook his head with a mournful expression. "They will have nothing, Ahriman, not even your life."

The shoulders of the prince slumped ever so slightly until he caught sight of the woman standing just behind Luke. A tall woman, built with muscle, she wore the attire of a lady of the house, down to the bronze collar around her neck. He nodded to her. "Why is she here?"

"They don't treat me like a prisoner, perhaps because I am the one who can translate best for you," Luke admitted, the words straining as they left his lips. His gaze fluttered up. "They are still treating me as your honored and she as my new attendant." He lowered his head. "I don't really need one, but she is the only other person I've met who speaks our mother tongue and I admit that I am fond of hearing it."

"I know what you mean. It is a happy thing indeed that I should hear your voice. Who is she?"

"Her name is Aleira Ritan. She is originally from our southern town of Jukad, near the border with Mavahan. She followed me here against my wishes. I suspect it was to get a glimpse of her husband." Luke nodded behind Keleir to the group of men, the tallest being Xalen Okara. If it were not for the longing stare the Droven slave offered in their direction, he probably wouldn't have known whom Luke spoke of.

"Slaves can marry?" Keleir asked, turning his attention back to the beautiful woman accompanying Luke.

As strong as any warrior, she had long, tightly braided brown hair, warm sun-tanned skin, and the eyes of a hawk. Mavahan slaves often possessed two jobs. Some of the house slaves pulled double duty as Challengers or gladiators. House duty, unlikely to break or weaken them before a fight, allowed plenty of time to train.

"Some can marry," Luke replied. "Those who earn the favor of their masters may be allowed to remain in relationships or build them. I imagine the masters like it, especially if it leads to prime pairing and offspring."

"Romantic," Keleir muttered. Slavery in any form disgusted him. He'd been a slave to the Oruke in him for so long, and Saran a slave to her father's will. There were many types of chains, some not always visible. He wrapped his arm over Luke's shoulders. The boy stiffened as he drew him in close. "We need out of here. Now. As soon as possible."

"Yes, I know, but—"

"Convince her to help," Keleir whispered. "Tell her if she helps I'll secure her freedom and her husband's."

"I don't think . . ."

"Don't worry, she'll help. She'll owe me." Keleir grinned, sly and devious as his eyes flashed to Xalen Okara. The contrast of such a wicked smile with the bloody hue of his eyes sent a shiver through the boy.

Luke shook his head. "Ahhh, n-no, I don't like that look. What are you going to do?"

Keleir ruffled the boy's hair. "Best you not know. Though, I do have a translation question . . ."

Luke scowled at the prince as he fixed his hair. "You know," he said, his warm brown eyes smiling, "you aren't what they said you'd be."

"Cunning?"

"A monster. I did not expect kindness in your eyes."

Keleir stiffened. His back straightened, and his shoulders rose. He watched the young knight leave, feeling a wave of disbelief and hope mingle in his chest. There were few people in the world—two to be exact—who would ever say such a thing to him. It startled him to hear such words from someone siding with the group that wanted him dead.

That evening Keleir did not seek his usual seclusion during dinner. When the guards delivered the gruel, he grabbed a bowl and plopped down next to Xalen as casually as he might his brother, Rowe. While a tall man standing, even the Fire Mage felt small next to Xalen sitting.

"A little bird told me you speak my tongue," Keleir said between mouthfuls of disgusting gruel. The slop had a putrid taste, but he'd eaten worse as a child.

Xalen angled his eyes at Keleir before cupping his fingers into the bowl and drawing food to his lips. It dripped down his hand, and he licked it from his wrist. "Did Aleira tell you that?"

"Her charge. He says she's originally from a border town in Adrid. He says you're married. I assumed you spoke our tongue if you were to communicate with her. Mavish isn't her native language."

"Nor is Droven, yet she speaks it fine," he said, tilting the bowl to his lips. "You know neither."

"No."

"Just like nobles, too good to learn languages when others can do the hard work for you." The Challenger threw his empty bowl into the sand. "What do you want, Ipaba?"

Keleir's red eyes narrowed on him. "I wasn't always a noble. For a while I was a poor, cursed boy who spent most of his days chained to the floor of his bedroom." Keleir rubbed his chest absentmindedly. He shook the memory off and continued, "I just want to talk. It's nice to see someone who speaks my language. It makes this less lonely."

Xalen cracked a smile, his dark eyes twinkling. There was mischief there, and his face glowed as bright as the sunbeam taunting them every day. "What is it you say in your tongue to flirtations—flattered, but married."

"Me too." Keleir grinned. "Married, that is."

Xalen snorted, and then his eyes lifted to the angry crowd gathering behind Keleir. "I'd find a dark hole to crawl in if I were you."

"I'm only trying to make friends," the Fire Mage replied, lifting his hands in peace.

"It's a bad day to make friends," Xalen muttered as he rose.

The dark, hulking Droven man lumbered past Keleir and snatched a prisoner in the crowd up by his neck and tossed him over his shoulder as if he were nothing more than a sack of rice. The man crumpled into the sand. A deep silence settled over the prisoners. Xalen raised his arms and turned in a small circle, looking over those gathered around, until he paused at the small group just behind Keleir.

Keleir turned his attention to them. They were a ragtag band of six men. Some knelt, some stood with arms folded, all of them glowered at Xalen. The edge of a smile tugged at Keleir's lips.

"*Dek togo roan?*" Xalen barked at them, spittle flying from his mouth. He took on a beastly pose, seemingly growing wider and taller at the same time. He huffed through his nose like a bull and stomped his foot forward. "*Dek togo roan?!*"

Keleir had seen it only twice in his time there. *Dek togo roan* meant "Am I challenged?" The phrase always ended with violence. The Fire Mage stood, turning to stand alongside the Droven man. Xalen sneered at him. "Back off, little noble."

The Fire Mage smirked. "Six to one are terrible odds. You could use the help."

"I need no help from an Ipaba," he said. "Six to one are great odds for a Droven Masodite."

Keleir eyed the bloodthirsty pack. Xalen, the strongest of the lot, had the most respect, the best food, possessed the favor of his master, and was allowed to keep a wife. If he lost the *roan*, he would surely lose all that. If a Challenger lost to mere thugs, outnumbered or not, he would not remain a Challenger for long. Either Xalen was very confident or too prideful to accept Keleir's help.

The Fire Mage smiled at Xalen and bowed his head before he stepped out from between the Droven man and his enemies.

Dust and sand skittered into the air as the six men clashed against the hulking, godlike frame of the Droven Masodite. Keleir found beauty in the brute force of Xalen's swing. He cleared three with one heavy swipe and stomped another down with a bare foot to the chest. The sternum cracked under his weight as he stepped across the scrawny prisoner and scooped up the man just behind him by the neck. The three he swiped away joined a fourth in clamoring up Xalen like a great old tree nestled in the forests of Adrid.

Keleir, content in watching the spectacle, spotted the glimmer of a weapon brandished high above the head of one of Xalen's attackers. He respected fair fights, and while he himself couldn't claim to be an honorable man, he would not stand for cheating. He stepped into the fray and, having no weapons, went for the sensitive spot between the man's legs. He grabbed the thin man by his genitals and pulled him down off Xalen's back with little effort. The man flailed at him, swiping with a sharpened rod stolen from the quarry. Keleir disarmed the prisoner, twisting the weapon from his grip.

The Fire Mage's hand quivered just short of plunging the rod through the prisoner's neck. Killing came easily, as natural as breathing. He had to consciously stop himself from doing it. He'd promised Saran that he wouldn't be that person and that he no longer harbored the hands of a murderer. Those hands belonged to the Oruke.

Keleir curled his fist tight around the dagger and drew back, punching the prisoner soundly across the jaw. He delivered quick short jabs to each of Xalen's attackers in less lethal areas of their bodies, areas void of arteries or organs. They dropped from him, grabbing at their wounds. The Fire Mage left the killing to the Droven Masodite.

But Xalen didn't kill them. He beat them within an inch of their lives and scolded the crowd in Mavish. When he finished, he turned his attention to Keleir, who'd chosen to step a distance away from the large angry Droven lest he be caught in the mix. Xalen did not appear angry that Keleir had stuck his nose where it did not belong. He grinned at Keleir and grabbed one of his shoulders tightly, shaking him. "A noble Ipaba! Who would have thought?"

"Do you get challenged often?" the Fire Mage asked while observing the mess the Droven man had made of his attackers.

"Every so often." He grinned. "But not so many at once."

Keleir sat in the gentle dip of the sand he'd occupied earlier, his attention caught by the clanking of keys against the barred gate at the top of the wide stairs leading out of the pit. Mavahan guards, in their rust reds and patinaed armor, rushed into the room, two by two. They surrounded the outer edge and swarmed in. Keleir quickly buried the weapon he'd stolen in the sand at his hip and smashed his fist against it as he stood.

"Stay down, Ipaba," Xalen muttered and held out a wide hand to the Fire Mage. "They collect."

The guards grabbed up the losers of the *roan* and dragged their half-conscious bodies from the chamber. Within minutes the only remnants of their existence were the crimson stains in the sand. When the metal doors clanged shut again and Keleir heard the heavy metal latch drop, he fell back into the sand and dug up his stolen weapon. He admired the small metal dagger before he pushed it into his boot.

"Don't get any ideas about that," the Droven man muttered, dropping down across from Keleir. "You won't get very far."

"I'll get as far as I wish," he replied with a wide grin. "I'd get farther with your help."

Xalen laughed. "Bold Ipaba!"

"Keleir," he offered, holding out his hand to Xalen. "Keleir Ahriman."

The warrior admired Keleir's outstretched hand before accepting it, grasping the Fire Mage by the forearm. "Xalen Okara, Chief Masodite of Droves. At least I was a long time ago."

"Masodite?"

"Chief General, in your tongue." Xalen smirked. "When Droves still stood, I was the leader of Death's Breath, the greatest Droven army ever known to the First. Now I'm a slave and I live here in the sand with the worms."

"Your master keeps you here?"

"Most of the time, so I remember my place. Though he has no need to teach me. But he keeps me here and keeps her . . ." Xalen glowered at the sand. "My wife, he keeps in his house. She is a female Challenger, and when she isn't fighting, he loans her out to the Keeper of the House as a companion or maid."

"How did you get a wife?" Keleir asked.

"She was my prize for beating the Ekaru o'Mortorten, the God of Death, a Dregs magician who fought in the Games. She and I did not love at first," Xalen said with the hint of a smile. "She beat me fiercely on our wedding night. I loved her after that."

Keleir laughed. "I was also beaten by my wife, long before we were married."

Xalen waved his finger at the Fire Mage. "That is the mark of a good woman!"

Keleir smiled fondly. "Aye, that it is."

Xalen's eyes misted. "I get to see her for a night at the end of every week. Until then, I spend my days here thinking of her and waiting to see her again."

"Do you ever think of escaping?"

"I've tried. I did not get very far, and it was Aleira who suffered for it. They beat her . . ." A darkness clouded Xalen's vision. He curled his hands in the sand. "We were running because she carried a child and we did not want it born a slave. In the end, it did not matter. They beat her, and she lost it. After that, I only see her once a week. The only reason I see her at all is that my master wants me to fight and win. Without her, I do not fight. I welcome death."

Keleir stared across the small space of sand between himself and the Droven warrior. The man was open with his tongue, but why shouldn't he be? No one but he could understand the language. A language taught to him by his wife . . .

The Fire Mage ran his fingers over the soft sand. "That is barbaric and awful. I'm sorry for your loss."

"It is best. No child should be a slave," Xalen muttered.

"No one, least of all children, should be slaves," Keleir whispered. "What if I told you there was a way to freedom? What if I said that if we worked together, we could all be free—you, me, a friend of mine, and Aleira. Maybe even all of the others. What must be done will not take the courage of a Challenger; it will take the steel and hardness of a Masodite. I cannot guarantee your freedom, or your life . . . All I can guarantee is a chance, and that's more than you're going to get sitting in this pit."

"They say not to trust Ipaba," Xalen muttered. "They say you weave lies."

"Who do you trust more, your masters or the man in the prison with you? I am going to escape with or without your help, Xalen Okara. All I'm asking is if you want to come along."

TWENTY-NINE

SARAN FROWNED DOWN at the bowl of potato soup. It steamed, the warmth wafting up to greet her cool face. She'd only had a few bites of it and already felt ill. She'd tried eating everything, but sometimes even the smell of food turned her stomach.

Today she felt too ill to leave her room. When she sat up, her head swam. After all, she'd eaten so little the past few days. Madam Ophelia visited often and brought her food, and Saran ate as much of it as she could stomach. The healer did not provide an explanation for the sickness, saying she needed more time to think on it, and instead only provided different types of soup for Saran to try.

Saran leaned heavily over the bowl and eyed the contents, trying to get her mind settled on swallowing what was already in her mouth. She mulled over it but couldn't seem to get the mental courage to roll the soggy lump of potato down her throat. This had been her life for the better part of a week.

A heavy knock on her door startled her into swallowing. The spoon slipped out of her hand, bounced off the rim of the bowl, and clattered against the wood floor. "C-Come in," she muttered, wrapping herself tight in her blankets.

Rowe appeared from the dark foyer, striding in dressed in his training leathers. He stood, wet from the cold rain, his black hair smoothed against his head and face. Fortunately he'd had the courtesy to dry his clothes enough that he didn't drip all over the floor.

"Have you eaten?" he asked, taking up the tiny wooden chair across from her small sitting table.

Saran motioned disdainfully at the food before her. "I'm attempting. Stop mothering me."

Rowe smiled, leaning his heavy arms across the tabletop. "Shall I spoon-feed you as you fed me long ago?"

She shook her head fiercely, turning a shade of green.

Rowe reached across the table and put an icy hand to her forehead. She jerked back and pushed his hand down. "Warm those first. Have you been holding hands with Odan?"

Rowe went to the fire and held his hands out over its warmth. "Have you spoken to Madam Ophelia?"

"Yes. It will pass."

"Are you sure?"

Saran picked her spoon up from the floor and wiped it with a rag before shoveling in another mouthful of potato soup. "Yes," she said just before swallowing. "See. Eating."

Rowe settled into the chair by the fire while Saran ate at the small table alone. He watched the flames lick around the logs, turning them black and orange, while the heat slowly dried his clothes. "I don't want to go to Salara until I know you're okay."

Saran sighed, dropping the spoon back into the bowl. "We don't have any other option." The princess stood from her chair, carrying the bowl of soup to the tray the servant had delivered it on. She paused against the bedpost, her heart thudding in her chest and her skin flush.

"Saran?"

Saran glanced up, peering through waves of red hair. She took a step toward Rowe, hand lifting, fingers grasping for him. Her knees buckled, and Rowe lunged up out of his chair. He caught her just as her knees banged against the wooden floor.

When Saran woke again, she lay in bed with the heavy covers tucked around her. The room was brighter than before. Rowe had lit every candle in her possession and added a few more of his own, until there were no dark shadows lurking in the corners or in the foyer.

Rowe sat on the edge of her bed, dressed in a warm, clean tunic with his now-dry hair pulled back behind his head. Concern creased his brow.

She shifted against the pillow, drawing her hands out from under the covers to run across her face and hair. "Perhaps I should speak to Madam Ophelia."

Rowe nodded. "She came by earlier to have a look at you. She asked questions I couldn't answer, and I told her I would let her know when you were awake." He moved to the table near the bed and took up a glass of water, holding it out for her. "Drink."

Saran drank without objection. When she emptied the glass, she passed it back to her caretaker with a trembling hand. "What questions?"

Rowe avoided her eyes and sat again near the edge of the bed. "Personal ones."

Saran laughed. "Personal ones? What sort?"

"Perhaps it is best for her to ask them? I'll get her."

Saran grabbed his arm just as he stood. Rowe's blue gaze fell on her with a mixture of worry and pity. "What questions, Rowe?"

"I believe she wants to know if you're pregnant. I don't know why she'd ask me. I thought it improper." Rowe curled his fingers around her hand.

Saran laughed again, shaking her head. "No, that's not possible. Whenever Keleir and I are together, I use mag—" The words fell off her lips. She blinked her gaze away and drew her hand from him, shaking her head firmly. "I'm very worried or I've eaten something spoiled, that's all."

Rowe sat nearer and draped his arm across her shoulders. He drew her hand into his and held it tightly. "You are, aren't you?"

Saran shook her head again. But even as she did, she felt her chest tighten. They were careful, and she always used magic to control the timing around her body's fertility. But since the Bind . . . she hadn't even thought about it, not with all that happened to them since returning to Andrian. Everything involving the task was so automatic . . .

Rowe's arms tightened around her. "This is a happy thing, Saran. Keleir will . . ."

Saran shook her head, quietly crying. "Keleir isn't coming back."

The Lightning Mage pressed his lips to her hair. "You can go to him."

Saran brushed the tears from her cheek. An odd comment from a man who last said that if Keleir didn't become the Vel d'Ekaru, she would die. "What about all this prophecy mess?"

Rowe held her hand tight and thought quietly for a while. "Maybe I'm wrong. Keleir would never abandon you, so if he chose to stay in Mavahan, it is because it truly is helping him. Perhaps staying there would nullify the prophecy or stagnate it. Maybe it will freeze the progress of the Oruke permanently, allowing you both to be safe. Maybe the Prophetess can't see him there, can't account for him."

There was a time, long ago, when Saran believed that Rowe saw this woman and that she spoke to him of the future. But

Saran prayed to the Prophetess for guidance on more than one occasion and had never seen or heard her, not once.

Saran knew that sometimes humans found patterns in places that didn't exist. There were many people over the years who had been born cursed with Orukes. Why did that make Keleir's destiny any different from theirs? Or her any more special than the millions who were born before her?

Patterns where they didn't exist.

Saran smoothed her hand across her flat stomach. "If it is true, and we don't know for certain it is . . . if my father finds out about this, he'll use it to bring Keleir home."

Rowe shook his head. "We're getting out of here. Tonight. I won't have you spending another moment in this place. I leave for Salara in the morning, I'll get you to our border with Mavahan before the attack on the capital."

"That's not possible," Saran muttered. "That's a two-week journey by foot, and I can't Port with this stupid Bind. Not to mention, if anyone runs Father through, I'm dead too."

Rowe stiffened. "I'll find a way to get the Bind off."

"You've read every book there is to read, Rowe! The Bind isn't coming off until Father gives us the key, and he isn't going to do that." Saran stared at Rowe's hand around hers. The Bind gleamed blinding bright in her blurring vision. If Keleir did return and she still had this thing . . . Saran couldn't take another moment of it being around her wrist. She needed it off once and for all.

"Move," she whispered, pushing him gently at first. Rowe's brow furrowed with confusion as her shoving grew manic. "I need this off. I need my element back!"

Saran shoved him harder than he anticipated. He slipped off the bed and landed on the floor. She brushed past him, heading to the fireplace opposite the bed.

"Saran, you shouldn't be—"

Saran ignored him and ran her hands along the hearth until she found what she sought, drawing the hatchet from a space between the fireplace and the stack of wood waiting to be burned. She whirled and slammed her hand flat against the small tabletop next to her sitting chair. Her eyes gleamed in the firelight as she lifted the hatchet and brought it down.

Rowe nearly lost a hand catching her wrist and drawing it back into the air. "What are you doing?"

"I'm getting rid of this awful thing!" she screamed at him, tugging on her arm. "Let me go."

Rowe shook his head violently. "I'm not letting you chop your hand off!"

Saran struggled against his harsh grip. His hand dug her skin against the bone. "I have to do this! I *need* my magic back. I need to make all of this right. If I don't, then I'm going to lose him. We are going to lose him, and *everything* will end because of me."

"Saran . . ."

Her eyes welled with tears. "He might already be lost. Rowe, I don't think I can do it twice."

The Lightning Mage frowned, appraising her thoughtfully. He did not let go of her wrist. "You've always said you didn't know what you did to him, Saran."

The look on her face said otherwise. Tears fell freely down her cheeks, the pain of what she'd done written on her face. It had never occurred to Rowe that she would have lied to them.

"What did you do to him?" he asked evenly.

She shook her head.

"Saran . . . what did you do to my brother?"

A mournful expression stole her face and she sobbed, shaking her head. Her knees grew weak and she leaned heavily on the table. "Something unforgivable," she choked out. Her grip tightened around the hatchet's handle. "I just want to be free of it all. I don't want to be the Princess of Adrid or the Equitas. Please let me do this. I only have you and Keleir. I'm alone, Rowe. If I lose you, if I can't stop what is coming—I don't care about my hand."

Rowe slowly pried the hatchet out of her grasp. "I care," he said. Saran gave a shuddering sob as he tossed it into the fire. He dropped to his knees and pulled her tight until she could barely breathe. "The Bind will come off this night," he swore. "I will find the key."

THIRTY

LIGHTNING FLASHED ACROSS a black sky. Pale white light exploded through the dark hall just outside Yarin's bedchamber. The hall, long and narrow and lined on one side with windows, had ten guards standing every six feet. Most of them relaxed heavily against the stone. They were bored or half-asleep.

The King of Adrid had a right to his paranoia. Soldiers guarded his chamber door day and night, even if the king wasn't there, to ensure no one slipped through to wait for his return. Secrets beyond Rowe's dreams hid behind that door, and only the maids and Saran had ever seen them.

Thunder shook the hall, startling a few of the sleeping guards awake. An angry storm brewed outside, an elemental representation of his feelings toward the infamous king. Rowe appraised the guards from where he stood opposite Yarin's door. His fingers flexed at his sides, glints of electricity crackling off the tips with a quiet static charge.

This would be easier if Rowe could Port into Yarin's room and question him. But Yarin was so worried about assassins that he had the whole castle warded so no Mage could Port into it. One could Port to any place outside the walls, like the roof or a balcony, but nowhere inside.

Rowe thought a quiet apology to the men lining the hall and let a burst of electric current rattle across the floor, traveling up through their metal armor and stunning them unconscious. They fell, one by one, to lie like logs across the floor.

The door to Yarin's chamber was unlocked. The room beyond had no light, not even a small candle flame, and the curtains were drawn closed. Rowe held up his hand. Static electricity crackled in his palm, growing out and warping into a small spherical ball of energy. It cast a pale blue glow against the walls as he used it to find his way through the large sitting room and to the king's bed.

A long time ago, Rowe would have feared sneaking up on a Mage like Yarin, who had been one of the most feared in all of the First. It was said that he once turned a whole army into deranged hundred-year-old men. Many, a long time ago, had suspected he was the Vel d'Ekaru. Looking upon the aged and slackened face of the king, Rowe felt little more than hatred.

Yarin took children from poor homes as payment for taxes that no one could afford. That was how Rowe came to be in his service. Yarin trained them, brainwashed them, and forced them to slaughter their own in order to keep what little control he had. He enslaved his own daughter and used her as a pawn in his twisted religion. He tormented Keleir by denying him the one thing that kept him sane. Rowe could end it all by driving a dagger through the old man's heart. If not for Saran's Bind, he would have.

War would be avoided.

Saran would be free.

Keleir would be safe from whatever twisted plan Yarin had for him.

He need only to find the key and set the princess free.

"Have you lost your way?" Yarin muttered through dry, thin lips. He cracked his eyes open and blinked at the harsh glow of Rowe's light. "Or has it finally come to pass? Has the soldier from the Eastern Mountains awoken?"

Rowe hesitated at Yarin's bedside, watching as the old man drew himself to sit. He lifted his hands to his face and shielded his eyes from the light. "I wondered who it would be . . . Out of all the children we dragged from that village, I did not think it would be the brother of the Vel d'Ekaru."

The Lightning Mage shook his head. "I need to release Saran from the Bind, and you're going to give me the key. No more games. No more riddles. I know there isn't any saving Keleir; I know he will be your Living God. So let me take Saran away from here. I promise we will not get in your way."

Yarin cocked his head to the side, a flicker of a smile stretching his aged face. "Does Saran know you're conspiring against her husband?"

"No," Rowe replied, lowering the light so that it no longer blinded the king. "I told her I was taking her to Keleir. However, I am going to keep her as far away from him as possible, by any means necessary. We both have our prophets, Yarin. Mine was wrong about Saran. It did not account for her love for him. She will never be the Equitas, and if she tries, she will die. You've won, do you understand that? So give me the key."

Yarin struggled with the blankets, shoving them off and slipping his gnarled feet to the cold stone floor. He hobbled to his desk and around it to the bookshelf near the window. "This is what happens when brothers love the same woman. How will Keleir handle your betrayal?"

Rowe frowned. "When Keleir returns to Adrid, he will no longer be my brother."

Yarin chuckled as he rummaged through the books. "No doubt, and if he does return the one you know, I daresay your betrayal will be just the push needed to send him over the edge. This works as much in my favor as it does in yours." Yarin stumbled on his feet, grabbing hold of the gold cord dangling by the curtains. He rested his cheek against the books. "Unfortunately." He sighed, "I don't need your help turning Keleir into the Vel d'Ekaru, and Saran can't leave. I will not let the Equitas free, nor will I allow the soldier from the Eastern Mountains to live."

Hate lit Rowe's eyes with blue sizzling light. The orb of electric current in his hand grew and bolts arched off to lick at the ceiling and the floor.

"Hurt me, and you hurt her," Yarin warned. The Lightning Mage's magic snuffed out, leaving them in the dark. "I've been at this game a very long time, Rowe. I know what is coming. I know every threat. No matter what you do, where you run, you can't win. You never win. You *always* lose. That is your fate and hers. Over and over, until the end of all time."

The wooden door to the sitting room broke open, and light exploded in from the hall. Rowe's eyes went to the cord that the king clung to, knowing that he'd been tricked.

Arrows whizzed past, and lightning arched off Rowe's hands, turning them to ashes around him. He threw a bolt against the floor, and it traveled to their feet, fizzling into nothing.

These were no ordinary soldiers. They were Saharsiad, the Mage hunters. They brandished their left arms, which bore spelled gauntlets warded to protect them from magic.

The Saharsiad circled into the room, flanked by regular militia. Each one had a dark cotton cloth drawn over their face so not to be identified. Rowe never understood that reasoning, for even if a Mage escaped when cornered, they would hardly seek out a Saharsiad willingly.

Magic crackled in a thick current around Rowe. He could not Port away, not from inside the room, and it had only one door. Getting through that door meant going through the wall of faceless mercenaries before him. His hand went to his hip and to the cold metal hilt of his sword.

"If you fight them, they will kill you," Yarin warned. "Surrender and live to see your brother become what was destined for him. Perhaps you will have your own transformation."

"I'd rather take my chances with the Saharsiad," Rowe muttered.

The Lightning Mage brandished the sword and lunged toward the door, into the fray. Even as a trained soldier, it was impossible to fight twenty men and win. Rowe used what magic he could on the line of soldiers standing behind the impervious Mage hunters. For the Saharsiad, he introduced them to the cold steel of his sword and the leather of his boot. Even so, avoiding all of them at once was impossible. Rowe, accustomed to pain, ignored the slicing rip of a blade through his back and leg. He kept pushing forward toward the open door and hall. If he could get there, he could Port away.

But the Saharsiad knew this and would not let him pass.

Rowe struggled to the door, feeling slice after slice cut through his leather armor and into his skin. He swung his heavy sword at them, kicked those who stumbled low and close. Their small numbers swarmed him. He dove for the door, crashing against the wood with a harsh thud before springing to his feet and throwing himself out the window. He called his magic to him as he fell, and a pool of blue crackling light exploded under him. He tumbled into its welcoming embrace.

Rowe reappeared, kneeling in a mushy combination of mud and horse shit, just outside the stables. He curled his hands in the soft wet earth, letting the solidity of it register.

"Rowe!"

Saran knelt near him and wrapped her hands around his arm, hoisting him from the mud. She drew her hands away to find them red with blood. "Prophetess!" The princess frantically examined the gaps in his leather until Rowe waved her away, looking sick.

"The horses?"

Saran released him and went back to the pale mare waiting by the stable door. She led the horse to him. "I only managed the one before you arrived. Did you get the key?"

Rowe pushed past her and mounted Saran's horse, smearing blood across the saddle. He grabbed her hand and tugged her up behind him, turning for the castle gate.

Lightning flashed across a smoldering black sky and rain fell in large cold drops, sparse at first, and then thick and heavy, soaking through their clothing in seconds. The castle bells tolled, their harsh ring echoing his failure off the brittle tower walls.

"Yah!" He kicked the horse forward through the castle gate and down a cobblestone street leading toward the outer wall of the city. Very little light illuminated the road. As the city sat mostly abandoned by its residents, no one took the time to light the streetlamps.

He blinked the water from his vision and glared at the closed city gate ahead. Electric current crackled bright and blue in his eyes as he raised his hand from the reins and threw a coiled ball of lightning through the rain. It crashed against the iron bars and traveled over the metal surface, wrapping like tentacles around the joints and melting them. The gate fell away, a broken puzzle of mangled, white-hot iron that quickly cooled black in the rain.

They bounded for the gate as the gatemen scrambled out of the stone bastion to see what had happened. He sent another ripple of electric energy across the wet earth and into their feet, dropping them to the mud with the gate. Saran's arms tightened around his waist, and he pressed forward through the passage until her grip tugged him backward, nearly off the horse, before her hold snapped free.

The warmth against his back disappeared, and Saran landed in the mud and metal behind the horse. He drew short and turned back for her. She struggled to catch her breath, wincing as she dragged herself from the rubbled gate and up to her feet.

Rowe slipped from the horse and went to her. "What happened?"

Her green eyes looked the archway over, but before she could give him an answer he began pulling her back to the horse. "They're coming." He jerked Saran abruptly into an invisible wall, the Bound wrist stuck in the grip of magic. He pulled harder until the metal bracelet cut into her skin, and she cried out and snatched away.

"I can't," she huffed. "The key. Give me the key, and I'll take it off."

The Lightning Mage froze, the glow of magic in his eyes faded. "I . . ."

Behind her, the Saharsiad gained ground on them.

"I didn't find it," he whispered to her.

Saran's jaw tightened. Her green eyes searched his horrified face, knowing that he couldn't stay.

They'd kill him.

But they wouldn't kill her.

"Go," she pleaded, pushing against his chest. "Go now!"

Rowe growled, grasping her hand and pulling her forward. "I'm not leaving you!"

"I can't go!" Saran jerked away and pushed at his shoulder. "Get out of here. They'll kill you. Go."

"No! I'm not leaving you here with him, Saran."

The princess took his face in her hands with a sad smile. "You have no choice. Sometimes we do what we hate to do what is right."

She brushed her fingers against his wet skin, feeling hot tears mingle with the cold rain on her cheeks. He shook his head, but she held him firmer. "Finish what we started. Find Darshan and finish this. He can't kill me, Rowe. He needs me. But he doesn't need you. Please go. Please!"

Rowe opened his mouth to argue, but the yelling of the Saharsiad behind her startled him out of it. He frowned at them, hate in his eyes. He brushed her cheek with a bleeding hand, as if his touch sought to memorize the curve of her face. He kissed her then, as he would have had she loved him, and she met it without coldness, but with warmth and longing and sorrow.

If only the world were different. If only they'd gone away like Keleir had wanted. If only he'd never told her that he didn't love her.

She pushed him away when he lingered too long. He felt the hooves against the earth. "Go!"

He nodded, torn and broken, but intelligent enough to know she spoke truth. He stepped back into a wall of blinding light before his poor judgment made him stay.

THIRTY-ONE

SARAN LOWERED HER hands from her eyes when Rowe's gate dissipated in a shower of blue sparks. In that second, she had never felt more alone. The metal bars to the city were gone, but she remained more a prisoner than ever before. She tried to push through the pass beneath the stone arch, just to test it once more, but the Bind on her wrist caught, as if an invisible hand held her firmly in place.

The Saharsiad rode up around her, circling menacingly on dark horses.

"Arrest her," one of them said, and two bound her hands together and tied her to the back of a horse.

Though it was a short distance back to the castle, the walk felt like an eternity. The closer they got, the larger and more hatefully the stone fortress loomed over her. The lightning flashing across the sky made the spindling towers look like black fingers reaching out over her. Her chest tightened; her stomach twisted.

The prospect of death did not frighten her. Being trapped frightened her. Not being able to escape to freedom, not being able to protect . . . She pressed her hands to her belly.

The walk from the bottom of the castle steps to the foot of Yarin's throne went by in a quick, rushing blur. The hard crack of a sheathed sword against her back sent her to her knees and brought her more aware of the throne room and the angry eyes of her father.

"He escaped?" Yarin muttered, drumming his fingers against the arm of his throne.

"Yes, Your Majesty," the leader of the Saharsiad said, placing his boot on Saran's back and crushing her against the gritty floor. "This one was with him. She is bloody, but it is not hers. He's badly wounded."

Yarin sneered, the light rhythmic drum of his fingers silenced with a final loud tap. "I'm saddened that you thought it would be that easy. Have I not taught you better?"

Saran lifted her head and struggled to push up from the floor with the heavy weight of the Saharsiad boot against her back. She offered him nothing but a black glare before spitting on the stone in front of her.

"He wasn't taking you to Keleir, you know." Yarin sighed, his brow furrowing with sympathy. "He was lying to you, Saran."

Saran clenched her teeth and turned her gaze to the floor.

"He planned to take you as far away from him as possible. He believes in the prophecy you deny. He would have betrayed you to fulfill it."

The princess did not meet the king's eyes. She stared at the stone, feeling a knot in the back of her throat choke whatever protest she could muster. Yarin could not be trusted, but Rowe did believe in that prophecy and he would lie in order to protect her from whatever he deemed a threat. The Lightning Mage had proven that already.

"Well, are you going to say anything?"

The weight of the Saharsiad boot grew heavier, until every breath she exhaled could not be fully replaced. She wheezed, struggling to breathe. Her hands pressed into the stone, and she shifted her legs beneath her to try to push the weight away.

"Teach my daughter the respect she has forgotten," Yarin sneered, resting his arms across his knees and peering down at her with a dark glare. "If you weren't a necessity, I would rid myself of your insubordination permanently. I can only hope that, with some proper tutelage, you will be better behaved in the future."

The weight lifted from Saran's back. She took a deep breath and slid up to her hands and knees. A dark shape moved quickly off to her side, and she caught sight of the boot just before it drove into her stomach. The sweet breath of air she'd stolen left her in a horrible gagging rush. She curled her arm around her belly and fell over onto her side, sucking air in wet and tight.

The next boot came for her, but she rolled so that her back took the lick. Each one that swung, she tried her best to make sure her ribs or spine took the punishment until she rolled flat on her stomach and covered her head with her hands. They stomped down around her, grinding her into the gritty throne room floor.

"Turn her over," someone said.

Saran struggled against the rough hands that grabbed her and forced her over onto her back. She curled her knees to her stomach and kicked at them, bit at them, screamed at them. When one tried to drive their heel into her gut, she tangled her legs around them and tripped them up until they ended up on the floor next to her.

She gave a feral growl, snarling like a savage animal, and tore her hands free from the Saharsiad. She wrapped her arms around herself and glared at them through loose strands of curly crimson hair. "It's easy to beat a woman when she's weaponless, isn't it, pigs?" She spat blood at their feet.

One kicked at her, and she offered him her back, rolling into the hit and repelling off hard enough to crack her head forward against the stone. She went still, frozen as a flash of bright white pain exploded through her skull. Vaguely she noticed the shuffle of feet, felt the hard leather of a boot shove against her until the Saharsiad rolled her over.

Her vision wavered on the cusp of black and blurry, but she saw enough to know the attacks weren't finished. She made a groan of protest, fumbled her arms up over her waist, and wrapped them like a shield about her belly.

Saran, born a woman of some privilege, had lived her life in a deserted city surrounded by soldiers and very few women. The women she did know were servants or healers, and while she had tried her best to befriend them, even they knew that it was safer for them to keep their distance. Despite her lack of female interaction, Saran knew enough. She saw and heard enough. She knew young servant girls who paid brutish soldiers to beat them so that they lost the child, since the healers refused to give them the proper potions to end it by any other means.

Saran knotted her hands in her clothes, locking her fingers tight and her arms like a protective vise. If she were pregnant, it was ill-timed. There were too many important deeds to be done and really no room for such a thing. But this was her child. This was Keleir's child. Her father had taken many things from her, but he would not take this.

"I'm sorry," she huffed. The words spilled out of her mouth before pride could snatch them back. She exhaled a ragged, angry breath. The room seemed infinitely quieter than before. Even the torches crackled with less enthusiasm. She gathered herself on her knees at the foot of King Yarin's throne and turned her face, marred by bruises and blood, up to her father.

Yarin's old, withered face sneered back at her. He rolled his eyes and ran a hand over his head. "Your words are insulting," he muttered. "I know you are not sorry, Saran."

Her fingers clutched at the stone beneath her, as if holding it tightly enough might give her the strength she needed. "I am," she said, her voice cracking. She bent forward slowly, wincing as every bone and muscle in her body protested. She couldn't tell if the pain were physical from the beating or emotional from the sheer will it took to grovel at his feet. She pressed her bleeding forehead to the stone and prostrated herself before the King of Adrid, not as a princess, but as a slave.

It felt like an eternity, and it was a number of minutes, but eventually the old man moved on his throne, shifting his bony body into a more comfortable position. "Curious," he muttered, drumming his fingers against the arm of his chair again. "I don't believe you. It isn't genuine. But what I would like to know is why you are so desperate to avoid your beating. Tell me, and I'll not let it continue."

Saran mulled over the words, slowly rising from the floor to her knees again. "It hurts," she muttered, smoothing her dirty hands over her clothes.

"It hurts, but that isn't why, is it? You've handled worse than this before without a word. So why?"

Saran didn't reply. She stared at him, trying to find the right answer that would please him.

"One last chance, my dear. Tell me the truth."

She weighed her options and the consequences of silence. She chose a lie—no, a halftruth. "I don't have my magic. What if they do something irreversible? Something I can't fix."

"Wounds heal, my dear, and they leave scars as a lesson to our faults. Perhaps scars are what you need to remember your place," Yarin said, a sympathetic look in his eyes. She wondered if it was for her or for himself, for having been cursed with her for a daughter. He exhaled a heavy, watery sigh and motioned to the Saharsiad. "Continue."

Hard hands grabbed her arms and pulled her back. Fear leapt up, sudden and scalding. It burned through her senses until it had hold of her heart and her mind and her voice. She yelped, the first real show of fear ever displayed before the old bag of bones that called her daughter. She kicked her legs out, tried to drag her arms away from their heavy gauntleted hands, tried desperately to wrap them around herself again. When she couldn't, she gave up on standing and instead let herself fall heavy to the floor, let herself dangle like a rock from their grip, and she drew her knees up to her chest and clenched her whole body tight, willing the joints to fuse into place.

A Saharsiad stepped forward and reared his fist back, his knuckles covered in sharp metal points that would tear into her flesh mercilessly. Saran closed her eyes and turned her already bruised cheek to him.

"Stop!" Yarin called, a strong tone in his normally feeble voice.

Her heart dropped and lifted again. Her body uncoiled like a broken spring as relief washed over her too quickly, turning her thoughts dizzy and her skin flush. She felt tears of relief, too shocked by them to notice her father leaving the comfort of his throne to greet her at the bottom. His aged eyes studied Saran before the concern left him and replaced itself with malevolent joy.

He laughed. The sound echoed off the walls, reverberating back and forth until it sounded as if he'd multiplied in presence. He laughed for so long that it became white noise in her ears. But then he laughed until he coughed, and he coughed so hard that a Saharsiad had to catch him before he fell.

"Does he know?" the king asked, clearing his throat and righting himself. He beckoned for his cane. One of the Saharsiad jumped quickly up the podium to collect it for him.

Saran turned her eyes away as Yarin knelt before her, his joints popping as he pressed his knees to the floor. He touched her bruised and bloodied cheek with a trembling old hand and then ran it over her damp, curling hair.

"Just like your mother," he whispered, uncharacteristic affection hanging in his voice. "If he doesn't know, he will. I'll send a letter to Mavahan tonight, once I wrangle someone to replace the departed messenger. Until Keleir returns, we'll find you a nice, cozy cell on the first floor of our dungeon."

THIRTY-TWO

YARIN, TO SARAN'S great relief, could not send a letter to Mavahan that night. While there were several individuals with the capacity to take over the role of messenger, none of them seemed to have the way with birds that the last messenger possessed. Short-range crows and long-range pigeons were different in temperament. She'd learned this from Madam Ophelia, whom Yarin sent down to her small dank cell just beneath the first floor of the castle to tend to the abrasions from her beating.

The cell wasn't so far down as to encase her in complete, hopeless darkness. It sat just at the edge of that bleak, inescapable prison, where the air wasn't too cold or the floor too damp. A bed made of straw sat tucked in the corner with a tin bowl to piss in. A metal grated window hung where the top of the wall met the short ceiling. A small beam of moonlight filtered in to bathe the torchless room in a pale glow. The storm had passed.

A guard stood at the open door, his arms folded across his broad armored chest, and a sympathetic frown marred his features. He watched Madam Ophelia tend to the wounds with the aid of a very weak candle resting on the floor near her knees.

Madam Ophelia's cold hands wrapped gossamer bandages about Saran's arms to cover the scrapes. The healer took greater care with the smaller wounds than she normally would, muttering about the conditions in which the princess would be kept and how they could lead to infection.

Saran hadn't spoken a word since the woman arrived. A hundred thoughts warred in her mind, some she felt the need to voice, but the heaviness in her heart made the idea of speaking them too exhausting. She resigned herself to watching the old woman, whose gray hair pulled so tight that her wrinkles stretched smooth.

"There are a few spells I can run on your blood to determine whether or not you are carrying a child," Madam Ophelia said. "Shall I?"

This startled Saran. She'd convinced herself so surely that it was true, she hadn't even considered the possibility that it wasn't.

"Yes." Her voice broke as she spoke and she coughed to clear her throat.

"It won't hurt to add another cut to you." The healer sighed, taking out a tiny blade and holding it up to Saran's finger. The guard at the door took a half step forward but stopped when Saran lifted her hand. Strange, she thought, that the man keeping her prisoner felt a duty to protect her from a tiny knife.

Madam Ophelia cut Saran's finger and drained the blood into a small glass vial, which she corked and pressed into the pocket of her cotton apron. "I'll come back when the spell is over."

Saran grabbed her hand as she stood and drew her low enough to whisper, "I'm not. Do you understand? Even if it says I am, I'm not. Tell no one the truth."

Madam Ophelia's eyes, often cold and distant, softened. She pressed her other hand to the top of Saran's head. "My loyalty is always and ever to you. Soon we will show them the light. When you are queen, we will rise."

Saran nodded softly, her lips parting with words she wouldn't speak. There were too many prophecies, too many conflicting religions, and too many people who believed in salvation derived from impossible idols. The healer was part of a sect of women who worshipped the Grand Feminine, a belief that men were inferior and had doomed the world, and that one day a woman would rise to power and the reign of man would be over. Women would rule over the world, bringing peace and justice. A fairy tale. Saran didn't believe in it, and she wasn't unwilling to use it to her advantage. But when confronted with Madam Ophelia's kindness and loyalty, it made Saran want to admit the truth.

But she wouldn't.

Like her father and his Living God, Madam Ophelia wouldn't be swayed from her beliefs. She wore this look in her cold eyes, a hardness as sharp as diamonds that said, if pushed, she had a terrifying desire for violence and a need to quench it. Madam Ophelia was dangerous, though her power could only ever be used for healing. Saran realized then how glad she was that healers only possessed the power for mending and not breaking.

"Thank you," she whispered.

Madam Ophelia scooped up her bag of medical supplies and the candle on the floor. She gave Saran a gentle curtsy before the guard let her out and locked the door behind her.

In the dark, quiet cell, Saran lay stiff and sore across the straw bed. It smelled of mildew and dust, and each breath she took coated the inside of her mouth and nose with dirt.

THIRTY-THREE

THE BUMPING AND jolting of the wagon woke Rowe to damp morning air and a gray sky glaring back at him. His mouth was too dry to swallow, and his body ached despite all the work that Darshan's healers had put into him. He ran his half-gloved hands over the wet tunic and the gaping holes in his garment.

"Healers are good at patching flesh, not so much with fabric," Darshan's voice filtered down to him. The Lightning Mage lifted his gaze to the back of the straw-bed wagon where the rebel leader sat tucked into the corner, one leg bent and the other stretched out before him. He wore a leather cloak over his shoulders with the hood pulled low over his brow. He was damp, but whether from rain or water magic, Rowe didn't know.

"Are we near Salara?"

"Not exactly," the older Mage said. "We're nearing the byroad to Salara that crosses the main road to Andrian. This is where we will part ways, you and I. I will lead the army to the capital and you will lead the diversion to Salara."

Rowe slowly drew himself up and against the hard-planked sides of the wagon. "Taking the main road isn't very smart, Darshan. The army will be using that road to get to Salara."

"I will not be on the main road. We will be diverting to the forest, and I've requested that our resident Earth Mage hide our tracks this far and onward. No one will notice a company of this size has been through the area. Your job is to get to Salara before Yarin's men. Logan, Desme, and Shalo will be with you. I would hope that four Mages plus a few armed peasants can subdue some military tax collectors."

The Lightning Mage scowled. "They are a bit more than that, and you know it. I really think we need to consider our other options now that Saran is completely a prisoner of her father, and especially now that I've defected. He's bound to know where I've gone and has to assume that I've given away our secrets. Aren't you concerned in the least that he will change his tactics or forgo missions all together to compensate for that leaked information? He might not be heading to Salara at all, Darshan, and you'll be walking into a trap."

"A poorly laid one. Andrian's walls are nothing more than wet parchment, and we've got the firepower to send it falling down around them. Yarin thinks his military is a force to be reckoned with, but it is nothing compared to the will of men who wish to be free."

"Let's be realistic here," Rowe muttered. "Numbers matter quite a lot, especially when you are pitting farmers against well-trained soldiers, men I trained as a matter of fact. At least let the others go on to Salara and allow me to go with you. If you are walking into a trap, I want to make sure you survive it."

Darshan pursed his lips together and turned his head toward the opening at the back of the wagon. "We will not deviate from our plan. We've prepared months for this. You will go to Salara, Rowe. That is an order."

Rowe frowned, studying the older man's indifferent form. Orders. He hated them, and he had to bite his tongue to keep from questioning who Darshan thought he was to give them to him. "You're risking much, Ishep."

"I will risk it all!" Darshan replied, ocean-blue eyes turning from the muddied road to the turncoat Lightning Mage. "With the Prophetess on our side, we cannot fail, and she has spoken of our victory. You said so yourself, my son. You are the voice of her visions. After the battle of Salara, the kingdom will fall. It matters not how Salara ends. Once it is over, we will have our victory. It is foretold."

"She hasn't spoken those words in years, Darshan, and she came to me again with a warning. She said, 'Remember my words, Rowe Blackwell, and know that you have been betrayed. The Equitas cannot exist without the Living God. For the Equitas to live, so must the Living God rise.'"

Darshan waved away his words. "She did not mention that we would fail in Salara, and you *were* betrayed, Rowe. Your brother abandoned you, abandoned us. He gave in to his own weakness, and now we are not one, but two Mages short. His betrayal is what she speaks of. Can't you see it, or are you still blinded by your love for him? Your brother is dead and has been dead since before he took his first breath in this world. If he wasn't, he is now. Her words speak truth to his lies. If I cannot convince you, perhaps she will."

Rowe felt a cold hollowness swallow him, colder than the rain-soaked clothes he wore. It reached in and wrapped around his heart. He slumped along the wagon wall, the world growing heavy around his shoulders.

Of course, he thought. That made far more sense than every other scenario he'd driven into his mind. Why hadn't he thought of it before? It was a warning, and it had come before

Keleir sent his letter proclaiming his abandonment. He felt so blind. The truth had been right before him all along.

The Lightning Mage struck the side of his fist hard against the wagon wall once, twice—over and over until a thunderous growl left him heaving heavy breaths into his lungs. Darshan did not flinch at his anger, but instead curled his lips into a knowing smile. "Are you ready to believe, my son?"

Rowe shook with rage, and pained tears blurred his vision. His brother, who had taken him under his wing, who had taught him to slaughter and enjoy it, who had turned his life around and swore himself to the path of redemption, had turned away from that vow. He'd turned away from his wife and, unknowingly, their child. He preserved himself in the Deadlands and left them to die at Yarin's hands.

He took a deep, calming breath. The crackle of electricity in his eyes dimmed. "I am ready."

THIRTY-FOUR

BLINDING GOLD LIGHT fell down the long square shaft, warming Keleir's face. He stood just beneath the opening, his arms relaxed at his sides, his head tilted back, and his eyes peacefully closed. The warmth of the sun chased away the chill dungeon air, and the hot wind blowing through the shaft smelled of salt. He imagined himself on the edge of the ocean, basking in the midday glow and relaxing along the shore with Saran and Rowe, just as they'd always dreamed. He could just see the small cabin nestled in the trees at the edge of the shore, where he would live with them, peacefully away from the Oruke. He smiled at the dreamy picture of what he'd never have.

Even without the ominous presence of the beast in him, he knew that it was too late for that. Once he returned to Adrid, the Oruke would be in control.

Besides, he was unlikely to survive the day.

He opened his eyes and let his gaze fall to the sandy dungeon and his malnourished neighbors. They minded their own business, as usual. None of them really liked him; they were too frightened of him to bother trying to make conversation, not that they would understand each other anyway. They were even more terrified to approach him now that he'd become friends with Xalen Okara.

Well, not exactly friends, he thought, but as close to friendship as Keleir was ever really able to get. Not for lack of trying, but no one liked an Oruke, least of all trusted one enough to befriend. He also wasn't blind to the Droven man's interests, and it didn't bother him that they were selfish. After all, Keleir's initial interactions had been for his own personal gain. But he'd grown to know the man in a very short time, mostly due to the Droven Masodite's peculiar knack for verbal vomit. If their friendship managed to carry any further than the stone walls that surrounded them, he would be sure to never tell Xalen a secret that needed to be kept. He counted his blessings from whatever god would have him that the warrior had kept the plans of their escape to himself and their party thus far.

In the distance, the faint roar of the crowd filtered down the shaft. He imagined Xalen Okara taking to the arena to play his part. According to Aleira, the entire palace, save the most necessary of guards, went to watch the Challengers fight. Xalen promised a spectacle to keep them entertained while the rest of Keleir's plan played out.

The Fire Mage flinched and stumbled as a heavy hand landed on his shoulder without warning. His red eyes flashed to the short, thin man standing next to him with a crooked grin and one blind eye. The old man pointed to the light and then motioned with his fingers like a rat scurrying across the floor. His smile broadened, revealing two rows of rotted teeth. He slapped Keleir's shoulder again and nodded to the light.

"You want me to climb it, don't you?" the Fire Mage asked the old man. He knew the Mavish man didn't understand him, and despite that the old man laughed and nodded. Perhaps he understood the tone in Keleir's voice. "Just to see me fall?"

The old one let out a wheezing laugh and scurried his fingers across the air.

Keleir shook his head and turned his face to the sky. "Nah." He sighed. "Not today."

Keleir ignored the old man as he kept poking at him, shifting to avoid his prodding jabs. In the midst of the bright light of the shaft, the Fire Mage spotted a shape toppling through the air. He grabbed hold of the old man and took three steps back just as an armored body plowed hard into the earth, crumpling onto itself feet first. Dust and grit filled the air. The old man coughed, raking his hand across his tongue to wipe the dirt off. He gave Keleir several hard pats on the back, tears in his eyes. He might have been crazed, but he knew gratitude.

The unexpected body brought a confused snort from the Fire Mage.

"Well, that is one way to get me a key," he admitted, glancing to look at the old man. "Good work, Aleira."

The body's arrival attracted his cellmates, but the old man seemed the only one brave enough to get closer. Keleir knelt and began to remove the unfortunate guard's belt, which held a ring of keys, a sword, and an empty dagger sheath. He helped himself to the dagger lodged in the guard's mouth.

"I'm going to assume you deserved this fate," the Fire Mage told the body.

The prisoners watched, silent and curious, as Keleir wrapped the belt around his own waist and buckled it. He took the knife and made a deep cut across the dead man's throat. Blood spilled fresh, and he cupped his hands in it. He took the blood and splashed it over his head so that it spilled down over his face in red rivers. The crowd around him took a frightened step back.

Well, all, except the old man.

They whispered among themselves about the Ipaba. The cursed. Keleir did not need to know their language to understand what they thought of him or what he intended to do with the blood. That reaction was of course exactly what Keleir wanted. Among their heated whispers, he heard it. The word he would use to get everything he wanted from them.

Dregs.

Blood magic.

He had no real power, not in this place. He didn't even know how to use blood magic, but he did have the gift of illusion, manipulation. He would use that to the fullest of his ability. They called him Ipaba, and that had power in and of itself. If he could convince him that he knew Dregs, perhaps the language barrier wouldn't be an issue, and they would follow him whether they understood him or not.

Keleir stood up, awash in blood, and drew the sword at his waist. He held his bloody hands in the air, one brandishing the dead guard's sword and the other grasping a ring of bronze keys. In an ill-practiced tongue, he cried the words taught to him by the Droven Masodite.

"*Dejeko tamaron os preve! Ru og preve! Deloro mak!*" Your path is freedom. I am freedom. Follow me.

The prisoners viewed him with blank stares, and part of him began to wonder if Xalen had lied to him about the meaning in those words. He waited a minute longer to gauge their reaction before he turned for the staircase leading up out of the pit. A twinge of disappointment bit at him. He doubted he would make it very far beyond the door without some sort of help.

When he reached the exit, he heard a soft padding of feet behind him. The old man, wearing a bloody handprint on his face, peered around Keleir at the door. Those who were free from chains stood over the dead guard and swiped their hands across the blood, painting their faces with it. Keleir wondered if they thought it gave them power. The trick had been to paint the facade of a Dregs magician.

And it worked.

Keleir choked up on the handle of the short sword he carried and slipped a key into the lock. On the loop there were many keys, but he'd paid very close attention to the ones the guards used to get in and out of the room, and he'd made sure to corroborate his findings with both Luke and Xalen. He knew the key, or at least he felt very confident in his observation.

Long, pointy-tipped, no middle bit, three grooves on the front, two on the back.

He knew he had at least three chances before the door swung open and a guard ran him through.

The Fire Mage held his breath, and the door clicked open. On the other side, wide-eyed guards sat clustered around a table, drinking ale from mugs and playing a round of chips.

Keleir was no stranger to fighting or killing, but he had promised Saran he would be a better man. He'd promised he would not kill unless to preserve his own life. He'd done very well with that promise for five years. But now he would break it.

He would kill.

Because he had to.

In the span of seconds, the shock wore off of the guards. They leaped from the table and brandished their weapons. Keleir spotted the remainder of the royal entourage that had accompanied him to Mavahan crammed into cells just behind the guards. A roar erupted from them in a tongue he could understand. They cried out for their prince to save them.

The Fire Mage greeted the first guard, swinging down on him with a hard, punishing whack. The metal in his hands felt light, the sword more ceremonial than useful. It shattered once it met real steel. Even fragmented, Keleir used it to his advantage and stabbed the man with the broken blade.

Behind him, a flood of blood-painted and ragged men flowed into the room, their numbers overpowering the small party just beyond the door. When all the guards had fallen to beaten piles on the floor, it still took several long, agonizing seconds for Keleir to come down from the rush of fear and adrenaline. When he did, he found they had successfully accomplished the first step to freedom. He stood over the bodies, heaving cooling breaths into his lungs in a desperate attempt to calm his blood. His hand clutched the broken sword, white knuckles bared and bright. The man he'd stabbed groveled on the floor, clutching a merciless wound to his gut. He'd die . . . slowly.

Keleir knelt near him and placed a hand on the top of his head. "I will not let you suffer," he told the guard, who quivered from pain and the fear of death. The guard begged, the words incoherent noise to Keleir. He wondered what he looked like to the guard, his face covered in blood and his eyes the color of it. He looked exactly as people had always seen him: a demon.

"I'm sorry," the Fire Mage murmured to the Mavish man. He took up the guard's sword and pressed the tip over the dying man's heart. Keleir pushed down quickly, ending his suffering the best way he knew how.

Keleir had slaughtered whole villages with a smile, long ago when his mind was not his own. This death, however, marked the first he'd taken with his own hands. It didn't feel natural to him. Guilt twisted his gut worse than when he thought back to those hundreds of lives he'd taken in the blurred fragments of the Oruke's memory. For the first time in his life, his hand quivered around a blade.

"Prince Ahriman!"

Keleir lifted his gaze to an Adridian soldier reaching through the bars to him. The prince took the large ring of keys hanging on a hook near the cells and went through them, one by one, while the prisoners he'd freed waited patiently for him. It seemed they still counted him their leader. When he found the correct key, he quickly went about freeing his men, who rallied around him with joy.

"Don't sing my praises yet," Keleir muttered. "We still have a ways to go before we reach any sign of an exit. We are lucky that fortune smiles on us. The biweekly games are being held, and a majority of the occupants will be in the arena. That works to our advantage in two ways, limited guards in the palace, and the Alar is confined to a central, inescapable location."

One of the Adridian soldiers smiled. "Do you mean to take Mavahan?"

"The Alar committed an act of war by locking away the future King of Adrid," Keleir replied, stern eyes staring into the floor. The Alar would not let him go. He knew well enough the power of a man driven by prophecy. "Adrid cannot afford another war. We will never win a direct fight with Mavahan."

"What do you suggest?" another asked.

"We win by different means," Keleir replied, boasting a clever smile. "At the end of this day, Mavahan will have a new king."

When Keleir opened the groaning exterior door of the prison to the first level of the ziggurat, he stopped short of Xalen Okara's warrior wife, Aleira. Her blue eyes peered like sharp diamonds through strands of brown hair. Blood splattered her tan face. She stood surrounded by four dead guards, wiping their blood off her sword on the fabric of her rust-colored dress.

"This better work, Ipaba," Aleira warned, lifting her gaze to him.

Keleir smiled. "Can you translate for me? I've got some orders to give."

THIRTY-FIVE

THE DUNGEON DOOR groaned open, remaining ajar for a long time before Madam Ophelia stepped into the room. The guard who dutifully watched the healer the day before did not follow her inside and closed the door behind her. The older woman stood tall and regal in her gray healer's dress, her white apron pulled snug around her narrow waist. She clasped her hands before her and turned a pitying look on the princess.

"I told him this conversation was personal," she said, answering Saran's unspoken question. "He agreed to wait outside. Obviously a healer cannot hope to help you escape."

"Obviously," Saran muttered, sitting with her back against the wall. Her breath caught in her throat. She hurt, but she'd felt truer pain than this before.

Madam Ophelia stepped forward and stood just before the straw mat that made up Saran's small bed. "You do *not* carry a child."

Something dropped in Saran, settling in the pit of her stomach before swelling in her breast. Her physical pain replaced itself in a wash of heated blissful relief. "I don't?"

"No," the healer replied, her voice an edge darker than before.

Too many emotions ran through Saran's mind in seconds for her to make any sense of what she felt about the revelation. A momentary pang of sadness fluttered through her breast at the thought of what might have been, but it warred with undeniable solace. Someday she would like to be a mother, but not today. Not when her life was so unsteady and dangerous. It left little room for a child. If anything, it would be cruel to bear one into her personal hell.

"This pleases you?" Madam Ophelia asked.

Saran glanced up from her thoughts. The healer looked primmer than usual, and the princess thought she spotted a hint of disdain in her eye.

"I'd be lying if I said that it doesn't make me happy," Saran replied. She willed herself to think no more of a child that had not been and would not be real for some time. Perhaps if she were someone else, someone with the luxury of time . . .

Saran snorted at the thought. How funny to think she once controlled time the same way a potter shaped clay. Now she had no power. She had no control. Even if she had, there was no room to mourn the loss of something that had not been real when she needed to escape a dungeon. She forced indifference into her voice and stretched her aching legs out in front of her, "I have no time for children."

A glimmer of light appeared in the healer's eyes. She straightened, a tall woman growing ever taller with pride. "And have you had enough?"

Saran cocked her head. "I'm sorry?"

Madam Ophelia took another step forward and peered down at Saran with a sharp gaze. "Have you had enough of this abuse? Enough of your father's depravity? Have you had enough of your complacency in it, and are you finally willing to accept what you were born for?"

Saran pressed her hands into her sore cheeks and smoothed her hair back. "I swear, if you give me a speech about destiny, I *will* kill you."

"I know nothing of your destiny, Saran D'mor, but I know of your bloodright." The healer bent ever so slightly down to her. "For years I have watched you and waited. I have patiently tended your wounds. I have healed every strike that crossed your flesh that you could not reverse. I soothed your flame-ravaged body after you faced the Oruke in Lifesbane. I have yearned for you to take what is your right and *burned* for you to free yourself from the boot of your father. I have forever been your quiet supporter since the moment that I helped bring you into this world. *I cannot be quiet anymore.*"

The princess lost her words. She had them on the tip of her tongue, and they fell away. The revelation stole the protest from her, and the healer took great advantage of it, along with another step forward. The woman nearly stood on top of Saran.

"You cannot run from this! You cannot hide behind Lord Blackwell or Lord Ahriman's demons. You cannot fix the broken and continue to break yourself, just as you can no longer shirk your path. A path chosen by blood and not heart, but *none* of us in this *horrible*, damaged world get the luxury of *choice*! Not even princesses! Sometimes we must be what we *hate* to do what is *right*."

Saran stiffened. *Sometimes we must* be *what we hate to do what is right.* It was a variation of the mantra that Madam Ophelia had pushed on Saran since she was a little girl. *Sometimes we must* do *what we hate to do what is right.* Sometimes we have to be uncomfortable in order to make progress . . . in order to see a better outcome.

Madam Ophelia continued, "You have no idea how much the people here long for you. Do you truly think that all those residing under this roof are followers of Yarin? If you asked it of them, they would lay down their lives to make you queen. You, who turned time back to save them. You, who took beatings and imprisonment to protect them. You, who walk among them, eat among them, live among them, while their king rests comfortably upon his ill-gotten throne, sending them to slaughter. His madness has ruined this kingdom, and he means to ruin you." The healer paused, letting her words sink through Saran like the cold of the dungeon managed to hours ago. "So I ask again," the healer began, looming over Saran. "Have. You. Had. Enough?"

Saran stared unblinking at the stern woman, at the emotion welling in her eyes. This woman who, for as long as the princess could remember, had never shed a tear, never truly smiled, nor shown an ounce of emotion. She hid them behind a mask pulled tight.

"Yes." The word burst out of Saran as if the healer had reached into her soul and snatched it out. "I have." Her hands shook with anger, but not anger at Madam Ophelia, not even anger at her father. She felt angry with herself.

Saran had never wanted to be Yarin's heir. She had never wanted to be queen. She wanted a cottage on a lake with the two men she loved, living their days out in peace. So she'd avoided that part of her life with every fiber of her being, because the closer attention she paid to it, the more she realized how inescapable it really was. She'd always, deep down, known the truth. There was no such thing as peace. Not for her. Not for Keleir. Not for anyone. Her life, and all the dreams beyond her reality, were a girl's dreams. They had always been a girl's dreams.

A part of Saran slipped away, passing like sand through her fingers. The dreamer in her quieted. Like the slow, graceful end of a season, the girl in her died.

The time had come, well past due, for her to be a woman.

No . . . that wasn't it. She was a woman.

She needed to be a queen.

Saran stilled the quiver of anger in her hands and with clenched teeth shifted to stand. Her body throbbed from the effort, still reeling from last night's beating.

The healer stepped back with a pleased smile and clasped her hands politely before her. "And what will you do?" she asked.

Saran took a slow, limping step toward the sunlight filtering in through the small, barred window in her cell. She admired the glint of dust dancing in the yellow beam. "In two days, Ishep Darshan will come to our walls with an army. If what you say is true, then have those who would wish me to be queen lower their weapons and join him. Those who would stand with Yarin will fall by our blade."

THIRTY-SIX

KELEIR AND THE small band of Adridian men he led crept through the ziggurat, following the directions that Aleira had given him before parting ways to go to her husband. They wound their way up the staircase from the bottom level of the prison entrance to the middle level that connected the ziggurat to the arena. The prisoners he'd freed had spread out and gone ahead of them to cause chaos in the halls and to draw the attention of the few guards left on duty. The result was an empty and painless trek to the balcony that the Alar occupied with Xalen's master, a few slaves, guards, and Luke Canin.

The knight sat in a chair just behind the Alar, a guard's hand planted on his shoulder to keep him in check. Keleir peeked through the red curtains into the arena. The thundering roar of the crowd filled his ears and fed fire into his blood.

The rattling groan of the arena door opening told Keleir that Xalen's opponent had arrived. He spotted the hulking Tomorron, with his white-painted skin and slicked-back black hair. He wore painted red marks across his cheeks and a leather cloth about his waist. Other than that, he was unarmored.

Tomorrons, like Droven warriors, refused the aid and restrictions of metal armor. It gave them an advantage in mobility, but a disadvantage in group combat.

While Xalen stood a tall man, the Tomorron stood a foot taller and twice as broad. Legend said that they interbred with giants that lived high in the mountains of Tomorro.

The Tomorron lifted a heavy wooden club tipped in long rusted nails. He slapped the smooth wooden side against the rough palm of his hand, a sneer curling his lip. Xalen's chest rose with pride before his gaze turned to the space that the Alar occupied with his master and their private guards. He sought Aleira.

Xalen's role in their escape was to deliver the greatest spectacle ever to befall Mavahan . . . at least until Keleir got his hands on the Alar.

The Droven Masodite choked up on his axe handle and held his arms out at his sides as a warrior greeting a warrior. The Tomorron did the same before rising to stand, if possible, even taller. The Tomorron warrior's laugh carried across the arena before being silenced by a long, bloody blade protruding from his chest. The painted warrior stumbled forward and dropped his heavy club to the sandy earth. He reached behind him, struggling to pull the hilt of the blade free. Before he could draw it away, his knees buckled and he collapsed face-first into the dirt.

Behind the fallen Tomorron stood the lithe figure of Xalen Okara's wife, a stern gaze creasing her beautiful brow. The crowd erupted in fury and delight, half hating and half loving the show. Aleira crossed the arena to meet Xalen, drawing the blade from the dead Tomorron's back.

Keleir made a sound in the back of his throat, almost losing himself to irritation. That wasn't part of the plan.

Xalen and Aleira greeted each other, pressing their foreheads together. They were too far for Keleir to hear what they said to each other.

Xalen and Aleira's master leaped to his feet, raging at the guards to grab them. None of the guards in the stand or the arena bothered to move at his protests. Perhaps they all thought it part of the game?

A deep growl rumbled up from the Droven Masodite, and he turned from his wife, clutching his axe. He took three long, heavy strides forward, curling the axe behind him, and, on the third step, he heaved his body and the axe forward.

His master only had a second of realization to widen his eyes before the axe buried in his sternum, and he fell backward between his chair and the Alar's throne.

The crowd erupted around him, the peasants rising to their feet with gleeful cheers. The guards, however, finally understood the point of the lord's angry crowing. They jumped to their feet and pushed past the crowd to reach the sandy arena floor.

The guards posted in the arena box with the Alar rushed out into the hall, where Keleir and his men ambushed them before they could utter a sound of protest. Then they rushed the small group left on the balcony while the army below attempted to regain control over Xalen and Aleira.

The Challengers were surrounded by hundreds of spectators now fully aware of their betrayal. They moved through them, dancing as deadly razorlike tumbleweeds across the desert earth. The soldiers clustered around, hacking and slashing with little expertise. They fell in droves about the husband-and-wife Challengers until a shrill Mavish cry echoed over the clang of metal and cries of the wounded.

"Inak!"

Time in the arena shuttered to a standstill, and all eyes turned to the royal arena box where the Alar stood with his back pressed against the chest of the blood-covered Ipaba, a dagger held to his throat. *"Inak,"* the Alar repeated.

"Put down your weapons," Luke Canin instructed in well-versed Mavish, standing at the Alar's side.

THIRTY-SEVEN

KELEIR HELD THE ruler tightly, though the Alar did not struggle. The man heaved angrily in the Fire Mage's grasp, too afraid of the blade at his throat to move. "They aren't listening," Keleir muttered, casting a glance to Luke. The knight shrugged and shook his head, offering no means for which they could gain control of the city other than pressure the Alar to order them to their knees. Keleir pressed the blade tighter to the Alar's throat. "Order them to put down their weapons and accept defeat."

The Alar growled. "So you *are* the Vel d'Ekaru. Clever actor."

"I am Keleir Ahriman. Nothing more."

The Alar turned a desperate glare on Luke. "You cannot let him be king! You cannot let him have the book. This is what he has always wanted! Don't listen to him! He's a demon."

"Shut up!" Keleir barked. "I am not a demon. You brought this on yourself. You locked me away! You threaten Adrid."

"He will take Mavahan's throne. He won't need the Adridian princess to make him king. He will have the book and with it he will have the Artifacts and keys to the universes beyond ours! He will destroy everything. *Kill him.* You know it is true! I see it in your eyes, boy!"

Luke's eyes widened, and he turned an unsteady gaze on the Fire Mage. Keleir knew that look well. In seconds, he saw his ally morph into an enemy. He could see the unsettled uncertainty falter in the boy's eyes as he tried to decide if killing him would protect the world.

"I'm not a monster," Keleir spat. "I don't want that stupid book. I don't want to be king of anything. I just want Saran safe, and an army is coming for Yarin's head in three days. They will kill her when they kill him, Luke. They will not care what it costs to see the king's head piked."

Luke swallowed and turned his eyes back to the Alar.

"Lies," the Alar growled. "Lies! Clever deceiver. Demon!"

Keleir's hand shook, and the dagger in his grip wobbled. Luke's faith faded by the second, and the Fire Mage knew only one way to restore whatever the young turncoat had left . . .

Keleir gritted his teeth and clenched his eyes. If he killed the Alar, he would be their new king. *Claim what is taken*—the basis of all Mavish law. That is how this Alar got his power, and the Alar before him. It was the source of the Deadlands curse on their kingdom. The Alars of Mavahan had not been legitimate rules or bound to the Core since stealing the throne centuries ago from the rightful king.

If Keleir killed the Alar to earn his freedom, it would not look like freedom to Luke. Luke would see it as the Oruke grasping for power, and he would turn on the Fire Mage. Keleir would lose what allies he had in Mavahan, and he'd die well before reaching Saran.

"Fuck," Keleir growled and drew the dagger away from the Alar's throat. He took a healthy step back, tossing the blade away, and fell into the Alar's throne with a heavy, sober sigh. Red eyes looked upon the king. Keleir could read the plan forming in the Alar's mind as if he'd drawn out a map on his face in bright red ink. Keleir settled comfortably into the chair—his grave—accepting of the end after struggling for so long. Better to die a quiet man on a throne than a power-hungry villain.

The Alar snatched the dagger at his feet and lunged for Keleir.

Just as he meant to plunge the dagger into Keleir's chest, a glinting sword swiped between them, and the Alar's arm fell away from his body. It landed on the stone flooring with a splattering thump. The Alar screamed and stumbled back into the balcony railing. Luke shoved forward, driving his stolen, bloody sword through the Mavahan ruler's belly. The Alar toppled over the arena wall, grasping hold of Luke's tunic. The knight yelped and fell after him. The Fire Mage bolted from the throne as fast as his legs would carry and grabbed hold of Luke's shirt. The fabric made a horrifying rip, but the Fire Mage managed to drag the knight back from the edge, and the Alar fell screaming to the earthen arena floor.

For a long while, Keleir could only hear the sound of his heart throbbing in his ears and Luke heaving great shocked breaths into his lungs. The poor young knight stared over the arena wall at the Alar's lifeless body. Slowly Luke lifted his brown eyes to the soldiers around the arena pit and to the crowd in the stands. Luke worked to find his voice before so many eyes, and Keleir gave his shoulder a strong, comforting squeeze.

"Say it," the Fire Mage goaded.

"I claim what was taken," Luke said in quivering Mavish. The Fire Mage squeezed harder, like he was squeezing water from a flask, until Luke shouted, "I claim what was taken!"

The crowd murmured among themselves, the murmurs growing louder until they were deafening. Keleir held his breath as they turned angry. In his mind, he'd imagined this part to be the easiest. He imagined they would fall to their knees and accept a new king, as they had all the others before. But who would accept an outlander as meek as Luke Canin?

"Strength," Keleir urged. "They will only respect strength." He pushed Luke forward. "Be strong."

Luke nodded. He bent and lifted the severed arm of the Alar and stepped toward the platform edge. He stood taller, if only by a bit, and held his head higher. He lifted the arm to the sky and cried his right to the people in their native tongue, "I claim what was taken! Blood on my hands. Body at my feet. I am Alar Luke Canin. I am your king."

The arena went silent, as if every man, woman, and child had lost the ability to speak. They stared at Luke and then between themselves. One by one the people in the stands fell to bended knees, and one by one the soldiers lifted their swords and pressed the blades to their hearts.

Xalen and Aleira locked hands and dropped their bloodied weapons to the sand. They walked through the crowd of stone-still soldiers toward the arena gate and their freedom. It sat beneath the platform that the new Alar stood upon, and they had to step over the lifeless body of the old one to cross its threshold.

Beyond the arena, the sun began to drift into night. The day ended, and Mavahan welcomed its new king.

THIRTY-EIGHT

KELEIR HAD IMAGINED the Book of Kings to be grandiose, but it sat unassuming in his hands. Bound in plain, well-worn leather, void of ornamental gold filigree or hard iron locks to keep out prying eyes, it was thick and heavy. A black, eight-pointed star had been branded into the cover. Keleir held it while Luke watched nervously next to him. The Fire Mage admired all the details of the binding and the weathered edges of the pages but never bothered to open it. Legend said that only a king could open the book. Even still, the Fire Mage didn't test it. He held it a second longer before handing it carefully back to the new Alar.

Luke relaxed, softening into putty as he clutched the book in his arms and passed it back to a servant who waited patiently next to him. "You don't want it?"

"No," Keleir whispered. "In fact, do as the old Alar said and ensure that I never have it." He turned to Luke, the newly crowned Alar of Mavahan, and met his eyes. Luke had a hard time keeping the contact, but the Fire Mage persisted. "Never let that book fall into my hands. You will do me this favor, from now until I die. Never let it come to Adrid."

Luke nodded, his face ashen. "I won't."

"Good."

The new Alar turned his eyes to the floor. "I'd heard so many stories about you. I'd prayed to the Origin God that they weren't true. I never believed my prayers would be answered. I was told that you and your brother were agents of evil, that you sought to corrupt our noble cause. I feel betrayed by my people and by my heart. I am so sorry to have thought ill of you."

"Agents of evil?" Keleir smirked. "Rowe is anything but. We have devoted ourselves to righting the wrongs we made long ago. He, most of all, seeks atonement."

Luke nodded, his face growing paler. He looked ill to the point that a servant pushed a chair behind him. He collapsed into it, clutching his head tight. "I've not been truthful with you."

Keleir frowned at the boy. "What do you mean?"

"You have to go. Now. As soon as possible. You have to stop them."

"Stop who, Luke?"

"Darshan, the rebels, you have to stop them. They're going to kill him."

Keleir nodded. "Yes, they'll kill Yarin. That's why I have to get back. As soon as I cross the border, I can Port there. I'll make it if I leave tonight and ride the horse to its end."

"No," Luke said, loud and angry. "They're going to kill your brother."

Numbness seized Keleir. He couldn't find the voice to ask, but Luke understood the shocked expression and continued, "Darshan planned to kill you both at Salara. But plans changed, and you went here instead. He sent me, not Princess Saran. He wants you and your brother dead so he can take Saran as queen and make his rule legitimate. He is going to kill your brother . . . and I was supposed to kill you."

Keleir stumbled away, his feet heavy as he went to the wall and braced himself there. In two days there would be two battles, one in Salara and one in Andrian, and he wouldn't be able to get to both. He couldn't protect his wife and his brother.

Darshan intended for Saran to make him a legitimate king. That would offer her some protection. Rowe would be blindsided by the plot against him. He was the greater risk.

Rage burned in the Fire Mage's eyes. After all that Rowe invested in doing the right thing, in believing in the rebel leader's voice, he would be betrayed out of greed. Darshan never intended to give Saran the freedom of choice. He'd lured them into his web of lies, knowing he'd inevitably do to Saran what Yarin had done to her mother: use her to make himself king—one that the Core would accept.

"I have to go," Keleir said, his voice too calm.

Luke nodded. "I'll find the fastest and strongest horse for you." He reached out to the Fire Mage. "I should have told you sooner, but I didn't believe until today. You didn't move to stop the Alar. You would have let him kill you rather than prove him right."

By midnight, Luke's men found a healthy black horse that the stablemen claimed to be the youngest and fastest of them all. Xalen, Aleira, Luke, and the other surviving Adridian party members that had traveled to Mavahan waited to send Keleir off. The Fire Mage ordered the Adridian soldiers to stay behind and ensure a peaceful transition for Luke. He firmly believed that assassins loyal to the dead Alar would attempt to take the young man's life and, if the assassins didn't, some other Mavahan noble might.

Xalen Okara wrapped Keleir in a burly hug that nearly suffocated the Fire Mage. "Ipaba isn't so bad!" He laughed at the struggling man. "Not bad at all."

Aleira offered Keleir a smile and curt nod, less warm and inviting than her husband. "Thank you, Ipaba."

"I have a name, you know," Keleir grumbled under his breath.

"Thank you, Keleir," Xalen returned, his jubilant demeanor growing more serious. "Truly. You kept your promise. We are free."

"And you will stay free," Luke added. "I'm going to free all of the slaves."

"One step at a time," Keleir told him, clasping hands with the new Alar. "I'd like to see you stay in power."

"I'll phase it out," the young Alar corrected with a dim smirk.

"Be strong," Keleir replied. "Predators devour the weak."

Luke nodded.

Keleir mounted the black horse and seated himself comfortably in the saddle. He gripped the reins and turned the stallion toward the city gates. "If we ever meet again, friends . . . I may not be the same. Remember that. Should my shadow darken your door, forget your fondness, forget my help, and kill me as you would any other man who threatened you. Believe me when I say it would be a mercy."

The Fire Mage did not allow them to argue. He tore across the desert, a speeding black shadow across pale, moonlit sand.

THIRTY-NINE

SARAN WATCHED THE dust dance in the sunlight. It was all she had to do for two days since speaking with Madam Ophelia. She found it soothing to watch the tiny sparkling particles, their glimmer a slight reminder of the magic she'd been without for months. Her magic danced like gold sparks when it wasn't invisible to the naked eye.

She missed it.

With her power, she could topple empires. She could've ended the war a long time ago. She could've rid the kingdom of her father, taken the throne, and turned back the awful tide of destitution and corruption that had ruined the land. Despite how much she hated and thought ill of her father, she truly was no better than him.

He selfishly spoiled the land, and she selfishly ignored it.

The realization weighed heavy on her heart. How many battles could have been prevented? How many lives saved, if she had only the courage and strength to accept a path she never wanted to tread? What good could have come from giving up the lust for freedom?

Madam Ophelia's words struck deep in her soul and marred the polished brand of pride she'd woven like armor around her identity. Saran had run from her blood as long and as far as she could, and it only made matters worse instead of better. Maybe that was the lesson in all of this? Running from what you are does little good.

Saran felt ill prepared for being the leader of an entire kingdom, even if she'd spent her life hearing the title *princess* wrapped around her name. She'd never learned the art of tactful diplomacy so needed in successful rulers. If anything, she fearfully carried her father's stubborn, unyielding ways. Saran was not graceful. She was not well-read, aside from spell books. She had never been tutored in anything but the basics of academics, war, and magic. Now that she thought about it, Yarin had only ever seen her as a means to get another man power. It explained why he'd never devoted much time to improving her life.

Saran lacked all the qualities to make a good queen, and perhaps that was why she'd run from it for so long. She carried the fear of being just as horrible as the man who spawned her. His blood, his derangement, flowed in her. It had all the potential to corrupt her into his image.

Though, there were qualities she possessed that her father did not. They offered the hope of salvation from becoming what she hated. Saran possessed goodness, courage, and love. She carried the light of her dead mother, Rebecca Vanguard, a woman she did not know, and all the qualities of her ancient house. She knew nothing of the Vanguard family, for they had been stripped from history within the walls in which her father raised her. He'd forbidden anyone to speak of them. But their blood flowed in her just as strongly as the D'mor line.

Saran focused on one sparkling particle in particular as it twisted in the air and caught just a bit more light than the others. She was the last tiny spark of the great Vanguard family that had ruled Adrid for thousands of years. Whatever she wanted, whatever she desired, she couldn't run from that blood either.

The people of Adrid had loved the Vanguards, and while they hated Yarin D'mor, she was still the granddaughter of Dante Vanguard. If she could convince them that his blood was stronger than Yarin's, maybe she could win them over.

Saran didn't know if there was such a thing as life after death. She was raised in the religion of the Vel d'Ekaru, though she'd stopped attending services when she was old enough to speak her mind. Darshan believed in the Prophetess and the Core. He said that when the living died, their energy returned to the Core to be one with the life of the world. He claimed the dead could hear the living if they were spoken to and called by name. Saran had little faith in religion. She liked to believe in what she could see and touch, and perhaps there lay the source of her hatred for prophecy. Still, on this day more than any other, she needed all the help she could get from ghosts and all the guidance the Prophetess could offer.

Saran stood in the warm light of her small barred window, closed her eyes, and spoke the prayer that Rowe taught her long ago, when she eagerly sought the woman of light. "Prophetess guide me. Prophetess speak truth. Prophetess light my path. Prophetess . . ." Saran's brow furrowed. She couldn't force the words out of her mouth. She couldn't recite such a silly prayer to a mystical entity who told riddles and made prophecies about her destiny but never once told them to her face. She clenched her fists, willing to give up. Instead she hardened her resolve to have the contortionist of destiny hear her words.

"Listen here," she said to the air. "I don't know what I am or what I was meant to be, and I don't really care what you claim of me. I've never worshipped you. In fact, I hate you. I hate that you decided my life for me, told everyone around me about it, and then never bothered to show yourself. For all I know, you are a delusion that exists only in the minds of those who choose to believe in you. I don't believe in you, but I have seen the power you have to sway others, and I need that power. I need those words that make men believers of fantasy, that turn villains into heroes, that set men on quests, and send them to die. So Prophetess guide me. Prophetess speak truth. Make them hear me. Make them see me for what I am, if I am worthy to be seen. Help me. Because if you don't, you can go fuck yourself. If you do not help me now, I'll never be what you want me to be. I'll fight and run as long and as far as I can from you. Understand?"

Saran turned her eyes to the dirty stone floor, listening to the clank of metal and leather boots in the corridor outside her cell. "Grandfather, if it is true that you can hear me, then I ask for your nobility, your voice, and your courage. I never knew you, but there are those that did, and I ask that they see you in me."

A jittering nervousness overtook Saran. The reality of her decision becoming more real the more she spoke to faceless figures.

"Finally I pray to whatever gods will have me that I live through this day. I pray that you protect Rowe and keep him from harm, and should harm befall him that you keep him alive." The clash of metal keys in the cell door sent her heart racing. "I pray to see Keleir again, and if it turns out I can't, do what I vowed. Save him from the beast. Keep my vow for me, when I cannot."

The door to her cell opened, silencing her prayer. She stood with her back to the guard, staring at the swirling dust stirred by the rush of air from the swinging door.

"It is time," Odan's voice called to her.

Saran turned to find a healthier Ice Mage than the one she'd seen days before. He had color in his pale cheeks, as much color as a man so cold could possess, and the dark circles under his eyes had lessened. He wore the signature leather armor worn among Mages in the field.

"Time for what?" Saran asked him, arching a brow. Odan was loyal to Yarin; she knew this without doubt. He believed in the old bag of bones, even worshipped him, and followed him without question. A cold uneasiness took hold in Saran, pushing out the nervous jitters she'd felt before.

Odan stepped into the cell, resting his hand on the hilt of his sword. His cyan-colored eyes hardened, and he cast them down to the straw bed. Then he looked her over, taking in her battered appearance, the cuts and scrapes from her beating. He frowned at her and turned to leave the cell, never bothering to close the door.

Saran waited a minute longer before inching through the threshold. He stood in the hall with six armored guards and an executioner. Saran's stomach dropped. She straightened her back and lifted her head high. It had been a stupid thing to ask Madam Ophelia to speak to those who might follow her on her behalf. If she'd spoken to the wrong one . . .

A guard stepped forward, holding in his arms a long, folded cloth. Another stepped out from behind him, holding a pile of roughly folded riding clothes and leather armor. The first guard uncovered the object he held, revealing just the hilt of her sword. No one attempted to justify the items offered. They looked at her with quiet, reverent eyes.

Odan stood at the back with a stern frown creasing his face.

The princess felt heat in her cheeks, felt fire in her blood. This wasn't an execution, but a rescue.

With Odan?

"My oath to Madam Ophelia binds me to this," Odan said, reading the confusion in her eyes. "As long as she lives I cannot bring you harm or help someone else harm you. Therefore, if

I want to live, my only option is to assist. Trust me when I say this is just as painful as dying, only less immediate and final."

Saran nodded slowly, even if his words did little to comfort her. She couldn't trust Odan, no matter what the healer had done to him.

The princess took the clothing from the guard and stepped back into her cell, where she carefully donned it over a weary body. Once dressed, they helped buckle her into the leather armor. The belt, sheath, and sword were the last items to be added, pulled snug about her waist.

No one said a word, the silence becoming the calm before a storm. Saran could almost imagine herself still sleeping on the straw bed, dreaming of her heroic rise to power.

"Thank you," she told the guards.

"My queen," they replied, bowing their heads and backing away.

The title jolted Saran. She'd gone her entire life being referred to as *princess*. She never imagined hearing someone address her as *queen*. She didn't feel like one. She felt exhausted, ragged, and beaten. The look in their eyes made her dig deep down inside for the smallest shred of strength.

"Tell me what you know," she forced out, curling a hand over the hilt of her sword. She gripped it tight to keep from shaking.

"Yarin waits for you in the throne room," the guard who brought her sword replied. Saran stiffened at the use of her father's first name, lacking the title *King* before it. Only she, Keleir, and Rowe had ever trifled with stripping it away from him. Hearing the king's given name from someone else unnerved her and made her feel more out of place than she already did.

"Darshan?"

"No sign of him."

Saran nodded, knowing there could be many reasons for Darshan's tardiness. She also acknowledged the strong chance that Darshan wouldn't come at all, especially if Rowe reached him. He may have changed his plans altogether if he saw the slightest chance of failure. They would have to do this without him, if that were the case, even if it greatly increased their chances of failure.

"I know your faces," the princess said. "But I regret I do not know your names."

"I'm Raener," the guard already speaking to her said and motioned to the others. "That's Coban, Velmier, Brock, Fao, Krevin, and our resident executioner Desmav. You are acquainted with Lord Marki."

"Very," Saran muttered, turning distrusting eyes on the Ice Mage. She took a step closer to them, looking at each one and attempting to memorize their faces with their names. "I'm not sure how many will stand with me today, but you are my strength now. You are my eyes, my ears, and my voice. A ruler is nothing without her people or their pride. I cannot express to you what it means to me that you stand here now and support me." *Because I have no idea what I'm doing*, she thought. "The truth is, Darshan very well might not come today. Lord Blackwell went to him wounded after trying to help me escape, so he might suspect that Yarin would know his plans by now."

"The army did not leave for Salara," Coban said.

Her heart fluttered. There were both good and bad aspects to that decision. Salara would be spared from collateral damage, but if Darshan continued to move on the city, he would face the full force of Yarin's army.

She needed to convince a substantial number of incumbent forces to switch sides. Or could it be even easier? Could she topple Yarin and claim her blood right with the few men in her possession? Hadn't her father achieved a similar feat to earn his crown? The idea brightened her eyes.

"Lord Marki." Saran turned her attention to the Ice Mage, a cool smile dancing on her lips. "I think it is time for the king to address his daughter. Can I count on you to keep your oath to Madam Ophelia?"

Odan sneered.

"Executioner, we will not be needing your services today, though I welcome your help. I need all of you to assure me that no harm will come to my father. This isn't sentimentality talking. In truth, I'd rather you slit his throat."

Odan winced away, but the others grinned gleefully at the idea.

"Whatever harm befalls my father will also fall on me. You are all charged with ensuring that, no matter what happens today, Yarin isn't hurt or killed. This is the greatest request I could ever ask of you, because it means guarding my life while protecting your enemy. Do you accept my request?"

All except Odan gave a stern nod. Odan's lips pursed tight together, his narrow face twisting with indecision.

Saran slapped him on the shoulder. "Cheer up, Odan. Your king will not die this day, nor any other, until the time that nature chooses. Well, that or until the Bind is gone. As I am without magic, you need to be my proxy. Are there any other Mages that would join us?"

"Lord Brenden, the Lightning Mage," Raener said. "I know of him for certain, but not of the others. He waits at the gate for Darshan."

Saran nodded. "Mages respect power, and right now they think Yarin has it." She took a few slow steps down the hall and turned back to them, mulling over the secrets bursting to spill forth from her lips. "What they don't know is that he lost his magic years ago with his disease. Everything that he has accomplished with magic since has been through a proxy—me. If they see Yarin for what he is, they will not accept a weak and powerless ruler."

It was a lie, to some degree. Yarin had not lost his magic. He just didn't use it because it was killing him. Just as one day, she thought bitterly, it would kill her.

The men before her took her words like swords through their stomachs. Each one went ashen before coloring blazing red with rage. This whole time Yarin had been a powerless bag of wind that anyone could rid the world of, and none of them had known. It was her father's one secret that she'd kept for him.

She'd never wanted Keleir or Rowe to know what fate waited for her at the end of the elemental gift of time. The lie she'd shared with them was the same that she told the men before her. If Keleir and Rowe ever knew the truth, they would not let her use her power ever again. But without it there was no one to keep the Oruke in check.

Desmav the executioner nodded off to Odan, whose stiff form leaned against the damp wall. "*He* accepted him."

Saran turned her gaze on Odan, who seemed paler than before and a bit green. She gave him a sympathetic frown, watching the light of admiration fade from his eyes. "I imagine he didn't know. Not many do. Those that realized it never lived long enough to tell anyone. I kept it secret because the repercussions of letting it out would have been . . . intolerable. People that I love would have died, and I would never have seen the light of day again, no matter how useful I was to him. My father's legacy means more to him than anything."

Saran placed her hand on Desmav's shoulder. "Lord Marki has his reasons for being loyal to my father, who has often been like a father to Mage orphans raised in this castle. But whatever those reasons are or were, he is Bound to me in this task by blood. You cannot trust him, but you can trust the curse that controls him. Understood?"

The men nodded, and Odan shoved off the wall to head toward the dungeon exit.

Saran had spent very little time in the dungeon compared to most. Rising to the main floor still made her feel freer than she ever expected to feel in the walls of her home. For the longest time the castle had been a prison, a monolithic symbol of the life she desperately wanted to escape. She could have run away years ago, but something always held her inside them, something always brought her back.

All those years of leading armies beyond the city walls, she'd always followed them back. After every secret mission, she returned. After every outing, every Port to another world, to another city, to another future, she returned. Did that mean destiny proclaimed it or that deep down she knew the course of her life, even as she denied it?

In the hall outside the dungeon doors, two long lines of Adridian soldiers stood ready at attention. Odan stepped around her and passed through to wait at the front, looking back at her with the patience of an irritated toddler. He loved her father, but he loved his life more, and at least she could count on that to keep him in line. The seven men who had been with him just outside her cell door joined the line of defecting soldiers, waiting for her to command them . . . to be everything they'd ever wanted in a leader.

Saran felt that nervous quiver in her hand begin again, so she curled it around the hilt of her sword and clutched the other into a white-tight fist. The length of the line of men lifted her spirits as much as it toppled them, because while it was a fair number of people, it was not enough to take a kingdom. Hopefully it would be enough to take a throne.

Longing wrapped around her heart, and Saran craved the presence of Rowe and Keleir. She wanted to draw from their strength and reassurance. She could let her guard down with them. She could question herself and her choices, but she could do none of that in front of these men. She would trigger doubt where she needed fealty.

As Madam Ophelia said, she could not hide behind the strengths and failings of Rowe Blackwell and Keleir Ahriman anymore. Saran drew on her own strength, on the hatred for the man who killed her mother, the man who tortured her, and the man who tore down the wall that had protected Keleir from the Oruke inside. She stepped toward her bloodright, each clunk of boot against stone growing surer than the last. The six soldiers, Ice Mage, and executioner fell in behind her, and the militia flanked their sides.

The halls emptied on the way to the throne room, with maids and servants ducking into open doors and empty corridors. The few soldiers that were in the halls made no move to stop them and pressed their backs firmly to the walls to get out of their way.

It wasn't until Saran reached the corridor to the throne room that any real opposition appeared. The Saharsiad stood at attention in two short lines just before the tall latched door. Their leader waited patiently behind them, his back pressed against the mahogany wood. He lifted his hand to the veil he wore across his face and dropped it, revealing a scarred visage and a pleased smile. Saran remembered him as the one who nearly crushed her face with his barbed glove.

His men wore deep hoods and veils about their faces, less Adridian and more Mavish in style. They had worked for Yarin since the night he stole the throne from her grandfather. Their expensive fee for protecting Yarin was nothing short of economic blight.

Saran stopped, and the procession behind her came to an abrupt, clanking halt.

"We heard whispers of revolt," the leader of the Saharsiad said, his boots echoing off the vaulted ceiling as he stepped from the long ranks of his men to just outside the edge of their protection. "We should have killed you. I'm sure His Majesty will see the error now. I'm sure he won't mind if you die here at my feet."

Saran appraised him quietly but did not give to his goading. She knew nothing of being queen or courtly grace, but she knew how to intimidate. She offered him unnerving silence, like the ethereal presence of death, and drew her sword slowly, letting the scrape of metal ring through the air. The men behind her followed the sound with a chorus of their own, drawing their weapons and letting the shrill sound signal their allegiance.

The princess admired the clean, sharp blade in her hand. Someone had taken the kindness to introduce it to a whetstone, as she'd ignored it of late. Her gaze flicked from the pale glint of steel to the dark-garbed Mage murderer.

"Four," she said, glancing to the floor and then back to the Saharsiad.

"Four what?" he asked, confusion creasing his tan brow.

"That is how many steps I'll take before you die," she replied, resting the tip of her sword on the metal toe of her boot. Saran concealed her self-hatred with a blank, unfeeling mask, walling away every part of her that hated killing. Now came what she dreaded, the part of this horrid life she'd managed to avoid with the help of her element. She couldn't avoid it this time, not if she wanted to live. "You see, Saharsiad, unlike all those other disobedient Mages you've slaughtered over the years, I had no mentors to teach me my element. I learned it slowly and with difficulty, and what I could not do with magic on the battlefield, I made up with swords and fists. Four steps, that's all I'll give you."

The leader of the Saharsiad sneered and drew the curved short swords at the small of his back. He charged her, and Saran took four strong steps forward, arching the long length of her blade up. But just as she did so, she twisted and ducked beneath his swings and brought her sword blindly behind her, taking off the Saharsiad's head with a strong, sure blow. Indeed, someone had taken care to sharpen her blade.

Saran stood in the midst of the Mage killers now, and they swarmed like hornets. Blood splashed across her face, and metal clashed against metal as her men met them behind her, punching through the line. Screams echoed. Limbs and bodies fell to pile bloody on the dirty stone floor. It only took a moment. The Saharsiad were good fighters, but today they'd chosen a poor strategy.

They'd grown cocky in their years of employment and had allowed themselves to be backed up against the heavy doors, becoming nothing more than cattle herded into the corner for slaughter. She lost two men for every one of theirs. While she had soldiers, the Saharsiad were better trained. When Saran tore her eyes from the last of the dead, she found her force roughly cut in half.

Odan had kept out of the fray, as she'd expected him to, since his magic would not work against the Saharsiad gauntlets. Saran counted him among the men who could handle a sword about as well as polishing his own boots, which of course he never did himself.

Two of her men grabbed the heavy rings that sat center each door to the throne room and drew back, putting their feet and knees into it. The doors slowly groaned open, and the dim firelight of the dark room greeted her.

Yarin looked up from his conversation with the scribe and various nobility at his feet. The king appeared calm, but his nobles shifted uncomfortably. She had no doubt that they were frightened from the screaming cries of battle, but they were also too frightened of the king to flee. Some of them brandished tiny daggers at their waists. She knew them enough to not feel threatened. If they were brave enough to fight, Yarin would not have stayed king long.

Yarin found his daughter wrapped in armor and hatred, emerging from the darkness of the hall with a lengthy procession of his own men at her back.

"What is this?" the king muttered, looking over his men as they filed out from behind Saran and formed a half circle around the king, the scribe, and the nobles that stood with him. Odan took his place just behind Saran but did not dare lift his eyes to see his unhappy master.

The princess looked each noble in the eye before she motioned harshly with her hand for them to leave. They scurried out of the way and fled through the open door. Seconds later, horrified screams flowed back into the room as the weak-willed men found the carnage in the hall.

Saran tilted her head at her father before speaking. "What do you think is happening?"

Yarin's mouth worked, his expression growing sour. He turned his eyes to the blood spilling in from the hall. "It seems I'll be hanging a lot of people today."

"No one's gettin' hanged today, my king." Desmav the executioner chuckled from Saran's right.

The King of Adrid drummed his fingers against the arm of his chair before he turned his glassy eyes to Odan with a sneer. "You? Of all people? You *hate* her."

"Aye," Odan muttered, barely lifting his eyes. "I do not want this, but I am Bound by a blood oath that healer witch Ophelia placed on me."

"Where is the key to my Bind?" Saran asked, moving another inch forward.

Yarin shook his head angrily. "You're not getting it. Not even when I'm dead. You'll search this castle over and you'll never, ever find it. It cannot be seen!"

Saran's jaw set tight. "Then I'll go through this life united as one with my powerless people. Now get out of that chair. You are no longer ruler of this land."

The king shook, rage turning his face a horrible shade of red. He struck his chest hard, and Saran felt it in her own. She did not wince, not even when he struck himself again. Did he truly plan to beat himself to death to get back at her?

"Odan," Saran whispered. "Detain our king for his own safety."

Odan's cyan eyes lit frost-blue, and a cool draft filtered through the air. Ice seized the king's hands where they sat and wrapped like protective armor around his body. It was, for Odan, a very kind gesture.

Saran started her ascent to the throne when the ground shook beneath her feet. The old stone walls cracked, and dust wafted from the ceiling, followed by a deep tremor. A harsh crash tore stone from the walls and rained it down across the floor, and a huge boulder rolled behind Saran, clipping her booted heel as it passed. Her men scrambled out of its way, some diving to the floor to keep from being crushed.

The boulder rolled to a stop, sitting still and quiet before shattering. Dust and rubble exploded into the air. As the dust settled, a woman of average height, with chestnut hair and deep brown eyes, emerged. She wore earthy toned leather and canvas, with mud smeared like war paint across her cheeks. She lifted her hands, and the rubble at her feet levitated from the floor and swirled around her legs.

Behind the Earth Mage, three rebels in patchwork armor emerged from the blood-soaked hall. She only recognized the old, kindly faced man in the center, whose eyes swirled ocean blue.

"Darshan."

FORTY

KELEIR BARELY STOPPED to rest the horse. He knew what that meant for the beast, who foamed at the mouth and charged forward on straining knees. The desert heat would kill them both if he didn't make it as close to the border as he possibly could. He felt shame and guilt for how hard he'd ridden the young horse. He tried to show mercy by keeping close to the shore, with its firmer sand and where the spray of seawater could cool him.

The rising sun on the second day sent Keleir's heart into his throat. He could just see the dark hint of forest at the edge of his horizon, miles and miles away. The gold light cresting the sky blinded him, but he rode for it with all the muster he could coax into the horse he abused.

Soon the brisk gallop of the beautiful creature began to break with stumbles and annoyed jerks of the head. Keleir murmured apologies to the horse and pressed him onward. He tried to ignore the horror in him for what he did and he promised the creature that, when death came, it would come quick. He assured the beast that it died for good, that he would not fail to reach the border or his brother. He begged the horse to go on longer.

Just as he felt the creature give in to exhaustion, its gallop grew stronger. Keleir knew the horse didn't understand him, and that it only appeared so by coincidence, but he wanted to believe that it willingly chose to give its life to help.

"Yes," he urged, patting the beast's neck. "Come on! That's it! Go!"

The gallop grew fluid and swift. Keleir's heart sang with hope. He laughed like a madman and sat up straighter in the saddle, thanking whatever gods would have him for their mercy.

Then the horse reared up with a great, horrible whinny and threw the Fire Mage onto his back before it collapsed sideways in the sand. Keleir rolled quickly to avoid the creature's crushing weight. The beast gave great watery, heaving breaths before it flattened into the sand and died.

Keleir stumbled to his feet, shaking his head until he felt dizzy. "No!" He turned his eyes to the distance and the trees still so far away. "Get up!" He scooped the reins from the sand and pulled hard. The horse weighed more than he could lift, and the head just drew up with each futile tug. The beast never rose. "Get. Up!" Keleir tugged harder on the reins until the leather snapped and he fell back into the sand.

He knew, deep down, that the beast had covered an improbable amount of ground in the last day. He knew that it should have died a while ago, and only by some miracle had it survived as long as it had. Perhaps the beast had understood his urgency and attempted valiantly to get him home.

Keleir knelt near the horse with tears in his eyes and patted its sweat-slick neck. "Thank you for your sacrifice, my friend. I am sorry. I promise, it will not be for nothing." He rested there a bit longer to offer the beast a moment of silence before rising to his feet and turning toward the distant green.

Then he ran.

FORTY-ONE

"PRINCESS." DARSHAN SMILED, his eyes twinkling as they always did when he greeted her. The twinkle dulled when his eyes turned on the captured king. The rebel leader grew tall and triumphant. "Your people have you surrounded. The gate that kept you safe is open. The men meant to guard you have bowed and let me in, and the few that fought against us met the sword. The empire you carved out of the remnants of a once-great kingdom is no more, Yarin D'mor, and it fell without a fight."

Yarin growled, wiggling against the cold bite of the ice that held him. "What I have made from the ashes of this lives on. You may have gained a castle, a title, and a throne, but the war, my friend, is won, and it is I who am victorious. This is fleeting compared to the glory that comes. The Vel d'Ekaru will rise."

"He has risen and fallen in the same breath." Darshan cocked his head high. "Luke Canin has seen to that. The Vel d'Ekaru will never return from the Deadlands. He is no more."

Saran's brow furrowed. She stepped hurriedly down from the podium, brushing past the rebel that stood protectively before Darshan. "What do you mean?"

Darshan's eyes cast her a sad, sympathetic glance. "It had to be done, my dear. It had to be. He turned into the monster, and I honored Rowe's last request. If Keleir could not be saved from the beast, he wanted me to end it before he hurt you."

Saran's heart dropped into her stomach. Her head felt light and her knees weak. "Last request . . ."

"His injuries were too grave," Darshan whispered, brushing her hair back with his hand. "He didn't make it. The healers had already been set to the road, and we did all we could to stop the bleeding. We couldn't get him to them in time. Rowe Blackwell died a hero to us. His history is now rewritten. He has absolved himself of his sins against us."

Saran shook her head fiercely. "No." Darshan reached for her, but she pulled away. "No. He is not dead. They are not dead!"

"Keleir didn't come back, because he'd already turned on you. He was the Vel d'Ekaru. Would he not be here, by your side, if he were himself? Would he have left you to this misery alone? No! Not if he loved you."

Saran roared at him. "You had no right!"

"It is for the best, Child. The Prophetess has guided us to this moment. Your husband is dead, which means that a legitimate marriage can happen between the two of us. The people will be united with the army once more. Your grandfather's kingdom will be united after all this time."

"You dare speak to me of marriage on the day you tell me you *murdered* my husband?" Saran shook with rage, wishing so much for the power in her blood, for the ability to age him to dust. She cared little if she cursed herself for it. Rage consumed her soul, killing what fondness she had for the man who had loved her mother, until cold realization dawned. "You planned this."

"This was all you," Darshan replied, motioning to the soldiers in the room. "You drew the rug from beneath Yarin's feet. I was surprised to arrive and find the gates open and the men ushering me in with open arms. This was you! You brilliant, beautiful, strong Queen of Adrid."

"You killed Keleir so you could be king!" She lifted her sword from her side and pointed it at him. "As long as I live, as long as I breathe, I will never let your deceitful ass sit on that throne. I care not what unity it destroys; I will see your blood, Ishep Darshan. I will paint myself in it. The demon's wrath you should have feared is mine, not the Vel d'Ekaru!"

Saran swiped her sword at him. The stone at her feet buckled and broke, and earth reached up before her in a great wall. The blade struck the stone and bounced off, chipping the metal. Darshan gave a heavy sigh behind the wall, and water trickled through the cracks in the rock and poured onto the floor at her feet. It swirled and danced around her before worming off, up the stairs to wrap about Yarin's legs.

The rock wall dropped with shuddering protest.

"I don't want it to be this way," Darshan said as his water magic soaked into Yarin's clothes. Saran, through the Bind, felt it constricting like a snake around his legs.

She turned to her men. "Remember what I asked of you."

They nodded.

She flashed Darshan a final look before bolting for her father, grabbing Odan by the scruff of his shirt and pulling him with her. They collided with the king and his throne, knocking it backward. They rolled into the far wall, near the tapestry that hung behind the throne. "The door!" Saran shouted at Odan, who ripped the great tapestry sigil of the D'mor house from the wall and kicked open the wooden door hidden behind it. He went feetfirst, coating the spiral staircase with enough ice to create a slippery slide.

Saran pushed Yarin's weak body through the door, feeling every bump and bruise made by the hard landing at the bottom. She followed close behind him, skidding round and round, down the never-ending ice escape. Desmav and Coban were next, leaving the others to keep the rebels from following.

A long, narrow corridor greeted them at the bottom, nearly pitch black save for narrow slits in the right wall where sunlight cast bright white lights on the stone. Odan waited until the last person slid to a stop, and then the ice melted. Water rushed in a torrent down the stairs and around their ankles.

"Coban, Desmav, bring up the rear," Saran ordered as she scooped her aged father up by his weak arms and dragged him to his feet.

He batted her away angrily, but she reasserted her grip on him, dragging him close to her face. "If you will not run, I will drag you. Understand?"

Saran pushed him forward, shoving him along with her body. "Odan! Come on." But Odan didn't follow, and when she looked back, she found him stalking in the opposite direction toward Desmav and Coban. "Odan!"

The Ice Mage grabbed the men from behind and drove ice-covered hands into their chests. Each one arched back, gasping on a dying breath as Odan wrapped his hands around the still-beating organ in their chests and clenched tight.

"Odan! No!"

Beside her, King Yarin D'mor laughed.

The light in Odan's eyes grew blinding bright. Ice sprouted from every pore and orifice Desmav and Coban possessed until their entire beings were covered in a hard, cold shell. Their bodies grew, limbs elongating until they stood eight feet tall. Each hand sprouted daggerlike fingers, and the hard ice shell that encased them slowly bled translucent. They stood like sea glass statues before their Ice Mage maker. Odan slowly removed his hands, revealing vibrant red beating hearts in the breasts of his creations. When his work was done, the Ice Mage slumped against the wall.

Above them the ceiling cracked. The stairs shook. Dust wafted through the air as the Earth Mage tore the walls down around them.

"Protect us," Odan told his Alikons. "Let nothing pass."

He collected himself and turned from them. The Alikons grumbled an unearthly agreement to his command and faced the opening to the stairwell, shoulder to shoulder, cold icy holes for eyes watching for trouble. Odan did not meet Saran's eyes as he brushed past her, grabbing hold of his king and dragging him off down the hall.

"You're a bastard," Saran seethed, skipping to catch up.

"I did what was necessary to protect my king, nothing more. Oh, and by the way, *Princess*, this is a dead end."

"Not entirely dead."

"The next levels are flooded."

"There is a way out; we only need to swim to it."

Saran eyed her weary father as he stumbled along, struggling with each breath. She couldn't remember the last time she'd seen him exert so much energy. Not since she was a little girl and he was healthy and whole.

They went down a short staircase but stayed straight along the outer edge of the castle and cliffside overlooking the Andrian Sea. The sound of running water grew louder, starting as a soft trickle before slowly transitioning into a gentle roar.

"This was an escape route centuries ago . . . a means to get the king out, should the palace be stormed. I used to hide behind that door to eavesdrop," Saran whispered. "When Father spent long hours in the room, I would go out this way. Then, one day, the old walls cracked and a spring opened, flooding the path. If we can swim past the flooded area, it comes out through a grate in the courtyard. We just have to avoid the tug of the water toward the cliffside, where the engineers opened another crack to try to rid the passage of water."

The Alikons behind them roared. The walls shook and chunks of stone rattled off the ceiling to plop down in the water ahead of them.

"Wonderful," Odan muttered. "We've got to try to swim a dangerous, pitch-black passage with a decrepit old man and hopefully not get sucked out the drain."

Odan paused as his feet sank into black water halfway down the stairs. He gauged the temperature of the water and turned back for Yarin, grabbing his arms and helping him down into the water, until it washed up around their waist.

"You should swim first," Saran said to Odan, propping Yarin against the wall. She eyed her father's hunched and silent form. He hadn't said a word since the brisk laugh he'd offered as Odan stole the lives of Desmav and Coban. While uncharacteristic of him, she thanked whatever gods had blessed her with his complacency.

"If this is some clever ruse to murder me . . ."

Saran glowered at him in the very, very limited light they had. "If I wanted you dead, I would have stabbed you when you turned good men into Alikons."

Odan scoffed and waltzed off down the passage before taking one step too far and plunging into the water. Saran edged away from Yarin, listening and waiting for Odan to pop his head up again. After several long, agonizing seconds, she almost believed he'd completely abandoned them until he finally shot out of the water with a wet gasp.

"It's a short swim and not hard to navigate. We won't be troubled by the drain."

"For a short swim, it sure took you long enough." Saran sighed, turning back to grab Yarin. "If we both take him, we can get him across with little effort on his part, aside from him holding his breath. You can do that, right, old man?" Saran grabbed Yarin and pulled him off where he sat on the steps, half-submerged in water. He hung as deadweight in her arms. "Yarin?" Saran shook him harder. "Yarin!" She stared down at the withered old king, shock stealing the words out of her mouth. She felt at his neck for the pulse. "Wake up, you old goat!"

Yarin didn't wake. Saran lowered her ears to his chest but heard no heartbeat. "Father?" The word slipped from her lips, belonging to some small part of her that still longed for him to be the father she always wanted, a tiny part not yet beaten into submission. After a long silence, Saran let him slip back down to lie in the water. "We ran him to death."

Odan rushed through the water, grabbing hold of Yarin's body and hauling him out to rest high on the steps. He checked the king, just as Saran had, his hand trembling ever so slightly as it rested on the old man's forehead. The Ice Mage glared at her. "*You* ran him to death."

Odan flopped into the water, sitting on the stairs just below Yarin's resting body. In the darkness, Saran could barely make out the Ice Mage's form, but she could feel his sadness in the change of temperature around them. The water grew colder.

Yarin had been her father, yes . . . but he'd been Odan's in some strange way as well. If truth be told, he'd been a far better father to Odan than he'd ever been to her.

"How is it you're not dead?" Odan's voice trembled out, half anger and half sorrow. She hated him for loving her father so much, for finding cause to love a man who had loved her so little.

Saran stared at their shadows in the darkness. "The rules. If he died of old age or sickness, and not another's hand, I would not be harmed. I'm free from his stupid curse, but not this stupid Bind. If I'd known that the key to my freedom lay in exercise, I would have made him run a long time ago."

Odan's eyes flared blue, and the water around her solidified for a second before melting away once the Ice Mage wrangled his anger, or perhaps because attempting to harm her hurt him.

Odan stood slowly, the water sloshing around his legs. "We will come back for his body," he decided. "We will bury him as a king." Saran imagined he needed to say that aloud to justify the need to abandon the corpse of his beloved adoptive father.

She fiddled with the metal around her wrist, frowning into the darkness. The one person who could give her the key now grew cold in the bowels of a broken escape tunnel built for the sole purpose of preserving his life. She was trapped within the city, and without her magic, for the foreseeable future.

Behind them, the Alikons raged and roared and screamed before finally silencing. The Ice Mage shivered, his cold eyes glowing as the power he'd given returned. The Alikons were no more. Odan grew quiet, listening behind them, absorbed in their deaths. The unfortunate part of creating life was that it always hurt when it ended.

Odan descended deeper into the pool with her. "I wonder what your Alikon would look like."

Saran stiffened. "Nothing special," she muttered, turning away from him and wading out into the water.

"Have you ever made one?" Odan asked, stepping up behind her.

"Once," she replied, feeling at the edge of the steps with her foot, looking for the point where Odan's feet had dropped out from under him before. The idea of dropping unprepared into black, icy waters didn't appeal to her, even on a good day.

"What did you do with it?"

Saran frowned at the water. She curled her fingers in it, thankful for the dark around them. "I married him."

Silence fell between them, with the cool rush of water filling the void. Odan broke the shocked pause with a loud, deep-bellied laugh. It echoed harsh off the walls. "Keleir? But he's not misshapen or transformed."

Saran clenched her eyes, regretting her admission. It slipped out, a secret she'd been holding for five years, and she'd admitted it to Odan of all people. "It is different! I didn't alter him into some elemental beast or something he's not . . . I simply changed what might have been. I reached into Keleir and found what he was without the Oruke. I made him that. He was there all along, trapped behind a wall the Oruke created, and I willed him into life. Without our connection . . ."

Odan gleefully finished the terrible thought for her. "That version of Ahriman ceases to exist."

"He ceases to have *control*. He always exists, trapped inside, helpless in his own body, able to experience without acting." Saran clenched her hands tight. She felt a shudder in her heart, a flutter that didn't beat quite right. The escape had been a perfect distraction from Darshan's admission, but now, as she spoke of Keleir, the truth came flooding back to her. "I suppose it doesn't matter now . . . He's dead. They're both dead."

The ache blistered her heart so profoundly that it stole her breath. She wanted to fade into tears, drift into the water, and grieve. But she wasn't that type of woman. There would be time to grieve, but not now, and not in front of Odan.

"Let's get out of here." Saran stepped down and readied herself to swim when Odan grabbed her arm and pulled her back a step.

"Can you do it?" His voice trembled with anger, but something else. Something hidden just beneath the surface of his quiet rage.

"Do what?"

His hand tightened on her arm. "Lead us?"

Saran looked aghast at Odan, who hated her and accepted her as his queen all at once. She could not see him well, nor could he see her, but she knew he had to sense her shock ripple in the water. "Why do you care? Why would you want me to?"

"Yarin raised me. I thought of him as a father. I think that is why I hate you so much. I would have killed for him to see me as his child, to adore me as his son. You were his blood and you treated him with such disrespect, and I couldn't stand to watch. You brought catastrophe and chaos to what he created, and I wanted nothing more than to prove my loyalty to him by showing him how unworthy you were. With him gone, I have no other purpose. I know no life but this one. I am bound to serve you because of Ophelia's curse. All I want to know is, will you lead us? Do you have that in you? Or will you give in to Darshan?"

Saran swallowed. Out of all the people in the world she knew, Odan was the last person she thought to ever have deep conversations with in the depths of such uncertainty. The princess stepped into the blackness of the water without providing Odan an answer.

FORTY-TWO

THE SUN HAD just burned off the morning mist when Rowe ventured to the edge of town and stood at the wide-open gates, staring down the empty road to the edge of the horizon. He listened to the wind, the trees, and the birds, but other than that he heard nothing. The villagers hid in their homes, or in cellars, quietly waiting for the worst to blow over. A few had joined his men at the village wall to wait for the Adridian army.

The rebels with him were at the blacksmith shop, just at the edge of town, near the gate. They gathered around the forge fires, despite his incessant urging for them to ready themselves for Yarin's army. Eventually he gave up. With a nearly empty village, he saw no reason to stand at the gate to block the army from entering.

But the army never came. Deep down, Rowe knew they wouldn't. Yarin, while crazy, wasn't stupid.

The Lightning Mage kicked the loose dirt with his boot. He couldn't stand being here in this place while Saran sat trapped in the castle. He watched time waste away before his eyes when he would be of better use there, with her. He lifted his gaze to the sky and listened once more to the world for any sign of an army. Finding birds and the rustle of trees, he turned back for the blacksmith's shop. They would all be of better use in Andrian.

When he turned to go to them, the rebels were already waiting behind him.

"I guess we're all thinking the same thing. Let's help our brothers in Andrian," he told them. "I'll Port us there."

"We don't need your help," the rebel to the far right said, spitting on the earth at Rowe's feet. "We can Port our own way with our own Mages."

Rowe frowned at him, ignoring the spit on the earth before his temper got the better of him. "Fine, I'll go my own way."

"That won't be happening either."

Rowe snarled. "And what makes you think you can stop me?"

A sharp pain struck him in the back, digging up beneath his ribs. He sucked in a breath and pulled away, stumbling on his feet to look behind him. Morning light glinted off the dagger in the scrawny man's hand. The Lightning Mage growled and drew his sword. "I am on *your* side!"

The man they called Joseph frowned. He wore a horrible scar across his face. "That may be true, but Darshan needs you dead. So . . . dead you shall be."

Rowe's brow knit tight together. An ache splintered up his spine and stabbed into his skull. His step faltered. "What?" The betrayal stole the strength of his voice, and it faltered on his lips as little more than a whisper.

"You're not useful anymore. Your visions aren't useful anymore. The Vel d'Ekaru is dead. Long live the King and Queen of Adrid, Saran and Ishep Darshan!"

Rowe shook his head, like the man's words reached inside his mind and scrambled his brain. He repeated them to himself, just to make sure he wasn't mad, that he wasn't dreaming, that he hadn't heard him say . . .

Remember my words, Rowe Blackwell, and know that you will be betrayed, the Prophetess's voice whispered in the back of his mind.

Again Rowe shook his head, feeling the trickle of blood down his back. Darshan wanted Rowe dead so that he would not come between the rebel leader and his ultimate goal: a union that would legitimize his rule as king. Rowe had laid his trust in the wrong man. Gods, a man he'd taken to like son to father. A man he'd idealized. A man he'd obeyed and loved.

Darshan had not been sneaky with his plans. He'd hinted to them. Time and again he'd mentioned transitioning power with marriage, and Saran always brushed it off as though it were a choice. The rebel leader had catered to them, indulged Rowe and Keleir, two men hated by his rebels, and pretended to let them help with his cause. He'd even pretended to care for Rowe. But he'd planned this all along.

The urgency to get to Andrian roared in him.

He had to find Saran.

Lightning ignited in Rowe's eyes, crackling bright neon blue. The warm hum of electricity ran through the blade of his sword. "Well, come kill me, then," he growled and slung his sword around at them. White-hot bolts of lightning arched off the metal, colliding with the twelve men. But energy expended reverberated back to him, as if they wore magic shields to protect them. It struck his chest, tossing him off his feet to land with a hard, rolling thud against the half-dried mud.

The smell of singed leather burned his nose, and smoke wafted off his body. He didn't move for a long minute, and the men, thinking him dead, crept closer. One of them that Rowe knew to be an Earth Mage rolled up his sleeve to show off the crude makeshift version of a Saharsiad gauntlet, the kind that protected Mage hunters against magic as much as it blocked them from using it. Each of the twelve men around him wore one to protect them from his magic.

Rowe winced at the gauntlets, disgust twisting his features. His eyes brightened with wisps of electric current, and above them the sky began to turn black with thunderheads. Lightning popped against the clouds, every crackle in Rowe's eyes reflected in a web across the sky. He knew it did him little good to use magic against them when they wore those bonds, but his rage would not be quenched.

"A Mage that wears the gauntlet of a Saharsiad willingly is an abomination," the Lightning Mage sneered. He moved his hands to his singed chest, rubbing at the ache in his bones. "You forsake your oath to the Core. Continue this, and she will abandon you. All things come with a price, and we were born of Her."

"It is you whom She has abandoned. The Core and the Prophetess. Where are They now in your hour of need? Where is your brother, the Vel d'Ekaru? Where is your princess?" The rebel spoke, but Rowe caught the shift in his eyes as his fingers began to remove the leather trappings on the gauntlet. Even these men wouldn't risk the Core abandoning them, no matter what they thought of him.

The wind grew harsh, tossing their cloaks and hair about. What little dry dirt remained on the surface of the earth became a cloud of dust around them. The lightning that danced across the sky crashed to the ground off in the distance, and the earth shook with thunder. One by one, the rebels dropped their gauntlets and took up their swords.

The lightning struck the roof of a cottage, setting the thatching aflame. It popped and danced down the main road. The men around him collected, but Rowe did not move. He clenched his fists against the leather he wore and straightened his spine against the earth. A tickle started in the air around him, a current of energy that sent the hairs on their skin out like spikes, and the hair on their heads floated in strands about them.

Poor, uneducated village men who did not know the power of a storm or that a man born of it could call down the fire of heaven upon them.

The one with the dark scar across his face, Joseph, glowered at Rowe. His scarred visage had always been vaguely familiar to the Lightning Mage but never more so than now. But the way Rowe remembered it, Joseph had been looking up at him. Joseph snarled, "Accept this fate, murderer. Accept the punishment you deserve for the blood on your hands! For murdering my family."

Rowe's stiff form settled in an instant. The light emptied from his eyes, and the storm around them quieted.

That's right. He'd murdered people. The faces of the dead and those he'd harmed in his devotion to Yarin blurred together until that moment. But now he could pick Joseph out of the thousands of memories he'd buried inside his guilt-ridden quest for redemption. He saw Joseph begging for his life and the lives of his family, and then he saw his own hands, his own sword, cut Joseph down. He'd killed Joseph's family in this very town. That was why Darshan had led him here to die.

Redemption.

A loud, ragged breath escaped Rowe. His gaze darted to them all, maddened in its realization. He'd spent many years trying to atone for his sins by helping Darshan on his path to the throne. But no matter what he did, it would never be enough payment for those sins.

He'd selfishly sought forgiveness. He'd broken promises. He'd lied. He'd risked his brother's soul and Saran's favor just to get to the end of his guilt. He'd worked to get to this moment, this day, and the price of his salvation would not be in Darshan's crown and Yarin's death. The price would be his life, and, after all the death and sorrow, it seemed the most fitting solution.

Rowe Blackwell had spent years desperately searching for salvation.

Now he'd found it in the sword of the man whose family he'd slaughtered.

The Lightning Mage settled into the mud. "I accept."

FORTY-THREE

KELEIR'S LUNGS HURT.

His sides hurt.

He couldn't breathe.

But he ran.

He ran across the shifting soft sand, struggling against the uneven ground and raging heat. The edge of the forest taunted him, just a few yards away at last. He pushed fiercely, tried to run harder, even as his knees began to give. His joints throbbed, and his lungs filled with fluid. He imagined the horse felt something similar before it died, and he tried to ignore the bubble of shame for murdering the beast in such a brutal fashion.

He counted in groups of ten, telling himself that he could go on for ten more, and followed that with another set and another. He did this until the shade of trees enveloped him. The thriving life of the world washed over his skin the closer he grew to the forest. The gift of that connection came with a dark price, as the Oruke stirred awake inside his mind.

Agonizing pain ripped through his chest, as if the Oruke were bursting out from his sternum. He cried out, his step faulting, and he clutched his chest as he ran.

"Let me do this," he roared at the creature. "Let me save him!"

The Oruke chuckled, writhing inside him.

"Please!" Keleir begged.

The Fire Mage ran blindly, focusing all his energy into his feet. He burst through the dry brush at the desert's edge, and as soon as the first foot touched the moist forest floor, he fell into fire.

FORTY-FOUR

JOSEPH STOOD OVER Rowe, the point of his sword pressing against the Lightning Mage's chest. "This might be the most honorable thing you've ever done," he said and lifted the sword into the air.

The world slowed. Rowe absorbed every detail, even down to the sound of the Joseph's leather gloves as they tightened over the hilt. It felt cowardly to close his eyes, so he watched, wondering whether or not Saran would ever forgive him.

She'd never willingly marry Darshan, not when she found out the truth, and she'd definitely find out. She was clever. But she was outnumbered and magically handicapped. She wouldn't live longer than today, and . . . he didn't want to live a day beyond hers.

This wasn't what the Prophetess foretold, but Saran had told him over and over that such things weren't real. If only he'd believed her. Maybe the deity was a figment of his imagination. Maybe he'd created her to help him atone for what he'd done. It hardly mattered now. At least he could find peace in death. At least he could find freedom from his demons once he returned to the Core.

Rowe focused on the sword as it fell and took a deep, calming breath.

The blade turned red-hot at the point before melting and burning away to tiny embers and ash. The rebel holding it shook, opening his mouth to scream, but fire consumed him from the inside out before he could utter a note. The twelve men burned away to glowing embers and ash before floating to rest on the damp earth around him.

Rowe's body registered what happened long before his mind did, taking in a deep, sharp breath. He bolted up and turned to the dark figure standing in his peripheral vision. Keleir, pale and clutching his chest, stood just a few yards away. Sweat beaded his forehead and soaked his clothes. He looked like a man who had run for his life. Keleir's eyes found Rowe. The Lightning Mage saw fondness and love in those demon red eyes, and he knew then that Keleir was not lost to him yet.

For just a second, Rowe spotted Saran, a rippling mirage between them, waving desperately at Keleir and begging to be seen. The moment Rowe thought he saw her, she disappeared. The Lightning Mage knew it to be his imagination, his desperate need to have them both safe.

Keleir took a step forward and winced, dropping to his knees. The ashes of the dead littering the ground fluttered and lifted and swirled up into a dark cloud. Rowe ran through it, bursting from the center to fall before his brother.

"Why did you do that?" he called to Keleir.

Keleir looked up to him, falling forward to rest against the hard grip the Lightning Mage had on his shoulders. The Fire Mage's eyes were wide with pain, and black seeped in from their edges. He'd fought the Oruke, but something worse came for him now.

"I saved you," Keleir whispered, relief bringing tears to his eyes. "I made it in time."

Rowe roared, shaking his brother. "Gods be damned, you are a fool! Do you know what will happen now?"

Keleir nodded, turning his gaze to the swirling ash behind his brother. "The Core will claim the price, a life for a life." Keleir had met this curse before, when he'd killed his father with magic as a child. The Core had claimed the price, but all it had done was give the Oruke control. Perhaps this time, he'd finally die.

Rowe shook his head, his fingers knotting in Keleir's tunic. "No . . ."

"It's too late," the Fire Mage murmured. "I feel it already. I feel them. I feel their pain."

"No!" Rowe wrapped his arms around his brother's waist and hauled him to his feet. "We'll outrun it."

"That's impossible."

"We'll outrun it, damn it!"

"No one can outrun death."

"Then we'll go to Saran. She can fix this. She fixed you before."

Keleir's legs barely held him. He sagged, heavy against his brother's side. He focused on forming words, speaking through gritted teeth. "You know she can't."

"We will try! Damn you, why did you do this, Keleir? Why did you do this? I was prepared to die! I'd accepted it. I chose it! Why did you do this?"

Keleir met his brother's angry gaze. "Because I love you. No matter our faults or fears, no matter your doubts . . . I have always, even in the blindness of rage, loved you. And if my last memory on this world has to be something, I want it to be that I saved you."

Rowe clenched his jaw so tightly it hurt. He held Keleir up, supporting Keleir's weight as the Fire Mage had supported him in everything else. How could he have doubted? How could he have ever doubted? His brother never lost faith in him, no matter how many times Rowe questioned him. He never stopped loving him. "You did. You saved me." *In more ways than one.* "Now let me save you."

As if all the thousands that the Oruke killed came to claim his soul, the swirling cloud of ash and death grew far larger than the ashes of twelve men. The ash swirled until it formed a face. The mouth opened in a great wailing motion, exerting a silent scream. It swooped up and down and opened wide to gobble them up, but Rowe took his brother away in a shower of sparks before the curse could claim him.

FORTY-FIVE

YEARS OF MUD and disuse had cemented the heavy iron grate above Saran and Odan's heads to the courtyard floor. She couldn't remember a single day when anyone bothered to show the courtyard an ounce of interest, least of all to clean from the stone the mud tracked in by horses. She beat her hands against the metal and mud rained down on her head in heavy wet globs.

Saran pushed with all her might, and beneath her, the Ice Mage pushed with all of his, his arms wrapped so tightly around her waist that under any normal circumstances she probably would have flayed him. But given their current predicament, she welcomed the help.

"Put your back into it, Princess," Odan muttered through gritted teeth as he strained to hold her and keep his balance.

"Shall I give you a boost and you try it?"

Saran shifted and did as he instructed, placing her back against the grate and standing with all her strength. The grate lifted away too quickly for it to be of her own doing. Hard hands dragged her from the hole and to her feet. Saran jerked from their grasp and whirled to take in her surroundings.

Darshan waited at the top of the staircase, standing between the castle's open doors. His men stood at the foot of the entry stairs, between the two great fire pits that topped the short pillars at either side of the stairs. A mess of haggard faces, as dirty as the muddied earth around them, filled the courtyard. For them, time stopped when they allowed Darshan into the city, and it wouldn't start again until they knew for certain who would take the throne.

Even the stableboy, who always greeted her when she arrived home, watched hopefully from his usual spot near the fire pits, along with his soldier friend who occasionally fed the flames out of boredom. The hatchet he used to whack small logs into kindling lay propped against the pillars. Saran eyed the tool, fiddling with the Bind around her wrist.

"I used that same route, you know, to escape your father the night your mother died," Darshan said as he sauntered down the steps.

Saran smeared the mud from her face. "It has seen better days, I'm sure."

Darshan eyed the hole darkly. "Tell the others to come out."

"Come out," Saran called down. The Ice Mage wiggled his spindle-thin body from the drain.

Darshan drew his sword. "And the king."

The king. Her father. Saran shifted involuntarily, as if he'd struck her, looking back to the black hole in the earth. Her father deserved no sentimentalism from her, and yet she couldn't stop the part of her from feeling sorrow at the lost chance to redeem him. Saran knew what he was, knew how she hated him, and yet some small childlike part of her loved him anyway. "The king is dead."

The courtyard hushed, the crackle of the fire pits growing like a roar in her ears.

"And you live?"

"He died a natural death, so I live."

Darshan's ocean gaze settled on Saran, and he sheathed his sword. "Then it's over. We have no cause to quarrel. The king is dead. Long live the queen."

No cheers followed his proclamation. The men and women around her glanced between themselves and murmured, but no one fell to a knee or shared in Darshan's enthusiasm. Perhaps they were in shock.

Saran spotted Madam Ophelia leaning out of an open window. The woman sported a deeper frown than usual, and Saran had to guess that she couldn't be pleased with how things were turning out. Her hopes of a Grand Feminine were lost if Darshan seized power through her.

Darshan whirled on his men. "I said, long live the queen!"

"Long live the queen!" they returned in one rattling voice that echoed off the bastion walls and rickety towers stretching to the sky. Saran stared at Darshan, burning her gaze through him and reading every part of him. He possessed great intelligence, a truly gifted manipulator who could rival Yarin in his coldness. He'd befriended her, befriended Rowe, and he'd used them. Knowing that every step she'd taken since joining his cause had been to get him to this very moment made her ill.

Saran knew that his men outnumbered hers. She knew that they were loyal to him. She knew that, if she did not go along with his ruse, he could whisper a word, and she'd be just as helpless and damned as her mother had been to Yarin. She couldn't fight him, not without magic. She couldn't fight him, not without numbers. She stood alone against him, and her only saving grace would be that she carried the courage of a Vanguard and the devious, conniving nature of a D'mor. Together, those traits had been what her father had hated and admired most about her. She understood that now.

Saran needed Darshan in order to earn the trust of the people, just as he needed her in order to earn the legitimacy of the throne.

She stepped away from Odan, waltzing languorously to where Darshan stood. The rebels parted for her. The princess stole a glance at Madam Ophelia, finding it hard to tell the woman her plan in such a fleeting manner. There wasn't enough clarity or emotion in the brief meeting of their eyes to put Madam Ophelia at ease for what would happen soon. Saran couldn't afford to have a vengeful healer with knowledge of poison on her hands—or, perhaps, she needed just that. A dark idea began to worm its way into her brain.

Saran turned her gaze back to Darshan and raised her muddied face high. "Long live the king."

The courtyard roared.

The cheers thundered through her chest. Just as quickly as they'd begun, they fell away to whispers. The clear sky turned dark at an unnatural pace. The courtyard, forgetting the proclamations of king and queen, turned their heads to the black cloud gathering in the distance. Blacker than any storm Saran had ever seen, it sped toward them like the angry rush of an exploding volcano.

Blue light flashed at the corners of her eyes, and two figures tumbled out of a crackling electric portal, one half dragging the other. Her heart seized in her chest.

"Rowe! Keleir!"

Rowe's eyes lifted, his gaze alive with his element and the static so thick in the air around him that she imagined, if she touched him without the bind, her heart would stop as easily as if he'd crushed it in his hand. He guarded his brother with a wall of current to keep out anyone willing to do them harm. He lumbered toward them, pulling Keleir's lifeless form with him until he dropped the Fire Mage in the mud at her feet. The field of power sparking around him fell away just as quickly.

She fell into the mud next to them, hugging and kissing them without worry for those who watched. Tears of relief and joy washed freely down her cheeks. Not until she saw Rowe's grave expression did she pause long enough to really *see* them. She turned her eyes to Keleir, who lay heavy against the earth. She hadn't realized it before, how his legs hadn't helped Rowe carry him, how he hadn't responded to her kisses and her words of love. He lay pale. Still. Like death.

"No . . ." She shook her head and patted his face harshly, trying to wake him. "No!" She reared back to strike him, and Rowe grabbed her hand. Saran struggled to look away from Keleir and meet his eyes.

"He's not dead. Not yet. He killed with magic to save me, Saran. It comes for him." Rowe pointed to the distance, to the great black cloud of ash that rolled across the sky and fell around them like rain. A hideous face appeared, a monster bearing down on them. "He sacrificed himself to save my life." Rowe's wide blue eyes pleaded with her, an unspoken request she read all too easily. He wanted her to save Keleir.

Saran looked down at the Bind around her wrist and then to the black cloud swirling above them. It hovered, moments away from devouring Keleir.

She'd promised to save him from the Oruke. She'd vowed to set him free.

Saran pressed a kiss to Keleir's lips. She loved him, he who called to her soul, he who fed it with fire. She would not lose him. "Hold Keleir. Keep him awake. Slap him. Punch him. I don't care what you have to do; don't let him accept this fate."

"What are you going to do?"

Saran scurried to her feet and looked deep into Rowe's worried eyes. "I'm going to get the key. I understand where it is now."

Rowe nodded feverishly, drawing his brother into his arms and slapping at his face to wake him. He slapped him hard enough to snap the Fire Mage's eyes open. Keleir gasped, struggling to breathe, as if he'd died and been brought back to life by his brother's raging need for him to exist. He searched the cloud above them. A sea of black threatened to steal the whites of his eyes. The ash that rained down on them disappeared beneath the Fire Mage's skin, each drop absorbed by him, each one taking him closer to death.

"Saran's here. She's gone to get the key. She's going to save you," Rowe promised.

Keleir shook. "No. Stop her." He struggled to sit up, struggled to push his brother away.

"Why?"

"There is no key!"

Rowe blinked and spotted Saran as she fell to her knees near the woodpile and grabbed the hatchet from the rubbish. She pressed her arm against the stone stairs and lifted the hatchet into the air. In one unflinching strike, she partially severed her hand from her wrist. She didn't scream, but Rowe did. Everyone did.

Saran didn't hear them over the roar of pain in her skull. She lifted the bloody hatchet again and brought it down a final time, severing the hand completely. She made a terrible sound, not quite a scream, and pushed to her feet. The Bind slipped off into the mud, and her eyes lit with white light. The Princess of Adrid cradled her bleeding wrist to her chest and turned to face the black ash cloud, lifting her glowing eyes to the heavens. The ash-formed face grew lower and larger over them. It opened its mouth and snapped ravenously at the air.

Darshan's men fled but he stayed, along with Odan. Madam Ophelia watched from the window with triumph in her eyes as the Time Mage, the Grand Feminine she'd made, lifted a shaking hand to the sky.

"I understand your anger," Saran told the storm, her voice quivering with pain. "I understand you want vengeance . . . but I can save you. I can turn back time. I can make you live again. All of you. Let me give you life. Let me forgive his debt."

Swirling, gold light tangled around her ankles and stretched up her legs to coil round her outstretched hand. Her injured arm bled heavily where she pressed it against her clothes, pouring in red rivers to the earth at her feet.

The Time Mage stretched her fingers out to the ash cloud and forced her will upon it. Saran knew no words to control it, no spell to undo it. She used her will and her will alone to change what could not be stopped. The cloud morphed and struggled, raging silently against her power.

Behind her, Keleir gripped Rowe's hand and struggled to watch. He shook his head fiercely at his brother and snatched a handful of Rowe's long black hair, pulling him low enough to whisper, "Stop her."

Liquid black stretched across the whites of his eyes as the Oruke grappled for control. Keleir struggled to hold it back, but he grew tired of fighting. He'd fought it for so long already. He couldn't keep up. The Oruke would win and, if Saran stopped the curse, it would be free to slaughter as it wished. Keleir's grip on Rowe's hair eased, and he wrapped his hands around his brother's protective arm. "Let. Me. Go. Let me die. Please."

Rowe shook his head. "I can't do that."

"Please stop her. Protect her. Love her, but let me go. *Please* let me go." Keleir settled into the mud. "Please, Brother, let me die. I want peace. I beg you. *I beg you.* Before it's too late."

Rowe had never seen his brother cry, never heard him beg for anything in his life. Not when their father beat him, not when the village elders carted him off to be tortured. Keleir accepted pain with pursed lips and cruel eyes, but he never begged. The look of fear and agony in his eyes tore a hole in Rowe's heart.

The Lightning Mage nodded to his brother, wincing at the pain of agreeing to such a terrible thing. With one hand, he squeezed Keleir's. He rested the other atop the Fire Mage's white hair. "As you wish."

Keleir smiled through pain. He dropped his hands to the mud and stretched his body upon the earth, where he accepted death and freedom as one. The black stole his eyes, swarming around the red, which lit with orange embers. The black swept over that, too, and passed away like a storm. The red burned as bright as fresh blood, and Keleir Ahriman was no more.

Rowe jumped to his feet and ran for Saran, calling to her over the roar of the ash storm. She turned her attention to him briefly and, with a voice like a choir of women, ordered him to stop. His feet planted into the mud against his will. He couldn't blink, couldn't breathe, even his heart stopped in his chest. He froze, while time carried on around him.

Saran struggled to hold back the cloud. It bore down on her in an arch, stretching out tiny ash tendrils in search of Keleir.

"I won't let you have him!" The world blurred before her, not from tears but the blood now covering her clothes.

The ash cloud opened its mouth and snapped at the air. Saran pushed forward, screaming, and plowed her foot into the earth. Blood ran from her nose, and her brain boiled in her skull. The world grew dark around the edges. A roaring started in her ears, so loud it blocked the rattling of her Bind as it wiggled angrily of its own accord near the steps where she'd left it.

Her vision failed her first. She went blind, and her knees buckled. The hold she kept on Rowe snapped, and he grabbed her before she fell. She fought to hold the ash back but ultimately lost the strength for that too. Her power snapped like a stressed rope. The cloud dove down and wrapped around Keleir in the same instant. It soaked into every part of him, his mouth, nose, and eyes, until it disappeared within his body, filling and destroying what life he had left.

The power Saran exerted over the cloud had built around her, like a pail too full of water and running over. The energy needed to go somewhere.

It exploded, reverberating out over every surface of the castle, city, and out into the grassy fields yards beyond the wall. It raced down corridors, over walls, windows, and roofs, turning ancient ruin into newfound glory, restoring the worn and broken city to a form it had not resembled in centuries.

Saran could not see Rowe, nor could she see her magic fix her broken home. She felt the Lightning Mage's arms tighten around her, heard his throaty roar of defeat. The pain she felt ebbed to nothing, and a cold metal band settled over her wrist.

FORTY-SIX

SARAN KNEW NOTHING of time or how much passed. Her eyes were too heavy to open, so she stayed in the darkness and half listened to the world around her. Voices jumbled together, indiscernible both in content and origin. They distracted her from the confusion. The days blurred together in shades of pain and fear, and she couldn't remember if she had died at the end or not. She felt dead.

She dreamed in dim colors of the Saharsiad beating her, Darshan wrapped in water and earth, and an angry cloud of ash. Within the ash, she saw a face, rage ripping its mouth open and snapping its jaws shut. She wanted to wake, to leave the darkness around her, but she could not move. Her limbs lay heavy at her sides, and the lids of her eyes wouldn't lift. Her lips wouldn't part. She groaned and cried from behind clenched teeth, begging for someone to shake her alive.

A hard hand grabbed her and shook until her eyes snapped open. She sat up too quickly and melted into warm arms. For a long time she lay there, wrapped in that warmth, staring at the blankets covering her lap, far too weary to lift her head. Eventually she gathered the nerve to look at the one who held her.

Rowe waited patiently, his gaze appraising her face with a deep frown. Her pale skin appeared nearly translucent, and deep, dark circles hung under her eyes. Her green gaze locked on Rowe, her lips parting to speak, but her mouth was too dry for words. They came out harsh and cracked. "K-Keleir . . ."

"Shh," he whispered, placing a cup of water to her lips. She drank slowly, choking at first. She lifted her hands to the cup when he attempted to draw it away.

Hands . . .

She stopped drinking and looked at the two hands in front of her, shock running cold down her spine. She had both her hands back, and the Bind dangled from her wrist. Had that all been a horrible dream? What was real? Where did the dream start? When she fainted in her room? When the Saharsiad beat her?

Rowe grabbed her hand gently and twined his fingers around hers, perhaps too unsettled by her shaking to let it hover in the air much longer. "Yarin's fail-safe, I assume. He might have guessed you'd try that eventually. As soon as you lost the power to hold time, it returned to your hand, with your hand. It actually saved your life. Even though you'd lost so much blood, it kept you from bleeding out."

"Keleir? Please tell me . . ."

Rowe froze, growing quiet. His lips parted, and he tried three times to speak, yet no words came out. His face hardened before he finally forced them free. "He went. You did all you could. Ultimately it is what he wanted. He begged for it. The Oruke won, and death saved Keleir."

Saran shook her head, tears welling in her eyes. She choked on a sob and buried her face against Rowe's shoulder. "After you blacked out, your magic changed the city and the castle. You wouldn't recognize it. I definitely don't. Odan and a few of the men who were left in the area overtook Darshan. He's

Bound and waiting in the dungeon for judgment. It takes every fiber of me not to kill him for what he has done to us. His people retreated to the outskirts of town when you stood to fight the curse. I sent a messenger to tell them to wait there until their leader finished with his negotiations. They were allowed to keep the messenger as insurance."

Saran wiped her cheeks harshly. "Who is the messenger?"

"Odan."

"He listened to you?"

"He listened to Madam Ophelia."

Saran nodded. "Of course he did." She pressed her forehead to his shoulder and knotted her fingers in his tunic. "I need to see Keleir, Rowe."

The Lightning Mage nodded. "When you're strong enough."

"I'm strong enough."

Saran wrapped herself in a robe, and Rowe carried her down to the dining hall. This late at night, it lay empty and dark, save the candles lit on the tables surrounding a long body draped in blue linen. Even before they reached the body, Saran began to shake. Rowe set her on her feet so that she could lean against the table while he drew back the cloth, revealing Keleir beneath it. The servants had cleaned him, left him naked beneath it. The fumes of heavy spice stole the air, and she knew then that they'd already performed the burial rights. She traced her fingers over the star-shaped scar around the intricate Oruke mark, a mark his village had attempted to remove over and over. It had always been a beacon of their failure and his ultimate doom.

"He's warm," she whispered, finding no shame in the tears that fell to splash across the tabletop.

"His element was fire," Rowe whispered, brushing his hand soothingly down her back.

"Shouldn't he be cold?"

"Maybe. I don't know."

Saran sniffed and pressed her hands to her eyes, collapsing against the table. Rowe grabbed her and lifted her off her feet, dropping her back down on the bench next to Keleir. She curled her hands around the Fire Mage's arm and held him tightly. For half an hour, she didn't move and barely blinked. Even when Madam Ophelia entered the room, followed by three of Yarin's councilmen, the healer's shoes clonking heavily across the floor did little to call Saran's attention away from her dead husband.

"We heard you were awake, my queen," Madam Ophelia whispered, bowing her head with a placid and unmoving gaze, the look of a woman bored with the view.

Saran continued to stare at Keleir's warm, tan hand. She traced her fingers over his skin. It felt so alive, such a cruel and horrible trick. "I am not your queen . . . not yet."

"Of course." Madam Ophelia sighed, rubbing her hands together. "We'll make it legitimate with a coronation. We'll invite the people on the outskirts of town to it. Darshan will agree and supply the needed goading for peace, with the proper incentive, of course."

Saran frowned. "Of course."

Rowe gave a deep, throaty growl, rather like a dog that disliked someone getting too close to his food. "He deserves death."

The healer ignored Rowe as if he hadn't spoken, as if he didn't exist at all. "Shall I make the arrangements?" she asked, an all-too-gleeful smile on her face.

"I'll make them," Saran replied, slowly releasing Keleir's arm to the table. She trembled as she pushed herself up with Rowe's guiding touch and placed a kiss on her husband's dead but warm lips. She drew the blue linen over his head. "We will have the coronation tomorrow. Afterward, Keleir will be put to the pyre as a king."

"What about King Yarin's body?" one of her father's advisers asked.

"Throw him in the pits with the rest of the unwanted," Saran replied.

"But he was the king!"

"I don't care," Saran said, acid in her voice. She lifted her green eyes sharp enough to cut his tongue. "He ran this country into the dirt because of superstitions about Living Gods and Equitases. He can rot with the worms, and the crows can have his eyes. He's left us with an unimaginable mess. He doesn't deserve the burial of a king. He doesn't even deserve the worms."

"You dare!"

"I dare!" Saran slammed hand down on the table near Keleir's body. "I have endured enough lectures from my father to last me all the rest of my days. I will not hear them from spineless weasels like you. You and your ilk allowed him to ruin the kingdom because you were too cowardly to do anything else. You enjoyed the limited luxuries of this castle while your people *starved*. You gave no voice to those who tilled your lands, who were in *your* keeping. You should count yourself lucky that I do not offer you to them like chum to sharks. Perhaps I could use the gesture to win the favor I need without resorting to making deals with Darshan!"

The three advisers who accompanied Madam Ophelia clamped their mouths shut, and the two quiet ones distanced themselves from the third. The healer, for her part, smiled, cold and proud, at her creation.

Saran sighed, leaning her weight against Rowe. At the moment, he supported her more than her legs ever could. "As much as I would like to think the people will fall in line and accept my rule without question, I know better. The proper arrangements will be made with Darshan to ensure his allegiance. I will discuss those arrangements with him."

"Shouldn't you build a collection of advisers to discuss this with you first?"

"No," Saran replied. "I will have none. You are relieved of your post, the lot of you. If I require your help in the future, I will be sure to find whatever rock you've crawled under."

"It's a dangerous thing to rid yourself of us," the adviser warned.

"Really? You've alienated yourself from the people who would have supported you. You've got no one to back you, and if by some miracle you were to find someone, I doubt you'd ever have the courage to do anything about me. If you could, you would have shoved Yarin from his throne long ago. I will be in touch when I require your droning voice, Lord Reland. Until then, I suggest you go find that rock, quickly."

The three advisers bowed deeply to Saran and excused themselves from the room. Madam Ophelia almost applauded. She lifted her hands and cupped them together over her heart. Her already tight skin pulled tighter with a smile. "It pleases me to see you accept your role. You were truly meant for it, whether you wanted it or not."

Saran smoothed her hands across the table, twisting the blue linen between her fingers. "Deep down, I think I always knew I'd end up in this place, cursed with this title. No matter how many times I told myself otherwise, when I spoke of the future to anyone but Keleir and Rowe, I was Queen of Adrid. I always thought I was acting, but now I know that I had accepted this fate, even unconsciously."

Madam Ophelia stepped forward. "Child, it isn't a death sentence."

Saran straightened. "No, it's a life sentence. One filled with decisions I'd rather not make. And speaking of those, I need you to take me to Darshan." Saran turned her head to Rowe, who remained a quiet perch for her to lean upon.

"Maybe you should rest a bit more before dealing with him?" Rowe muttered.

Saran scowled. "I want to show him that I am impervious, that not even blood loss can stop me, that I am stronger than death. He thinks me easily toyed with, after toying with me for so long. I will face him, weak and strong at once. You will take me, and you will not say a word of protest to whatever you hear. Do you understand?"

Rowe pursed his lips together, cocking his head back questioningly at her. "Is that an order?"

Saran set her teeth tight. "For the first time, Rowe, yes. That was an order."

Very few guards stood at the dungeon doors. Most of them waited inside, in a line down the halls of the dungeon, or stood outside Darshan's cell door. They bowed to her, one by one, as she passed with Rowe's aid. The door to the Water Mage's cell groaned open, and Darshan turned from his dark corner to step into the light. He waited with a cold smirk turning up his salt-and-pepper beard.

"I see you got your hand back," he mused.

Once inside the cell, Saran nodded to the guards, and they shut the door behind them. A heavy silence settled as the Water Mage began to pace. "My people?"

"Waiting on the outskirts of the city. I suppose the Core's curse and the rapid change in the city spooked them." Saran sighed, taking a slow, quivering seat on a wooden stool along the stone wall.

"They won't like it if they find out that you locked me in here, you know. You're treading on very dangerous ground."

Saran leaned heavily against the wall, turning her gaze on Rowe. He stood rigid, his hands clenching so tight that his knuckles turned white. She reached out and brushed her hand over his arm. "Step out."

"No."

She pursed her lips together but possessed little energy for arguing. Instead she turned her attention to Darshan. The Water Mage and rebel leader smiled, but the longer she sat silently waiting for him to stop his prideful pacing, the more that smile faltered. When he settled into one spot, she clasped her hands over her lap and began, "I will be crowned queen tomorrow. You will stand by my side. You will accept my reign."

"What do I get in return?"

"Your life?"

Darshan laughed. "I'll need a bit more incentive than that."

Saran had many years of practicing a facade, but tonight she had little patience for it. The distaste wrote itself in the hard glare she wore. She wanted to kill him, but her soul felt too guilty from the deaths by her hand the day before, and her heart too heavy with grief. She pressed on with what needed to be done. "My husband is dead. You will allow me my year of mourning, as is custom. You will support me in all that I do. You will turn your people to me, and in return, after my year of mourning, I'll make you king. Just as you always wanted."

Rowe jerked away from her touch. "Are you mad? You will do no such thing!"

"Stay out of this, Rowe," Saran snapped.

"No, I will not! I'll never let you marry him. I won't let him get what he wants, not after what he did."

"This is our chance to finally bring peace back to Adrid, Rowe. We can stop everything that has plagued this kingdom. I don't want this life, but it is mine. These people are my responsibility now." Saran ignored the pleased smile on Darshan's face. "I should have taken the throne from my father long ago. If I had, I wouldn't have to resort to this. I have no magic with this Bind. The Mages will only support a ruler of power, and the rebels will only accept Darshan. He has both power and respect. It is the reasonable and responsible choice, albeit one that makes me ill."

"Saran . . . we'll find the key to your Bind."

"No, we won't. Father said so himself. It is nowhere that can be seen, which means he destroyed it."

"Then let me be your power. Let me be by your side. It is what Keleir wanted."

"Keleir has no say in this matter. He's dead." She hated the words as soon as they left her mouth. She winced at them and tried a warmer tone. "Sometimes we must do what we hate to do what is right."

Rowe shifted at her bluntness. He bowed his head sharply and excused himself from the room. Darshan faded into warm laughter well before the door slammed, stepping back into the shadows to lean against the wall.

"Do you accept my terms?"

Darshan kicked at the hay tangled over his boots. "Accept your terms? Of course. How could I refuse?"

"If you do anything to jeopardize this or to undermine me, I will kill you and find myself a new rebel Mage to marry. You're not special, Darshan. You're convenient. As convenient as I am for your legitimacy concerns, but the only problem is that you are a silver a dozen and I am rare. I could step outside these walls and make the offer to six of your men. I am the only one that can make you king, not just in title but in soul. The Core will accept nothing else."

Darshan's cleverness washed from his face. He bit at his lip, his aged expression growing stern. She could tell by the lengthening lines of his face how seriously he understood his situation.

"You loved my mother," Saran continued. "You tried to save her, and I found you endearing for it. I looked to you as a father, and Rowe did the same. You will never gain back the trust that was lost between us. You are no longer the man that loved my mother. He is gone. The man who has replaced him holds no favor in my heart and is expendable. Do we understand each other?"

"Yes," Darshan replied.

Saran moved to stand but found that her legs wouldn't obey her. She hated the idea of calling Rowe back to help, worse than admitting weakness. She pressed her hands into the sides of the stool and pushed with all her might, thankful for the robe and dressing gown to hide her quivering legs. She knocked harshly on the door and walked slowly through it, using the wall to carry her weight. Rowe waited outside, pressed against the stone hall. When he saw her, he offered her his arm.

As angry as Rowe seemed, he didn't stray far for the rest of the night. He only disappeared for a short while to order the guards to tear through Yarin's room. "Empty everything out," he'd told them. "Down to the last crumb, the last puff of dust, until it is empty, and bring any key found to me." When he returned, he found Saran sitting near the fireplace, staring into the flames.

"You should be resting."

Saran nodded but did not let her eyes roam from the embers and the long, hot fingers of fire wrapping around the logs. She knew he was right. She had to rest. She had a whole day ahead of her and needed strength to make it down the length of the throne room to her place at its end. She needed to be able to walk on her own. Anything else would show weakness before those who could sense the limp of prey.

Saran sat in an overstuffed chair unfamiliar to her or her room. Actually nothing in her room belonged. She imagined the whole city had a similar issue, after her magic turned it from a barely standing ruin to a newly constructed mecca. All her trinkets, all the little beautiful things she'd collected over the years from her visits to the Second and Third were gone. All the books she pored over and absorbed by reading thousands of times, even her favorite one that reminded her of Rowe, had been replaced with different books that were both new and old all at once. The scratches and dents on the floor where she carelessly discarded Keleir's armor on nights of passion were polished over. New, clean boards replaced them. She'd never even seen her bed before, and impossibly it stood even more opulent than her old one.

"I think this was my mother's room," Saran admitted. "When she was a girl. Perhaps even my grandmother's . . . It is old enough. Everything in here is ancient and new all at once. There are some things that oddly haven't changed, like the dagger in the wardrobe and my wedding dress. I knew it had to be old, but I didn't think it that old. I wonder what magic seamstress could weave fabric that would stand a hundred years without disintegrating."

Rowe admired the room down to the deep blue curtains that he'd never seen before. "I haven't bothered to look at mine."

"You won't find the key in his room," Saran whispered. "If it wasn't there before, it definitely isn't there now. Nothing is in any place that it was before. Everything is different, down to the smallest details."

"This scale of magic should have killed you."

"But it didn't."

"Why?"

Saran shrugged her shoulders. "I am stronger than you think."

"Obviously. You've recovered from Keleir's death fast enough."

Saran's green eyes shot up to him, narrowed and sharp. She had a hardness to her face that he didn't recognize. "Get. Out." Short, demanding words spoken after several long, agonizing seconds of silence. Tears brimmed her eyes, and she held her jaw tight to keep her lips from trembling.

Rowe felt shame at his words. He'd spoken them against his will and couldn't repair the damage fast enough. "I didn't . . . I'm sorry."

She shook her head, losing the war with her tears. When Rowe shifted off the wall to go to her, she held up her hand to him with a look in her eyes that said she wished her magic could stop him. He stopped of his own accord. "Saran, I'm sorry."

"I can't," she gasped, wrapping her hands around her neck. "I can't. I can't. I can't." She couldn't breathe.

Rowe knelt next to her and wrapped his hands around her arms and held her tight. She sobbed, wild and hard, until her lungs seized with sorrow. "I couldn't save him."

"You tried," Rowe whispered, brushing her tears away. She only cried harder.

"I wasn't strong enough. I couldn't save him. I promised I'd save him. I'm sorry, Rowe. I'm so sorry."

"Shhh," he pleaded, wrapping her up in his arms. "Don't . . ."

Saran shook her head. "I did so many horrible things to get to my father. I killed and I couldn't reverse it. I couldn't bring them back. I couldn't save anyone. He's gone, and I can't bring him back."

"You haven't lost him. Not completely. There is a part of him in you. In your child."

Saran froze, hiccupping through tears. Her expression turned mournful. The feeling welling in her wasn't sadness for a child that had not been, but the stinging reminder that she and Keleir had been robbed of that joy with his passing. "No, I don't."

"You . . . lost it?"

Saran shook her head again, harder. "I wasn't pregnant. I was sick with worry or food poisoning, something, but it was not a child. Madam Ophelia confirmed it."

Rowe pressed his hand to her cheek. They hadn't discussed what the possibility of a child meant to her, she knew that. She read it in his eyes. He fought to find the right words to soothe her. Saran took his hand, unable to tolerate the uncertain anguish in his eyes. "It's okay . . . I'm okay. It is better this way."

She believed those words, without a shadow of a doubt, and hated herself for it.

FORTY-SEVEN

THE NEXT DAY started early for the servants in the palace. They had much to do to prepare for the coronation, a ceremony that had not been performed in so long that only a few of the remaining priests who understood the rites were available, and most were too old to attend to it themselves.

The servants had trouble locating many of the items familiar to them. Storage rooms lay empty of the usual supplies. Instead they held completely different ones. Some storage rooms weren't for storage at all anymore and held empty beds in them. Saran's magic had turned the palace upside down. Some servants spent the entire night searching it over just trying to find their quarters and their belongings, which, of course, no longer existed.

Time had changed in the city by a hundred years.

The benefits outweighed any price paid by the change, because when the servants searched the typically empty vault for the crown belonging to the queen, the last real wealth Adrid possessed, they found chests of gold and silver, trays of jewels, and racks upon racks of jewelry. They pocketed some of it for themselves, collected the crown, and ran off to tell the queen the good news. Adrid was no longer destitute.

Rowe left Saran in the care of her new personal guard, led by Raener, one of the soldiers who let her out of the dungeon. The Lightning Mage spent the morning rummaging through the king's chamber. The servants had obeyed his order and emptied it out. Only fitting for them to do it anyway, since Saran would be moving into it by the end of the day. He spun around an empty room with polished wood floors, crisp curtains, and perfectly clean windows.

Clean windows . . .

The palace hadn't had those in all the years the Lightning Mage lived there. It wasn't so much that they didn't have the man power to clean them before, but the fact that Yarin had specifically ordered them not to.

Rowe went to the window and peered out at the courtyard where they stacked dried wood for the pyre that Keleir would rest upon that afternoon. He watched them methodically arrange the logs and limbs around a wooden platform built specifically for the body to rest upon. The platform stood ten feet tall, high enough for all that would stand in the courtyard to see the Fire Mage burn.

He doubted many people would attend Keleir's funeral. Not many liked him, even among his own men, much less Darshan's rebels. Perhaps they would attend, if only to watch the famed Vel d'Ekaru burn away to nothing, thereby relieving any fears held that he might rise and wipe them out. Rowe winced at the idea, at the mental image of his brother disappearing in the flames. He'd seen Keleir walk in fire, seen it wrap lovingly around him as a woman might, but the fire never hurt him. He was born of it, and after today he would return to it, return to the Core that granted him her most precious gift.

"Lord Blackwell," a meek voice murmured to him from behind. Rowe turned to find a shy servant girl, no older than fifteen, standing just behind him. "We didn't find the key you are looking for, but we found these. I'm not sure what they belong to." She held out a ring of keys and placed them in his outstretched hand. "Might I suggest talking to Madam Ophelia, m'lord?" There was an uneasiness in her eyes, a tinge of fear when she spoke of the healer.

"What's your name, girl?"

"Betha, m'lord, his majesty's chambermaid. I was, at least."

Her name felt familiar to him, and he searched his mind for what he should remember of her. "Tell me, do you know what the king did with the key, Betha? You can tell me. No one will hurt you, I promise."

FORTY-EIGHT

SARAN ADMIRED HERSELF in the mirror, something she never really took the luxury of doing. Ora had outdone herself this time. Despite the heavily embroidered, corseted dress she'd worn for her wedding, she felt comfortable. Perhaps it had a lot to do with the fact she'd accented it with armor.

The brown leather armor of her breastplate, gorget, and pauldrons covered the top of her dress fittingly, along with the metal and brown leather bracers around her arms. The curls of her deep red hair were piled up with the elaborate headdress worn by the Adridian queen woven across the crown of her head. Ora painted her face to mask the paleness and bruising. She looked just as unfamiliar as she had on her wedding day, with deep-colored lips, rose on her cheeks, and black around the rims of her eyes.

Madam Ophelia stood just in the doorway, waiting patiently for Saran to address her. The whole situation felt oddly familiar. Saran thought back to her wedding day, musing over the healer's joy at the idea of a woman on the throne. She imagined Madam Ophelia felt very happy to finally see her dream come true.

"Ora, would you leave us?" Madam Ophelia asked, offering the girl a tight half smile. "If you're finished, of course."

Ora smiled at Saran's reflection. "Never have I made a finer masterpiece in all my life. The armor was a lovely touch. Great idea, Your Highness. I'd shiver in my boots if I were your enemy. You are a warrior queen if there ever was one." The servant girl bowed deeply and scurried off past Madam Ophelia, who closed the door behind Ora and allowed herself farther into the room.

"Warrior queen, indeed," Madam Ophelia echoed. She looked extra prim in her gray healer's attire, which seemed washed and pressed nicely for the occasion. Her hands clasped tight, she held her head higher than normal.

"What can I do for you, Madam?"

"I just came to admire you," Madam Ophelia admitted with an empty sort of reverence, the voice of a mother who could not believe her dreams had come true.

Saran fiddled with the armored bracers on her forearms. "Is the pyre being prepared?"

"It is almost complete and will be ready for the funeral after the coronation," the healer replied, taking a step forward. "It was such hard work, but it all worked out in the end. You are here, taking your place as you should. I had my doubts, but I never should have."

The queen paused in her fidgeting, staring at the mirror, at Madam Ophelia's proud expression in its reflection. "Hard work?"

"I worked hard to separate you from them and look how you flourished! Look what you became!" Madam Ophelia's eyes welled with tears. "You don't know how hard it was to keep your magic from you, but I needed you to understand how strong you could be without it. I worried when you wasted away as soon as it was gone. I couldn't stand your phlegmatic attitude toward life—it nearly drove me mad." A happy laugh involuntarily burst from her. A laugh from a healer was like watching a goat sprout wings. "I almost carved the key out of your father's body and gave you your powers back. But Darshan told me to be patient. He knew that you'd come around once Ahriman was out of the way. You wouldn't be blinded by girlish ideas. And then he was away, and you were even worse. I mourned it and I nearly lost hope."

Anger boiled in Saran, but she couldn't force herself to stop the woman's monologue. A desperate part of her needed to hear it all, wanted all the frayed edges of information made whole. Madam Ophelia cried happy tears and cupped her hands over her heart as if she prayed, as if she worshipped Saran as those who worshipped the Vel d'Ekaru. Saran allowed the healer to worship herself straight to her own doom.

"Blackwell held you back more than Ahriman ever did. I poisoned your food, just a little, to make you sick and convinced him I thought you were pregnant. I knew he wouldn't let you stay here in that condition. But I also knew you couldn't leave the city. Blackwell would either die trying to free you or abandon you."

"You did all that just to get me alone?" The calmness of her own voice startled Saran, but the surprise did not show on her face. "You've been working with Darshan all this time? You knew where my father hid the key to the Bind? You did *all* that, just to see me rise to this?"

"I only worked with Darshan up until yesterday. I used him to help me get you here. I knew you'd never let him have control. I trusted you." Madam Ophelia grinned, joyful tears rolling down her face. "It all worked. As soon as you were separated from all those crutches, you flourished. You *flew!*"

Saran stepped closer to Madam Ophelia and cupped the woman's face, brushing her tears away. A deadly calm settled in her soul. "Do you think I deserve to have my powers back now? Now that I've proven myself to you?"

Madam Ophelia nodded. "Yes. I do."

"And you hid it in my father's body?"

The woman smiled. "The wound in his leg. We hid it there after your wedding. Once the coronation is over, I'll retrieve it for you."

Saran nodded hollowly and turned from the woman, going to her wardrobe as stiff as a puppet with no strings. "I have very few things in my possession," she murmured, numb and broken. Her hand swiped across the top of the wardrobe. "But I think I have just the reward for your cleverness."

Madam Ophelia pressed her hands to her heart. "I am astounded. I half expected my account to be suicide. But I felt compelled to tell you so you would understand the depths of my devotion to you, to the Grand Feminine we've longed for."

Saran paused. The numbness she felt began to crumble. "Of course I understand. Without you, none of this would have been possible. You, Madam Ophelia, are the root of all of this." *All of this pain. All of this. All of this. All of this!*

Saran stepped out from behind the wardrobe door, tucking her hand in her skirts and easing them around the furniture. "Everything, from the moment you soothed my wounds with tea to this brave confession. I know only one way to reward such devious cleverness."

Madam Ophelia bowed her head low. "I am at your disposal."

Saran smiled, cruel and beautiful. Her father's smile. "I killed for the first time yesterday, did you know that? I've hurt people before, I've killed before, but no one ever stayed that way. Every life I've ever taken, I've restored . . . until yesterday."

For so long she'd been powerless, unable to exact revenge on her father, unable to have control over her own life. Rage built against a woman who had been Saran's advocate, a woman who had practically raised her. Madam Ophelia orchestrated the destruction of Saran's dreams of escape and the death of her husband. She created the lie that Saran carried a child, gave the princess the brief thought of that ill-timed future, all for the sake of leaving her hopelessly alone. The real villain in all of this was Madam Ophelia.

Saran's hands shook, and the quiver spread through her whole body. *She is the reason for all of this pain. All of this sadness. Helplessness. Death. All of it.*

The healer caught the glint of a dagger before the princess drove it up into her stomach. Shock washed over the healer's face. She lifted her eyes to Saran's blank stare before stumbling away and falling backward to the floor. Madam Ophelia cupped her hands around the wound, gasping and staring in disbelief at her creation. Saran shook with rage, unable to quell it in her heart even to see what she had done.

The healer drew the dagger from her stomach with a sharp gasp and pressed her hands to the wound. Saran offered a sympathetic frown, her hands and legs quivering. "That helplessness you feel? I know it well now. It is a horrible feeling . . . watching something you care about slip away because you don't possess the power to mend it."

The rage that consumed Saran broke like a wave crashing over the shore. It washed out of her, creating a void that quickly filled with regret. Her eyes finally saw Madam Ophelia bleeding out onto her bedroom floor.

The princess's chest heaved with shock, and she broke with a sob, wrapping her arms around her stomach. Bile crept into the back of her throat. She went to Madam Ophelia and pressed her hands into the wound. The healer covered those hands with her own, smearing blood over Saran's fingers. Saran's lip trembled as she tried to form words. She willed her magic to mend the wound but could not call it forth to do so. Helplessness consumed her, ate at her until it stole what was left of her composure.

"I'm sorry," Saran murmured, looking deep into Madam Ophelia's gray eyes. "I . . ."

"I did it for you." Madam Ophelia nodded. "You are what you need to be."

Saran shook her head at those words. She was not her father. She would never be her father. "Guards! Someone, help!"

The healer smiled. "Sometimes . . . we do what we hate . . . to do what is right."

Pain squeezed Saran's chest, and she couldn't breathe. As Madam Ophelia slipped away, her eyes went dull and lifeless, and her hands fell from Saran's fingers. The princess shattered with a horrified scream that repeated until her voice grew ragged and silent. Raener, her guard, burst into her room. She didn't register his presence, not even after he drew her away from Madam Ophelia's lifeless body.

Every step Saran took down the lengthy hallway echoed with the clank of armored guards at her side and back. The familiar sound she'd known all her life ticked on as white noise in her ears. She stood stoic and regal between the lines of armed men, while she broke apart inside.

Saran had never killed anyone as coldly as she'd done to Madam Ophelia. Up until yesterday, she'd never really killed anyone at all. In her grief over losing Keleir, she hadn't given it much thought. Now it consumed her.

Lost in the focus needed to keep putting one foot in front of the other despite exhaustion and emotional instability, she didn't see Rowe bounding down the hall toward her until he grabbed her shoulders and stopped her.

"Ophelia knows where the key is."

Saran's eyes lifted, half hearing him. His nostrils flared, urgency and anger creasing his face. "I know," she replied, turning her eyes back to the stairs. "She just told me."

"Where?"

"My father has it. In him. In his leg."

Rowe growled, his hands tightening on her shoulders. "I'm going to kill her."

Saran lowered her gaze shamefully. "I already have."

"I'll get the key after the ceremony."

"Now," Saran whispered, tears in her eyes. "I cannot handle another moment of this torment. Find it now."

The Lightning Mage nodded. "Now." He touched her hand, gave it the faintest of squeezes, and rushed off down the hall.

Saran took a moment to collect herself. She swallowed the heavy lump in her throat, straightened her spine, lifted her head high, and carried on with her long walk to the throne room. The queen flexed her fingers at her sides, feeling the leather of the fingerless gloves worn with the armored bracers. She'd go down in history as the first queen to ever wear armor to a coronation. Her dress felt heavy, the corset too tight, and the red cloak she wore caught on the roughness of the stone floor. Every detail hyperrealized and dreamy at once.

The heavy doors to the throne room groaned open, and bright golden sunlight spilled into the hall from the large windows at either side of the throne. The room went silent, like a wave of mud washing over her. Her feet grew as heavy as lead plates, and she forced herself to meet the eyes of the coronation attendees.

She put one foot in front of the other, passing down the center of the room as gracefully as she could muster with the unmanageable tremble in her knees.

Darshan stood on the granite podium to the right of the throne, wearing a borrowed deep blue tunic. An Ekaru priest stood to the left of the throne, the same one who had performed the marriage rites with Keleir. The line of soldiers stretching the length of the aisle snapped to attention once her feet brushed the short steps leading up to the throne. She nearly tripped, but by some miracle or force of will, she caught her balance. She welcomed the throne, wanting to sit after exhausting every ounce of stamina she possessed, both physically and mentally, just getting to it.

The throne didn't look the same as the one her father occupied all these years. Times had changed. This one, the one her father sold to pay for wars so many years ago, had finally returned to where it belonged. It was ornate and gold, with a plush red cushion.

Maybe the spell she'd woven to reverse Keleir's curse was not just of time, but also of purpose. Maybe the castle had everything exactly where it belonged, even herself.

Despite her hatred for the idea of a preordained life, she couldn't help but feel that everything she'd ever done led her to this moment, to this end . . . or this beginning. She was the heir to the throne. Her kingdom was tied to the Core and she to her kingdom, and thus that connection sustained the life of Adrid. In that moment Saran knew she could never bring herself to leave her home because she was tied to her world and this throne as surely as if someone had bound her with rope.

She passed the last step and stood before her throne. Taking a deep breath until the corset pulled uncomfortably tight, she turned to face the people. *Her people.*

She expected to see angry faces, for flying vegetables to rain down and pitchforks to rise up with torches. Darshan's presence soothed them. The hopeful expressions they wore were not for her—she knew that. They were for him. She'd fought so hard for them, endured the punishment of her father for them, and yet they hated her. She'd sacrificed her life, Keleir's life, in order to see them freed, and they wanted Darshan for their king.

Saran sat stiffly as the Ekaru priest began his ritual. He announced, in the old tongue and the new, her right to the throne, her lineage. When he touched on the Vanguard line, the lines of their faces eased. It gave her some hope that in the future, after many years as queen, she might win their favor. That they might love her as much as they loved Darshan.

Her fingers curled over the arms of the chair, and she clutched it as the incense wafted from the brass thurible the priest waved back and forth. She disliked the strong smell and held her breath as it passed.

Normally in a coronation, the crown would be placed on the head of the ruler, but Adrid's crown for its queen had been made so intricately that it needed to be woven into the hair. It proved to be a tedious process that she had no intention of enduring every morning. She would wear the crown meant for the king instead. Another could be made for Darshan, now that there was gold in the vault.

Gold.

Everything had changed in a day. No more debt. No more corruption, at least for the most part, and they were no longer at war with themselves. Everything had been made better, and yet she could not find happiness in it. She could not feel joy at her accomplishments, not when her husband lay waiting to be put to the pyre. She'd failed to keep her promise.

Her heart grew heavy in her chest, and her throat closed tight. She found it hard to breathe but focused all her attention on remaining as calm and controlled as she could. She kept the facade but felt it cracking with each second she had to look out at the faces watching her. She didn't want to be there anymore. She didn't want them to see her break. Saran fell into a void so deep that she didn't hear the celebratory bells tolling or the cheers from the crowd as the Ekaru priest finished his ritual. The world blurred as Darshan took her hand and led her from the throne, down the short steps and through the crowd, to the eight men with Keleir's wrapped body balanced on a flat board resting against their shoulders. She followed them numbly, staring at the deep blue linen, clutching Darshan's arm painfully tight.

Her breath came too quickly. She felt light-headed, almost drugged as she forced one foot in front of the other, scraping them against the floor. Saran stayed with Darshan at the top of the steps leading into the courtyard, while the castle emptied out around her and filled the space around the pyre.

"It is okay to grieve," Darshan whispered to her. "You loved him."

Saran turned teary eyes on the older man, wanting to choke the life from him, wanting to turn back time so far that he were never born. She could not stomach the thought of marrying him, of binding herself to him and only him for the rest of her life. She looked away, back to the eight men as they carried Keleir's body up the steps to the flat place where he would rest atop the wood. The place where he would burn.

Beyond the pyre and the castle walls, the sun began to set.

FORTY-NINE

KELEIR KNEW IT wasn't night. He knew that the deep unfeeling darkness around him, so quiet and still, belonged to the hollowness of the Under, where the dead rested for eternity. He'd lain in it for hours, or at least it felt like hours. He felt no ground at his feet, nor soft bedding at his back, nor even the brush of air across his skin. He called out in the darkness, cried out for someone to hear him. When he'd begged for death, he hadn't expected it to feel so isolating, so unending.

Only after hours of silence, of lying in the blackness of his ever after, did he finally accept his death. But just as he accepted his fate, a spark of orange light lit off in the distance. Keleir ran for it, a fleeting hope of escape buried deep inside him.

He ran until his feet trod across molten, swirling lava. He did not sink beneath it but stood upon it as he often had in his dreams. The Core beneath his feet lived, a bright and thriving beauty to behold, a vision he'd never been allowed before. Was this a gift for ending himself and saving the world? Keleir bent and touched the molten rock with his bare hand, smiling at the way it wrapped painlessly around his fingers.

"You've always felt tied to it," a voice whispered to him, coming from just behind him. Keleir tilted his head up to the black-clad figure standing next to him and to the face that was his own. "That's what they say of Fire Mages, right? That you are closest to the Core. Favored by her."

"I thought I'd endure death in peace," Keleir muttered, standing slowly. "It seems you'll be allowed to torment me well into eternity."

The Oruke frowned. "I never meant to torment you."

Keleir laughed. "You just made my every day a constant battle. You desired to murder my wife. You tried to force me out of existence!"

The Oruke tilted his head at Keleir and then glanced down at the fire. "I was wrong to do that, but I knew no other way. You weren't meant to exist, Keleir. I can't imagine that torture, you being in here when it was only ever meant to be me. Now I have the chance to do away with you completely, and I cannot bring myself to extinguish you."

"We're dead."

"You're dead. The body lives on. I keep it going. I'm a creature of time, Keleir. Not even the Core's curse can stop that. Right now, they place this body on a pyre to burn, but it will not. I will rise. It is your choice whether you rise with me."

Keleir glowered at the Oruke. "So not even that could stop you? Not even death?"

"I told you," the Oruke replied, "this body will live on."

The Fire Mage's calm demeanor melted into rage and sorrow. "So you're just going to wake up and slaughter them all? Conquer the world? Enslave humanity? And nothing I did mattered?"

"I'm going to save the world, Keleir. But of course you don't believe me. You've never believed me. You've never listened to me. I've tried desperately to show you the truth, and you refuse me!" The Oruke stomped forward across the rippling

Core. "You can continue to exist, or I can crush you. It is your choice."

Keleir laughed. "Now you're giving me a choice?"

The Oruke seethed. "You were never supposed to exist! She created you, and I grew to love you as my kin. I feel pity for you, because I understand what it is like to live a half life. I need you, Brother. I want you to exist alongside me. I know of a way that we can live separate from each other, if you would only follow me."

"What do you mean, she created me?" Keleir sneered.

The Oruke stilled. "Let me show you what you've refused to remember. Then decide whether you want to live or die."

Keleir appraised the mirror image of himself for a long time before he gave a harsh nod. "Fine. I don't have much to lose, do I?"

"Simply much to gain," the Oruke replied and waved his hand out away from them, toward the darkness.

Fire erupted across the earth and swallowed him. The darkness rippled and reformed into burning buildings lining a main road through an indiscernible town. Keleir's body moved of its own accord, lifting a hand and spreading the fire. He heard screaming but saw no one. The smoke blotted out the stars in the sky, and through it he could just begin to make out the shadows of his army surrounding him. He saw their faces, a mixture of horror and awe, and he looked each one in the eye until he found Saran and Rowe.

Rowe looked thin, sickly thin. He knew Rowe had been ill. Those were his first memories after waking with control over his own body. This moment, where he stood, was at the beginning of the rebellion against Yarin and before Rowe had healed from his illness. Before Keleir knew Saran as his lover.

Rowe held the princess back as she struggled to escape, glaring through the flames at him. In his heart, the Oruke hated her. He loathed her. But underneath that, the Oruke felt longing. Desire.

Love.

Saran snatched away from Rowe and ran into the flames. The Lightning Mage screamed for her to stop. The fire burned her clothes and ate at her skin, but her eyes lit white, and her flesh regrew. Each lick of flame burned her, and she replaced it with new skin. The agony wrote itself in the tension of her face, but she did not scream. She walked through the fire to him, twenty yards of slow and agonizing torment. She let her clothes burn away and focused her energy on repairing her body.

"A terrible way to die," Keleir's voice growled without his control.

Saran didn't reply. She took one agonizing step closer to him, reaching out her left hand toward his heart. He tried to move, but her power froze his arms to his sides. The Oruke panicked. Time had never affected him so strongly, him of all people, a creature of time itself. He struggled against her power as her hand pressed in against his chest. He felt her fingers reach inside him, wrap around his heart and his soul.

Saran's skin burned away and regrew. Her eyes brightened until it blinded him, and he could only look down at her hand inside his chest. A pale glow wavered around the hole she'd made, and he could almost see his heart thumping in her hand. He lifted his gaze to her, growling and thrashing, but Saran held him fast.

Realization dawned, noted in the faltering expression of her face. She could not protect herself from the fire and finish what she'd started. So she chose. He felt the full force of her power settle over him, and her skin burned. The fire took layers of flesh from her legs and her hips and her chest, until the flames licked at her face and melted her hair down to the scalp.

She screamed as she clutched his heart and pressed her will upon him until the darkness in him receded.

"By my will . . . thee be mine!" Her smoke-damaged voice cracked, but the words were no less powerful. The Oruke receded, and Keleir replaced him. The Fire Mage remembered this part, the part when he woke from his dark slumber to find a burned woman withdrawing her hand from his chest. The fire snuffed out, and he had his first real memories after thirteen years with the Oruke at the helm.

He stared down at her crisp, black, flame-ravaged body, realizing now what he'd never thought to wonder before: Why he found it so easy to obey her when she asked him to. Why he felt drawn to her so intensely. Why he could feel her in the air around him. She mastered him. She created him.

"Now do you see?" the Oruke whispered.

Saran's burned body disappeared from his arms and the world returned to the molten landscape of the Core. The Fire Mage stood hollow on its surface.

"I'm . . ."

"An Alikon."

The Fire Mage watched the orange swirling beneath his feet, unable to find words to express the complexity of emotions warring in him.

"There is a way to make you real, Keleir. The Book of Kings will lead us to a power that can separate us and make us both very real. I offer you this, Brother. I offer you truth and life, a real life. Saran manipulated you and tormented you with the illusion of existence. I will never do that to you. Nor will I question you or distrust you as Rowe has done. He planned to kill you, you know."

Keleir covered his ears and clenched his eyes. "Shut up."

"She never loved you."

"Shut up!"

"She controlled you. You were her pet!"

"STOP!"

"The fire's being lit, Keleir. It is up to you whether you live or you die. But when I wake, if you have not chosen, then I will let you disappear as you were meant to when her power over you broke! It is by my will alone that you still exist. Choose. Live or die. Exist or disappear."

Keleir turned tearful eyes on the white-haired Oruke. Excruciating pain tore his heart asunder. Anger filled the void, anger so hot he couldn't speak. He breathed panicked, heated air into his lungs and pressed his hands harshly to his eyes. He roared, indecision tearing him apart.

Who could he believe? Which was the liar? He loved Saran, couldn't bring himself to believe that his life with her had been a lie. Yet it made more sense now than ever before. Why his dreams of the Oruke got worse when her father Bound her. Why his control slipped the moment the Bind wrapped around her wrist. Why Yarin wouldn't yield to her release until after the Oruke woke. The old bastard knew. He knew . . .

"Have you chosen, Keleir?"

The Fire Mage dropped his hands slowly, embers burning in his eyes. "Yes."

FIFTY

FIRE ATE AT the logs, growing higher and hotter. Fast, destructive, aided by dry wood and lamp oil, it filled the sky with thick gray smoke. The courtiers and peasants watched the body burn, and not one shed a tear for him. Saran didn't expect them to. No one liked Keleir, not really, save those who thought of him as a god. Brother Povish, the Ekaru priest, waited eagerly near the fire with his hands clasped, praying feverishly for Keleir to rise from the dead. If any satisfaction could be found in his death, it was that they would find no joy in seeing Keleir become the Vel d'Ekaru.

The new queen, regal next to the rebel leader, stood serene as she watched the blue linen wrapped around her dead husband catch flame. She fixated so maddeningly on it that she barely noticed a bloody hand wrap around hers and draw it from her side. Saran blinked at the sweating figure, who'd seemingly appeared out of thin air next to her. Rowe held her hand firm and pressed the smallest of keys into the Bind lock.

He twisted the key, too angry to care about his violent grip, and the thin metal manacle fell from her wrist to clatter against the stone stairs. It rolled down step after step, each fall providing a sharp ringing echo in Saran's ears.

The world came back in one overwhelming rush. She hadn't noticed it before, when she'd severed her hand. The agony of that act had blocked the feeling of being reconnected to the Core. Nothing blocked it now. She felt everything anew and multiplied, even down to the weakness of her anemic form. Her knees buckled under her. She reached out and grasped hold of Rowe's arms, steadying herself as the world settled back to normal. Tears of relief burned her eyes.

Her skin tingled with a familiar and impossible hum. It had been so long that it took her a moment to place the sensation. Shame washed over her for forgetting. The Time Mage straightened and turned her attention to the fire, where the linen burned away but the body remained. Immediately her left hand felt heavier by a fraction, and she looked down to find the fourth finger of her hand wrapped tight with a gold wedding band. Without the Bind, the marriage spell finally completed.

"He's alive."

"What?" Rowe muttered, not quite hearing her.

Saran shoved past him, nearly tumbling down the stairs in her dress. The Lightning Mage seized her, half falling and half running to the bottom, where he held her fast before she bolted for the flames.

"He's alive!" she cried, tugging her arms against Rowe's grip.

"Saran, he's dead!"

Saran shook her head and pulled harder. She turned and beat at Rowe. "He's alive! I feel him! I feel him, Rowe!"

Rowe wrapped his arms tightly around her and held firmly in place. "If that is true, the fire will not hurt him. But it *will* hurt you. We will see when the fire is gone. If he remains in the ashes, then he lives."

A startled cry rippled through the crowd, followed by horrified gasps, as the dead body on the platform sat up in the flames. The Ekaru priest fell to his knees, lifting his hands to the sky with a loud thankful wail. The body rose to stand naked upon the burning wood. The fire wrapped around him, tender and loving as it licked harmlessly against his flesh.

Saran struggled to escape Rowe's arms and, in the Lightning Mage's distraction, she managed to wiggle free.

The figure standing in the flames looked out over the crowd and stepped off the crumbling altar. He sauntered lazily down the steps, the fire moving with him like a river. It washed down the pyre, out and away from him, into the crowd, where the flames caught on those closest. Their screams stopped Saran short. The courtyard broke with panic, and people scattered in chaos, like ants from a crushed mound. They knocked each other down and stomped over the bodies to escape the fire.

"That's not him," Rowe called. "Saran, that's not him!"

Saran watched Keleir slowly make his way down, him watching her in turn. He looked like Keleir, but he lacked the softness in the eyes. This Keleir wore a pointed glare of hate. A cruel smile sprouted on his lips. The darkness in it caused her to take an involuntary step back. She could almost read his thoughts, could almost see the terrible things he longed to do to her. The Ekaru priest kneeling before her jumped to his feet and sang the praises of his god, even as the fire swallowed him whole.

Rowe drew her back, the fire washing up around her feet. They moved swiftly enough that it had no time to catch on her clothing. He pulled her toward the castle stairs. "We've got to go!"

"I can stop him," Saran argued, pulling him to stop.

The Lightning Mage shook his head. "There isn't any time to stop him. He'll kill you!"

Saran's eyes lit white with light. "Don't argue."

"Keleir told me to protect you. I'm not letting you get killed because you think you can stop him. He's dead, Saran. There is nothing left of him to save." Rowe's blue eyes burned into her, searing in a truth that tore her heart in two.

She shook her head. "There is a piece of him in there, I know it. I can *feel* it."

Rowe's shoulders slumped, like a beaten man. "You won't ever give up, will you? You won't ever stop trying to save him . . . You'll die, you know that?"

"I love him," she pleaded.

Fire filled the courtyard, wrapped around the stairs, and surrounded Saran and Rowe before they could make their escape into the castle. The heat singed their skin.

Keleir emerged, naked, standing at the edge of the flames and letting them curl around him. Rowe hugged her tighter, burying his face in her curly hair. "I won't let you kill yourself. The Three need you. I need you."

Rowe pressed a hard kiss to her forehead, a static charge sparking off their skin in a flash of blue light. Then he gave a violent shove to her chest, sending her falling back down the stairs toward Keleir. A crackling blue Gate swallowed her before she met the stone.

Rowe turned a bitter glare on his brother, and the fire closed in around him.

TO BE CONTINUED

EXCERPT:
THE BOOK OF KINGS

New York City, United States—The Second

IT WAS AN unusually cold day for the fifth of May and marked a year and some odd months since Sara Jane Doe arrived at Fairmount Hospital, where she'd been placed in a medically induced coma after surviving being hit by a car. Today they were transferring her to a different, less familiar part of the facility. Her escorts referred to it as the "psychiatric ward." The term was hard to understand, as it was not a language she felt truly fluent in. She came to realize that it was a place where you put those who were no longer physically ill but had not recovered their wits.

No one in the hospital could understand her. She spoke eloquently and confidently in the language she knew, but no matter what sort of man or woman they put before her, no one understood what she said. Sara muddled through what little she knew of their tongue, speaking to those around her in broken sentences that made her seem unintelligent. Eventually she stopped speaking at all.

The language barrier in Fairmount happened to be the least of her worries. She soon discovered that she knew absolutely nothing about her surroundings. Her first days in the common room were spent squatting beneath a rectangular box mounted to the wall just out of the reach of patients. The pictures on the front moved and changed, with different faces, costumes, and voices. She listened to them and slowly but surely began to teach herself their language. This did not help her case for sanity, as she spent a lot of her time mumbling repeated words from where she sat before the box.

The only possession she had, aside from the hospital gowns she wore, was a gold ring around the fourth finger of her left hand. They told her that, despite every possible means, they could not remove it. They called it a wedding band, but of course she could not remember having a husband.

Sara had weekly meetings with a doctor named Andrea Davis. At first there was very little communication between them, and Sara spent most of the meetings listening to the idle tick of what Dr. Davis referred to as a clock. At the end of each meeting the clock gave a shrill ring, one so loud that, no matter how many times she heard it, sent Sara leaping out of her skin. Dr. Davis eventually made it a point to make the bell quieter or resort to a different means of keeping time.

After the meetings, Sara took her medicine and spent the rest of the evening in the common area with the other patients until she felt too drowsy to keep her eyes open. She liked to look out the window, tracing the bars that lined them with her finger. She knew what bars were, yet she did not know how to use the big metal box in the hall with the colorful food lined in rows. She knew that the metal bars held her prisoner, but she did not know that one could put green paper or silver coins into the box in the hall and get food, not until someone showed her. Sara didn't understand why she knew some things so surely, but not others. It frustrated and frightened her. So rather than investigate and show her relative ignorance to the world around her, she stood at the window and looked at what she did know. When she wasn't observing the small park square outside the hospital, she was sitting in front of the rectangular box with the pictures.

It wasn't long before Sara began to wonder about the images, especially the ones that touched some part of her that she could almost just remember. She didn't understand what the box was, only that it appeared to be a window to a world she felt she belonged to, at least during the hours of a 9:00 and 10:00 p.m. on Sunday.

On the fourteenth of August, a little over three months since arriving in the ward, Sara broke the box. She climbed onto a chair and clubbed it three times with a cane she'd stolen from Mrs. Myrtle, an elderly patient with what the orderlies called dementia. The men in white clothes tackled her before she could climb through the broken glass and escape into the black void beyond. When she screamed at them in the tongue she knew so well, they made her sleep with a sharp prick to her neck.

ACKNOWLEDGMENTS

Thank you to Kathy S., who has read every single version of this tale and never once complained (at least not verbally, haha). You've stuck through my obsession with the story and the characters. I've had so many projects I've worked on, but you understood that I couldn't let this "love affair" go.

Thank you to my mother, for instilling in me a love of fantasy, science fiction, reading, and writing.

Thank you to my beta readers: Andrew, Carrie, Kathy S., Kathy W., and my husband, Scott.

Thank you to all the book supporters on Inkshares for making this possible.

GRAND PATRONS

INKSHARES

INKSHARES is a reader-driven publisher and producer based in Oakland, California. Our books are selected not by a group of editors, but by readers worldwide.

While we've published books by established writers like *Big Fish* author Daniel Wallace and *Star Wars: Rogue One* scribe Gary Whitta, our aim remains surfacing and developing the new author voices of tomorrow.

Previously unknown Inkshares authors have received starred reviews and been featured in *The New York Times*. Their books are on the front tables of Barnes & Noble and hundreds of independents nationwide, and many have been licensed by publishers in other major markets. They are also being adapted by Oscar-winning screenwriters at the biggest studios and networks.

Interested in making your own story a reality? Visit Inkshares.com to start your own project or find other great books.

CPSIA information can be obtained
at www.ICGtesting.com
Printed in the USA
LVHW041530270519
619152LV00005B/908/P